one fine day
in the middle
of the night

one fine day in the middle of the night

christopher brookmyre

LITTLE, BROWN AND COMPANY

A *Little, Brown* Book

First published in Great Britain in 1999
by Little, Brown and Company

Reprinted 1999 (two times)

Copyright © Christopher Brookmyre 1999

The moral right of the author has been asserted.

A CIP catalogue record for this book
is available from the British Library.

HARDBACK ISBN 0 316 84864 6
C FORMAT ISBN 0 316 84867 0

Typeset by Palimpsest Book Production Limited,
Polmont, Stirlingshire
Printed and bound in Great Britain by
Clays Ltd, St Ives plc

UK companies, institutions and other organisations wishing
to make bulk purchases of this or any other book
published by Little, Brown should contact their local
bookshop or the special sales department at the address below.
Tel 0171 911 8000. Fax 0171 911 8100.

Little, Brown and Company (UK)
Brettenham House
Lancaster Place
London WC2E 7EN

For Andrew Torrance

Thank you: Gerard Docherty and Allan McGuire, who know where all the bodies are buried (including the real owners); Pete Symes for kitting out the bad guys again; and Marisa for joining the dots at table 42.

The following is based on a true story.

William Connor was standing outside a disused cattleshed on a bright Highland summer's morning, ankle-deep in cowshit, liquidised mercenary raining splashily down about his head from the crisp blue sky above. He wasn't an overly superstitious man, but this was precisely the sort of thing that tended to make him wonder whether fate wasn't trying to drop just the subtlest of hints.

He reached up reluctantly and wiped the gore from his eyelids, then, grimacing, ran a hand through his caked hair, shaking it at the wrist in a whiplash motion. The slick red goo made a wet snicking sound as it licked the dung-carpeted ground. Sighing, he turned around languorously to face Dawson, who was as inevitably likely to be right behind him as he was extremely *un*likely to be impressed. In fact, Dawson's state of impressedness had begun at its default low and pursued a steepening downward trajectory since his arrival an hour back. At that point, he had given the assembled unit a cursory few moments' scrutiny, then signalled Connor to join him out in the yard.

'Who the fuck are these clowns?' he'd asked.

'This is the crew, Finlay. These are my men.' Connor had tried to sound persuasively confident, but only managed slightly miffed.

'Men? They look like a bunch of thugs. Where did you get them? Ned Warehouse?'

'Don't judge them till you've seen them in action,' he

countered, throwing in a knowing smile to disguise the fact that his teeth were beginning to grind. It had been a few years since he'd seen Dawson, but it had taken only moments for the backlog of irritation and resentment to catch up. 'Believe me, mate, these guys are sharp.'

'You've worked with them? All of them?'

'Individually, yes,' Connor offered confidently, until Dawson's sodium-pentathol stare had its inescapable effect. 'Well, most of them, anyway,' he adjusted.

'Never together, never as a unit?'

Connor sighed, ever his most consistent means of expression in Dawson's company. 'No, but I can assure you—'

'Who actually are they, Bill? What's their background?'

'Christ, Finlay, we don't have time. Do you want a pile of fucking CVs? You're the one came to me at about five minutes' bloody notice. You wanted a team – I got you one.'

The display of petulance failed to deflect Dawson's stare. Connor guessed an extended tenure attaching electrodes to anyone who disagreed with him couldn't have done much to mellow the man's notoriously uncompromising nature.

Dawson glanced across to where two men were unloading a crate from Connor's truck.

'Those two, for instance. Which half-derelict council scheme did they escape from?'

Connor looked across to the diesel-reeking vehicle. Both of the men stopped a moment and gave him a salute. He wasn't sure whether it was paranoia induced by Dawson's withering disapproval, but he couldn't help thinking there was an element of sarcasm to the gesture.

'That's Mailey and McKelvie.' Dawson's penetrative gaze demanded he elaborate. Balls. He'd been hoping to put off

2

this particular revelation until Dawson had seen what the pair could do. 'They've both been in, em, active service,' he mumbled.

'British Army?'

'British Army was involved, yes.'

'*Involved*?'

'Yes, they . . .' Connor sighed, yet again, and rolled his eyes. 'All right, they're ex-paramilitaries,' he admitted.

Dawson's eyeballs began to inflate. 'Paramilitaries? Terrorists? Good God, I need soldiers, not amateurs, man.'

'I'm telling you, Finlay, these guys are far from amateurs. It's a bloody stunning track record they've got. You should see the list of places they've blown up. It's like the back of a roadie's t-shirt, I'm not kidding.'

'So what are they doing here, working for you? Were they kicked out or something?'

'No. They went freelance. They got bored. Too many cease-fires and peace agreements, not enough action. They're not really interested in politics. They just like the pointing-guns-at-people part.'

'And presumably you feel you – or rather *we* – can trust these pyro-Paddies?'

Connor's frequency of sighing was starting to make him sound like an asthmatic. He'd heard there was now a particular form of torture named after Dawson in the Middle-East; presumably it had to do with the rectal region.

'Look, I'll come clean with you right now,' he told him. 'Yes, I've hired ex-terrorists. And yes, before you ask, there's more republicans than just those two in the unit. There's guys in there with loyalist paramilitary backgrounds, as well. *Ex*-terrorists, get it? *Not* interested in politics – *like* action. What they've done before doesn't matter – it's just previous employment, if you like. No longer relevant.

3

They work for me now. And yes, I do trust them, because I know I'm uniting these guys like no politician ever could, by offering them the chance to get well paid for doing what they do best and enjoy most: threatening unarmed civilians.'

Dawson closed his eyes and exhaled at length, a hint of a smile finally appearing at the corners of his mouth.

'All right, Bill, my man,' he said, slapping Connor on the shoulder. The gesture was nauseatingly insincere, but he was grateful nonetheless. At least it meant he'd knock off moaning for a few minutes. 'It's been a while, a damn long while, but I'm still me and you're still you, right?' Dawson continued. 'If you trust them, that's good enough for me.'

He sounded like he was trying to convince himself. Connor doubted he'd managed it. The moaning would resume soon enough.

'So what about the rest of them?' Dawson asked, lighting a cigarette.

'A few ex-army. Worked with them in various African shitholes, the usual cycle of coups and rebellions. Gaghen in there has got the record, I think. He helped Matsutu to the presidency, then joined the rebels and deposed him, then got the contract to put him back on top. An exemplar of mercenary professionalism. Absolute ideological detachment at all times. He'd be back with the rebels again now except he got Triso . . . Trypaso . . . Tryoso . . . Ah, fuck it, that nasty business with the tsetse flies – you remember, McGoldrick got it that time.'

'I thought McGoldrick got elephantiasis.'

'Maybe that's what it was. Whatever, Gaghen says he's feeling a lot better now. Anyway, there's a few more from either side of the Ulster bomb-tennis match and a couple

4

of Yanks, used to be in one of those militia capers until their particular Brownie pack got forcibly disbanded. A Norwegian, too. Roland something. Can't pronounce his surname.'

'And what about the bloke with the video camera?'

'Oh, that's Glover. He's shooting our promotional video.'

'Your *what*?'

'Promotional video. This is the future, Finlay. The mercenary market's a busy place these days. If you want the contracts, you've got to be able to show people what you can do. Things have changed while you were sunning yourself in that wee Arabian sinecure. The competition's absolutely fierce, and so many of them are complete fucking cowboys. All these ex-Soviet and Stasi guys for a start – wouldn't trust them to kill your budgie, neither you would. And the worst of it is they've had a knock-on effect for the reputation of the business as a whole. People are very nervous of dealing with a new outfit, so we're filming the crew limbering up here, handling the toys. Then when we tender for a job in future, we can show them what they'll get for their money.'

Dawson made no attempt to disguise a sneer. 'So you see this . . . crew, as you called them, as a long-term venture? I thought you were complaining to me two seconds ago about only having five minutes' notice?'

Connor was determined not to sigh, frequent exposure to Dawson's haughty expression having cultured in him a certain immunity to it. Unfortunately, his recent years of apparent good living meant there was more of Dawson's face for the expression to take up. If offered a choice between a million quid or Dawson's head stuffed with fivers, it would be a tough call.

Connor sighed. 'I wouldn't say this is my envisaged

first-team line-up,' he admitted. 'I wanted Gerry Thomson, for instance, but it turns out he's in jail in some place hot and sticky. Got involved in drug running, silly boy.'

'Drugs,' Dawson said with obvious distaste, flicking ash from the end of his fag. 'He should have known better than that.'

'And Nigel Dixon was meant to be here too, but the Sonzolan air force went in the huff and bombed the army's HQ, so he reckons the coup's going to take another couple of weeks at least. He says hello, by the way. Truth is, a few of these guys are really only stop-gap appointments, but they'll get the job done, don't worry.'

Dawson shrugged his shoulders, about as uncharacteristic a gesture as Connor could imagine. 'Well, it's a fish-in-a-barrel affair, I suppose,' he reflected. 'As long as they know one end of a gun from the other, there's not really a lot can go wrong.'

He did seem to be lightening up. Connor was evidently doing a remarkable job of masking his own misgivings about the patchwork assembly he'd thrown together. But, like the man said, it was a fish-in-a-barrel deal.

'So do many of these guys know each other?' Dawson enquired, incidentally pinpointing the very aspect of the assembly about which Connor had his misgivings.

'Some,' he managed, half-heartedly. 'A few have worked together before, a few haven't but know who each other are, and a few have never met in their lives. But in my experience, it's amazing what the smell of cordite and the promise of a few bob can do to generate team spirit. This time tomorrow they'll be ready to name their children after each other.'

Dawson gave that laugh of his, that wheezy, gravelly effort, like jackboots coming up your garden path. Connor could never tell whether it was amusement or dubious derision.

'Well, I suppose you'd better introduce me to this elite unit of yours,' he said. 'Then we can get on with explaining our evil masterplan.'

'Soon as you're ready, yeah.'

Dawson paused a moment, looking quizzically at the half-smoked cigarette between his thumb and forefinger. 'Never know what to do with these things when there isn't a dissident to put them out on.' He shrugged and dropped it to the ground, grinding the dowt into the mud beneath his boot. Connor looked to the heavens, thinking, Count the hours, count the money.

They walked back towards the cattleshed, slaloming the voluminous country pancakes that lay scattered about the yard like an infestation of some cold, damp, parasitic alien species. Just as long as they didn't attach themselves to your face.

'I thought you said this place was disused,' Dawson grumbled. 'There's shit everywhere.'

'It is disused. But the area around here is still farmland. There's cows all over the place, and they come wandering through whenever they fancy. There's one there.' He pointed to an impressively horned specimen about fifty yards away, watching the munitions truck with bored disinterest. Dawson drew a pistol and pointed it at the beast. It glanced his way for a similarly disinterested moment, then back at the truck with uniform ennui, then dumped splatteringly with a jaded absence of enthusiasm.

'Not much sport to stalk, are they?' Dawson commented.

'No, but they make some size of trophy. Come on, white hunter.'

A second later there came the unmistakable sound of a

shot being fired from inside the cattleshed, followed by a crash of splintering wood. Dawson looked at Connor accusingly.

'I know we're out in the middle of nowhere, Bill, but do the words "clandestine" or "discreet" mean anything to you?'

Connor bit his tongue and stomped purposefully towards the entrance, almost grateful to have some idiot to take it all out on.

'This isn't a bloody firing range,' he began shouting, then had to dive for the floor as a volley of bullets pinged through the massive, side-rolling corrugated iron door, puncturing whatever bombast he'd worked up but fortunately nothing else. He lifted his head and looked up from where he lay on his stomach. Inside the shed there were men lying similarly flat on the ground, while others sheltered behind crates and still others scurried frantically for the exits. He noticed that one of the men on the floor was missing the back of his head, the crate he'd presumably been carrying lying smashed open beside him, polystyrene packing shapes spewing out of it.

Glover came crawling out on his hands and knees, camcorder slung around his shoulder, as several more shots echoed through the dilapidated structure.

'What the fuck's going on?' Dawson demanded, arriving at Connor's rear.

Glover gestured to the pair of them to back up further from the doorway.

'I was doing interviews, like you asked,' he said breathlessly. A couple more fugitives scrambled out the doorway and into the yard, one muttering something about 'fucking mad Irish bastards'.

'I was filmin' McKelvie. He were carryin' in a crate,

and I got him to talk to the camera a little, you know: name, experience, bit of background. Anyway, another of the Irish blokes must have overheard. McWatt, his name was. He come up to me and asks – *fuck's sake!*' Glover flinched as another shot tore through the corrugated wall, leaving a hole less than six inches above his head. Dawson slapped a mag into his pistol and slid the bolt. Connor pulled his own handgun from the back of his trousers, a relief as it had been no friend to the palinodal sinus he'd been inadvertently cultivating between his arse-cheeks.

'He asks whether the guy I'd been talking to was *Antony McKelvie*,' Glover continued. 'I goes: "Yeah, mate, d'you know 'im?" Cunt says, "Sure, he shot my fuckin' cousin", then walks up behind him and blows the back of his fuckin' 'ead out through his face. So McKelvie's mate, Dailey, or Mailey, or whatever the fuck his name is, he sees this and has a shot at McWatt. Then McWatt's mucker joins in as well and suddenly it's the fuckin' OK Corral in there.'

Dawson glared at Connor, who thought for a brief second about shooting him rather than suffer the inevitable onslaught of withering remarks.

He signalled to Pettifer, the last of the evacuees. 'Who's left in there?' Connor asked.

'Dunno. There was one or two stranded in the crossfire, I think. Apart from that, just the shooters.'

'Right,' Connor said, standing up and flipping off the safety as five more rounds were loosed inside. There were times when death seemed preferable to sheer embarrassment.

He dived through the doorway into a practised roll, righting himself against an empty water-storage tank. None of the gunmen was in his line of sight, and presumably not in each other's either, given the temporary lull in

9

firing. From where he squatted, he could more clearly see McKelvie's outstretched arms a few yards in front and his brains another few feet in front of that. It was a profligate waste of talent. He'd have McWatt's balls in a blender for that. Just beyond the cerebral purée, Jackson was lying flat with his arms around his head. He noticed Connor and gestured with his empty hands that he didn't have a weapon, the look in his eyes communicating further that Connor was a considerable distance from his good books at that moment.

'Yeah, okay,' Connor mouthed, tutting. Why was everything always fucking *his* fault? He took a deep breath. 'All right, this is Connor,' he called. 'Cease firing and safety your weapons now. That's a fucking order.'

Four bullets drummed into the side of the water tank in instant reply.

'I mean it,' Connor shouted. 'Anybody fires one more round and they're off this team. We've got a job to do here – a very lucrative job, I'd remind you – so put your bloody toys away and save your parochial tantrums for your spare time.'

This time there was no hot-lead riposte, which he took to be an encouraging sign. 'Come on, guns on the floor, now. Throw them into the middle, there, where Mr Jackson is waiting patiently to collect them. Then we can all walk outside and cool off. DO IT!'

There followed an age of silence, throughout which Connor tried not to think of phrases like 'Hume-Adams', 'decommissioning' and 'Dayton-style peace agreement'. Eventually, a Glock came arcing from the shadows and landed next to Jackson, kicking up a foot-high spray of dust. The motes continued to swirl in the sunlight and silence as the weapon waited for a companion. A Nagan clattered into it a few seconds later, in a Nobel Peace Prize kind of moment. Finally, and with more than a suggestion of begrudging defiance, a Browning automatic was lobbed accurately at Jackson's head. With the safety still off.

The Browning discharged a shot into the dust, inches from Jackson's right temple, causing him to howl in pain and spring reflexively on to his knees, holding a hand to his ear. Blood was trickling out of it by the time the first of the shooters edged tentatively from the shadows. It was Mailey, his hands held either side of his face, his eyes looking to the doorway for assurance that someone was coming in to mediate. Dawson, Pettifer, Glover and others quickly took position around him, while at the other end of the cattleshed, several more men moved swiftly inside to circle McWatt and his fellow loyalist, who turned out to be Kilfoyle.

'All right, children,' announced Dawson acidly, 'I want everybody's firearms on the floor over there and I want all of you standing to attention in three seconds. *Everybody*,' he repeated, coldly eyeing a few who hadn't grasped the newcomer's role in proceedings. Guns began thudding into the dirt amid a grumbling spate of sighs, shrugs and 'fuck's sake's. Dawson gestured to Connor to collect them, doing so with an I'll-see-you-about-this-later headmasterly glower.

'And you'll get them back when you've learned how to play with them properly,' he continued. The disarmed troops eyed Connor balefully as he marched past their dishevelled line, carrying their beloved playthings outside in a wooden box. Dawson began to address them in parade-ground register.

'For those of you who don't know, my name is Finlay Dawson. I am the man ultimately in charge of this operation, which means in short that I and only I tell you who to kill and when. What you do in your own spare time has nothing to do with me, so if any more of you feel like killing each other or indeed killing your*selves*, you're perfectly free to do so when your shift finishes tomorrow morning. But right now, it's office hours, got it?'

There were a few grudging 'yes, sir's, their lethargy causing Connor to wince. Dawson was used to a degree more effusiveness, his man-management style being based on somewhat hierarchical principles.

'Okay, which one of you is McWatt?' he enquired casually.

McWatt lifted a hand shiftlessly. Dawson took a step towards him and shot him through the forehead.

Kilfoyle made a lunge for Dawson but found himself nose-to-barrel against his automatic.

'What's this one's name, Mr Connor?' he barked.

'Kilfoyle.'

'Kilfoyle. Well, Mr Kilfoyle, is there any business between yourself and Mr Mailey that you feel can't wait until after office hours?'

Kilfoyle swallowed. 'No,' he said, his word barely a whisper.

'No what, Mr Kilfoyle?'

'No, sir,' he corrected, his would-be defiance wilting predictably in the heat of Dawson's unflinching stare.

'Stand down,' Dawson told him. Both men took a step back. 'All right, now that everybody's "on-message", perhaps we can get on with unloading the gear. Then, if we pull that off without any further casualties, we'll maybe move on to the challenge of an inventory. And if we complete *that* mission successfully, who knows? I might even progress to debriefing you on this evening's itinerary. But let's not get carried away with our ambitions, given that fatality-free freight-loading proved beyond us at the first attempt.'

Connor chose this moment to step in and attempt to recover some remnant of authority. 'Dobson, Fleming,' he ordered tartly. 'I want small arms and ammunition in that corner. Pettifer, Jardine, all explosives over there. Quinn, McIntosh, comms equipment—'

'What about the bodies, sir?' asked Glover.

Dawson intervened before Connor could speak. 'Messrs Mailey and Kilfoyle will place them in the truck once it's been emptied. We can't bury them around here – we'll dispose of them later.' The pair moved off towards their respective fallen comrades, but Dawson stopped them. 'No. Back you come. Mr Mailey, I'd like you to take charge of the late Mr McWatt, and Mr Kilfoyle, I'd like you to look after the late Mr McKelvie. If you both pay close attention to the state of the bodies you'll observe that Catholic or Protestant, a bullet to the head has much the same effect. On you go.'

'What was that?' Connor asked him. 'Your attempt at reconciliation?'

Dawson tutted. 'Merely reminding them they're both on the same side today, seeing as this *esprit de corps* you were waxing lyrical about has manifestly failed to materialise. Never mind *esprit de corps*, even plain old mercenary materialism seems beyond these morons. I just hope the rest of your shower turn out to have some idea of what they're doing. Especially as we're now two men down.'

'Well you're the one who shot McWatt.'

'And if I hadn't, Mailey'd have popped him, first chance he got. Then Kilfoyle would have popped Mailey, and so on. There are more nationalists here, aren't there?'

Connor nodded reluctantly. 'Different faction. Can't

remember which one. But they didn't get involved back there, I hope you noticed.'

'Yes, but that's because they're used to shooting at people who can't shoot back.'

Connor had had enough. This prick had breezed in at the eleventh hour needing *his* help, after all.

'Look, Finlay,' he said angrily. 'Don't fucking kid yourself that I don't know *exactly* how many options you've got right now. What else are you going to do, eh? Who else are you going to go to? You came to me looking for an outfit, and I got you one. So it's not been a dream start this morning, so fucking what? Don't judge me on one screw-up, and don't judge these guys until you've seen what they can do.'

Dawson shrugged. 'It's a fair point, Bill,' he said patronisingly. 'Consider my judgement "reserved".'

Arsehole.

Dawson walked off to talk to Jackson, who was squatting on the ground, still holding his ear. Connor headed for the door, reckoning a dose of fresh air was in order if he wasn't going to punch somebody. He passed Kilfoyle, who was crouched between McKelvie's corpse and the crate he'd been carrying when he got shot. He was staring at Dawson with emotions not too different from Connor's own. The Ulsterman looked like he'd dearly love to have his gun back.

'Save it till after payday, pal,' Connor advised, checking his stride and moving to one side as Pettifer and Jardine approached from the truck, supporting a cumbersome box between them. He noticed Kilfoyle reach a hand into the broken crate and pull some polystyrene shapes from it, staring fixedly at what was beneath. Suddenly unfixed, Kilfoyle pulled out the rocket launcher that had been contained within, momentarily eyeing the tailfins and hefting

14

it to his shoulder to point the other end directly at the man who'd executed his comrade.

There were several shouts in that moment as Kilfoyle pressed the button, all but two of them too-late warnings to Dawson and Jackson to get out the way. Of the two dissenters, one was Connor's too-late warning to *Glover* to get out the way, having noticed that Kilfoyle's tailfins were in fact forefins and that therefore the launcher was back to front. The other was Glover going 'Aaaaaaaaaaaaaaaah!' as the rocket hit him in the chest, picked him up bodily, flew him thirty metres across the yard and detonated against the concrete wall of the barn opposite.

Connor ran uselessly after him. He made it through the gaping doorway in time to see Glover's head and arms fly off in different directions, and a few seconds later for his sautéed insides to pay their due respects to the late Isaac Newton.

Dawson was so intent upon getting to Connor to express his disgust that he almost forgot to stop and shoot Kilfoyle on his way past.

■ 09:09 ■ kilbokie brae ■ return of the mac ■

Former Lothian and Borders Police Inspector Hector McGregor took a deep, satisfying breath of the Cromarty Firth air and looked at his watch, which told him he was officially about ten minutes into his retirement. He hadn't actually worked a shift for three weeks, but that had, strictly speaking, been holiday time, most of it spent organising and executing his and Molly's move from Islay. Yesterday had been his last day of paid leave, and he'd toyed with considering himself a gentleman of leisure as of tea-time then, but an August Saturday at nine had sounded far, far more satisfying. Somewhere in Edinburgh right now, a copper was turning up to start *that* shift, with the Festival in full swing, Princes Street mobbed, and Rangers due at Easter Road.

The morning was cool and clear, with a warmth in the wind that seemed to promise the sun would get stronger and that a hot summer day was in prospect.

Lovely.

Perfect, in fact. Another half an hour's brisk walk and he'd be at the kitchen table, enjoying one of Molly's no-holds-barred fry-ups, before deciding how to spend the rest of this momentous day. A leisurely eighteen holes, perhaps, or possibly a seat by the water, meditating in anticipation of the unmatched pleasure of a tug on his line; perhaps even phone his brother-in-law in Portmeddie, see if he was taking his boat out later. Or maybe he'd just sit on his arse in the sun-trap back green, pipe in one hand, can of export in the other, contemplating the fact that if anyone in the vicinity decided to do something unpleasant to anybody else today, it was no longer any worry of his.

The smell of pine filled his nose, the twitter of birds his ears; that and the wind the only sounds to be heard, it seemed, in the whole world.

He was due this. Christ knew he was due this.

His posting on Islay hadn't turned out to be quite the peaceful valedictory sinecure he'd hoped. First of all, there'd been that horrible stooshie over the wifie in Ballygrant with MS who was growing her own cannabis in her greenhouse. Having spent three decades policing a city whose name had become synonymous with heroin

16

and AIDS, McGregor's perspective on both drugs and disease had prompted him to be forever too busy to investigate rumours of something that seemed common knowledge throughout the island and something no-one in the community wanted to make a fuss about. Even the occasional pointed suggestion that it was 'a helluva big greenhoose, right enough' remained insufficient to pique his professional curiosity, until a 'concerned citizen' made a formal complaint and he was obliged to take action.

The concerned citizen, a Mr Charles McGinty, was not in fact a resident of Islay, but owned a holiday home there, which he visited most weekends. Through a telephone call, he furnished McGregor with the information not only that Stella McQueen was growing cannabis for personal use, but also that she was selling the excess to the island's impressionable youngsters.

When he arrested her, the whole thing turned into a three-ring media circus, with reporters, photographers and news crews descending instantly on the place, closely followed by a waftingly stinky mob of long-haired protesters in the most life-endangeringly ramshackle convoy of motor transport outside of a Mad Max picture. The dictaphone-and-flashbulb brigade only tarried long enough to interview Stella and file their 'senseless victimisation' stories, buggering off again before the real senseless victimisation began.

The crusties kept pelting him with lumps of rancid bacon (him being a pig – ho fuckin' ho), which he thought might have more usefully been fed to the diseased-looking mutts that followed them around. Some farmer friend of Stella McQueen (McGregor had no witnesses, but everyone knew fine who it was) sprayed slurry all over the front of his wee station in the middle of the night, and he was even hit with the time-honoured jobbie-inside-a-blazing-newspaper-left-on-your-doorstep routine. Time-honoured it may have been, but when the bell rang and he opened the door to find flames licking his trousers, he automatically began stamping on it – in his bloody slippers – before remembering.

As if that wasn't enough, he also had the islanders on his back, complaining about the mess and general nuisance the crusty encampment was causing, and practically a pitched battle on his hands when the locals decided to confront the visitors over whether Jock Gibson's missing sheep and the barbecue they'd had the night before might be in some way related. Having been thus aggravated by the indigenous population, the crusties rightly anticipated that the most damaging response would be to announce their intention to stay even longer. McGregor successfully persuaded them otherwise using a phoney ferry timetable, with which he pointed out that if they didn't piss off on the next boat they were going to be marooned there during Glastonbury.

Nobody said thank you. In fact, the only civil gesture he received came in the form of a cake baked and sent to him by, of all people, Stella McQueen, with a note to say sorry for all the bother he'd had. He and Molly polished it off between them for dessert, and very tasty it was too, but he did begin to fear the worst a wee while later when he realised the pair of them were laughing away at an ITV sitcom. Stella sent another note the next day to tell him exactly how much gear had gone into the cake, her idea of a practical joke. At least someone on the island still had a sense of humour. That sense of humour was doubtless painfully tested when the less-than-understanding sheriff imposed a custodial sentence, but for McGregor at least it seemed to draw some kind of line under the matter.

Being in jail – on top of being in a wheelchair – meant Stella McQueen therefore had a stoater of an alibi for the night Charles McGinty's house had all its windows shot out by an estimated three hundred rounds of ammunition, evidently intended to harm more than just glass. Traces of blood were found in several locations along a trail leading from McGinty's back garden to the Kilchiaran road, despite the inhabitant himself not being injured in the attack. This tended to suggest one of his would-be assassins had come to some harm, but Mr McGinty was unable to furnish McGregor with any explanation as to how this might have come about, nor why the policeman had found a number of spent shotgun cartridges around the premises' back door.

It was around this time that McGregor discovered his concerned citizen to be better known around Glasgow as 'Mad Chic McGinty', currently holding the strongest hand at the West of Scotland's drugs-and-doings table. He'd grassed up Stella McQueen partly to maintain his duplicitous public image, but mainly because he didn't want impressionable teenagers wasting their money on cannabis when his boys could be supplying them with something that was more of a long-term investment.

The word from Glasgow was that a rival player had attempted to destabilise McGinty's operation via the direct and often effective decapitation method. For a while McGregor wished they had succeeded, but that soon gave way to wishing plain old murder was all it had been about.

As the Islay nights became ever more frequently lit up by small-arms fire and, on several spectacular occasions, exploding boats, it became inescapably apparent that some kind of territorial battle was being bloodily fought, with

McGregor handed the blue helmet and the role of use-less UN peacekeeper. Of course, it wasn't long before Strathclyde sent reinforcements, followed by cops from London and Amsterdam, plus a small army of customs officials. But his Edinburgh fireside fantasies of being a one-man police force with nothing to do evaporated into a blurred haze of gunplay and politics as his poky wee station became the hub of an international narcotics investigation.

McGinty hadn't bought a holiday home on Islay simply because he liked the place. The knuckle-dragging bampot was hardly the scholarly type, but had evidently been a keen student of local history, and of that subject's incorrigible tendency to repeat itself.

Think Islay, think whisky. Rich, dark, peaty stuff. The place was hoaching with distilleries, and once upon a time there'd been even more. The reason for this was not the excellent quality of its fresh water, the aforementioned peat or any other factor conducive to fine malt-making. It was that for a period during the nineteenth century, there wasn't an exciseman posted there, so every bugger had started his own still.

In more recent times, the customs men's numbers had been slashed back to save money, with attention centred on certain high-profile airports and harbours, 'intelligence' rather than diligence relied upon to thwart the smugglers. McGinty had reasoned that nobody would be paying much attention to Strathclyde's most westward point, and had cultivated links with European exporters to land heroin at a wee jetty just north of Portnahaven. From there the gear was transported to Port Ellen for the ferry to Kennacraig, then driven off the boat, uninspected, on to mainland British soil.

It had been the key to McGinty's bludgeoning progress

through the Scottish drugs underworld, and his local power was such that it turned out the battles on Islay hadn't been instigated by any native rivals but by a major European firm who fancied making use of his trade route and wanted both ends of the incumbent arrangement out of the way. Hence the small-arms fire. And the exploding boats. And the mortar attack on McGregor's polis station, forcing him to work out of a Portakabin for the rest of his attachment.

But that was over now. It was *all* over now. Edinburgh was behind him. Islay was behind him. The future was the undisturbed tranquillity of the Cromarty Firth, and it had only just begun.

He took another satisfied breath and resumed walking. The sound of gunfire erupted suddenly from somewhere beyond the cover of the trees. One shot, then, moments later, a few more. Then a lot more. He caught himself panicking, peering nervously into the woods, then stopped, remembering both his geographical location and the date. It was August the 12th – the glorious 12th – and here he was in the highlands. The grouse season started today. He laughed aloud, relishing the moment for its timely symbolism. From now on, shooting meant sport. Loud bangs meant hunting. And none of it was his problem.

He strode contentedly down the path for another quarter mile or so, following the trail until it passed close to a couple of rather run-down farm outbuildings, occasionally visible through breaks in the trees. Another glance at his watch told him he was still officially less than half an hour into his retirement, and it just seemed to be getting better and better.

A few seconds later, barely preceded by the startling blast of an explosion, a severed arm came hurtling down

21

upon him from the sky, its clenched fist knocking him unconscious with a solid blow to the side of his head.

■ 09:17 ■ auchenlea ■ the start of a great adventure ■

Dear *Alastair McQuade*,
      'Let's meet up in the year 2000!'
Your former classmate Gavin Hutchison cordially invites you to an unmissable reunion event. Join your fellow ex-pupils from St Michael's Auchenlea in the incomparably luxurious surroundings of Delta Leisure™'s Floating Island Paradise Resort on Saturday, August 12th, for an evening of food, drink, dancing, reacquaintance, reminiscence and nostalgia . . .

August 12th. Today. Now. Annette pulled the Audi over about a hundred yards from the entrance to the school car park, where the coach would pick everyone up. She was seriously taking no chances about being seen as she dropped him off. He looked across at her and they both laughed.
'Last chance,' he said.
'Yeah, right.'
The invite had arrived about three weeks back, which at the time had seemed indecently short notice. Not in terms of clearing a space in his social diary, which generally worked on a free-form improvisational basis, but in terms of growing up, which was something Ally felt you were optimally supposed to have achieved before attending a

fifteen-year school reunion. Even if you hadn't achieved it, you were at least supposed to have given it a shot.

It was Annette's fault, really. They'd been living together for nearly two years now, throughout which she had been neglectfully remiss about her duty to nag him incessantly on the subject. No whining about his immaturity, no accusations of childish self-indulgence, no tutting disapproval of his alcohol and fast-food consumption, no arguments about the part his disposable income was playing in propping up the Hollywood studio system, not even a tantrum when her mother had to be rescued by helicopter from the foothills of his sell-through video collection. And this woman expected him to marry her?

Still, give the lassie her due, after this growing-up deadline came through the letterbox last month, she had done her belated best to assist him by declaring herself irrevocably up the jaggy. That the announcement should have come as a complete surprise had ramifications for his otherwise reliable powers of observation and deduction: Annette drinking Virgin Marys on a Friday night was barely less ambiguous than if she had come home with a Silver Cross pram.

It would be inaccurate to say it wasn't planned: that would give the impression that it had actually been discussed. They hadn't even talked about the possibility in a yes/no/don't know/let's-have-this-conversation-in-six-months kind of way. That was entirely symptomatic of their relationship to date, right enough. They weren't much given to state-of-the-union summits, in keeping with the 'pleasantly winging it' philosophy that characterised what they had between them. The upside of this was that it always felt new, it always felt like they hadn't been together long, despite the calendar stating its regular, irrefutable objections. The downside was that Ally occasionally entertained a fear that Annette would wake up one morning with a sudden clarity of vision, take a deck at what was around her, scream 'Jesus Christ, I'm living with Ally McQuade!' and run directly for the street in her goonie and slippers, never to return.

Admittedly, this wasn't exactly the manifestation of a crippling inferiority complex that stood in the way of their mutual emotional development. And that. It was just a thought Ally had from time to time, to remind himself of his status on the shortlist of the world's jammiest men. All the reasons and all the scenarios by which it would become obvious why the two of them could not possibly work out had serially presented themselves and inexplicably failed to produce the logical result. Even at the beginning, their relationship had been founded on enough misunderstandings, misconceptions and misapprehensions to fuel a dozen ugly break-ups and as many straight-to-video Jennifer Aniston vehicles.

They met at the opening 'reception' for a new art gallery just off Great Western Road. It was a champagne and canapés affair, attended by local journos, PR smile-a-whiles and a populous delegation of the effetely pretentious goatee-and-navel-ring types who gave rise to an indigenously Glaswegian application of the word 'poof' that was entirely indifferent towards sexual orientation. Ally was standing before (according to the card) a 'post-cubist' triptych entitled *Love, Honour and Obey*, which he decided had less to say to him about marriage than it had about the artist's unspoken sufferings at the hands of a deranged geometrist. He was bursting to say something crude, ignorant and uninformed, but he didn't know the gallery owner well enough for it to be worth embarrassing him.

24

That was when Annette appeared at his elbow, attracting his attention with a wave of her fingers and saying: 'I'm sorry, I can't remember your name, but we've met before, haven't we?'

Recognising her now that she was separate from the throng, Ally put her unguardedly warm approach down to her inability to recollect also *where* they had met before, which was St Michael's RC Secondary, Auchenlea, Renfrewshire. Geographically, it was only a few miles from an art gallery on Great Western Road, but sociologically, it was a long time ago in a galaxy far, far away.

Her name was Annette Strachan. Ally could have rhymed off the names of everyone who was ever in one of his classes, but even had he not been what Annette referred to as 'the human database', it was unlikely he'd have forgotten hers. Every year-group had its beauties, and in his, Annette Strachan and a girl called Catherine O'Rourke walked head and shoulders above female-kind. Not that thoughts of them kept Ally awake at night in those days: Annette and Catherine existed in a different dimension, so the notion of a crush on either was as hopelessly abstract as fancying Phoebe Cates or Victoria Principal.

It was a slight relief, if hardly a surprise, that she did not so vividly remember him, as his distinguishing characteristics throughout the awkward age had amounted to little more than a smart mouth and a weak stomach. Memories of an irritating wee bastard who puked when he got nervous would hardly have proven an enticement to the sort of informal approach she had just made.

He came clean on their previous connection, which had roughly the opposite effect to the undignified retreat he'd anticipated. Maybe that was actually what hooked them

together: if you did traverse the galaxy and you met someone from your home town, you were likely to find them
twice as fascinating as all the punters with three heads
and eight tits, if only because they'd made the same epic
journey. Arthur Dent travelled not just the universe but to
either end of time, and three books on he was still fixated
by Tricia McMillan – but then Londoners always were very
parochial that way.

They got blethering, small-talk and smiles, with maybe
even a hint of mutual flirting, and soon blew the gallery
for a pub round the corner. Ally was just placing the first
round of drinks on the table when Annette casually asked
what he was doing at the reception. Her failure, once again,
to cool her interest upon the revelation that his invite was
a courtesy after rewiring the place, suggested he might be
the one carrying the misconceptions.

He'd admit that a small, sour part of himself was disappointed by her reactions. Both when he told her the St
Mick's link and when he told her he was a spark, the
inverted snob in him was looking forward to seeing her
embarrassment, her discomfiture, as a confirmation that
as well as retaining her looks, she had held on to the other
aspect he well remembered her for. Annette Strachan had,
throughout her schooldays, been somewhat aloof in the
company of her peers, or in the local parlance, 'a fuckin'
snooty bitch'. She'd lived in one of the big 'bought hooses'
up on the Springwell Road, and neither her socio-economic
status nor the benefits of her physical attributes had made
her particularly disposed towards sharing much time with
the likes of Ally.

It was, Ally grew to learn, nothing personal. Annette
had simply hated being at school and spent the whole
time counting the days to when she could spread her

wings. She detested the miniature totalitarianism enforced by the staff, the mentality that punished the whole class if one culprit wouldn't own up. She found the curriculum frustratingly restrictive as well, with everything so geared towards exam syllabuses and exam technique that learning for its own sake seemed a decadent luxury. But mostly she hated the junior fascism among the pupils, the way the wee buggers mercilessly cracked down on every minuscule transgression of a social code that only its adherents knew. From the make of your schoolbag to the colour of your lunchbox to the type of wallpaper covering your workbook, you never knew what might mark you out as a leper tomorrow. (Ally didn't remember Annette ever having to ring a bell herself, but then you didn't have to be on the receiving end to abhor it.)

She knuckled under big-time in fifth year, making sure she got the Highers she needed to access Glasgow Uni, the West End and as much student bohemia as she could lay hands on. After that she 'did the London thing', and sought work as a journalist. She started off on one of the temps' weekly giveaway mags, writing features and advertorials, as well as laying out ads and even selling space when things got tight. In time she made it up to the glossies, got the big-city lifestyle she'd long aspired to, and after a few years a bidey-in 'partner' to share it all with. He was handsome, ambitious, sophisticated, connected, the works. He was also, she inevitably discovered, just about the most shallow human being ever to exist in the three-dimensional world. Annette made it a considerate policy not to talk to Ally about him, but he still picked up the gen here and there: the lying, the backstabbing, the mistrust and, of course, the cheating. This last Ally had some difficulty getting his head around: previously he'd thought the male tendency to stray was symptomatic of a fundamental dissatisfaction caused by not sleeping with someone like Annette Strachan.

The break-up was very messy, and her work was contaminated by the fall-out. This precipitated 'the life-crisis thing', which in turn gave way to a year or so doing 'the travel thing', at the end of which she decided she was utterly scunnered with London. In defiance of Dr Johnson, she was not correspondingly tired of life, but she did feel she needed to scale things down a little, so opted to move back to the West End, somewhere she'd often returned to for weekends even during the height of her metropolitan phase. She'd been living back there a wee bit less than a year, working freelance, when she went to that art gallery, ran into Ally, and commenced their unlikely but confoundingly successful relationship.

Ally hadn't lacked for female company before that. The cheeky wee bastard of youth had evolved to be a charming wee bastard when appropriate; and the evidence suggested that women actually found him either quite cute or at the least too short to be threatening. However, it still required a steeply descending lack of subtlety in Annette's overtures for him to grasp that she didn't want them to be just good friends.

The morning after they first slept together, she said that she had been one date away from asking if he was gay, as he had set a new heterosexual record time for not making a pass at her. He confessed he'd been slightly intimidated because of how inaccessible he'd regarded her in their youth. Fortunately, he drew short of sharing the Phoebe Cates and Victoria Principal comparisons, as Annette was finding it hilarious enough already. He decided then that their relationship might just have a chance, provided, of course, she at some point stopped laughing at him.

Ally knew what her friends thought of the situation, mainly because early on he'd been wary of it himself: she was on the rebound. Not from her ex-partner, but from her ex-life, so Mr Down-Home Spark – the genial skilled tradesman who could read books *and* knew who Krzysztof Kieslowski was – would be both lap-dog and bit of rough until she'd sorted herself out; upon which he'd be humanely put down to make way for someone who read books and actually *liked* Krzysztof Kieslowski.

There were some who still thought that way, or at least, in the face of overwhelming contrary evidence, adapted to discreetly sympathise for poor Annette's downfall. These tended to be – ironically or significantly, according to your individual regional prejudices – her Glasgow friends rather than those she knew from her London days. Perhaps this was because the former, being closer to the reality, were that bit more afraid of a similar disastrous fate befalling themselves.

The others' sympathies were often surrogately lavished upon Ally. They tended to be so pleasantly surprised by his literacy that they were always trying to suggest ways to unshackle his gifts from the chains of his workaday existence as an electrical contractor. The notions that he quite liked what he did and that he might be making more money than any of them were thoughts that he patiently resisted sharing. This was only fair, as he knew he was occasionally guilty of encouraging them. It hadn't escaped Annette's notice that company from the big smoke often provoked in him the familiar Scottish working-class ostentation of wearing your esoteric intellectualism on your sleeve. This worked best in conjunction with an uncompromising refusal to refine your accent for mainstream consumption, and often piqued an entertaining reaction in those who'd never heard the names Plato or Aristotle pronounced with a glottal stop.

Not much escaped Annette's notice, right enough. For instance, in company, Ally could no longer get away with showing off his encyclopedic knowledge of Woody Allen scripts or De Niro's *oeuvre*, because she knew he also had an encyclopedic knowledge of *South Park* scripts and Van Damme's *oeuvre*. That she didn't consider either of these reason enough to dump him was, he considered, a true miracle of modern living.

And in return for this saintly degree of tolerance, Ally provided . . . well, he wasn't sure. He had to be doing something right, he knew, but he wasn't aware of it being anything he consciously went out of his way to achieve. He would occasionally reason to himself that he must, on the whole, be a pleasant and considerate guy to have around, but this always led inevitably to the question of why none of his previous girlfriends had noticed this. One of his more observant (if admittedly unreconstructed) pals had reasoned back then that his girlfriends *did* find Ally pleasant and considerate: the problem was that having landed such a rare specimen, they very quickly decided he would do as a husband, then became frustrated when he didn't, with reciprocal haste, advance matters along those lines. This in turn, Jake reasoned, had Ally reaching for the ejector seat.

Ally tended to take most of Jake's sexual-political theories with a pinch of post-modernism, but a retrospective analysis of his break-ups did unearth certain recurrences in the preceding days or weeks, notably a tendency on his girlfriends' parts to dwell in front of estate agents or Pronuptia outlets. It was very possible, therefore, that he and Annette had made it so far because for so long he'd have found it hard to believe she could have such designs on him.

Christ, maybe she hadn't, but it was moot now. She was pregnant and glowingly happy about it. That, in fact, was the greatest compliment Ally had ever been paid: that when she told him about it, she did so with a big, cheeky, bad-girl grin. Whatever fears she was naturally bound to have for how he'd take it, she masked them behind a show of assumption that he'd be as astonished but pleased about it as she was.

And she was right. He'd have to confess that his initial unmanly show of emotion was partly in response to the shock of the news and partly in ecstatic appreciation of its long-term ramifications (principally those affecting the likelihood of that sudden-clarity/dressing-gown/slippers/street scenario). However, in the week that followed, when he actually had time to consider the reality of what he was facing, he was even more surprised to find that he was unreservedly, uncomplicatedly, utterly fucking delighted about it.

None of which made sense. In fact, for about four days, nothing in his head made sense. Responsibility suddenly sounded like a fourteen- rather than four-letter word. Parenthood sounded like a great adventure rather than a waste of Steve Martin. And growing up sounded plausibly achievable.

Once his whizzing brain had calmed down a wee bit and he discovered that such ludicrous thoughts were actually there to stay, he appreciated that he shouldn't really have been so amazed at the strength with which his paternal instincts had suddenly kicked in. It was hundreds of thousands of years of genetic programming against a brief decade or so of late-twentieth-century pseudo-individualism.

Besides, bottle feeding a wean at three in the morning would provide a unique opportunity to revisit the *Moonlighting* back-catalogue.

At the end of that week, Annette asked him to marry her. It was the sort of moment that made him think the real secret of their relationship might lie in 'McQuade' turning out to be Gaelic for 'Faust'. Ally knew this was largely down to his Catholic upbringing and the guilt it made you feel over anything good that life allowed you. However, he was able to counter his fear with the rationalisation that, as an atheist, he hadn't accounted for having a soul anyway, so Meph was welcome to whatever was going. Eternity seemed a price worth paying for one lifetime of what he was signing up for when he said yes to Annette.

Of course, she did very openly add the proviso that this meant he'd have to sell all his CDs, videos and computer games, and that they'd never have sex again, but he'd taken that as read: marriage is marriage. Similarly sticking with tradition, it was decided that they should proceed to the main event fairly swiftly in order that Annette should not be 'showing too much in the photies', and the date was accordingly set for a month hence.

Annette sympathetically observed that this didn't leave much time to organise a stag night, sympathy that Ally considered misspent as he had never expressed any desire to put himself through such a thing. His now-fiancée (oh, how he loved that word) elaborated that it was an important and time-observed custom for the groom-to-be to undergo a night out so thoroughly ghastly and traumatic that he would wish to spend the rest of his life exclusively in the company of someone who hadn't been there. She then concluded that she could think of no occasion more convenient or appropriate than Gavin Hutchison's school-reunion party. Ally took this to be a final confirmation – as if there had been any ambiguity – that Annette would not be joining him on the Floating Island Paradise Resort.

'It sounds like the most bloody awful nightmare I could possibly imagine,' she'd said, after her email invite was forwarded from the London offices of a magazine she still strung for. Ally's, via plain old snail-mail, arrived at the flat, being his registered business address. He found her print-out and his postcard lying side-by-side on the kitchen table when he came in from work, Annette washing dishes at the sink.

'I honestly can't think of anything worse. If there's one thing in my life I have never looked back on, it was getting out of Auchenlea, getting out of *that* school and getting away from *those* people. Now this clown, who I don't even remember, is suggesting getting together with all of them – overnight – on a place you can only escape from by boat! It would be like . . . like . . . actually, I can't come up with a metaphor. In fact, in future, people will *use* this *as* a metaphor. How awful's that? That's as awful as cooping yourself up on a bloody oil-rig with thirty or forty people you've never stopped hating in all the fifteen years since you last had the misfortune of sharing a room with them.'

'So,' Ally had ventured, 'not up for it then?'

She laughed, but Ally knew she wasn't kidding. Realistically, apart from visits at her parents' place, the only thing likely to reunite Annette and Auchenlea was a bad Monday, a tower and a high-velocity rifle.

'And I take it you are?' she stated, almost accusingly. The almost-accusation derived from Annette finding Ally 'irritatingly well balanced' when it came to his schooldays, or indeed anything; he never having confided the sudden-clarity/dressing-gown etcetera scenario.

'Of course,' he said, feigning a wounded look. 'This could be my only chance to tell all those people that I've shagged Annette Strachan.'

Ally had to dodge a wet handful of water and suds.

'See, I know you're joking about that, but that's what these things are about,' she told him. 'That's the single reason anyone would go: the only people who turn up will be the ones who think they've done quite well for themselves one way or another and want to compare scores with the rest. This Gavin Hutchison idiot obviously wants to show off this ludicrous holiday resort he's built, probably to compensate for the fact that he was so anonymous at school. I can't even remember who he was.'

'You can never remember who anyone was, Annette,' Ally reminded her. 'I'm surprised you remember the name of the school.'

'That's not true,' she countered, grinning. 'I remember Matthew Black. *And* Davie Murdoch.'

'Oh, well, we'll just call you Miss Mnemonic, then. Imagine bein' able to simply pluck *those* names out of the ether.'

'Easy for the human database to say. And besides, you remember everyone because you *liked* everyone.'

'I did *not*.'

'You did. You *do*. You get on with everybody. You don't have many character defects, Ally McQuade, but that is definitely one of them. And don't argue with me, I know you too well – you'll already be looking forward to this thing because you *genuinely* want to know what happened to everybody, what they're all doing with themselves. You can't help it: you're a people person. If I didn't love you, it would make me sick.'

34

So there they were, three weeks later, parked a short walk from the St Mick's school gates on a dry Saturday morning.

'You'll be the only one there, I'm telling you,' Annette said once more. 'I'll pass by again on the way back from my mum's, and I'll bet there's just you and the coach driver, both looking lost. If you look pathetic enough, I might stop and offer you a lift home, but I'll need to see some *big* puppy-dog eyes.'

Ally leaned over and gave her a kiss, then opened the car door. 'I will *not* be the only one there,' he told her, climbing out. 'Because there were two crucial words near the bottom of the invite that you have obviously failed to take into account.'

'And what might they have been?'

'Free drink. I'll see you tomorrow, baby.'

Ally closed the door and began walking towards the car park. Annette caught up with him in the Audi a few seconds later, the electric window sliding down as he turned to see her.

'Remember,' she called out. 'Ghastly and traumatic.'

'I'll do my best.'

■ 09:50 ■ glasgow airport ■ lost soul in transit ■

The trickiest thing about not killing yourself is knowing that if one day you decide it was a mistake, then you'll always be able to rectify it. Opting against suicide may be a choice *for* life, but it's not for *life*. It's kind of like parole after a murder stretch: you're walking around free but you'll always be serving the sentence, knowing one screw-up is all it takes to send you back down. And therein hangs the burden. The worry that one bad day could be all it takes to put the pills back in your hand, like one drink could be all it takes to send the alcoholic spiralling down Bender Avenue once again.

If so, Matthew Black had reason to fear. He was on his way to a school reunion. How bad could a bad day get?

He was also an alcoholic, whatever that meant. He'd read it in the *Daily Record*.

Not that he should be dissing the tabloids, right enough, given the crucial role they'd played in coaxing him back from the brink. Because, when he was a bawhair's breadth from the precipice and leaning teeteringly forwards, before he'd embraced all the life-reaffirmation shite and cried himself through to that beckoning dawn, those much-maligned newspapers had given him a reason to go on. When there seemed nothing else to cling to, the thought of those sanctimonious bastards enjoying that told-you-so moment as they gleefully reported his senseless, tragic death, resurrected some nuance of self he'd so long ago buried.

People seldom appreciated just how vital and positive raw hatred could be.

He eyed the conveyor belt patiently, waiting for his wee black sports bag to trundle modestly into view, thinking how old habits were hellish hard to shake. These days, people would apparently prefer to risk hernias and coronaries heaving monolithic baggage about departure terminals and on-board aircraft than stand around a carousel for five minutes at the other end. He kept picturing Atlas at a check-in desk: 'Can I take this on as hand-luggage?' Five minutes at the end of an hours-long flight – how big a fucking hurry would you need to be in?

Matt usually travelled light. One wee sports bag light. And the old habit he hadn't shaken was of checking the scrawny thing into the cargo hold, even though it was hardly much of an encumbrance. This was a throwback to a more colourful period in the Matt Black life history, and was based on the international aviation protocols stating that once a passenger's bag is onboard, the plane is not allowed to take off without him, just in case he's checked a bomb on and buggered off. In practice this meant he could go and get obliviously wrecked in the airport bars without fear of missing his plane, as the ground staff invariably reasoned that it was easier to make a few angry PA announcements or even send their most stern-faced and matronly stewardess to retrieve him than to unload the entire cargo hold and root through all the bags until they found his.

A plooky adolescent male eyed him shyly as he picked up the holdall, or holdnov'rymuch might be more like it, bearing as it did only most of his worldly belongings. He pulled back the zipper and had a quick check of the contents, like there might be two identical, unlabelled and empty-looking black leather sports bags coming off the same flight. Neglecting to label his minimalist luggage-item was another historical habit, especially flying into Glasgow, ever since some baggage-handler had evidently recognised his name on the tag and shat inside it. His just-ever-so-slightly controversial sitcom pilot had gone out the week before that on Channel 4, and presumably the bloke had considered the jobbie more direct than going on *Right to Reply*. Matt had to admit, right enough, the show got worse reviews than that.

Plook made his move as Matt headed for the car-hire desk.

"Scuse me, any chance of an autograph?"

He stopped, caught off guard, staring at the guy like he had addressed him in Mandarin, feeling for a second like he'd no idea how to respond. 'Eh, sure,' he eventually said, sounding anything but as he patted his pockets for a pen. There was reciprocal confusion on the adolescent's face, turning to embarrassment as it became evident that the kid had nothing to write on. That was when Matt remembered: there wasn't supposed to be anything to write on, because an autograph was the last thing Plook was expecting. He was expecting to be told, 'Get tae fuck', then he could run off and impress all his pals in the student union bar, if they believed him.

'Hey, Matt Black, can I have your autograph?' – 'Get tae fuck.'

He couldn't remember quite when it had gone from attitude to standing joke, but ultimately it had reached the stage where it was so much expected that any other response would have been impolite.

Matt Black: darkest, sharpest, cruellest, scariest stand-up comic Britain ever spawned.

Aye, right. Very good.

Even his name now sounded like a fucking caricature: Matt Black, the cartoon comedian. Chalk another one up to Seemed Like A Good Idea At The Time. The excuse that it really *was* his name didn't score more than sympathy, because it was still his choice to use it: in fact, if he had actually made it up, it might at least seem half ironic. He'd saddled himself with it early on, when he first started trying his hand at open-mike nights. The moral of the story was that if you're trying to make a name for yourself, you ought to think more carefully about what that name's going to be, because pretty soon you'll be stuck with it. Once there'd been a bit of press and he was being offered proper slots, no-one was going to book him under any other handle: they wanted the guy people were starting to talk about.

It all fitted together back then, anyway. The energy, the ferocity, the edge he had in those days – you couldn't do that stuff, you couldn't say those things and be called anything *but* Matt Black; same as you couldn't call yourself Matt Black without doing that stuff, saying those things. It was dark as hell, vicious, vengeful, reckless, and too excessive to be taken as anything other than wild, scary fun. The material had to live up to the name, the name had to live up to the material, and the fact that both were over-the-top was crucial.

The symbiosis should, in fact, have been bomb-proof, career wise. You get up there, you be the bad guy who says the wrong thing: half the audience laughs because they don't believe you mean it, while the other half laughs because they've thought it themselves and they sincerely believe you do. Half the crowd thinks you're laughing at your subject, the other half that you're laughing at yourself. And all of them are right. And all of them love you.

Yeah, the symbiosis was bomb-proof, but only as long as both halves stayed intact. Which meant, as he critically failed to anticipate, that you couldn't get on a stage and be the scary bad guy after the audience had seen you taking it up the arse on US network television. According to the credits for NBC's lame but lucrative *There Goes the Neighborhood*, 'Mad Matty', the grouchy-but-loveable Scottish bartender, was played by Matt Black. However, the truth was that once Matt Black had played Mad Matty, Matt Black, as was, no longer existed.

Matt Black had sold out. The man who'd so gleefully

lobbed boulders at other comics' undignified lack of integrity had moved into his own villa on Glasshouse Row. The only difference was where the rent was coming from.

The sin he'd condemned Jack Dee, Vic Reeves, Allan Davies and all the other usual fucking suspects for was doing ads. ('It's not just them endorsing the product, you have to understand: it's the product endorsing them. It's the fuckin' BSA approval stamp on a comedian-safety certificate. Guaranteed: no sharp edges.')

Matt hadn't done any ads, but then neither had he particularly needed to, financially. He was filling every hall in the country, selling CDs and videos by the truckload. But perhaps more importantly, he didn't covet the cash. This was, he appreciated, symptomatic of a middle-class upbringing on the Springwell Road. If he'd known what it was really like to be skint, like half the folk he went to school with, then maybe he'd have instinctively gone after every penny too, no matter what he had to do for it. No, not maybe: definitely. Because whenever something he did want had been dangled before him, he'd jumped like a daft wee dog. Women, booze, drugs – and most of all, fame.

He'd made some ripples Stateside with a couple of controversial appearances on a late-night talk show, enough to start earning him bookings in New York. Then the sitcom role was offered, which was when he bent over and spread his cheeks.

LA. Tinseltown. Celebrity pals. Movie-star girlfriends. All that stuff. He'd depicted himself as impossible to impress, iconoclasm personified, but when those things came within touching distance, he was just another small-town boy from Auchenlea, dazzled by the bright lights.

He could barely remember the lies he'd told himself at the time in justification: maybe something along the lines of him taking them for mugs, or it being a means to an end, widening the potential audience for his *real* work. That was until he tried to go back and *do* his real work.

A joint in New York, a place he'd fucking slayed them a year before.

Dead on stage. No vital signs. Pronounced at the scene.

What the fuck, he told himself. There were film scripts on his desk now, for Christ's sake. He'd moved on from that stand-up stuff anyway. It had been a means to an end.

'Course it had. All that work developing his craft, it had really just been so that he could pull women and party with the in-crowd. All those years writing his material, building up a following, cultivating a unique and widely envied reputation had merely been an overture to being the second-string bad guy in a straight-to-video cop thriller, or playing Mad fucking Matty on *There Goes the Neighborhood*.

That disastrous show in New York had been almost eighteen months back, but he could see it now as the bright cold dawn of one long, messy day that ended on a Mexican beach less than a week ago. A long, messy day and a very long, dark night.

Matt reached out and grabbed Plook's *NME* from under his arm, then signed his name across Greg Dulli's forehead. He drew a smiley face beside the signature and handed back the paper.

'My new image, pal. Mr Sunshine.'

The hire car was a bit of a sales-rep job, a Mondeo, but it would make smooth work of the A9, and what's more it had a CD player. It was probably the same juvenilia synapse in the male brain as made him read newspapers from the sports pages backwards, that had Matt sussing out how to work the stereo ahead of adjusting the mirrors or figuring how to get the thing into reverse. It wouldn't accept his disc at first, and he was on the verge of taking the keys back to the hire desk when he clocked that there was already a CD in it, left there by whichever numpty had driven the car last. He ejected it and cast an eye over the track-listing. Mariah Carey, Celine Dion, Michael Bolton, Simply Red, M People . . . 'The Best Insipid Corporate Ballad Album in the World . . . *Ever!*' Music for people who don't really like music. He reassessed: maybe the last customer hadn't forgotten it; maybe the hire company supplied it with this particular kind of car, having completed a demographic study of who generally tended to drive that model.

He had pulled away and into traffic before it became apparent that the thing was on a randomiser setting, one of the electronics industry's more sacrilegious innovations. He knew songwriters who spent countless hours arguing with their fellow musicians and the A&R men over their album's running order, then tortured themselves once it was too late over whether they got it right – yet here was a machine that could do it for them, and better yet, make it different every time!

It took a few seconds to suss that the loud, brassy noise he heard each time he leaned over and tried another of the CD player's buttons was, in fact, other drivers parping their horns as he swerved into their paths along Love Street, and at that point he decided to give up and let Mixmaster MC Sony make the selections. Rejecting suicide only to kill yourself by accident a few days later was the kind of irony that was far funnier if it happened to someone else.

It was only once he had passed the Theatre of Suffering on his right-hand side that he became aware of having driven off in entirely the wrong direction, ignoring the M8 entry ramp at the airport and habitually heading into Paisley. He reached Causeyside St before there was any opportunity to turn back, which was when he saw the road-sign for Auchenlea.

Well, what the fuck, he thought. This was supposed to be about going back, wasn't it? About remembering where he once was, who he once was. Something like that, anyway. Plus humility, penitence and self-flagellation. Plenty of self-flagellation. He indicated and pulled into the right-hand lane. The randomiser was unimpressed by his sentimental intentions, playing 'Archives of Pain' and the Manics' admonishment that there was a bit more to redemption than merely regretting your own fuck-ups. Matt punched the thing with his left hand, walloping a cluster of buttons. The randomiser retaliated with 'Die in the Summertime'.

Fucking machine. He gave the thing another belt, which seemed to establish who was boss. It dropped the 'tude and played 'Faster', his one-time adopted personal anthem, which he realised he hadn't heard for far too long. Listened to it, yes, but *heard* it – different story. Self-disgust. Self-obsession. Same difference. He knew that now. Worked it out in time to survive the former.

Therapy for the latter was starting today.

St Michael's RC secondary sat on a promontory overlooking the town of Auchenlea. The choice of site was an indirect consequence of a past mistake in vocational guidance, leading someone who had a pathological hatred of children into town planning, rather than the more traditional field of teaching. Before construction began, it had been the kind of spot that you saw unwary and hypothermic ramblers being rescued from by helicopter on the news. Unsheltered by trees or any natural relief, wild winds pummelled it, blowing in from the north Atlantic and strafing the weans mercilessly with rain, hail and Ayrshire farm smells. It was also a popular spot for lightning strikes, even more so after the school installed a dozen 'lightning conductors' about the building. While failing to disprove the adage that lightning never strikes in the same place twice, these devices did demonstrate, however, that it never strikes a lightning conductor. Ever. Not when there's a wide choice of children to char instead.

Matt drove his rep-mobile into the car park, relieved to see a number of empty vehicles but no luxury coach, which meant the full-service school-trip party had already departed. He was going to have to face them soon enough, but all the way up to Cromarty in the one bus constituted too much, too soon.

He got out of the Mondeo and walked to the school's main entrance, which looked down a concrete exterior stairway that Eisenstein would have been impressed by. All it was missing was the runaway pram and some blood, but the latter would be supplied next week when the kids started back after the summer. The steps led down to the school's football pitch, a hard, unforgiving, compacted grit surface known as red blaes, which remained in use despite being outlawed by – at the last count – UEFA, FIFA and the Geneva Convention. It wasn't much use for playing on, but it did have the potential for exploitation as a cosmetic exfoliation treatment, just as long as the flayed look was in that year. It looked calm and quiet today, no hint of the grapeshot effect that the wind and the red ash could sadistically combine to produce. Just the thought of it was enough to make Matt rub at his eyes in painful memory.

The only activity out there that morning was a guy tormenting his dog with a frisbee and an expert wrist, firing the thing for the mutt to chase, only for the disc to come arcing back to his own hand every time. Matt figured five more throws before the dog went for his balls instead.

Separated from the football pitch by a concrete path was St Michael's other playing field, 'field' being the appropriate term as it was used for cattle grazing during the summer months when the school was closed. Its only other formal use was as a rugby pitch for the two weeks that the curriculum stipulated the males in each class be subjected to the dull-but-dangerous sport. There was probably therefore some calculated psychological reason why the PE teachers chose to schedule it for that first fortnight after summer, when the churned and muddy mire was strewn with fresh cowpats: literally stomping you down into the shit to let you know that the fun was over and you were back under the staff's boots for another year.

Certainly there couldn't be any more wholesome explanation, like trying to drum up interest for a different sport before the football season got fully underway: nobody in Auchenlea, nobody in Renfrewshire, Christ, nobody in the west of Scotland was the slightest bit interested in playing or even watching the game. The only time it got paid any attention was if England were losing at it, but then shove-ha'penny and 'best man fall' would be accorded similar heed if they ever attained international competitive status.

There were a few black-and-white bovines loose on the rugby field just then, chewing the cud and working hard at turning what grass there was into watery big tolies for poor first-year midgets to land in during tackling practice the following week. Back on the football pitch, a slight breath of wind tossed just enough grit into one of the frisbee-thrower's eyes for him to suddenly double over in

45

delicate rubbing. The frisbee whacked him on the top of the head, eliciting a yelp of delight from Fido, who promptly fucked off with the thing and began energetically mangling it a measured distance away.

Matt had a glance through the locked glass doors at the empty and unrecognisably clean 'social area' allocated to the first- and second-year inmates. He hadn't laid eyes on it in fifteen years, but the smells of half-eaten apples and wet snorkel-parkas came vividly to mind, along with hollow feelings of impotence and timid vulnerability. Rain and hunger dominated his memories, generously interspersed with random violence. Back in the wee diddy days of S1 and S2, it had always been pissing down, and he'd always been starving, despite daily consuming enough rolls, pieces, crisps and Mars bars to burst an elastic tapeworm. Theoretically this ravenousness was fuelling his pubescent growth-spurt. Except that he didn't seem to get any taller, broader or even just fatter.

Matt wandered along the covered walkway that skirted the building, connecting the main entrance he'd just passed and the doors to the larger third- and fourth-year bearpit. He picked his steps carefully, finding the surface underfoot to be unaccustomedly dry and tractable. In his schooldays – no doubt no different now, when the current incumbents amassed – the passage was a hazardously slippy route, slickly coated in a slimy amalgam of mildew and accumulated groggers. The male and female bodies each underwent their complex and dismaying changes throughout those stressful few years, with the distaff's boob-, pube- and bleeding-related ones coming in for the greater academic research and discussion. This had unfortunately led to a frustrating neglect in exploring also why puberty caused the teen male's saliva glands to increase production by a

46

factor of four, at the same time as restricting the previously effective ability to swallow the stuff back. Some time around thirteen, spitting transformed from an anti-social habit to a survival reflex necessary to avoid drowning in your own phlegm.

Perhaps a greater sensitivity to masculine needs or merely sharper awareness of a historic marketing opportunity would one day see the development of the male oral-tampon, and the introduction of a comparable rite-of-passage in commencing their regular use. Soft, absorbent, ergonomically shaped and discreet, apart from a modest length of hairy string hanging out the side of your gub. Drawbacks would include not being able to talk, but as most teen males were several years off saying anything worth listening to, this was hardly a great loss, and indeed would cut down on their embarrassment-recall quotient for later life.

Matt smiled at the image, automatically shunting it to his brain's routines-in-progress workshop, which was, happily, still open for business.

He walked past four sets of glass double-doors, the statutory minimum one of which was boarded up with plywood, a janitorial operation more often than not paralleled by lengthy suturing work at the Royal Alexandra Infirmary. Inside he could see the distinctive terraced benching arrangement where S3 and S4 spent their lunchbreaks and intervals. This was where he had achingly discovered why his preceding years of unsated guzzling hadn't put an ounce or an inch on him. All proteins, fats and fluids had evidently been diverted into advance sperm production, as by the middle of third year he was wanking enough to fill a small swimming pool on a weekly basis.

He remembered the boys at St Michael's – particularly

the 'bright' ones – being frequently berated over their failure to match their female classmates' academic standards. Such admonishment was generally at the hands of female teachers who could not understand (and a select few males who had presumably forgotten) how much greater a workload was unavoidably being processed by the teenage male mind. Given the exhaustive mental effort required to relentlessly visualise the breasts, buttocks and pubes of the at-least fifteen girls present in any given class, Matt considered it laudable that he and his peers had had enough brain cells spare to notch up *any* O-grades between them.

Such reflections had formed the basis for one of his early open-mike routines, expanding the night a woman in the audience shouted out that he was being sexist. 'No, I'm being honest,' he countered, adding that his mental undressings had been entirely PC and subject to no prejudice. 'I mean, hear me out, get the full picture – I fantasised about the hounds as well.'

Rain and hunger had given way to rain and hard-ons. The random violence kept up its reliable back-beat, but the omnipresent fear of an occasional doing was sweeties compared to the lingering agony of fancying everything before your eyes and being too ugly, awkward, shy, spotty, uncool and thoroughly terrified to do anything about it. Ms PC in the audience would have had nothing to fear from the young Matthew's anguished and fevered libido. The greatest fantasists are often the greatest realists, and at that stage even a kiss was straining the plausible limits of his aspirations.

He used to be such a sweet thing . . .

Matt slowly circumnavigated the place: walkways, doorways, playgrounds, grass bankings, kitchen bins, railings,

48

stairs, windows. The initial standard impression of every-thing being smaller than he remembered wore off as each square foot yielded up a long-stored recollection. To anyone else the walls might look like plain brickwork, but in Matt's eyes they were lined with brass plaques:

On this spot, during some miserable, drookit
lunchbreak in Autumn 1981, Paul Duff
stuck the heid on Ally McQuade, having demanded
satisfaction over a matter of honour (slagging his
Clark's Commandoes once too often).

Davie Murdoch battered Paddy Greig on this
banking, Spring 1980.

Local legend records that in this passageway, on the
night of the 1982 Christmas disco, Maggie Turner
did famously allow Barry Cassidy to get three
fingers up her, giving rise to a tediously oft-repeated
gag about Kit-Kats.

Davie Murdoch burst Jai Lynch's nose in this
doorway, Winter 1981.

Eddie Milton knocked himself unconscious against
this pillar playing tig, Winter 1979. He remains
officially still 'het' to this day.

Davie Murdoch leathered Jai Lynch's big brother
Mick beside this fence, Winter 1981.

Ally McQuade spewed his ring next to this drainpipe
after pochling a suspect scone from the Home
Economics department, Spring 1980.

Davie Murdoch leathered Mick Lynch's two

mates, also beside this fence, same day as above,
Winter 1981.

Davie Murdoch smacked Tommy Milligan's face
against this kitchen bin, Autumn 1980.

Davie Murdoch punched Allan Crossland down these
steps, Spring 1982.

Davie Murdoch burst Matthew Black's nose and
mouth against this banister, Winter 1981.

And so on. Until:

Davie Murdoch threw Deek Patterson out of this
second-floor window, for reasons never disclosed by
either party.

That one would have a more specific date, ingrained as it
was on everyone's memories: Saturday, March 24th, 1984. It
was the last day Davie Murdoch set foot inside St Michael's,
and the last day Deek Patterson set foot at all without
someone else's assistance, confined to a wheelchair for the
rest of his life.

Davie Murdoch. Or Davie Fuckin' Murdoch, as it probably read on the bastard's birth certificate. Sociopath, psychopath, whatever you like, Matt had always preferred
bampot. Not *a* bampot but *the* bampot; the absolute quintes-
sence of bampottery. The more technical diagnostic terms
had always seemed too sophisticated for describing a crea-
ture who was, uncomplicatedly, a violence-dispenser: an
inexhaustible fount of rage, like some abominable force of
nature striking out arbitrarily and impersonally at anything

50

in its path. There was no cause and effect with Davie, no way of predicting what would set him off; and consequently no course of action guaranteed to keep you safe. As far as appeasement went, from Matt's memory, copious bleeding usually did the trick.

The familiar comedian's story, 'I was a little guy at school so I developed the ability to make the bigger guys laugh as a form of self-defence', didn't really apply either, not in a part of the world where the phrase 'You 'hink you're a smart cunt, daen't ye?' carried such portent. When Matt had his exterior respiratory outlets rearranged through their rapid application to a sturdy length of aluminium, it was because he had raised his own profile sufficiently to be singled out the next time Dilithium Davie's main reactor blew. Matt had been, he would admit, grandstanding a wee bit, giving it plenty of *esprit de l'escalier* with some classmates after a double Maths period. The lesson had been overseen by the aneurism-burstingly tedious Mr Jones, a man so reliant upon cliché for communication that his joining the teaching profession was an enormous loss to ITN.

'"I'm not doing this for the good of my health,"' Matt had mimicked, then added his own imaginary reply: 'Aye you are, because it pays the mortgage, feeds you and keeps you in mingin' cardigans.

'"It's no skin off my nose whether you get your exams or not." Well, that's not strictly true, is it, sir? Because if nobody in the class passes, there's bound to be one or two questions asked about your teaching abilities.'

Smart-arsed wee wank. Maybe he'd deserved a doing. Whatever, Davie M had shown him *his* version of the spirit of the staircase soon after. Why? Ha!

Davie Fuckin' Murdoch. Dilithium Davie. DM and his DMs.

51

'Mad Dog Murdoch' the tabloids had called him, straining their imaginative capacities to come up with a hackneyed moniker that no-one had previously referred to the bloke by in his life. (And therein lay another grudge Matt held against him: the bastard had notched up more press in his time than *he* had.)

Upon incarceration, Davie gradually developed into a model prisoner. Unfortunately, his model appeared to have been Jimmy Boyle. His record of violence involving screws and fellow inmates earned him years more time, widespread notoriety, a slew of vilifying headlines, and ultimately a place in the Barlinnie Special Unit. This last was a unique penal innovation that seemed to function by sheer force of paradox, as it seemed hard to think of a crazier idea than taking the most violent men in Scotland and giving them chisels, craft knives and flammable liquids.

The tabloids might have seethed with condemnation of his previous conduct, but it was the sin he committed in there for which they would never forgive him: he reformed. Took the Jimmy Boyle thing the whole way: discovery of artistic talent, Gandhi-grade renunciation of violence, marriage to award-winning American documentary-maker who'd been allowed access to the Bar-L to make a film for PBS. Far as Matt had read, he now lived with the wife and weans in New York state, his paintings paying the bills and keeping them in society invites while he spent his days working at some sort of parolees' outreach centre.

In spite of all his professed liberal sentiments, some small part of Matt – possibly an artificial part, like where the rest of a shattered tooth used to be – had always resented how the guy's life worked out. Today, though, outside that school, things were looking a little different. Previously, he thought he'd never believed in redemption;

now he was wondering whether he'd just never needed to.

Besides, Davie Murdoch might have banjoed him, but it had only been the once. There were those at St Michael's who'd blighted Matt for months at a time, and he hadn't borne *them* a grudge. However, this was mainly because they'd been utterly oblivious of the havoc they were wreaking through their thoughtless and irresponsible acts, such as walking along a corridor, asking what you'd put for question four, or sitting within perfume-breathing range.

Simone Draper. Lisa McKenzie. Eileen Stewart. He was surprised at the ease with which he could recall their names and faces, given that they'd lain buried in some disused memory repository for a decade and a half. Presumably his current location had a lot to do with that, compensating for the rust of time and the ravages of dedicated substance abuse. Looking through the windows into the unlit and empty rows of desks, he could still see them in their school uniforms; or Christ, worse, the gear they wore at exam time when the dress code was relaxed. He remembered Eileen Stewart in a Simple Minds t-shirt outside O-grade English Paper One, a sight enough to make him consider reassessing the band's worth (the effect lasting until he gave his borrowed copy of *New Gold Dream* another spin that night and concluded that they were, in fact, still pish). Lisa McKenzie's flat-but-nonetheless-beguiling chest advertising *Combat Rock*, thus rendering her even more impossibly perfect. Simone Draper wearing, well, anything at all.

Matt never tortured himself by fixating upon the truly unattainable class (and classic) knock-outs, the ones everybody else was fantasising about night after night. Not for him the Catherine O'Rourkes, the Annette Strachans. He suffered the far more excruciating affliction of precipitous, unheralded infatuation with girls no-one seemed to have previously paid much attention to (including himself), his eyes suddenly opened to traits and beauties he'd apparently been too blind to see before.

Simone was the absolute worst. She must have been in various of his classes for years without drawing his notice, then one Sunday evening he and some pals watched *Fast Times At Ridgemont High* on video in Allan Crossland's bedroom, less attracted by the prospect of digesting the young Cameron Crowe's insightful observation of American teen mores than the chance that there might be some tits in it. Matt fell asleep that night utterly captivated by thoughts and images of Jennifer Jason Leigh, and by Monday morning she had turned into Simone Draper. The two of them were never going to confuse anyone in a line-up, but this wasn't a rational matter. Something about one clearly reminded him of the other, and within a day or so he couldn't be sure which way it swung: whether he'd actually gone gaga over JJL in the first place because subconsciously he had already fallen for Simone.

And, of course, the worst of it was that there was no chance whatsoever of him doing anything about it. He was still a good few years away from the review that would describe him as 'instilling the room with a presence that wavers precariously between hit-man cool and psycho-killer chilling'. At that age, he had all the physical presence and coordination of a baby giraffe; and besides, Auchenlea was hardly the environment for teen dreams to come true. It was far easier in the movies. For a start, the kids all seemed to be born with fucking driving licences, and their puppy love could flourish amid ice-cream parlours, soda-fountains and drive-ins. Somehow the thought of the corporation bus, the Napoli chippy and a sticky seat in the Paisley Kelburne didn't seem a prospect likely to cement a tentative, fledgling amour.

So he'd just suffered instead, seeking consoling distraction in records, Betamax pirate videos and ZX Spectrums. You couldn't have the girl of your dreams, but you could always go round to your mate's house and play *Manic Miner*, *Lunar Jetman* or *Attic-Attac* to the constant accompaniment of The Jam, The Skids and The Clash, in between arguing whose turn it was to go downstairs and make toast. It was a travesty that women thought men naturally obsessed with such trivia: taking football too seriously, playing video games, building record collections. They weren't. It was what they did because they couldn't get a girlfriend, and unfortunately they got addicted to it like a crocked footballer gets hooked on painkillers, then keeps taking them once the injury's cleared up.

'So, ladies,' as Matt had been fond of saying on stage, 'it's your own sorry fault. If your man seems more excited about the prospect of finding a limited-edition 10-inch remix of a fuckin' Thompson Twins single than he is about the prospect of going to bed with *you*, then I'm afraid you're just reaping the whirlwind for the time you knocked back one of his worldwide brethren for a dance at the 1982 Halloween disco.

'Sure, like I wouldn't have swapped any of those *memorable* nights sitting in a cramped bedroom with my emotionally retarded and hormone-addled school friends, watching each other's boils gradually reach critical mass as we huddled round a portable TV set, endlessly rearranging our newly hairy tackle through the pockets of our jeans . . . Like I wouldn't have swapped all that *every* night to be in the company of some sweet teenage girl, just talking, enjoying the sound of her voice, listening to her laughter, watching her smile . . . Long as there was a shag at the end of it, anyway.'

Yeah, that money-shot punchline. Got them every time. Everybody thought the gag was the 'real' Matt Black coming bursting through, but maybe its genuine purpose was to protect the nasty, dark comedian's secret true identity. Maybe the purpose of the whole fucking thing had been to protect that: a sensitive wee guy with a fragile romanticism and an imprudent tendency to give a shit.

What was he doing standing here outside this building otherwise, if not hopefully seeking to discover whether that individual still existed? If not to discover whether, buried under the crumbled detritus of a besieging ego's rampage – beneath the empty bottles, the powder-flecked shards, the headlines, the vicious lies, the worse truths, the friends alienated, the women used, the spotlights, the veneration, the notoriety (hurts so good), the indulgence, the decadence, the waste, the self-disgust and the self-obsession (honey) – there were still fragments of someone he'd once been?

And why else could he be even contemplating putting himself through the unspeakable horror of a school reunion – an invitation he'd have ceremonially incinerated less than a fortnight ago – if not to sift for traces of that person in the memories of the people he'd meet?

Matt completed his circuit and walked back to the hire car. He flipped open the glove compartment and reached for the road map, then fished the invite out of his bag. 'Pick-up point: Kilbokie Bay, Cromarty Firth', it stated on the topological diagram. He figured five hours would be plenty, even allowing for the caravan-convoys you'd inevitably hit on the A9 this time of year. A few patient moments disabled the philistine randomiser function before he popped in *London Calling*, ruling that such an otherwise despicable indulgence in nostalgia was excused by the context.

Pulling away from the row of parked cars, it occurred to him that there were two other constructive reasons for attending this absurd off-shore bash. One was that Simone Draper might not turn out to be married. The other was that he was bound to run into someone who'd fucked their life up worse than him.

■ **11:04** ■ **fipr charter coach** ■ **road to (inver)nowhere** ■

'But it cannae be a fuckin' oil rig. Naebody's gaunny go their holidays tae a fuckin' oil rig. Be worse than Blackpool.'

'It's no' *actually* an oil rig, Charlie. It's aw built on an oil-rig *platform*.'

'An oil rig *is* a platform, Eddie. Oil rig, oil platform. Same thing.'

'Aye, but I mean, they've stripped it doon tae *just* the platform, then built everythin' up again fae there. I read somethin' aboot it in the paper.'

'But whit's the point? Buildin' a hotel or whatever on a big hunk o' metal? Whit's wrang wi' dry land?'

'It's so it's exclusive, big man. So's scrotes like you an' maself cannae get near the fuckin' thing. Like wan o' thae wee islands, whit dae ye cry them? There's hunners o' them. The Endives.'

'Maldives, ya fuckin' eejit. Endives are in salad.'

'So that would be thousands of islands then?'

'Aye, very fuckin' funny, Eddie.'

57

'Anyway, in the Maldives, ye've tae get a boat oot tae your hotel, an' your hotel is *aw* that's on the island. You're isolated, away fae it aw. So they've used this oil-platform affair instead of an island. It's like *buildin'* an island.'

'Be fuckin' freezin', but, will it no'? The Cromarty Firth's no' exactly the South Pacific. Cannae see many folk lyin' oot in their bikinis in May. Have tae wipe the snaw aff the sunloungers first.'

'Have you been listenin' tae a word I've said? It's no' *stayin'* in the Cromarty Firth. That's just where they've been rebuildin' it. Fittin' it oot, an' that. When that's aw done, they're towin' the whole shebang aff tae somewhere it's warm aw year roon. Coast of Africa, I think.'

'Oh, I get you noo. Wee bit hotter than Rosstown, then. Still, whit's the point o' gaun aw that way, tae Africa like, an' then coopin' yoursel' up in this wan wee place the whole time? Seems a bit ay a waste, to me.'

'Well, Charlie, that's how we've no' made millions oot the tourist business and Gavin Hutchison has. I mean, personally, I think it's the stupitest fuckin' idea I've ever heard in my life, but that just proves I know fuck-all.'

'It doesnae take an oil-platform holiday resort to prove you know fuck-all, Eddie.'

'Aye, very good.'

'But I take your point. I wouldnae be seen deid in the place if it wasnae aw bein' laid on.'

'You couldnae afford it if it wasnae aw bein' laid on.'

'Good shout, aye. But you know what I mean, Eddie. It sounds hellish.'

'Some place for a party, mind you. I think this could be a rerr terr, the night. Nae neighbours tae tell you tae keep it doon, nae polis, free drink.'

'Aye, but if it turns oot it's shite, it'll be a cunt tryin'

58

tae get a taxi hame. Be a good laugh phonin' for wan, right enough. Givin' them directions: "Aye, you just take a right at the lights, then first left, then hauf a mile across the water. It's the second oil rig efter the kebab shop."'

'Aye. "Name on the door's Hutchison."'

'I have to say, though, Eddie, I still don't mind o' the cunt at aw.'

'Who, Gavin?'

'Aye. Drawin' a total blank here.'

'Come on, Charlie, fuck's sake. You must remember him. Mind, the guy that got a knock-back aff Hound Henderson in first year at the Christmas party when everybody was up dancin' tae the fuckin' "Hucklebuck" or some shite.'

'I mind o' *her*. Fuckin' horrible beast, so she was. Christ, I hope she's no sittin' two seats in front. Did I say that loud?'

'Naw, you're awright. But d'you mind him noo?'

'Naw. 'Cause it wasnae him, it was Paddy Grieg that got knocked back aff Hound Henderson that time.'

'Fuck, so it was. Right enough. An' *he* cannae be on this bus, cause we'd've smelled him by noo. Fuckin' hell, man. Paddy Grieg. I mean, gettin' knocked back affa Hound Henderson – it doesnae get any lower than that, does it? Seriously, you'd have tae stick your heid in the oven efter that wan, wouldn't ye?'

'Aye, Eddie, says you that shagged Linda Clark thon time.'

'That's different. At least I got a result.'

'Some result. She'd a face like a melted welly.'

'Well, you don't look at the mantelpiece when you're pokin' the fire.'

'Poor, Eddie, poor. And does your Margaret know you shagged Linda Clark?'

59

'It was afore we were merried. I was eighteen.'

'Aye, but does she know? 'Cause the two o' them werenae exactly pals, like, were they?'

'Fuck's sake, keep your voice doon. Margaret's got ears like fuckin' radar, even *if* your Tina's burnin' them aff doon the front the noo.'

'You leave ma Tina oot this. Answer the question: does she know?'

'Am I still alive? Is Linda Clark still alive?'

'I'll take that as a No, then.'

'You, me and Linda are the only folk that know. I'd everybody else that knew professionally murdered a few years back.'

'So, is Linda Clark on the bus?'

'You're fuckin' hopeless, Charlie. Linda Clark went tae Auchenlea High. She wasnae at oor school. Heidin' fitbas must have knackered your memory.'

'Ach, pish. I can mind as much as you. Wait a minute. I know who Gavin Hutchison is noo. Wasnae he the guy that knocked himsel' oot playin' tig wance, when he ran intae thon big pillar?'

'Naw. That was me, ya daft cunt.'

'Well, was he the wan that got stung wi' a deid wasp in the art class, pickin' it up?'

'Naw. That was me as well. You're takin' the piss, ya fuckin' prick.'

'Hing on. I've got it. Was he the wan that got a doin' aff Davie Murdoch?'

'Noo you're *really* takin' the piss. Every cunt got a doin' aff Davie Murdoch. I 'hink the Pope probably got his baws booted aff Davie when he came tae Bellahouston Park.'

'Well, in that case, as I says, I don't mind him at aw.'

'Actually, noo I come tae think of it, I'm no' sure I mind him masel'. I thought that was him wi' the Hound Henderson cairry-on but it wasnae. An' I thought mibbe it was him that spewed his ring in RE, mind, like the fuckin' *Exorcist*, but that was Ally McQuade. Fuck. Total blank.'

'Tell't you you were as bad as me.'

'What the fuck, but. Free pairty. We'll mibbe recognise him when we see him.'

'Either that or we'll just have tae kid on. "Awright, Gavin? Howzitgaun? No seen you for dunkey's. Whit? You don't remember us? Whit kinna pal are you, ya cunt?"'

'You've some brass neck, Charlie my man. You don't remember anybody. I'm surprised you remember me.'

'Come aff it. I remembered Davie Murdoch, didn't I?'

'*Everybody* remembers Davie Murdoch. Same as Matt Black. Hard tae forget when they're in the newspapers aw the time.'

'D'you reckon it's true aboot aul' Dilithium, then, Eddie?'

'Whit?'

'Aboot him turnin' ower a new leaf? Renouncin' violence, becomin' a painter an' aw that?'

'Fuck knows. Everybody changes, I suppose. I mean look, there' Ally McQuade five seats doon, bein' dead pally wi' auld Mrs Laurence. He was a cheeky wee shite, used tae make her life a misery.'

'He's still a cheeky wee shite.'

'Aye, but you know whit I mean. Davie was awright sometimes. I sat next tae him in Geography in second year. We'd a laugh noo and again.'

'Whit are you talkin' aboot, Eddie? Davie leathered you in Geography in second year. Dished you wi' that big atlas.'

61

'Aye, right enough. But still. He must have reformed or they'd never have let him oot, would they? An' sure there's that story aboot when he was released. Deek Patterson's brother, Panda, attacked him ootside the jile an' he never fought back. Just stood there an' took it until the polis pulled Panda aff.'

'Aye, I remember hearin' aboot that masel', Ed. Still, if Davie turns up tonight, I don't see anybody puttin' it tae the test by tryin' tae settle any scores, do you?'

'Well, I never cried him Dilithium Davie tae his face back then, so I'm no startin' noo. He might have a flashback. A fuckin' "regression", know?'

'Naw, I wouldnae worry, Eddie. On the off-chance that he's actually there, if Davie went mental again, it's odds-on it would be Kenny Collins that got the doin'. His mooth was aye writin' cheques his arse couldnae cash.'

'Him or Ally McQuade.'

'Naw, at least Ally was funny. Kenny was just ignorant. Horrible wee bastard, so he was. Sneaky as well. No redeemin' features. Face you could punch aw night.'

'Shoosh. Keep your voice doon or he'll come back up here again. I thought he was gaunny sit doon beside us earlier. I couldnae have handled him aw the way up the road.'

'Aye, you're right there, Eddie. My heart sank when I saw him gettin' on the bus. I suppose that's whit you're signin' up for, though, goin' tae a thing like this. The drink might be free, but you're still payin' a high price puttin' up wi' some of the company.'

'Still, it's gaunny be mental seein' some o' thae folk again.'

'That's if anybody else turns up. The pairty could be just us that's on this bus, plus this Gavin Hutchison bugger that we cannae remember anyway. I cannae picture Matt Black comin' back fae America just tae see us arseholes again, eh? An' Davie Murdoch – he lives in fuckin' New York or somewhere. He's no gaunny be there either. No tae mention aw the wans that are in the jile.'

'Ach, never mind. Free pairty, innit? Overnight stay an' everythin'.'

'Aye. Overnight stay on an *oil rig.*'

'It'll be fine, big man. It'll be better than that, in fact. Forget the oil rig: it's a *resort*. This guy obviously knows what he's doin', knows how tae make folk feel comfortable. That's how he's rakin' in the millions, an' I'm fittin' fuckin' wardrobes.'

■ 11:08 ■ fipr charter coach ■ five seats doon ■

'Good guys get shot in the shoulder,' Ally was explaining. 'It's the first rule of engagement for action movies. Allows that aw-naw-he's-been-hit fright moment, renders the hero apparently vulnerable, gives everybody a quality wince, but crucially does no real harm. Headshot is obviously oot, as is the chest; leg wound limits mobility, stomach puts you on a dead-withoot-medical-attention timelock, and forearm is just too wimpy. Thus, the upper-arm-to-shoulder area gets it every time, and doesnae affect either the aiming or the punching ability of the aforementioned good guy. Bruce Willis in *Die Hard* – bullet in the shoulder courtesey of Alexander Godunov. Michael Beihn in *Terminator*, courtesy of Arnie. Linda Hamilton in *T2*.'

'That was a stabbing weapon.'

'True enough, but same difference. Arnie himself in *Commando*.'

'Grenade blast, if I remember correctly,' Mrs Laurence clarified. 'But nonetheless, it *was* the shoulder.'

'Indeed. Then there's Arnie again in *Predator*. Danny Glover in *Predator 2*. Danny Glover again in *Lethal Weapon*. Carrie Fisher in *Return of the Jedi*. The golden era was, of course, your Joel Silver Eighties – I suppose that should be Silver era, shouldn't it? – but the rules are still bein' observed today. Nick Cage in *Con-Air*, Guy Pearce in *LA Confidential*, Robert De Niro in *Ronin*.'

'Yes, but it goes back a long way before the Eighties. Before cinema, even. Might I offer Jim Hawkins in *Treasure Island*?'

'Of course. Knife through the celluloid sweetspot on the mast of the *Hispaniola*. An' if we're openin' it up to books, there's Frodo Baggins in *Lord of the Rings*, with the added discomfort of the blade breakin' aff an' giein' him the Orc equivalent of tetanus for a good two hunner pages. But it's important to stress that this is a convention we're talkin' aboot, not a cliché. Admittedly, there' an awfy fine line between the two, but good guys gettin' shot in the shoulder is the right side of it.'

'What would be a cliché, then?'

'Eh, let me think. Aye. Bad guys comin' back for one last fright. See, your hero gettin' wounded is part of the mechanics of the story – the baddie comin' back is just a cheap shock. Fortunately, the *Scream* movies put a bullet in the head o' that wan. Literally.'

Ally was well into his stride, feeling buoyed by the experience of having a sensible conversation with Mrs Laurence: it constituted valid, independent confirmation of having achieved grown-up status. Never mind jobs, money, wives or weans: you knew you were a man when you could contradict your former English teacher without her giving you a punishment exercise.

Well, not that sensible a conversation, maybe, but an enjoyable one. Mrs L had surprised him by confessing her devotion to action flicks, unwittingly triggering an onslaught of Ally's in-depth theses on the genre. This was something that seldom required much provocation, and under these circumstances he was really going for it, making the most of that Vader-to-Kenobi moment: 'Now *I* am the master.'

'You know, I never really had you down for a post-structuralist, Alastair,' she said.

Ally laughed, thinking back to all the things Mrs Laurence had called him in his time. That had not been one of them. It seemed he wasn't the only one pleasantly surprised by their mutual civility.

'Ach, naw,' he told her. 'This isnae deconstructionism, it's pure, anorak-class obsessiveness. Aw the theorisin' goes right oot the windae when I'm actually watchin' a film. I *want* to get carried along for the ride, which is where clichés ruin it, but conventions are part of the structure.'

'Suspension of disbelief.'

'Aye. That kinna thing. I'll swallow any scenario, as long as the film sticks to its own bullet-deadliness quotient.'

'Its what?'

'An action film establishes its own rules of gunplay. In some, every bullet is potentially lethal – even the old shot to the shoulder can look worryingly close to the upper-chest area. But in others, machine guns can seem the least deadly weapon known to man. To illustrate, at one end of the spectrum there's your Tarantino movies: reputations aside, there's not *that* much gunplay, so when somebody lets off a shot, it's for real, and it's usually fatal. High bullet-deadliness quotient. At the other end, there's your John Woo movies: zillions of rounds goin' off an' the only thing they ever hit is glass. Low bullet-deadliness quotient. In a high BDQ film, if the baddie draws a bead on somebody, get ready for ketchup. In a low BDQ film, that's just a bad day for the janitor. And both types are fine by me, as long as the rules are followed consistently.'

'But you can't establish a high BDQ and then have a low BDQ showdown at the end, that's what you're saying?'

'That's what I'm saying. And you cannae establish a low BDQ then have the hero take oot the baddie wi' wan shot while the air roon about him fills up wi' lead.'

'I agree. So, as you've got a term for everything else, what do you call it when that happens?'

'I call it a Renny Harlin film, usually. Worst fuckin' action director – excuse the swearies—'

'Oh please, Alastair. I'm not your teacher anymore.'

'Fair enough. Worst fuckin' action director in the world. No idea whatsoever. Just blows a few things up and links it together with badly blocked – and always badly lit – dialogue sequences. And the worst of it is he makes money, so they let him go and do it all over again.'

'I'm not so clued up on the names of the directors – who is he?'

'Renny Harlin. Never to be forgiven for *Die Hard 2*. A sequel so unworthy, John McTiernan kidded on it had never happened when he made *Die Hard With a Vengeance* – even came up with a title that got around callin' it *Die Hard 3*. Further Harlin crimes include resurrectin' Stallone's career with *Cliffhanger*, and the absolute mortal sin of wastin' a script by Shane Black wi' *The Long Kiss Goodnight*.'

'Oh come on, I thought that one was funny.'

'Aye, it was – that was down to Shane Black, though. As a thriller it was pish – and that was down to Renny Harlin. I mean, Shane Black, that's precious material. You don't give it to just anybody. There should be an approved list of directors for his stuff.'

His tone of indignant reverence had Mrs L highly amused, evidently recalling the level of respect he had previously afforded the written word.

'You know, if I could have got you just a fraction as observant and analytical when you were in my English class, my job would have been a damn sight easier.'

Ally, having seen this one coming, wasn't for backing down.

'Christ, what did you expect, inflictin' that Grassic Gibbon damage on us? You'd be up on an abuse charge for that these days. Besides, I needed all my powers of observation and analysis to keep comin' up wi' new slaggin's for my classmates. It was hard work bein' a smart-arsed wee bastard – you teachers never appreciated that.'

'Oh, believe me, we did. We knew exactly how much effort you put into that – rechannelling it was our impossible ambition.'

'Well, you could have made it easier on yoursel's. I know it was the curriculum, but I mean, if it was up to you and you were tryin' tae get teenagers interested in books, is that what you'd throw at them? Grassic Gibbon? Teuchter farmyard dreichness?'

'Well, no, I must admit . . .'

'What was wrong with Stevenson, then? Or Tolkien? Bit of hobbit action. Plenty of pyrotechnics to keep the weans interested. Mibbe it was a Catholic thing – it had to be borin' an' depressin' or it wasnae daein' you any good.'

'That sounds as much a Protestant ethic to me. And before

you say it's a general Scottish philosophy, it was the same down south when I was growing up. The only difference was we got our rural depression from Hardy and Eliot.'

'George Eliot? That's the one whose husband jumped oot the windae on their weddin' night. She must have threatened tae read him her new book.'

'Well, I must say, Alastair, I'm impressed at you knowing that.'

'It's no' the kinna detail you're likely to forget. Anyway, I'm the one that's impressed at *your* movie knowledge. Never pictured you wi' a bucket of popcorn an' a bandana, you know?'

'Oh, James and I were always big on the movies. We went all the time. Must have kept a few picture-houses open between the two of us during the video boom.'

'Aye, I can appreciate that much, but I mean, Arnie and *Aliens* and all that?'

'Oh don't be so ageist. I was watching *The Enforcer* when you were in short trousers, remember. And I saw *A Clockwork Orange* when you'd have still been in a pushchair. To me, cinema has always been more about spectacle than anything else. I loved reading *The English Patient*, but on a Saturday night out, if it was between the *film* of that and *True Lies*, give me guns and explosions every time.'

'Your husband must be awfy keen on that stuff as well, then.'

'He was. He died almost four years ago.'

'Oh, I'm sorry. I didn't know.'

'Now, now, don't mention it. Before he passed on, James made two requests of me for when he was gone, and one of those was "don't be a widow".'

'Sounds like good advice. What was the other?'

She gave him a conspiratorial look then produced a

half-bottle of Glenfiddich from by her side. 'Grow old disgracefully,' she said with a grin. She took a quick swig and passed the bottle.

'Cheers,' he said.

The choice of seat had been kind of forced upon Ally, not that he was complaining about how it had worked out. When he got on the bus and started moving up the aisle, he'd soon noticed that he was one of very few people not to have brought along his or her significant other.

There was a guy sitting alone two seats from the back. He had his head down, so Ally couldn't place him, but then there were lots of spouses in tow who hadn't had the pleasure of a St Mick's education. The bloke was probably waiting for one of the gaggle of females currently under the impression that the reunion was taking place outside the coach's front steps.

Ally had clocked Mrs Laurence on her tod three rows ahead of that. There were still a few empty double seats on offer, most of them in eavesdropping distance of several one-time classmates and their undoubtedly better halves. That was when he glanced out of the window and spotted the instantly recognisable Kenny Collins swaggering alone towards the coach, trademark four-pack of Cally Special Brew swinging from one hand. Sitting alone in a double seat would be an invitation to the alky bastard to plague him for the next five hours, so Ally swiftly opted to forgive and forget *Gumble's Yard* (she was only obeying orders) and very politely reintroduced himself.

Kenny's appearance was an unwelcome vindication of Ally's contention that the offer of free booze would tease all sorts of creatures out of hiding. More surprising, really, was the attendance of others such as himself who would, generally, have better things to do on a Saturday night. Allan Crossland, Mick Thorn, Karen Nelson, Jennifer Finn, all known to have successfully escaped Auchenlea for the world beyond. Maybe Ally wasn't the only one with a sentimental streak. Either that or Annette was right and they wanted to survey their successes in the context of what they rose above and left behind. Whatever, they'd all be pissed and best pals by midnight. Then after tomorrow they'd never see each other again.

Throughout the journey gossip and rumour filtered back and forth as to who else might be showing up later, as well as grim facts about who definitely wasn't. Janice Brennan, breast cancer, '95. Markie Roberts, car crash, '92. Eddie McGinn, heroin OD, the super-strength batch that took out dozens in '96. Vera Murphy, two ODs proving a warm-up for suicide, '98. Peter Cullen, shot dead in a Paisley drug-war retaliation hit, '96. Franny Smith, life, murder. John Donnelly, eight years, armed robbery.

At one point Mrs Laurence enquired as to whether Ally knew anything of what had become of 'that lovely girl, Annette Strachan. Very bright. Very pretty.'

Ally barely resisted the temptation to say that, last he'd heard, she was barefoot and pregnant, and opted sensibly to change the subject.

'Do you reckon there'll be any other former St Mick's staff at this thing tonight?' he asked.

'I doubt it. As far as I'm aware, none were invited.'

'So why were you?'

'I wasn't. I'm gatecrashing. Oh for God's sake, stop looking so shocked. You're like an old woman with that face on, Alastair. I just heard on the grapevine that this reunion was taking place and I thought it sounded rather a hoot, so I decided to invite myself along. It *will* be fun, don't you think? All those familiar faces, all grown up. And on this bizarre floating resort place, too.'

'Aye. I have to say, though, I've got my reservations about the timing.'

'What?'

'Well, this floating island affair is *almost* complete. You hear that crucial word? *Almost*. Not half-finished, not up-and-runnin' either, but *this* close to ready.'

'So?'

'So, "almost finished" is the most vulnerable time for disaster. Nakatomi Towers, Jurassic Park, the second Death Star, Deep Core . . .'

■ 11:19 ■ three seats back from that ■

Nobody had recognised him. He'd been among the first to climb on board, making his way to a double seat near the back. Most of the subsequent arrivals had eagerly scanned either side of the aisle, looking for faces from the past, but they'd all passed him over. Maybe it was the sunglasses; it was a bright, warm day, the kind you always got in August as a kid when the schools were ready to go back, it having pissed with rain all through July. Or maybe it was that he'd kept his head down the whole time, not ready for eye contact, not ready for recognition.

It was hard to know whether he'd have been recognised anyway, particularly if they looked in his eyes. There weren't many photographs of him at that age, but those few he'd seen looked like a different person. A person he knew well, admittedly; a person he remembered with

71

little fondness but much sympathy; but a different person nonetheless. His wife had once written, touchingly, of his eyes as 'placid pools, calmed by the depth of their secret sadness', though the sadness was no secret to her. In those old photographs, they raged and boiled, permanently energised by the volcanic activity below.

There was one picture he still had, a class line-up from maybe Primary Four, which looked like a Gary Larson cartoon. Teacher standing tall on the right, big glasses, two rows of weans beside her, teeth missing in action from a few of the beaming smiles, knee-patches on all the boys at the front, bunches sticking out like jug-handles on the girls. Then you looked at the photo again and noticed John Lydon Jr, second-left in the back row. No caption required. He wouldn't be surprised if they had a copy of it in every social work department in Scotland as a test for prospective employees: Spot the Looney. If you don't get it in one, it's probably time for a vocational rethink.

There was also the possibility that he *had* been recognised and was being blanked. He had so instantly remembered many of the faces around him, yet he remained unhailed as they shuffled up the bus and took their seats. He stole his own glimpses once each gaze had scanned and rejected him. Jawlines filled out, waistlines filled out. Lines of age like pencil scribbles on old photographs, the images beneath nonetheless familiar. Twinges in his stomach, the heart-quickening surges of excitement, surprise. Moments of anticipation, stilled with the reminder that for him there was nothing to anticipate. For him, there would be no mutual recognition, no laughing or tearful reunions.

He had not been their friend.

Still, going in the huff wasn't really Auchenlea style if someone bore you a grudge. Nor would it ever be, unless it one day became possible to dish out the silent treatment *and* declaim your foe as 'ya cunt' at the same time. Even allowing for reputations, fear had seldom kept an Auchenlea mouth shut. It was the kind of town where guys would insist on the last word even if they were speaking it from the deck, through a shattered jaw. You may break my feeble body, but my blow-hard ego marches on.

Confirmation that he simply hadn't been IDed came when he heard Charlie O'Neill and Eddie Milton talking about him, clearly oblivious to his being within two thousand miles of earshot. There they'd been, up the back, reverting to class-trip protocol despite being past thirty – even ditching the wives for the duration of the journey because a school coach's backseat was an inviolable male preserve.

Eddie was only belatedly enjoying back-row privileges, having presumably become more pally with Charlie in adulthood than they'd been at St Mick's, where the latter's midfield prowess and the former's all-round dunderheidedness meant they'd moved in mutually exclusive circles. Well, maybe that was going a bit far, but it was still fair to say the younger Eddie had never been invited to join the Lad Elite along the rear-most window, not least for fear that he'd contrive to put his head through it.

Even from the brief glance he'd got he would guess Charlie was still lithely performing that libero role for some local outfit. No hint of fat beneath the tight, white t-shirt; taut, robust shoulders for shielding that ball; and above those the bright features of a tirelessly cheerful face, the guy who convinces you that a three-goal deficit is still recoverable with ten minutes left to play.

Eddie, by contrast, looked more like the guy who convinces you that three rounds are still drinkable with ten minutes left to last orders. He hadn't blown up or anything, but he had that fullness of face and that paunch on top of a skinny frame sufficient to suggest that if it was between his dinner and another pint with the boys, Eddie wouldn't waste drinking time on the deliberations.

The notion crossed his mind to stand up, turn around, face the pair of them and, say 'Awright, boys? Guess who?' with a big let's-kid-on-we're-all-pals grin, but it passed without action. He just wasn't ready. The coach wasn't the right place, either. For some, sure, the reunion started here – look at Ally McQuade, bubbling with chat for old Mrs Laurence, no doubt complimented and delighted that she had time for him after what a wee shite he'd been as a pupil. But for himself and doubtless a few others, it was a mobile ante-room, somewhere to prepare before entering a place where such surprises were in context. He'd bet he wasn't the only one who'd clocked a few familiar faces but not let on, not yet. They all knew it would be easier at the party. Attendance was itself consent to such awkward intercourse. Plus there'd be booze.

He had taken the charter coach rather than hire a car because it brought forward the point of no return. Either way, he knew he'd spend most of the journey asking himself why he was making it, but only one option allowed him to pull into a lay-by, swing around and head back the way he'd come.

So why was he making this journey? What did he want from these people, who he'd only known as children, however old fifteen might once have felt?

His favourite of his paintings shared its name with the intended title of his autobiography.

Seek No Absolution.

It was his lesson to himself, a code by which he had

learned to live. It was his penance and his protector. His pain and his strength.

'I came from the same background as Davie Murdoch, the same kind of council scheme, and I never turned out like that. So don't talk to me about poverty or about deprivation, because that's nothing to do with it.'

A thousand people, a thousand quotes, a thousand tabloids. And know what? They were all right. It was nothing to do with money, or class, or streets, or schemes. He knew that. Always had. It wouldn't have mattered whether he'd grown up in a council house in Auchenlea or a mansion in Newton Mearns, Davie Murdoch would have turned out exactly the same – long as you didn't take his parents out of the equation, anyway. Well, actually, perhaps that was unrealistic: if his father was working in a position remunerative enough to pay that Newton Mearns mortgage, he probably wouldn't have had quite so many spare hours to drink all that El-D. Quality time with his family would have been at more of a premium, too. Far fewer memorable evenings together, by the fire, or round the dinner table, or down at Accident & Emergency.

Killing the budgie stood out. He didn't know why – maybe because it only happened the once and most of his da's other party tricks happened on a regular basis. Maybe it was the absurdity. It sounds quite funny, almost. Budgies *are* funny. Daft wee things. Mr McCrae in number 24 bred them, gave Davie one for his seventh birthday, plus an old cage. Davie spilled a glass of Alpine cola over his da's fags that night, after the shop had shut as well. Joseph Murdoch esquire wasn't best pleased, and felt his son needed to be taught a lesson about the irreplaceability of certain fragile things.

He clapped his hands together hard on the wee green

bird and dropped it on the coffee table, where it twitched for a while, then lay still. After that his da battered him 'for greetin' aboot a stupit fuckin' wee spyug'.

Ah, the memories. You couldn't buy stuff like that.

There had been a squalid inevitability about his da ending up dead in a gutter with bootprints all over him. When Davie was informed of it in prison, he'd wanted to meet whoever it was and shake his hand. That lasted the second and a half it took to realise that the bloke would only be another angry and sadistic wee cunt, with another vodka-and-Valium-blitzed wife and another junior protégé learning violence as his only means of expression.

'My father was a violent alcoholic too, and I never turned out that way.'

Good for you, pal. Good for you.

Seek no absolution. Offer no excuses.

He would not present his childhood as mitigation, only context. Your environment might help make you who you *are*, but what you *do* is all your own work. He knew who he was and he knew what he had done. He knew also that he could undo none of it. So though every day he repented, he never asked forgiveness. Forgiveness, if successfully solicited, seemed a thing not earned but cheaply bought, and that from the goodwill of the wronged, to whom the cost was far greater.

All of which was, of course, just as well and by the by, because there was never likely to be much forgiveness going round – not while Scotland's moral arbiters remained the *Daily Record* and the *Sun*. Forgiveness is not a front-page lead. It's a slow-day inside feature at best. According to the tabloids, Davie Murdoch had gone from hard-man to con-man, convict to con-merchant, pulling the wool over the eyes of whatever gullible liberals in the penal regime

76

saw fit to parole him. Guys like that don't change, they just learn to play the system.

Well, maybe that was true. If the system involved not hurting anybody anymore, trying exhaustively to understand yourself and striving to make some kind of amends, then sure, he'd like to think he'd learned to play it. But had he changed?

Everybody changes, according to the sage Eddie Milton, two seats back.

Certainly, he'd 'put his past behind him'. He now had a life that at fifteen he wouldn't even have had the imagination to aspire to. His wife, Collette, his greatest, closest friend, was a Yale-educated, New England blue-blood. Theatre directors came to dinner. Galleries exhibited his paintings, which hadn't made as much of a splash or as much money as was reported back home, but they *were* his work, and he had enjoyed the satisfaction of reading New York critics argue over them in glossy magazines. And beckoning him towards a bright and loving future were the three kids who were so much the children of his new world that they didn't even talk like him.

The trouble with putting your past behind you, however, is that sometimes you can feel like you *have* no past. Collette understood that, the way Collette understood everything, belying as she always did the notion that an absence of adversity in your life was any impediment to either wisdom or empathy. She knew that a past so filled with mistakes and regrets can be overcome, but can't be erased. His might be a shitey past, but it was the only past he had, and no matter how he tried, he couldn't get by without one.

St Michael's held a special status for him. He had gone from secondary school to incarceration with very little in the way of 'normal' life intervening, so his schooldays were the

77

closest he'd come to living as part of a functioning society, closed and microcosmic though it was. Consequently, his recollections of this period seemed not only more vivid but more poignant than of any other time. Memories of petty playground thuggery elicited deeper shame than of certain later, greater brutalities, and it was only recently that he'd appreciated the simple reason why: at school, he *liked* the people he was hurting.

He never knew that at the time; all he knew was anger. Anger at their laughter, at their friendships, at their achievements, at their boasts, or anger at their posturings, at their aspirations, at their trivialities . . . but mainly anger because he didn't know how to be part of them, one of them. Their friend.

He liked those people. It felt like a revelation when at last he articulated this to himself, but it had been staring him in the face for years. For years he'd often found himself wondering what became of them: who they married, what jobs they'd found, whether they had kids, what experiences they'd known, where in this wide world they might have wound up. Matt Black was the only one he knew anything about. Davie had all his CDs and videos, had even gone to see him at a club in New York (although he'd sat at the back and quite definitely didn't introduce himself after the show).

So when the invitation arrived, it appeared to offer some kind of possibility; he wasn't quite sure what. 'Closure,' Collette suggested, invoking the American term for tying up such psychological loose ends. It was presumably their record of mauling and disfiguring the English language that made them feel they had nothing to lose when it came to conveying things other cultures had written off as inexpressible in words. The results were seldom elegant, but you always knew what they were getting at. However, in this case closure seemed wrong: to him this was more about openings, beginnings.

Seek no absolution.

He couldn't change who he'd been, what he'd done. He didn't want to ask their forgiveness. He just wanted to know them again.

He watched the road go by, listened to the chat around him. Familiar names were mentioned, incidents recalled, characters reassassinated, old jokes revisited. He wasn't ready yet, but he would be. By the time they got to their destination, he definitely would be.

There was only one wee thing still bothering him.

In common with both Eddie and Charlie, the name Gavin Hutchison meant absolutely nothing to him.

■ 12:23 ■ floating island paradise resort ■ ■ behind a great man ■

Simone Hutchison knew that nothing made a party memorable quite so much as a surprise. Her husband, Gavin, had of late devoted almost all of his spare time and energy towards making that evening's soirée the biggest social event of his life, so she felt it was the least she could do to match that with the biggest surprise of his life. She estimated that standing up before the assembled throng and announcing she was leaving him should probably do the trick. At the very least, it would be a honey of an ice-breaker.

The key word was 'almost'. Almost all his spare time,

79

almost all his spare energy, almost all his spare cash. Almost. As in not absolutely. As in still leaving enough of all three to send his dick on frequent fact-finding trips to foreign genitals.

She wasn't leaving him because of the affair; she hadn't left him over any of the previous ones, and although this one was simply overflowing with signposts and significance, when it came down to the fundamentals there was nothing new to get especially upset about. The betrayal and the humiliation might have seemed unusually poignant, given the latest away-day fuck's identity, if Simone hadn't recognised them as a mere pastiche of the greater betrayal and humiliation that characterised her entire marriage.

That was why she had been biding her time, waiting for tonight instead of confronting him with it weeks back: not just because it would be embarrassingly public, but because the occasion represented everything that was wrong with Gavin, and there could be no more appropriate moment to serve up his balls on a plate.

He'd been like a kid on Christmas Eve all the way up the road, so uncontainably jumpy with anticipation that she'd feared he might wet the car seat if they drove over a bump. Ordinarily, she'd have found it pathetic, but she lapped it up that morning, entertained by the knowledge that the more inflated he got, the bigger the bang when she burst his bubble. He thought the reunion would be his triumph. He was wrong.

It would be her revenge.

He had, typically, no inkling that his daft-but-sweet wee wife could be harbouring any mischief. With him driving (of course), she had control of the Lexus's stereo, and he'd failed, for instance, to detect any significance to her repeating the same track several times as they journeyed north, other than to ask whether there was something wrong with the CD player. It was a Ben Folds Five song, a typically rinky-dinky number entitled 'One Angry Dwarf and 200 Solemn Faces', about a guy who was bullied at school coming back to lord it over his former classmates, now that he's grown up and become a success. The parallel escaped Gavin, but then he seldom paid much attention to Simone's music purchases anyway, frequently opining that if a record wasn't available at Tesco's, then there was probably a damn good reason. The same consumer principles had also lined his bookshelves with the complete works of Clancy, Grisham and Archer.

They parked at the Kilbokie Liftings Jetty and travelled the half-mile or so out to the Floating Jobbie by power-launch, several of which would ordinarily be shuttling back and forth while construction work was underway. Refurbishment activities were now suspended at weekends, Delta Leisure having found the overtime outlay to be the only thing more expensive than the interest payments. This meant that all the boats were at Gavin's disposal, but he had instead sprung for a helicopter charter to take the guests out to the platform that afternoon. This was presumably in accordance with the philosophy that ostentation was its own reward, even – maybe especially – when you're skint.

'Darling, would you mind taking the gear up to our suite?' Gavin said, stepping out of the elevator and handing her the overnight bag. 'I'd better make my presence visible to the staff, check on a couple of things. And maybe you should give your mother a call, make sure the twins are all right.'

'I shouldn't imagine anything fatal's happened to them in the five hours since I last saw them, dear.'

'Indulge me, darling,' he added, giving her a peck on the cheek and a thin smile, ostensibly a gesture of affection but translating in the language of their marriage to 'Fuck off out of my face, can't you see I'm busy?'

Indulge him. Indulge what? Gavin could often go a fortnight at a time without seeing Rachel and Patricia; one morning was hardly going to leave him wounded by their absence. The true intention of his remark was to restate (once more) that *she* ought to be with them. This was less motivated by any fears over her mother's child-care competence than by Gavin's never explicitly spoken – but nonetheless bluntly obvious – desire that Simone shouldn't be at the party tonight.

Not that he wasn't concerned for his daughters' welfare. He loved them and treasured them, undoubtedly far more than any of the material accoutrements his success had garnered. However, he didn't love them *differently* from those material accoutrements: he wanted to take them out and admire them – even play with them – while the mood took him, but once he was finished, he wanted to put them back in their boxes again and play with something else.

His wife was the box-keeper.

Simone watched him skip off towards the administration suites, impatient to start pushing the buttons and flicking the switches on his latest, biggest toy. She picked up the overnight bag and began walking towards the Laguna Hotel, the most luxurious of the accommodation blocks and so far the first to have its furnishing and decoration completed. She took the most direct route, using the ornate footbridges to cross the network of water-channels, islets and cascades that fed in and out of the largest of the resort's swimming pools. A breath of wind found its way between the buildings and the screens, the briefest smell of salt a welcome natural intruder amid the interchanging wafts of chlorine, fresh paint and gypsum.

She arrived at the Laguna's lobby doors, which obstinately failed to open for her. Through the glass she noticed one of the skeleton staff gesticulating at her from where he sat behind the reception desk. He was pointing with a bored expression at the unlit chandeliers and wall-mounted uplighters, communicating not only that the electricity was temporarily off but also that she must have the visual acuity of a pipistrelle not to have noticed.

She shifted the bag to her other arm and walked to the right-most door, which sported a blue triangular handle in the shape of the Delta Leisure logo. Neither pushing nor pulling yielded a result. The receptionist pointed with a pencil towards the other side of the entrance, this time not even looking up from his paper. Sighing, she changed her grip on the bag once more, the bloody thing getting heavier with every pace, and headed for the allegedly functional door on the far left.

'You with catering?' the receptionist mumbled as she approached the desk, more by way of statement than question. 'Kitchens are through that door on your right, then down the stairs, but nothing's working yet, obviously, because—'

Simone dropped the overnight bag on the tiled floor with a loud slap, and began rubbing her reddened palm. 'No, I'm not with "catering". I need the keys to the Orchid suite, please.'

'The Orch . . .' He looked perplexed. 'But that's Mr Hutchison's suite.'

'Yes, and I'm *Mrs* Hutchison.'

This seemed to worsen the confusion. 'You're Mrs . . .

Oh. *Oh.* Right. Orchid suite. Orchid suite. Right. Here you are, Mrs Hutchison.'

The receptionist passed her the plastic keycard with the rapid over-eagerness of passing a buck, handling it as though it was hot. He looked suddenly terrified, and not, she understood, of her.

Gavin had been screwing *her* here. The bastard had been using the place as his own private, five-star love nest, and the skeleton staff on duty, keeping an eye on the place and taking out the empties, had assumed *she* was his wife. Simone gave a short, bitter laugh and stared upwards at the ceiling, calming herself so as not to take it out on the unwitting and undeserving lackey. Besides, she didn't want any ire going to waste. Drink back the gall, she thought, all the more to spit in his face.

'W-would you like a hand with your bag, Mrs Hutchison?' the receptionist asked with a jumpy disquiet and a north-east English accent. 'The suite's on the top floor, and because the electricity's down, the lifts—'

'It's all right, Jamie, *I*'ll see to our ever-beautiful hostess.'

Simone turned around to see where the voice had suddenly come from. Timothy Vale was standing not three feet behind her, at presumably the spot Scotty or La Forge had beamed him down. It warned her how immersed she'd become in her wrathful thoughts that she hadn't noticed his approach, not even footfalls on a tiled floor.

'Mr Vale,' she greeted, resourcefully finding a smile several hours earlier than she'd anticipated managing one. She offered a hand, which he clasped between both of his as he gave a small bow.

'At your service, madam.'

Her next smile came easier. 'Well at least someone is. It's

84

nice to see you again. But I thought you were supposed to be on holiday. A shooting trip somewhere in the highlands, wasn't it?'

Vale picked up her bag and led her towards the stairs, placing a light hand against the small of her back. The gentility of his touch defused any awkwardness – or indeed thrill – to such unaccustomed familiarity. To say Vale had always struck her as the perfect gentleman was to illustrate how devalued that expression had become, so far short did it seem to fall. There was something of the man that belonged to another era, an effortless, unaffected charm that allowed him to say things like 'our ever-beautiful hostess' or 'at your service, madam' without sounding like a complete tit.

On first sight, her impression of him had been that he looked like either James or Edward Fox, a notion she in time revised to conclude that he resembled both of them plus at least a good half-dozen other male relatives they might have. Other than that, he was an extremely difficult man to get a measure of. He was no taller than she (five-six at the most), and appeared as slight of frame as he was light of foot, yet up-close his arms struck her as taut rather than skinny. There was restless, mercurial energy about his aristocratic features, a mischievous, almost incongruous geniality to his face, which possibly took years off an accurate estimate of his age. At the same time, his skin had a deeply sun-weathered tint and texture that suggested greater exposure than an annual fortnight on the Med, which possibly stuck a few years back on. She guessed if you went for a number between 55 and 70, you'd be wrong, but you'd get marks for your working.

'Oh, don't torment me with thoughts of what I'm missing,' he chided. 'The glorious twelfth, grouse in season, clear skies

85

on the moors, country-house cooking, open fires, single malts . . .' He sighed, smiling ruefully as they climbed the stairs. 'And let me assure you, my good lady,' he continued, 'there's nothing piques the tastebuds for a meal and a dram quite like a long day blasting defenceless creatures out of the skies.'

Simone laughed. 'So why are you still here?'

He produced a compact disc like a conjuring card. 'This is why,' he said. 'Beta version of our surveillance program, hopefully with one or two fewer bugs than the alpha release, which had more than Doctor Fleming's celebrated cheese sandwich. It arrived yesterday, more than a fortnight late, but that it arrived at all is reason for tearful gratitude when you're dealing with software engineers. The sooner I've given it a full run-through, the sooner I can be out taking pot-shots at your native birdlife.'

'If it works,' Simone cautioned, showing him crossed fingers.

'Oh good God no, my dear, it won't *work*,' he said with a grin and a shake of his wispy fair hair. 'But once I've listed everything that's wrong with *this* version, they can get on with fixing it while I'm off doing my bit for the distillery trade.'

Vale and his company had been contracted as security consultants shortly after a Delta marketing focus group uncovered 'certain misgivings' (Simone had seen Gavin personally Tippex the word 'baulked' from the report) about the consequences of assembling hundreds of strangers in a confined space with several miles of water between themselves and police intervention. Vale's task was to assess all the ways in which the paying guests could harass, rob, assault, rape, kill or eat each other, then implement the means to minimise the risks of them doing

86

so. He was charged with designing and installing a state-of-the-art surveillance system, as well as devising control and containment procedures, all of which had to be operable by whichever dopes Gavin hired locally once Vale signed off.

Simone had first met him in the spring at an outdoor afternoon reception Gavin hosted for the project's many and various contractors. Such social functions were normally held indoors after dark, meaning she had to stay home with the twins and thus not cramp her husband's dynamically virile image. However, on that occasion, Gavin had been playing the casual-sweater family-man card, intended to convey a sturdy responsibility to businessmen who might have reservations about their chances of ever getting paid for their involvement in such a radical project. Simone suspected Gavin was also half hoping the wife-and-weans, cherished-dependants bit would appeal to his contractors' own paternal instincts and get them to knock the odd zero off their tenders. It was a desperate ploy she'd seen attempted by car salesmen: you went into their office and there was a photo of the missus and the adored offspring on Daddy's desk, except it was facing *away* from Daddy's chair, so the prospective customer would notice it. Simone had often wanted to ask these guys whether the picture was turned the wrong way because they found their kids too ugly to look at.

Vale had 'materialised' beside her that day too, with a spare glass of champagne, while Gavin was off wearing Rachel and Patricia. It was an act of attentiveness her husband had neglected throughout the afternoon, something Vale had unquestionably noticed. Noticing things was, after all, his business. His solicitude might, in anyone else, have seemed clumsy or ulterior, but the sense of observed propriety about the man put her immediately at ease.

Soon enough there came moments when she fleetingly wished his conduct and his motives not so proper; but only moments, only fleeting. The truth, she understood, was not that she fancied Vale (he could be twice her age, for God's sake), but that she liked the idea of him fancying her. Of *someone* fancying her. Christ knows Gavin didn't.

'Anyway, enough about me. How are *you*, Mrs Hutchison?' Vale asked, pivoting on the landing to ascend the next flight.

Simone stopped the word 'fine' in her throat. She was sick of pretending, of suffering in dignified silence – whose dignity was it preserving anyway?

'Well, not at my best, I have to admit,' she said. 'I understand from my brief exchange with the lad downstairs that my husband's been skewering his latest tart in the room I'm about to spend the night in. But then, you probably knew that, didn't you?'

Vale said nothing, but gave her an apologetic look. She appreciated the honesty.

'I'm sorry,' she told him. 'I'm not having a go. Besides, this place has only been functional a few weeks and he's been banging her longer than that, so it's not as if you knew before me or anything.'

'No,' he assured. 'But now I know you know before he knows you know. You know?'

She couldn't help laughing. Vale's gentle humour had an irresistibly calming influence. Nonetheless, one thought did trouble her as they reached the door to the suite.

'Mr Vale, I appreciate that you're sort of working for Gavin, and in surveillance even, but can I trust you to keep—'

'My dear Mrs Hutchison, I should remind you that while I have been contracted to install a surveillance system, I am not being paid to actually survey anything. Therefore neither your husband's unconscionable behaviour nor my evaluation of him as a self-deluded buffoon are matters for my professional concern.'

'Thank you,' she said, sliding the plastic keycard into its slot.

Vale followed her into the spacious suite and placed her bag delicately down on the luggage rack. 'Now, are there any more courtesies I can offer today, ma'am?' he asked, standing with his back to the open door.

'Not unless you stretch to professional killing.'

'Ehm, I'm afraid that's not a service I offer here in the private sector, no.' He smiled.

'Oh, that's all right. I'll just have to divorce him instead.'

'Are you serious?' Vale asked, the levity temporarily vanished from his voice.

'Oh yes,' she said, nodding. 'Very much so.'

'Good for you,' he told her.

Simone took off her jacket and placed it carefully on the king-size bed. When she turned around again, Vale was gone.

She closed the door and sat down at the suite's bureau, looking around the opulently decorated quarters. She had to hand that much to Gavin – he might not have any taste himself, but he did know to hire people who did.

There was a rumbling, grinding noise from somewhere below, heralding the return of the Laguna's electricity. The bureau's angle-poise came on, as did the ceiling lights and one of the bedside lamps: the one on the right. Gavin slept on the left. She pictured the scene and smiled acidly to herself. He might be playing on a different instrument, but he wasn't making any better music. The last time they were here, the poor girl was doubtless reading to pass the time while Gav took his scarcely earned post-coital snooze.

His last request to her, regarding the twins, drifted irritatingly to mind, and she cursed herself for allowing it to bully her into reaching for the phone. However, the tone went dead every time she dialled for an outside line, and a call to the still-stammering receptionist confirmed that the resort's landline telecom links were temporarily down. She retrieved her Motorola from her jacket, flipping it open to be told, familiarly, that the battery power was too low to support a signal. Gavin was always nagging her about recharging it, which was precisely why she made a point of letting it run down. She could have lived without the thing altogether, as its principal function was to allow him to satisfy himself from a remote distance that she was at all times attending to her motherly duties.

Simone tucked the mobile back into her jacket and hung up the garment inside the spacious walk-in wardrobe, then she began unpacking the overnight bag, unfastening the hooks and unfolding the canvas lengthwise. She removed Gavin's shirt and suit first, holding them up on their plastic hanger and eyeing a fountain pen on the bureau with calculated malice. No, she decided. Maximum self-inflation for a maximum bang when he burst. Then she took out her own evening wear and surveyed it with a smile. It had suffered a few minor creases in transit, so she hung it up in the bathroom rather than the wardrobe: an old travel technique. Leave it there while you steamed the place up and it had roughly the same effect as an iron.

Grabbing a bottle of fizzy water from the mini-bar, she noticed a small strand of orange foil snagged just inside the door. Veuve Clicquot, she identified, presumably the bimbo's purchase, in which case Simone had to admit she shared her taste. Gavin always went for Moët, on the assumption that if it was the one Freddie Mercury sang about, it must be the most famous and therefore the best. The fact that the average supermarket Cava tasted better was not a consideration that troubled him.

She poured the water into a tall glass and dropped the empty bottle into the nearby bin, wondering at the absurdity of the little fridge being stocked as though the hotel was open for business. It was the same in all the guests' rooms tonight, Gavin going the whole nine yards to convey what the place would be like when it was finished. Perhaps he'd argue that it was effectively a test-run ahead of forthcoming similar events for investors and travel journalists, but Simone knew which party he was most keen to impress. Still, at least it meant that the suite's sheets had been changed since its last adulterous occupation.

Simone slid open the door to the private terrace and walked outside. There were still remnants of transparent polythene where the edges of the sunken jacuzzi abutted the terrace's tiles. A smattering of plasterdust betrayed that the tub had never been filled; nor was it likely to be until the whole monstrous hulk was ultimately towed somewhere a damn sight warmer. On either side, shallow channels cut in the floor optimistically awaited earth and pot-plants. Simone walked to the end of the balcony and swept the dust from its rail with a paper hanky from her pocket. She leaned forward on her elbow and sipped from her glass, looking down upon the absurd sprawl that was the Floating Island Paradise Resort.

Hutchison's Folly.

It was the consummation of Gavin's ambitions, and one rare thing they both agreed on was that there could be no more appropriate monument to the achievements of his career. Their perspectives upon said monument and said career were where they diverged.

The history of tourism was replete with horrible ideas, most of which had unfortunately been horrible enough to succeed. In his time, Gavin had implemented just about all of the established ones and contributed a few stinkers of his own. But now he had come up with possibly the most horrible idea yet conceived in an industry that had made a sacrament of vulgarity.

When the technology allowed, Simone believed, we would one day see rotund Glaswegians in garments bearing the legend: 'My pal went to the second moon of Jupiter and all I got was this lousy t-shirt' – these being gifts from their radiation-blistered neighbours, who will have at length regaled them of where to get the best full English breakfast on Neptune, while complaining that the Martians *still* haven't learned to do a decent fish supper.

'Make the world England' had been the motto of imperialist ambition. Where invasion and colonisation had failed, tourism was rampantly succeeding. The poet Hugh McDiarmid once said that England destroyed nations not by conquest but by pretending they didn't exist, words which went a long way towards explaining, for instance, why centuries of Spanish culinary heritage had been wiped off menus to make way for 'bubble and squeak'.

Meanwhile Scotland had neither alibi nor mitigation for the charge of complicity. It might offer its usual excuse for absolutely everything – 'a big boy done it and ran away' – except that too many witnesses had seen it helping the aforementioned big boy, and not just on this occasion either. For every Balearic bar-pump dispensing Watney's Red Barrel or Tetley Bitter, there was one spewing McEwan's

Lager or Tartan Special; nor were the locals going to flog the Jocks much paella until they'd sussed a way to batter and deep-fry the stuff.

Gavin appreciated this, although he'd phrased it differently: 'People don't like anything foreign at the best of times; they certainly don't want to be bothered with it while they're away their holidays.' He had built a career on pandering to the great British sense of unadventure. The success of Flyaway Holidays was propelled by his uncompromising belief in giving people what they wanted when they travelled abroad, viz: exactly the same things they got at home, but with better weather.

While the major holiday firms attempted to improve their market share through price wars, brochure redesigns and expensive TV campaigns, the smaller Flyaway carved out a steadily increasing slice for itself through the widening cycle of customer satisfaction and word of mouth. People who don't like anything different aren't going to risk a different holiday firm if they trust yours to deliver what they want; and what's more they'll have lots of friends who think the same way.

Flyaway had been dawdling myopically towards bankruptcy before Gavin arrived, or at least that was how he liked to tell it. Certainly Simone remembered he'd been advised against taking the post – even though it was the first he'd been offered – because the company wasn't expected to be around much longer. As it turned out, he wasn't so much their new graduate recruit as their last roll of the dice, but he came up double-sixes. On Gavin's advice, they pulled out of everywhere but Spain, and even there abandoned destinations deemed too small or 'too ethnic', with the rule of thumb being that if there was a fishing village still surviving in the

93

vicinity, forget it. They concentrated activities on the big resorts, and further focused their market by booking up a larger number of rooms in a smaller number of hotels. There was no point, Gavin reasoned, in buying up a few slots in a complex where Thomsons had half the joint to themselves, because not only could they undercut you in the brochures, but they would always have bigger clout with the hotelier.

Gavin's strategy was to monopolise the premises Flyaway booked into, so that they could then tell the locals exactly how they wanted the place run: no point endeavouring to make the punters feel at home if some dago's going to offer them *huevos con chorizo* when they wanted sausage and eggs. The Flyaway brochure consequently became the first to offer 'guaranteed British menus' in its hotels, but it was perhaps some of the smaller touches that cemented the firm's reputation, such as always supplying sachets of Nescafe (or even better, Mellow Birds) at breakfast as an alternative to freshly brewed coffee, which everyone knew the continentals couldn't get right.

It wasn't a recipe for overnight success. Gavin's scaling-down and focusing policies kept the company afloat that first sticky summer; growing back up again was going to take a while, but this time they were building on stronger foundations. Within five years Flyaway were setting new records for repeat visits to the same hotels, and their customer-loyalty figures were becoming the envy of the industry.

They expanded slowly but successfully in Spain, then had an initially cautious go at repeating the formula elsewhere. Cyprus was first, an obvious choice given its established British connections and the helpful fact that most of the natives spoke English. Malta followed, for similar obvious reasons. Then they had taken a leap of faith in having a crack at the more developed Greek islands. This had necessarily seen the company invest in its first purpose-built 'resort hotels', the extant local accommodation having proven unsuitable. There had been a great deal of nervousness at Flyaway about broaching this more developmental aspect of the industry, but it wasn't shared by Gavin, who saw it as a natural progression. They had been knocking hotels into shape all along, so building them from scratch presented nothing but opportunity. His own reservations were about the destination, as despite all the bars, discos and reinforced concrete that had sprung up on Aegean shores, he feared the Greek islands might have too many connotations of rusticity in the minds of his target market. Even on Corfu, the fishing-village factor was still worryingly high.

As it turned out, he had nothing to worry about. The company name carried enough trust to fill the first hotels on their debut summer, then the crucial second-year figures bore out that word-of-mouth had been good and the Flyaway formula had prevailed even in Greece. With confidence soaring, a larger-scale strategy was planned, with the Black Sea outlined as the next area of expansion.

However, in Gavin's view there was still one major obstacle to providing the perfect foreign holiday: foreigners. Flyaway's brochures might be able to guarantee British food, but one thing they couldn't guarantee was that when you went down to the beach after eating it, there wouldn't be German towels draped imperialistically over all the sun-loungers.

Wasn't it possible, he'd wondered aloud, to somehow harness the benefits of a foreign climate without the inconvenience of foreign living? Cruise liners had always aspired to this, but in Gavin's experience they'd never quite managed it, as they traded the inconveniences of foreign living for the inconveniences of maritime living. No matter how big they built them, however many casinos and restaurants they incorporated, the whole affair tended to have an inescapable 'indoors' feel to it, like one big building that happened to have a swimming pool on the roof.

The cruise companies called their liners 'floating hotels', but the problem was that they were just that and nothing more. Gavin's vision, Gavin's truly, unprecedentedly horrible idea, was to build a whole floating resort. Or rather, more accurately, *not* floating – an entire, self-contained holiday destination built on what he called 'a free-standing aquatic platform structure'.

Also known as an oil rig.

Hotels – plural – of differing size, design, standard and price range, set amid a vast, picturesque lido of interconnected swimming pools, waterways, sunken bars, jacuzzis, flumes and slides. There would be restaurants, pubs, shops, cinemas, bowling lanes, an ice rink, casinos, games arcades, bingo, a laser arena, a sports complex . . . every modern British urban leisure activity, but without the British urban clouds and rain. A resort where all the staff didn't merely speak English, but spoke it in comfortingly familiar accents. A resort where you didn't have to change money, because you could pay for everything in pounds, shillings and pence. A resort where there was no fear of being mugged or broken into by the local residents, because the only local residents had either wings or gills. And, crucially, a resort where you *could* be guaranteed never to see the front page of *Bild* staring back at you from your desired poolside spot.

To Simone, it sounded like hell on earth, or at least hell

on water. Unfortunately, in accordance with the Goldwyn Principle, Gavin was seldom wrong about the popularity of such abominable notions, and he had little doubt about the viability of this one, not even when Flyaway refused to back it. They had already committed to their Aegean and Black Sea strategies, and in any case saw this as too radical a departure for a company now reaping benefits yielded by previous years of patience, prudence and stealth. The advance outlays would be enormous, it could be years before the facility began paying for itself, and all the while their core revenues might well be gobbled up by servicing the debt. The words 'eggs' and 'basket' featured prominently on the Flyaway feasibility document.

Gavin's belief in his vision proved stronger than his belief in Flyaway. He resigned, cashing in all his share options and selling out his interest in the company to provide seed money. He went in search of backing elsewhere, and found it from an American firm called Delta Leisure. Delta had built a chain of plastic paradises in Mexico, eradicating all trace of local colour bar the tequila, in order that American tourists could escape American winters without forsaking Pizza Hut, Mickey-D's or ESPN. Naturally, Delta and Gavin had a lot to say to each other.

Delta's CEO, Jack Mills, viewed the project as a trial run: they'd back Gavin to give it a shot, and if it proved a hit, then there'd be Floating Island Paradise Resorts sprouting all along the Gulf Coast and the Baja California a few years hence. As far as Gavin was concerned, there was no 'if' about it. He had seen the future of holiday-making. He had believed in his vision. Now time and money would realise it.

A lot more time, as it happened, and a hell of a lot more money than he or anyone else imagined.

The project got off to a promising start when Gavin was able to negotiate the purchase of a decommissioned oil platform from Norco for the nominal fee of one pound. He had stepped in with opportunistic timing when Norco found themselves facing a PR catastrophe of Brent Spar proportions over the undecided future of their disused facility, and sealed an agreement to take further rigs off their hands if – when – the resort was a success.

However, it wasn't long before he understood why Norco had been contemplating just sinking the thing, protests or not, as stripping all their crap off of it proved almost as costly as – and even slower than – building a new platform from scratch. By the time the thing was towed into Kilbokie Bay to begin the rebuilding and fitting operations, the budget was being revised upwards on a daily basis, and the projected completion date got further off rather than nearer as the months went on. The sheer size of the thing, for instance, meant that it had to remain half a mile out in the firth, rather than in the shallower waters within the Kilbokie yard perimeter. Out there it was attended constantly by lift-ings barges, as prefabricated sections were slotted into place and vast hoppers of materials were supplied to the small army of tradesmen who ferried out and back each day.

Fortunately for Gavin, Delta still retained faith in the eventual success of his idea, and eschewing accepted wisdom about throwing good money after bad, they reasoned instead that further outlay was the only way of recouping what they had already shelled out. Such logic, however, can generate a very costly spiral, and there were soon an awful lot of zeroes on the figure under 'Unforeseen Logistical Expenses'. Worsening matters still, the delays meant that the resort was going to miss its first summer, and although its planned site – the Gambia – enjoyed sun and high temperatures all year round, most people didn't enjoy time off all year round. The most optimistic projection said the place wasn't going to be open for business until November, so not only did this mean a delay in generating any revenue, but it set the crucial word-of-mouth effect back a year at least.

The pressure mounting on Gavin was not eased by grumbling disquiet Stateside regarding how exposed the project was rendering his backers. Delta's ever-increasing investment had left them over-leveraged and there was much concern that the company would be vulnerable to corporate predators as a result. The news that there would be no revenues that summer was therefore hardly music to their ears, and Gavin's constant assurances that time would vindicate their belief started to ring a little hollow, as seeing their project succeed five years down the line wouldn't be much reward if they didn't own it anymore.

It became imperative that the resort start providing a return – any kind of return – as soon as possible. Gavin had consequently been panicked into rechannelling much of the marketing budget into a summer advertising and PR offensive, pitching the facility's year-round sun credentials in an attempt to maximise winter bookings and thus at least get the ball rolling. Problem was, visually they were still heavily reliant on virtual reality graphics and artists' impressions of what they were offering. Even once the Lido was complete, the Cromarty Firth hadn't cooperated with much in the way of blue sky for taking photographs, and neither was it easy to find an angle that didn't also include cranes, scaffolding and bum-cleavage.

Interest was proving slow to develop, and actual bookings were worryingly thin on the ground. Gavin blamed this on the frustrating inability to fully convey what kind of holiday experience the resort had to offer. Simone wasn't so sure, reckoning the failure to fully convey what people would be letting themselves in for might be the only reason anyone had been daft enough to book at all. And despite his continued profession that time and bloody-word-of-fucking-mouth would ultimately prove the resort 'a money-rig', Simone suspected Gavin had begun to suffer his own pangs of doubt, most clearly manifest in this school-reunion nonsense. Admittedly, it was something he'd often talked of organising, but in Simone's opinion, the reason he'd never actually done so before was the on-going thought that if he waited another few years, he'd be even more impressively successful. Far more than the hosting opportunity afforded by this unique and available venue, she guessed the reason he'd bitten the bullet now was the secret fear that this might be the last time he could play king of the castle.

One angry dwarf right enough.

Gavin had, as the Americans might say, 'some issues' regarding his schooldays.

Simone had known him since pre-nursery age, their mothers being sufficiently close friends for each other's children to call them 'auntie'. So although Gavin wasn't literally the boy next door, the pair of them did have that ambiguous childhood pseudo-cousin status, which diminishes through the primary-school years but can kick back in when mid-teen awkwardness renders everyone else of the opposite sex an unapproachable alien.

No-one would say Gavin was bullied at school; at St Michael's, all but a select few behemoths were subject to violence and ridicule on a rotating and fairly equal basis. He didn't find himself singled out for doings, like the unfortunately effeminate Martin Clark or the loathsome and suicidally obnoxious Kenny Collins. Neither did he suffer more than the average volume of verbal abuse, such as was levelled at Tommy Milligan for his academic prowess or Paddy Greig for his apparent aversion to modern toiletries. In fact, Gavin didn't stand out for *any* reason, and that was the root of the problem.

He wasn't a hard-man like Davie Murdoch; he wasn't a great footballer like Charlie O'Neill; he wasn't trendy and good-looking like Barry Cassidy; he wasn't funny like Ally McQuade; he wasn't a brainbox like Tommy Milligan. He was just Gavin Hutchison, skint in the currencies that purchased popularity, notoriety or even merely distinction. An unremarkable wee guy to whom nobody paid over-much attention.

People might remember him as quiet, probably because they didn't recall much of what he said. They might also assume he was shy, and maybe he had been a little, but just because Gavin was never in the limelight didn't mean he wasn't jealous of those who were. In truth, Simone now knew Gavin had craved the limelight – he just hadn't had any means of attracting it.

He'd made a bid for cred at primary school by trying to get himself nicknamed 'Hutch', in the days when David Soul and Paul Michael Glaser reigned supreme over the Saturday night viewing schedule. None of his classmates cooperated. Kids grasp every stick they can to beat each other, so an irretrievably uncool handle like 'Gavin' was not a handicap they were prepared to relieve him of. Paul Stark got to be 'Starsky', but Paul Stark was in the school team *and* he had a Raleigh Grifter.

Brainbox, hard case, beauty, athlete, psycho, slut . . . in every school there would always be those who achieved prominence for certain remarkable properties, good or bad, but only within that limited context: both of circumstance and of age. For that reason, social microcosm that it might be, school was no reliable predictor for later life, not even simply on a physical level. Simone's now head-turning friend Alison had once been a fifth-year ugly duckling like herself, while conversely (and with not a little *schadenfreude*), she had seen the adolescent faces, bodies and dress-sense of certain others fail to realise the early-teen promise that had once granted them unassailable in-crowd credentials. And, of course, there were those who found success – even fame – in the real world following comparative anonymity at school (Matthew Black, she remembered, had always been well behind Ally McQuade in the class-comedian stakes). This was often due to late development, but sometimes it was because school had offered no vehicle for these people's talents. Gavin, clearly, fell into this latter category, 'travel industry visionary' not having been one of the archetypes in *The Breakfast Club*. However, the difference between him and everyone else who made their mark later in life was that *they* never looked back.

He hadn't always been that way: his pursuit of success was not driven by a crusade in search of self-vindication. Rather, it was his success that indirectly drove him to start looking back in, if not exactly anger, then at least ill-concealed indignation. Simone didn't remember Gavin as being a particularly egotistical teenager, adolescent or even 'young man', but when the money and the status began to accumulate in his mid-twenties, his sense of self-importance started growing in proportion. Then out of proportion.

It was as though his late-blooming ego had back-dated itself, expanding to claim his past because there wasn't enough room left for it in the present. Grown used to people

102

taking him *dreadfully* seriously, he became retrospectively outraged at the indignity, disrespect and – worst of all – lack of recognition endured by the younger Gavin. Consequently, he began to harbour a resentment towards all the people who had, back then, failed to appreciate what a remarkable person Gavin Hutchison was. And this number included – perhaps not as bizarrely as it might seem – himself: the self who'd put up with all that crap, the self who'd so under-represented his potential, and, most loathed of all, the self who'd been content to land Simone Draper when he could have done a lot better than that.

She and Gavin had started dating over that summer between when she finished fifth year at St Mick's and started at uni. The remnants of that one-time pesudo-cousin status had probably made it easier for him to ask her out, and certainly easier for her to accept: the whole boyfriend-girlfriend thing seemed very daunting at that age, so the fact that they were pals made being stumbling beginners that bit less awkward. In fact, it was quite exciting really, as well as pleasantly flattering. She hadn't imagined anyone was crying himself to sleep at night over Simone Draper, certainly not the guys she'd had her own curious thoughts about, such as Andrew Reilly (already driving, already seeing the very gorgeous Laura Heaton from Auchenlea High) or Matthew Black (*far* too wittily cerebral to take any interest in a dweeb like her). Gavin wasn't the man of her dreams, but she knew she could do a sight worse too. She realised that having never previously been made to think of him that way, she did actually find him quite attractive, but more importantly she enjoyed his company and he clearly liked her, which was what truly made her feel good.

No thunderbolts, though. No shooting stars.

She'd thought about that the night before their wedding. No thunderbolts, no shooting stars. She'd never been swept off her feet, never met that tall, dark and handsome stranger, never been consumed by some passion that meant the world made no sense without *him*. But then who did any of that really happen to? What she did have was a good man, someone who loved her, someone who'd been a faithful companion on the road they'd travelled so far, and would be on the longer one ahead.

They'd known each other since they were toddlers – perhaps they were always meant to be together. Perhaps all that passion and pyrotechnics stuff was just people getting a concentrated dose of the sense of togetherness she and Gavin had built over years.

Yeah, right. Shame no-one told him that.

The affairs started soon after the twins were born. Golly, what a surprise. He'd hit that 'Oh Christ' realisation so many new fathers go through when they see living, binding proof that this marriage business is now for real. But what made it worse for Gavin was that this realisation dawned at the same time as his financial success. The moment at which he found himself with the money, the respect and the kudos to attract all kinds of women was also the one at which he found himself tied down to dull wee Simone, plain of face and sagging round the middle following her recent dual tummy-tenancy.

It was always the glamorous types he went for. Simone would think of them as bimbos but they usually weren't. They tended to be career women he met through work: attractive, intelligent and single. After the initial hurt of finding out he was cheating, that was what made it easier to feign ignorance, hide the pain and think of the twins. He wasn't going to run away with any of them: he wasn't fucking them because he loved them, he was fucking them because he wanted to feel like a guy who could bed attractive, intelligent single women.

He didn't love her either, though: that was increasingly clear. He even stopped buying her flowers, once the guilt-tinged giveaway that he'd been a naughty boy on his latest foreign trip. Not, of course, that there weren't plenty of other giveaways. Discretion wasn't something Gavin had ever mastered, or if he had he'd evidently thought Simone too stupid for it to be worth the effort, a misapprehension she'd admittedly worsened through pretending not to notice. In truth she'd thought she could get used to it, even that in time he'd get over it, his childhood inadequacies one day finally compensated. She knew that sounded dippy and pathetic, but when you've given up your job and there are two toddlers at your feet, it's hard to see yourself as spoiled for options.

Nonetheless, it still *was* dippy and pathetic. The twins were nearly school-age, and with such emancipation at hand, her vision was cleared enough for her to see the single-most salient fact that she'd been missing: *she* didn't love *him*.

If she needed proof of this, then it came in spades when she discovered the identity of his latest concubine: Catherine O'Rourke, the face that filled a thousand hankies once upon a time in Auchenlea. She felt amused by this rather than hurt. Put together with the school reunion, there was just something so embarrassingly desperate about it.

Gavin had crossed paths with Catherine after all these years because she was working at the PR firm handling publicity for the resort project. She was still quite the clotheshorse, but if truth be told she was no longer the knock-out Simone remembered. However, that wouldn't have proven any deterrent to Gavin. Poor Catherine – he wasn't screwing her, he was screwing a memory. Screwing what she represented, and no doubt frustrated that everyone in their fifth-year Chemistry class couldn't be there to see it.

But soon enough they would be.

Simone knew that was why Gavin had tried so hard to put her off attending the reunion. He wanted all his ex-classmates gathered here on this marvellous creation of his, where they would see how much more successful than they he had been, and where they would see also that Catherine O'Rourke, who the boys had all fancied and the girls had all envied, only had eyes for him. It would slightly spoil the effect if wee Simone Draper was hanging around, pointing out that she was the one he was actually married to, but that was something Gavin had been forced to get grudgingly used to.

Little did he know that there would be a couple more things spoiling the effect, too. Such as the fact that she'd secretly added David Murdoch and Matthew Black to the list of individuals Gavin had instructed the PR firm to track down and invite. How very odd, she'd thought, that their names should slip his mind, considering they were the two people from Gavin's yeargroup who had, in their different ways, gone on to achieve the most renown.

And, of course, there would be one further upstaging that evening.

Simone walked back inside the suite to the bathroom, where she turned on the shower and stripped off her clothes. She looked at the black dress hanging up against the wall, then with satisfaction at her taut, flat stomach and lithe, slim thighs. Several hours in the gym every day, while the girls were at nursery school. Gavin hadn't been the only one doing plenty of preparing for this party. Couldn't do much about the boobs, right enough, apart from firm things up a bit, but then that's what she'd brought the wonderbra for.

She had decided it wouldn't be enough merely to leave him, even in front of all those people and in his moment of triumph. She wanted him, and everyone he'd been so keen to assemble there, to see exactly *who* was leaving him: the smartest, brightest, sexiest woman in the room.

Simone Draper.

■ 16:18 ■ rosstown nick ■ cromarty's most wanted ■

McGregor wasn't enjoying his retirement much any more. He sat in the interview room, arms folded, malevolently eyeing a lukewarm polystyrene cup of watery tea, his simmering gaze occasionally straying to PC Carrot-Cruncher on the other side of the desk. Carrot-Cruncher didn't seem very comfortable either, nervously glancing at the door every few seconds as he impatiently awaited his superior, Sergeant Mutton-Molester, who was presumably about to bring his unique teuchter policing genius to bear upon this perplexing matter. The juvenile-looking cop flinched every time McGregor shifted in his chair, seemingly terrified of becoming the Beast of Kilbokie's next mutilated victim. At one point McGregor had coughed and the skinny drink of water involuntarily slid his chair back from the table. It was hard to tell whether the accompanying shriek came from the chair legs cr the post-pubescent polisman.

The irony was coming out his arse. His first official

civilian day in close on four decades and here he was on the wrong side of the interview table, faced with a far-from-inspiring representative of the future of the force. He was beginning to appreciate a certain twisted plausibility to the Pink Panther films, understanding vividly how Chief Inspector Dreyfus could progress from respected senior police official to misanthropic arch-criminal. It didn't take a Clouseau; it just took a day like this.

He had come round lying on his side in some long grass, his head throbbing with a sharp, insistent pain, his mouth raspingly dry. His first thought was a nagging worry that he couldn't even remember whose stag night it had been. Then he was disturbed to find that he could open only one side of his mouth, and feared that this was due to a facial palsy resultant of the stroke that must have scythed him down suddenly during his morning stroll. An exploratory hand reached gently to his lips and discovered that the restriction was in fact caused by a large quantity of dried blood that had oozed from his nostrils and pooled on one side of his face. He picked at it with his fingernails to loosen its edges, then peeled the clotted mass off like a giant scab. It was almost a shame to throw it away: he had a young nephew who would have enormously appreciated it, and the look on his sister-in-law's face would have been a picture too.

Sitting up, he felt the damp weight of his shirt tug upon his chest, and started a little when he saw that it was coated down one side in drying but still-sticky blood. He pulled rashly at the buttons, sending several of them popping off into the grass as he ripped open the garment and examined the skin beneath, his right hand patting down the area in frantic alarm. To his relief there was no injury, no wound, and not even any pain. He rested his hand back upon the grass at his side, then suddenly sprang three feet sideways like a startled crab, having felt foreign fingers beneath his own. Looking down, he saw that there was a messily detached human arm lying beside him, scorch-marks on the skin near the end where such appendages normally connected to their owner.

McGregor climbed tremulously to his feet, memories of a loud bang beginning to form in his aching head. Recovering from an initial wave of dizziness, he commenced the hangover walk, cushioning each footfall against shaking his agitated brain. After a few tender yards, he reached the edge of a clearing and could see two outbuildings downhill from where he stood. The building on the left was missing the best part of one wall, and there were bricks scattered in a wide arc around it. Cows stood nearby looking uniformly unimpressed; presumably they'd all seen much better explosions, tons of times.

He picked his way delicately back to the spot where he'd come to, and lifted up the arm. The unexpected weight of the thing caused him to wince, and the very thought of it seemed to make his skull ache all the more. It was a hell of a thing to get hit with. He took a deep breath, steeling himself for the walk ahead and the unenviable task of finding whatever else might remain of the redundant limb's former employer among the rubble.

His eyes were fixed upon the site of the explosion as he trudged woozily down the hill. Going by the state of the building and the distance the arm had travelled, it was short odds an open-casket funeral would be ruled out at an early juncture. Poor bugger. Some farm worker probably, paying a high price for a fly fag in the vicinity of several drums of agricultural chemicals that would have about three different Brussels departments in collective apoplexy when they found out.

109

He felt a squelching sensation underfoot and stopped dead, looking down reluctantly as the cows' lethargic lowing rang in his ears like a taunt. Examining his spattered boot, he observed that the colour, texture and consistency were not what he had been expecting. Admittedly, being from the big city, he was no connoisseur of cowshit, but even a dilettante could detect that this was something even less pleasant than a freshly laid steamer. Besides, it wasn't the first time he'd found himself standing in a puddle of blood amidst a scene of carnage and devastation. The difference today was that nobody was paying him for it. He looked again at the severed arm, then back down at the puréed gore. Never mind an open casket, they'd be burying this guy in a jug.

McGregor extricated himself from the puddle, the slightest wave of queasiness rippling through him despite decades of practised detachment. It was at such moments that he often worried about the possibility of it all catching up with him one day in some almighty, cumulative attack of squeamishness that would have him arcing boak for six yards before collapsing into a quivering, gibbering heap. Then again, he thought, switching the arm to under his left oxter, if this kind of thing didn't bring it on, chances were it wasn't going to happen.

He noticed that the sliding door to the building opposite was open slightly, and decided to have a look inside. Maybe the puddle had left his jacket in there or something. Certainly they were going to have a swine of a time identifying him if he hadn't, not unless the bugger had been fingerprinted. McGregor shouldered the door open further, noticing as he did so that four small holes had been drilled in the corrugated metal. They weren't grouped or spaced in any uniform manner, so he was clueless as to what they were for. The thought of some teuch finding ways to relieve the rural monotony using a power tool was not one he wanted to dwell upon, so he ventured inside cautiously.

It was gloomy in the shed, the sunlight prodding through in shafts and streaks where the metal panels didn't quite meet. There were other, smaller beams, leading to further round holes in the walls at consistently random positions. McGregor scanned the area just inside the door until he found a forebodingly ancient-looking light switch, connected to a frayed and tape-bound length of cable, an arrangement straight out of a cautionary BBC public information film. He stayed his hand an inch from the switch, the ach-fuck's-sake-it'll-be-all-right impulse overruled by thoughts of the puddle saying much the same thing a few hours ago, back in his pre-puddle incarnation.

McGregor looked around for something non-conductive on the floor, and spotted a splinter-edged length of wood. He bent down to pick it up, feeling his fingers sink into something wet on the underside. Shuddering at the combined effect of the sensation and the lingering thought of what lay outside, he picked up the piece of wood, liquid running off the back of it as he did so. It was flimsy, packing-case stuff. He turned it around so that he was holding a dry section, and jabbed it at the switch, which flipped downwards with a stiff click. Nothing happened. He threw the piece of wood away in disgust, skelfs embedding themselves in his flesh as the departing ragged edge scraped along his palm. The stick clattered against the sliding door and landed outside, where the sunlight revealed its liquid coating to be an unmistakable shade of dark red. McGregor walked back to the doorway and examined his hand. It too was streaked with blood.

'Jesus fuck,' he muttered. 'Whit's the score here?'

He shouldered the sliding door and pushed it open as far as it would go. Sunlight invaded impatiently. It picked out several packing crates lying discarded on the ground, straw and smashed lids spilling over the sides. McGregor walked towards them, bending over to have a closer look. He remembered the skelfs currently wheedling their way ever-deeper into his right palm, and prodded carefully at the straw and shards to see whether any clue remained as to the crates' former contents. There was nothing. Beside the last one, however, there was another very small, dark, damp patch. He knelt down to examine it, putting the arm down on the floor so that he could lift the crate to one side. As he'd suspected, there was a larger reservoir of the red stuff hidden beneath, dripping off the underside of the container as soon as he lifted it.

McGregor grimaced and dropped the crate back down, unavoidably splashing himself as he did so. He felt the blood spray his face and neck from below, and spat as he recognised a hint of the taste on his lips.

'God 'michty. Eurgh.'

Another thing he recognised was the sight of an initial simple explanation heading speedily for the hills. By the time he reached for the arm again and found a shell-case glinting nearby, it had disappeared over the horizon, never to return.

From the sober, detached perspective of the Rosstown interview room, it was easier to see how his subsequent actions might have inadvertently courted maybe the merest possibility of misinterpretation. At the time he'd been more concerned with the immediate necessity to inform the authorities of his discoveries and his suspicions, now that he wasn't the authorities himself anymore. He had stuck the shell-case in his pocket, lifted the arm once again, and headed purposefully for the main road, which was the best part of a mile from the farm down a crater-pocked track. Emerging sweaty and pink-faced from the hedge-shielded junction, he had attempted to flag down an approaching minicab, realising only as he saw the horror in the driver's eyes that he was waving at the vehicle with the dismembered limb. The minicab swerved almost off the road as the driver attempted to give him as wide a berth as possible, before righting itself with a screech of its tyres and accelerating insanely away.

About two hundred yards further on, a Renault with foreign plates came hurtling round the bend and into view. It was upon him before he reacted to hide the extra arm, but he could appreciate in retrospect that even without it, he wasn't looking much like anyone's idea of a safe hitchhiker. The Renault swerved much as the minicab had, except that it over-compensated in righting itself and ran off the road, bouncing violently along the clumpy grass for a few dozen yards before coming to an abrupt stop against the tall, unkempt hedge. McGregor bounded wheezily towards it, intending to check that both of the occupants were all right. As he approached, he saw the driver emerge and clamber across the bonnet to reach the passenger-side door, yanking it open and practically dragging his female companion from within. Once safely extricated, the pair began running along the road, looking back every few paces at the bloody and terrifying figure who was now bearing down on their forsaken car, shouting after them as they fled.

'Aw, for Christ's sake,' he grunted, giving up the pursuit and panting heavily as he watched them hare off, the female figure frantically punching at a mobile telephone as she ran. McGregor turned around in disgust, then allowed himself

113

a smile as he noticed a plume of exhaust-smoke spiralling wispily from the rear of the car. He walked slowly towards the Renault, wiping sweat, grime and gore from his brow with his left sleeve. Placing the arm on top of the car's roof, he climbed into the driver's seat and checked out the controls. It was an automatic, which explained why it hadn't stalled, but with no pressure on the footbrake since the driver scarpered, it had been determinedly nosing its way deeper into the hedge.

McGregor stuck it into reverse and pressed an ever-heavier foot on the accelerator. The car moved back less than a foot before one of the rear wheels sank into a rut and began burrowing itself into the sod. He put the gearstick into forward again and turned the steering wheel hard away from the hedge, but the front remained both obstructed and ensnared by the robust and unruly privet.

It was around about this point that the local police were formulating a response to the distressed and resultantly garbled messages they'd been receiving in the previous few minutes. The first had been via radio from a rabid-sounding cabbie, and they'd been inclined to disregard it until it was followed shortly by a 999 mobile call from a near-hysterical French tourist. Neither report sounded particularly lucid or even entirely comprehensible, but both were undeniably terrified, and referred consistently to the presence of a blood-covered madman on the road to Kilbokie.

The cabbie had come on literally screaming murder, his static-crackled stream of consciousness only randomly throwing up nuggets of coherent speech. 'He's cut up the body!' he kept babbling. 'He's kill't them an' he's chopped them up!'

The tourist's already feeble English was not assisted by her panic-stricken condition, but she nonetheless managed

114

to communicate a sufficiently corroborative story for the police to take the cabbie's report seriously. However, even more alarmingly, she added that 'the man . . . 'e 'ad . . . how you say? An arm.'

'He was *armed*?'

'Yes, 'e 'ad an arm.'

'Oh Jesus Christ. Sarge! Sarge! . . .'

Meanwhile McGregor had unfortunately succeeded in jamming one of the Renault's rear wheels into the rut, but upon close examination reckoned it just needed a wee bit of rocking for the thing to pull free and haul the car back on to the tarmac. However, he couldn't drive it and rock the back-end at the same time. This was definitely a two-man job.

Hope teased him for a second as a delivery van came by and drew to a stop alongside. The bloke even went as far as opening his door before he clocked the severed arm lying on top of the car and the general condition of the man at the wheel.

More screeching tyres.

However, it did give McGregor an idea. He didn't really need a second man, just something to keep pressure on the accelerator while he applied his shoulder at the rear of the left flank. He put the Renault into reverse once more and reached for the roof.

'Right,' he muttered darkly. 'Aboot time you gave me a hand.'

His theory worked well enough in practice, the car dislodging itself suddenly after half-a-dozen spirited heaves, but illustrated a limitation around the area of slowing down again. He enjoyed the most fleeting moment of satisfaction at feeling the vehicle overcome the rut and move clear, before having to start tearing after the thing as it began lurching backwards with the familiar bronchitic whine of rapid reverse acceleration.

McGregor caught up with it and yanked at the handle as the Renault bobbled along, two wheels on Tarmac, two on grass. The door swung suddenly open as the rear grass-side wheel encountered a particularly unforgiving pot-hole. McGregor shimmied to avoid it, but it had been at least two decades since his last such manouevre, probably on Leith Links, and there was more body to swerve these days. The door caught him a glancing blow, enough to send him sprawling into the grass as the Renault, driver's door a-flap, trundled slowly back off the road on the other side and came to rest against a fencepost with a gentle bump. From his prostrate perspective he could see the dislodged arm hanging out of the car, hand-first, like there was an unconscious motorist still attached.

'Sufferin' God.'

With a diminishing sense of determination, McGregor picked himself up once again and walked across to assess the latest developments. He climbed clumsily into the driver's seat and tossed the arm into the passenger-side footwell.

'Some fuckin' driver you were,' he told it, sticking the car into forward one more time. The Renault crawled labouringly up the grassy incline and was finally on the open road again. He executed a dozen-point turn on the narrow tarmac and headed off in the direction of Rosstown.

It was a single-track road with passing-places, so he was relieved, if a little surprised, not to meet any traffic coming in the opposite direction. Still, it wasn't exactly Princes Street round here, so presumably it wasn't that much out of the ordinary. As he passed a sign denoting that he was two miles from town, the spell ended and he at last encountered another vehicle. Less comfortingly, it was a helicopter, swooping down from nowhere and dogging him less than ten yards to his left, flying about thirty feet above the fields. He craned his neck to look upwards out of the window, snatching glances back at the road to ensure that he didn't lose control. It looked like a police bird, with a bloke staring back down at him through binoculars, talking into a hand-mike as he did so.

McGregor reached down automatically for a radio handset, the years of habit and conditioning prompting a now-redundant action. His outstretched fingers found only an open ashtray with a moist, half-sooked boiled sweetie in it. There was a bend approaching. He slowed the car a little and had another gander up at the chopper before he hit the turn. The man with the mike was still doing his Peter O'Sullivan, by the looks of it. When McGregor fixed his eyes back upon the road, it was just in time to see two police cars slewing across his path in front of the junction he was nearing at – according to the speedo – Christ! Ninety! There seemed no time to brake, and he'd kill himself and both the polis drivers if he hit them head-to-side like that. He had no option but to swerve to his left and aim for the hedge.

The Renault burst effortlessly through what turned out to be an anorexic privet, and immediately encountered something more substantial in the form of an astonished and transfixed Cheviot. McGregor heard a gassy groan – half-baa and half-burp – as the sheep was bounced into the air, the Renault bludgeoning onwards beneath. The ewe flew over the hedge, into the roadway and crashed through the windscreen of the next arriving squadcar, which consequently ploughed into the two units forming the make-shift roadblock.

McGregor grappled with the squirming steering wheel as

117

the Renault thumped along the grass, somehow managing to aim the car through an open gate and back on to the Queen's highway. His detour had taken him diagonally across a section of the grazing field before emerging forty yards down from the junction, where steam and smoke could now be seen rising above the hedge. He trundled the car slowly up towards the crossroads, above which the helicopter was now hovering.

Choppers and roadblocks. Jesus. Something very big was going down, almost certainly related to whatever he'd stumbled upon back at the farm. He could see two more police cars arriving at speed, blue lights and sirens. They pulled up at the junction and six men exploded out, kitted in full body armour and bearing automatic weapons. Christ, an Armed Response Unit! He remembered the shellcase in his pocket and decided his suspicions must have been bang-on. Someone extremely dangerous was on the loose.

The ARU guys filed across the road ahead of him, he assumed to take up covered positions behind the roadblock. But instead they knelt down in formation on the tarmac, pointing all of their guns directly at the slow-approaching Renault. Then they shot out all his tyres.

'In the name of the wee man,' McGregor yelped, jumping on the brakes and ducking down behind the dashboard.

'This is the police,' came a hailer-amplified voice. Like there might be hunners of other blokes running about in kevlar around Rosstown. 'Turn off your engine and step out of your vehicle with your hands up.'

'Aw, for fuck's sake,' McGregor muttered, a grim realisation descending upon him as he eyed the spare body-part lying across the passenger-side floormat.

'Step out of the vehicle, I said. Come out right now with

your hands in the air. Slowly. Come on, let's see those hands. I want to see those hands.'

McGregor looked again at the arm and decided he owed it to himself.

'If we can go over it once again, you're claiming that at this point, whilst out walking, you were suddenly attacked?'

McGregor was getting bored now. His head was still sore and he wanted to go home to his bed. He hadn't had anything to eat all day and the only liquid refreshment on offer was tea that he wouldn't have foisted on a mass-murderer back down the road in Edinburgh. He'd used his phone call to ring Molly and ask her to come down and collect him, guessing he'd have explained his way out in a matter of minutes, but that had been reckoning without Sergeant Mutton-Molester.

Playing the dunderheid could sometimes be an effective interrogation technique: you pretended you didn't quite understand, made yourself out to be slow on the uptake. It forced the suspect to repeat himself and get frustrated, and that's when the inconsistencies started to come out. Unfortunately, as this particular interview wore on, it was becoming depressingly clear that Sergeant Mutton-Molester wasn't pretending.

'I was knocked unconscious, yes,' McGregor said steadily, using his experience on the other side of the table to keep his emotions in check. 'I'm assuming it was the arm that hit me, but I don't think I'd call it an attack. It's not as though the bloke had a lot of say over where his arm was going at the time.'

'So you're saying your assailant was out of control?'

'No, I'm saying my "assailant" exploded.'

'He exploded, yes, he exploded with *rage* and he attacked

you. Set upon you in the woods when you were minding your own business. But you retaliated, didn't you, Mr McGregor? You exacted terrible revenge.'

Oh for Christ's sake.

When he'd first set eyes on his interrogator, McGregor pegged him for some young up-and-comer who'd be heading south for greater things once he'd cut his teeth in the sticks. However, a closer look at his coupon betrayed that the red hair and freckly chops had conspired to knock a deceptive few years off his appearance, and a few minutes of witnessing the numpty in action told McGregor that the bright lights of the big city would most definitely not be beckoning. In fact, if at any point in the past this tube had made it down to civilisation, there was little doubt he had been posted back north to sheep-shagging country to keep him the fuck out of the way of serious police work.

McGregor took another long, slow, deep breath.

'Look, Sergeant, I've told you this three times now, and if you play the tape back you'll see my story's been entirely consistent—'

'Ah, so you admit it's a story. Now we're getting somewhere. So why don't you save us all a lot of time, forget about your *story*, and just tell us where the rest of the body is?'

McGregor leaned forward until his forehead touched the plastic table-top. Maybe if he went to sleep he'd wake up in his own bed. He helped himself to yet another long breath. The calming effect was diminishing every time.

'I don't know where the rest of the body is,' he mumbled, his head still resting face-down on the table as he spoke. 'And I really think you should start to address the issue of what caused it to disappear in the first place, especially as there's ample evidence of some kind of firefight having taken place at the same locus. I mean, that to me would seem to be the most pressing matter, but then maybe I'm lacking the advantage of your detective skills.'

Sergeant Mutton-Molester slapped his hand down on the table-top, close to McGregor's ear. In a saner parallel universe, McGregor throttled him to death for it. In this one he remained still and listened.

'What you're lacking, Mr McGregor,' the eejit announced loudly, 'is a plausible explanation for why you were apprehended in a hijacked vehicle with a severed arm in your possession, and why in your crazed desperation to evade capture, you contrived to wreck three police cars, injure four men and inflict fatal injuries upon a prize-winning and highly regarded local sheep.'

McGregor sent the bucket down the deep-breath well one more time. It hit the bottom with a dry clatter and came back empty.

Right.

He had been entirely cooperative, lucid, forthcoming, truthful and generally everything that suspects, in his vast experience, were dedicatedly not. He had, quite definitely, up to this point, done everything he could to help, and it had not proven rewarding. It was now his moral right to be a pain in the arse.

His head still resting face-down on the sweaty plastic, he began mentally composing the most lengthy, tediously elaborate, irritatingly detailed, thoroughly fib-filled and utterly outrageous statement it would ever be this half-wit's misfortune to transcribe, at the end of which he would refuse to sign. It was only a matter of time before hard evidence intervened on his behalf, proving his original story true and forcing them to let him go, so he might as well keep himself amused.

However, at that point there was a knock at the door, and Sergeant Mutton-Molester was drawn outside for a brief conversation in the corridor. McGregor couldn't make out much above mumbling, but the words 'Lothian and Borders' were definitely uttered, as were 'decorated officer'. The words 'your arse is oot the windae' were not, but the import was clear from the sergeant's failure to return and his replacement with a highly apologetic and obsequious more senior detective, DS McLeod, who'd just come on shift via the farm at Nether Kilbokie.

Fifteen minutes later, McGregor was being driven home in Molly's Primera, powering back along the same road he'd travelled earlier but this time without airborne accompaniment. The polis were satisfied that his story about the explosion was true, having been out and checked the site themselves, but they still didn't share his evaluation of the significance of the spent shell. Tomorrow, they would have people examining what had been found at the farm to try to determine what caused the explosion and – if possible – the identity of the fatality. However, they remained conspicuously unworried about the possibility of foul play.

There'd been much arse-kissing by D S McLeod regarding how long it had taken to confirm that McGregor was indeed who he claimed to be, and more regarding the scepticism shown in the interim. However, the patronising bastard had nonetheless let slip something about retired policemen occasionally having over-active imaginations. 'I don't think we need lose too much sleep over mad bombers, Mr McGregor,' he'd offered glibly. 'I mean, what could terrorists find to interest themselves around here?'

Smug prick.

Molly gunned the engine to climb Kilbokie brae, taking them above the liftings yard. As they came over the brow, that daft floating-hotel fiasco loomed enormously into view.

■ 17:38 ■ 'tropics' bar ■ cocktails and aperitifs ■

'There you are, big man. Grab a pew. Whit you fur?'

'Eh, pint o' heavy would be lovely, Eddie.'

'Right you are. Two pints of heavy, please, Jim.'

'Coming right up, sir.'

'Grand.'

'So, is this whit you've been dein' wi' yoursel', Ed? Mighta known. Where's the wife?'

'She's upstairs gettin' the good frock an' the warpaint on.'

'Aye, Tina's the same. I thought I'd best leave her tae it. She's bad enough at the best o' times, but she's really gaun for it the night. Brought two dresses an' she's changed in an' oot o' baith o' them aboot five times already, no' sure which wan looks best. Of course, then she asks me. It's wan o' thae questions you can only get wrang, no matter whit you say. You say you like the blue wan, so she says does that mean you don't like the black wan? And she's no' even *started* on the shoes yet. I had tae get oot. She's up tae high doe, so she is. You know whit it's like. Says she doesnae want tae show hersel' up in front o' aw these auld schoolmates.'

'Bit late for that – look who she came wi'.'

'Aye, very good. Comin' fae Man at Poundstretcher sittin' there. How long have you been here, anyway?'

'Ach, don't look at me like that, Charlie. It's a free bar, for

123

fuck's sake. You've got tae make the maist o' these things. I'm just surprised you wurnae in here sooner.'

'Aye, well, Tina wanted tae see roon the place, so we took the wee tour. Were you no' curious for a wee swatch yoursel'?'

'You kiddin'? I mean, I know they've spent a lot o' money buildin' this place an' aw that, but I find it hard tae believe they've installed anythin' on it that could possibly be mair of an attraction than Jim, there.'

'How's that, then?'

'He pours you drinks an' he doesnae ask you for money.'

'Better than Disneyland, then, Eddie, eh?'

'Sure is.'

'There you are, gentlemen. Two pints of heavy. That will be . . . nothing whatsoever.'

'Ooooh, I just never get sick o' hearin' that wan. Keep the change, pal.'

'Thank you, sir, most generous of you.'

'Cheers, Eddie.'

'Cheers, big man.'

'So, have you been in here yoursel' the whole time? Just you an' your new best pal here?'

'Naw, there's been a few familiar faces drifted in an' oot. Kenny Collins, of course. He was here for aboot hauf an 'oor, durin' which, bless me, Father, I must confess for the first time in my life I began to have doubts aboot the merits o' free drink.'

'So how's he no' here noo? Cannae see Kenny poppin' in for a quick Dry Martini then poppin' back oot.'

'There's two bars in the hotel, thank fuck. Somebody tell't him you could get snacks at the other yin. Oh, which reminds me. You'll never guess who *did* pop in for a quick wan. Matt Black!'

'You're kiddin' me on.'

'No shit, Charlie. Matt fuckin' Black is *here*. Came by, had a wee blether.'

'Christ. Did he remember you?'

''Course he did. He was brand new. He's no' changed, really. Had tae tell him, right enough, that American programme he's on is fuckin' shite – an' he never even took the huff. He was askin' for you, by the way, says he'd make sure he got a word wi' you later.'

'Serious?'

'Aye. He even asked who you were playin' for these days. He was well impressed when I says it was the Arthurlie, but I didnae want you gettin' big-heided, so I tell't him aboot you gettin' sent aff last week as well.'

'Thanks a bunch.'

'Never bother, it was a blessin': you wouldnae have been able tae come here the day if you werenae suspended. Besides, I tell't him it was against Pollok, so you only went up in his estimations.'

'That's mair like it. So, whit's it tae dae wi' food?'

'Oh aye, right. Kenny was still hingin' aboot like a bad smell when Matt came in. Matt goes up tae Jim there an' says, "Can you make me a large cappuccino, pal?" Jim says sure. So at this point Kenny pipes up an says, "Aye, gie's wan o' them ower here as well. I'm fuckin' starvin'."'

'You're a fuckin' liar, Eddie. Christ, last time I heard that wan it was Lorenzo Amoruso an' Barry Ferguson. An' before that, it used tae be Mark Hateley an' *Duncan* Ferguson.'

'Aye, an afore that it used tae be Butch Wilkins an' *Iain* Ferguson, but I'm no jokin', it fuckin' happened. You tell him, Jim. What happened in here earlier wi' Matt Black?'

'Oh don't, please. I almost gave myself a palsy trying to keep a straight face.'

'See?'

'Aye, ferr enough. Class act, the boy Kenny. Jesus Christ.'

'So whit aboot yoursel', big yin? Whit faces fae the past have you run intae so far?'

'Eh, no' many that werenae on the bus, tae be honest. Lisa McKenzie, I saw her. She was on the tour. She's a lawyer noo, lives through in Edinburgh. Works for the procurator fiscal, she says.'

'Married?'

'Naw, she was on her own. Lookin' very well. No' as quiet as I remembered her. I suppose you'd have tae come oot your shell if you're prosecutin' crooks, right enough. Oh aye, an' I saw Tommy Milligan, speakin' o' lawyers.'

'He a lawyer as well? He was always a brainbox, right enough.'

'Too true. Daein' well for himsel' by the look of it. Dear-lookin' watch on one arm an' a dear-lookin burd on the other.'

'He must be *defendin'* the crooks, then.'

'Aye, must be. He says tae gie you his business card.'

'Very good. Cheeky bastard.'

'Naw, just kiddin', Eddie. Noo, who else was there. Aye, Eileen Stewart.'

'Oh aye, I remember Eileen. How was she?'

'Much the same, just a bit rounder. She's still a cheery wee soul, but to be honest, I can only take so much of hearin' aboot other folk's weans, you know whit I mean?'

'What's her man like?'

'Well, he cannae shut up aboot them either, so I didnae really get tae fin' oot much else.'

'An' presumably you got a closer look at Gavin.'

'Aye. I recognised him once I saw him, but it's nae wonder we didnae remember him that well. He was awfy quiet at school, far as I can recall. Nice o' him tae remember aw us, right enough.'

'So whit was the tour like, big man? Was I the only wan that missed it?'

'Eh, naw, no' exactly. I think Gavin's nose was a wee bit oot o' joint aboot the numbers, actually. Bit daft o' him tae organise it for when everybody's just got here, though. Maist folk want tae unwind efter the journey, have a lie doon or a shower, you know?'

'Aye. Bit daft o' him organisin' anythin' in competition wi' a free bar, if you ask me, but I know what you're sayin'. So how come you went?'

'Politeness, I suppose. Plus Tina insisted – she wanted a nosy.'

'Are you comin' here your next holidays, then?'

'Aye, that'll be fuckin' right.'

'So's it a dump?'

'Naw. Naw, far from it. Everythin' – the bits that are finished, I mean – everythin's really posh, lot o' money been spent. It's just . . . I don't know. It's . . . it's . . . it's a fuckin' *oil rig*! There's just nae gettin' away fae that. Well, that's no' fair. It's no' like there's any trace o' whit it used to be: there's nae drillheids lyin' aboot roon the swimmin' pools, or nothin'. But it's so kinna enclosed. You've got these big hotels loomin' ower you on all sides, an' at the parts where you *can* see ower the edge, it just freaks you oot. It's as if that's where there should be a road oot the place, but aw there is a fuckin' sixty- or seventy-fit drop.'

'Nice view, though, is it no'?'

'Aye, lovely. An' I'm sure it'll be lovely doon in Africa an' all, but it's . . . it's the fact that you cannae touch it, you cannae get any nearer it, so it might as well be wallpaper.'

'Sure, but is that no' the idea? Nice views, warm weather, an' loads o' stuff tae dae roon the resort?'

'Aye, I suppose so. There's plenty of activities, right enough.'

'Like what, then?'

'Well, there's the Lido first of all. You'll have seen some o' that yoursel' on the way in. Aw thae swimmin' pools connected up wi' wee channels an' tunnels an' bridges an' that. The weans'll love it, that's for sure. Folk'll never be able tae find the wee buggers again, but then mibbe that's another sellin' point for the parents. The Lido's no particular tae any wan o' the hotels – it's the kinna centrepiece o' the whole resort. I think he said two o' the hotels have got their own indoor pools as well, but the Lido's the main sunbathin' area. There's a wave machine in wan o' the pools, an apparently aw the wee totey wans dotted aboot the place are actually jacuzzis. An' aw roon the Lido there's terraces, so's you can sit ootside an' have a drink or a bite tae eat.'

'That sounds quite nice.'

'Aye, quite nice if you like McDonald's an' Pizza Hut, 'cause that's whit you're gaunny get.'

'Aw, you're kiddin'.'

'That's whit Gavin says. But if you fancy somethin' mair traditional, there's gaunny be eight chippies dotted aboot the resort.'

'*Eight*?'

'Eight. Eight fuckin' chippies, aff the coast o' Africa. I think they're gaunny use wan leg o' this place for storin' the tatties, an' another yin for the lard. So it's no' an oil rig noo, it's a cookin'-oil rig.'

'Jesus. Eight chippies, man. Whit aboot kebab shops?'

'Oh aye, four or five o' them as well. Plus six curry hooses an' four chinkies, but they're aw indoors, doonstairs. In fact aw the proper sit-doon, bottle-o'-wine restaurants are doonstairs, below decks, if you like. Gavin says some o' them are at the ootside walls, so there'll be windaes lookin' oot tae the sea. An' there'll be another yin at the top o' wan o' the hotels that looks oot baith sides, oot tae sea an' doon tae the Lido.'

'So apart fae eatin', drinkin' an' sunbathin', whit else is there tae dae?'

'Eh, well, there's cinemas doonstairs, a multiplex. An' bingo halls – a bloody multiplex o' them as well. Grand prize is a free week at the resort. Second prize is a fortnight. Oh aye, an' there's ten-pin bowlin'. We walked past that, but it's no' quite finished, so Gavin never let us get a look inside. There's an ice rink as well. We got a wee gander at that, but obviously there was nae ice yet. I'd imagine there'd have tae be a casualty department an' all, but it wasnae on the tour. There was wan o' thae laser places, though.'

'Whit, tattoo removal?'

'Naw, Eddie, lasers, ray-guns. You know, for kid-on gunfights.'

'Oh, heh, I wouldnae mind a wee go at that. Bit o' target practice. Is it open?'

'Naw. Nothin's open, no' until they move this thing tae Africa. Just as well, tae. If somebody gied you a ray-gun, you'd end up blindin' yoursel' wi' it. You'd be better aff stickin' tae the video games.'

'Oh, is there an arcade?'

'We passed aboot five, but before you ask, they're no' open either.'

129

'Where are they, though?'

'Same as everythin' else – doon in the sub-levels. I think Gavin said it's three or four floors deep, across the whole surface area o' this place. We only saw a fraction of it, which was enough. There's dozens an' dozens o' corridors doon there, linkin' aw the facilities, an maist o' them are lined wi' shops.'

'Whit kinna shops?'

'Well, they're no' stocked yet, thank Christ. I think if Tina had seen them in aw their glory, she'd have been askin' Gavin for the brochure for next summer. He was sayin' there'll be franchises o' aw the big high-street chains, plus souvenir stores an' hairdressers an' beauticians an' you name it. There's gaunny be a special sports area as well, wi' a big bookie's an' a sports pub wi' giant telly screens. Turns oot Celtic, Rangers, Man-U, Arsenal an' Chelsea are aw gaunny get shops tae themsels.'

'God. He's gaunny make a mint, in't he?'

'Gavin? Sounds like it.'

'Still, big man, I mean tae say: the pictures an' the bingo an' the bowlin' an' the shops – you might as well be at hame, apart fae the weather.'

'Aye, but I think that's the point. Every room's gaunny have satellite telly showin' British channels aw day, plus the place is gaunny have its ain press.'

'Its ain newspaper?'

'Naw, a mini printer's. Seriously. Gavin says they're negotiatin' deals wi' the *Sun* an' the *Mirror* tae download their pages affa computer every night, so's they can print their ain special editions for the punters on the rig.'

'Well, that's understandable, Charlie. You might start tae feel a bit oota things if you couldnae keep up wi' who was shaggin' who back hame.'

'Pretty hellish, though, the whole place. It's like Butlins meets ethnic cleansin'.'

'So what was everybody else sayin' tae it?'

'Fuck, some o' them were right intae it. Eileen Stewart an' her man, they were practically bookin' up on the spot, goin on' aboot how great it would be for the weans. Paul Duff as well, he thought it was the best thing since flush lavvies, but you know Paul – mair brains in a puddin' supper. Lisa McKenzie, though – I thought her eyes were gaunny come oot her heid aboot five times.'

'Was she impressed?'

'Well, Gavin seemed tae think she was, but the poor bugger was gettin' the wrang end o' the stick. By the end the lassie was tryin' that hard no tae laugh, she was aboot greetin'. It was murder. Every time I caught her eye, I was nearly away masel'. She's a good laugh, Lisa. Need tae make sure we get a wee word later.'

'So, same again, big man?'

'Eh, naw, no thanks, Eddie, keep your haun in your pocket. I'd better get back up the stair an' get intae the tin flute.'

'Ach come on, just wan mair. It'll no' take you a minute.'

'Naw, seriously, Eddie, that's the part I'm worried aboot. I'm watchin' how much I drink the night.'

'How?'

'Well, think aboot it. There's times you get blootered an' it doesnae matter whit you dae or whit you come oot wi', because naebody knows who you are, anyway. Let's just say this is no' wan o thae times. This is the last group o' folk in the world that I want tae make an arse o' masel' in front of. I might never see any o' them again, but just knowin' would be enough.'

131

'Aye, well, big man, it's times like this you appreciate the benefits o' havin' a reputation for makin' an arse o' yoursel'. I can get as pished as I like the night, 'cause I've got fuck-all tae lose. Same again here, Jim.'

■ 19:30 ■ moran cove ■ three men in a boat ■

After Dawson shot Kilfoyle, Connor had remarked that if he didn't knock off the summary executions, it was going to end up being a Rambo-style one-man assault. At the time his intention had been sarcasm, not soothsaying, but then, as a military man, Connor should have known the one about careless talk.

They'd lost four men back at the farm through assorted variants of homicidal mania, and now two more were threatening to desert. Not just any two, either, but specifically two of the team assigned to execute the initial infiltration. With that being a three-man op, the rather unforgiving arithmetic left Connor in the aforementioned Sylvester Stallone role.

He looked back across the water to the spur, behind which the rest of the unit was on standby, waiting for his green light to begin the second stage. It was that smoke-'em-if-you-got-'em moment, except that nobody in their right mind would be lighting up with all those rockets lying around. He thought of how he'd felt, standing there on the sand maybe less than ten minutes ago. The horrors, indignities and stupidities of the morning had seemed forgotten, the smell of sea air even purging the scent of fried Glover, which had enveloped him all day like an everlasting fart. The adrenaline had started coursing through him as he pulled on his gear and checked his weapons. He'd watched Jackson and Gaghen do likewise – slapping mags into breeches, clipping spares to bandoliers, adjusting the shoulder-straps on their automatics – and he felt like a soldier again.

This was what it was all about. The golden idea of running his own outfit had been tarnishing steadily up until that moment, having already proven a tedious burden of administration and busy-work before this morning added worry and embarrassment to the load. His vision was of orchestrating an elite unit's operations in the field, but so far the only field his unit had seen action in was the one behind those outbuildings, where the military operation he'd orchestrated involved five men chasing the highland cow on whose left horn Glover's head had impaled itself. (Christ knew where his right arm ever got to.)

But once he felt the cold steel of an Ingram's in his hands, smelled the petrol from the outboard, all of that faded. This was the part he did best, and this was the part that mattered.

All of which made Gaghen's timing pretty fucking choice.

They'd climbed into the dinghy, the three of them, and set off into the firth. Jackson had the tiller, Gaghen sat at the bow. Connor was in the middle, partially unfolding the plan of the installation because he wanted to double-check their secondary route.

'Look, ehm, Bill,' Gaghen began, with a sheepishness that would have sounded less uncharacteristic coming from Ian Paisley. Connor looked up from his map, noticing that the boat was slowing down now that it was out of sight of the beach. 'I'm sorry, mate, but we're not going.'

'*What*?' Connor spluttered, grasping for some other possible interpretation of this remark in which the juxtaposition of the words 'not' and 'going' had fewer consequences for their imminent assault on the resort complex.

'I mean, we'll drop you off first, like, obviously, but we're legging it after that.'

Connor was about to laugh to show that he'd seen through their wind-up, when he noticed that Gaghen's machine gun was pointed straight at him, his finger round the trigger-guard. Then he remembered seeing Gaghen and Jackson engaged in rather furtive discussions throughout the day. He'd thought little of it at the time, imagining they were catching up on each other's news or exchanging off-colour tales they'd heard about various of their comrades, but now it all added up. Neither of them had been acting very pleased since this morning, and Jackson kept giving Connor the stink-eye every time someone asked how his ear was.

'It's nothing personal, Bill,' Gaghen explained. 'It's the job. It's just not right for us.'

Connor decided, particularly in light of the 9mm levelled at his abdomen, to view this as a man-management challenge, and reacted in as conciliatory a manner as he could manage. In practice this merely amounted to him asking 'why on earth' rather than 'why the festering fuck' they had waited until this excruciatingly inopportune juncture to voice their disquiet.

'Well,' Gaghen said, in an absurdly reasonable tone, 'I suppose partly because we didn't want to make a big scene and damage the *esprit de corps*, but mainly because we didn't want your man Dawson shooting us as deserters. He's a bit over fond of the theatrical gesture, your mate. Spent a bit too long in the company of dictators, if you ask me. We thought it best – and safest – if we just slipped away quietly. We didn't want to bail out in front of everybody, because we know this is your gig and we didn't want you to look bad. Sorry, Bill. No hard feelings, eh?'

Man management, he kept telling himself. Man management. Deep breaths, deep breaths. Count down backwards from, ah fuck it.

'No hard feelings? You didn't want me to look bad? Just how much of a fucking elephantine wanker do you think I'm going to look when I radio back and ask them to send out a couple more guys because I seem to have lost the two I set off with? And what in the name of Queen Guinevere's quim do you mean "the job's not right"? What, were you scrubbing around looking for Glover's arm and you found a conscience instead?'

'It's not like that, Bill. Look, we don't want to go into the reasons. Just take it from me, the job isn't right and let's leave it at that.'

Searching for a rational explanation for this abhorrence, Connor's sense of logic finally burned through the obscuring mists of his indignation.

'You want more money. That's it, isn't it? You want a wider wedge. That's why you're springing this out here, it's the ultimate seller's market. And you're playing it cool, too, not asking, just waiting for me to offer. Christ, I can't believe you could be so, well, you know, *mercenary*.'

'It's not the money, Bill. You know both of us better than that. And it's not a matter of conscience. It's a matter of not ending up in jail – or worse.'

'Oh come off it, Dan. I told you right from the start that this would be A, British soil, and B, highly illegal. You could have knocked it back long before today. So at what point did you suddenly decide you've a problem with that?'

'Probably around the time that we found out what a bunch of fucking half-wits we'd be working with,' Jackson said bitterly.

'This whole op is from page one of the cluster-fuck recipe book,' Gaghen added. 'And that's the only thing about it that isn't half-baked. You're in too much of a hurry, Bill, and that's because Dawson's in too much of a hurry. It's under-planned. His tip came in late, but he figured it was too good to pass.'

'Bollocks it's under-planned. We've done ops together at much shorter notice than this, Dan. Remember Kanayo? And when have we ever had this level of technical info about—'

'You can have as many maps and blueprints, as much inside gen as you like,' Gaghen interrupted, 'but it's not going to matter if your personnel literally don't know one end of a rocket launcher from the other. Sure we've gone in at short notice before, but we weren't carrying any fucking passengers. Most of these guys you've got, Bill, they're not professionals, they're adventurers. No training, no discipline, just a taste for action. Christ, did you see some of them when the guns came out? It was like fucking Christmas. They all dived for the stuff before they'd even heard the brief, before they'd any fucking clue what kind of hardware they were actually going to need.'

Connor winced with embarrassment at the memory. He'd been kind of hoping no-one else had noticed.

The engine had calmed to a purr, the dinghy no longer moving forward at all, just bobbing gently with the waves in the warm wind. The light was fading, a late summer's evening glow gradually dimming around them.

'Yeah, all right,' Connor conceded, 'they're not pros, but they've all seen action. I didn't get them down the fucking labour exchange. Africa or Ulster, they've been in amongst it and they've come through. Do you think I'm *that* fucking stupid or *that* fucking desperate that I'd throw my lot in with people I didn't think could handle it? I'm not sitting back somewhere, watching this unfold, remember. I'm leading the fucking assault.'

'I know you're not stupid, Bill,' Gaghen stated. 'Desperate I'm not sure about. You're saying you think these guys can handle it, but I notice you didn't pick any of *them* to be in this boat alongside you.'

'No, of course I bloody didn't. I picked the best men for the most important job. Once this part's been executed successfully, we could hand the op over to schoolkids and they'd pull it off. For Christ's sake, come on, it's unsuspecting, unarmed civilians. It's fish in a barrel.'

'Yeah, and that's the part that's worrying me,' he retorted. 'If it *was* schoolkids I'd be less concerned, because you could rely on them to do what they're fucking told. As far as I can see, the success of this job relies on nobody on the outside finding out what's going on until it's all over. That means total control. No hysteria. Hysteria leads to mayhem. Mayhem leads to fuck-ups. Fuck-ups lead to jail. It's a fucking miracle the show's not over already, after the pantomime we put on for the world this morning. Now you're talking about a situation where you've got unarmed civvies in the same room as a bunch of psychos who're just *dying* to shoot somebody.'

'They're not psychos. They're after a purse, same as you. They know the score: they follow orders or they don't get paid. And Jesus, do you think any of them are going to step out of line and cut loose on the civvies after Dawson's display earlier? If the two of you are running scared of pissing him off, imagine what the others'll be like.'

'We're not running scared,' Jackson interjected, inadvertently offering Connor an angle of attack. 'We're just being prudent.'

'Oh, that's the subtle difference between mercs and adventurers these days, is it? They're scared but you're "prudent". Fucking amazing, guys. From soldiers of fortune to soldiers of caution. I'll just call you the Mild Geese from now on, shall I?'

God, it was cheap psychology, but, like squeezing someone's nuts, when you're prodding at an ego's most tender spot, the obviousness of your approach doesn't make it any easier to withstand.

'Come off it, Bill,' Gaghen said defensively. 'You know us better than that.'

'I know you *used* to be better than that. Now I can't say. I never had you down for shiters before . . . I don't know, maybe you're just not following the logic. You're concerned the new boys might fuck up and the alarm could be raised, but as the new boys aren't being brought in until we've cut off all communication channels, then I don't see where the danger lies. Do you?'

There was a long silence, only the slapping of the waves and the idling engine to be heard. Connor stared insistently at Gaghen, who was avoiding eye contact.

'Ah, fuck it, I'm in,' Gaghen eventually announced.

Jackson nodded, a little unsurely. 'Yeah, okay. Me too.'

'Right,' Connor sighed. 'And let's have no more of this shite, gentlemen, eh?'

'Sorry, Bill,' Gaghen said with a shrug. 'Just not been feeling myself lately. This trypanosomiasis thing knocked me off-kilter a little. A bit of action's probably just what I need. Look, you won't tell anyone about this, will you?'

Connor sighed again. 'No, lads, your secret's in safe

hands.' God strewth. 'So now that the matter's closed, are you ready to do some work for a living?'

'Yes.'

'Good. Then let's kick some botty.'

■ meanwhile ■ fipr ■ humility and that ■

The evening was proving slightly less horrific than Matt had feared. Maybe it was a lot easier to move freely and 'mingle' without the encumbrance of lugging a monolithic ego around. He'd checked his in at that beach on the Baja. Tonight he was hand-luggage only: the wee black sports bag of the soul.

He might even have ventured tentatively to concede that he was, to his enormous surprise, maybe just possibly slightly kind of enjoying himself, and not just because of the ostentatious wealth of new material he was being gifted. The potentially disconcerting strangeness of being confronted at once by so many faces from the past was tempered by fascination at the way those faces had changed, and in many cases also by an uncharitable amusement at the size or shape of the body underneath. His conscience tried to rein him in on this last, particularly in the case of beer-swollen males, reminding him with a little internal finger-poking that not everybody could afford cocaine. Still, at least he wasn't lying when explaining that his own slimline appearance was down to a Californian lifestyle.

He had come here to be humble, to exhume daft old stories and to hear what had happened to everybody else in the time when he was lost in the mirror-maze of self.

He'd had images of standing there, nodding and smiling – but principally just listening – as other people did the talking. He'd hear all about their lives, their experiences, their weans, whatever, then they'd walk off thinking he was a nice guy, and maybe he'd walk off feeling like one. He used to be a nice guy, once upon a time. The teachers used to tell his mum that. He was polite, well-behaved, considerate, hard-working . . . all that stuff.

He used to be such a sweet thing . . .

So far it wasn't quite going according to plan. This was perhaps because he'd failed to anticipate that everyone else might not share his currently low opinion of himself. He'd also failed to anticipate that they would be fairly interested in hearing about *his* life, too. And he'd utterly failed to consider that their first-hand memories of him were of an approachable, easy-going and fairly likeable person. Consequently, rather than be humble, he was feeling humbled: they were chucking warmth at him by the bucketload. And as for getting to hear about *their* lives, forget it.

'Matt Black! Howzitgaun! I cannae believe it. We were just talkin' aboot you. There was a rumour goin' aboot that you were here the night, but I didnae believe it until I saw you. I cannae believe I'm staunin' here talkin' to you efter aw these years. Absolutely mental. I must have bored her silly aboot you, eh? This is my wife, by the way, Maureen. Maureen, this is Matt Black. See, I bet you thought I was makin' it up aboot bein' at school wi' him. We've got aw your videos and CDs, Matt man. I cannae believe you're *here*. I thought you'd be far too busy to bother comin' oot tae a thing like this, but it just shows you, eh? You're livin' in America noo, is that right? But you were ower two year ago for the tour. We saw you at the Theatre Royal. I nearly died laughin', didn't I, Mo? Whit was I like? Absolutely mental. So how are you? Are you tourin' again? Aw, man, see that thing you did aboot Mandelson's boyfriend an' the pager? Wi' him readin' it tae see whit tae scream durin' orgasm? Aw, Jesus, I was on the flair, so I was. Or that bit aboot Cardinal Winning? Absolutely mental. Wonder whit aul Father McGinlay would have made of it, but. Mind that time we were in first-year Science an' he came in tae tell aw the guys aboot how we wurnae allowed tae wank? I'm surprised you never done a routine aboot that. Mibbe you're workin' on it, eh? Or mibbe I'll get credit for suggestin' it. It's magic to see you, by the way. Are you ower for long?'

And so on.

It was a while before Matt even got to move from the first spot he'd taken up, a few yards from the ballroom's main door, where two waiters were welcoming everyone with glasses of champagne. He'd automatically taken hold of one before he could commence any internal dialogue about his current drug abstinence or worry whether anyone had read the tabloid stories describing him as an alcoholic. If nothing else, he'd felt he needed a prop. With all the guests arriving accompanied, he thought he'd look and feel less of a haddy standing on his own if he had a celebratory drink in his hand. But he'd barely managed a sip before catching the first familiar eye and being hailed with an enthusiasm so solicitous that it made him forget to dwell on how scarcely he deserved it.

Couples were circulating and interweaving as though part of a great eightsome reel, quickly congregating into new groups each time one broke up. Jim Murray and his wife Maureen were joined by Anne-Marie Dougray (née Taylor) and her husband Derek, beckoned by Jim as they passed. ('C'mere, Anne-Marie. You'd never believe it – look,

141

it's Matt Black. Matt, do you remember Anne-Marie from Mrs Laurence's class at O-grade?') When Jim and Maureen were buttonholed by the newly arrived Andrew Reilly and partner, their places were quickly taken by Paul Duff and his wife Angela. In turn that couple was loudly hullaaaw!ed from behind, and as they turned to see who had called, Matt, looking elsewhere, found himself in the glare of another God-look-who-it-is smile, and on it went.

The majority of them knew little of his work beyond that he was a comedian, and a few weren't even aware of that: once this would have felt like a sturdy boot in the only place more sensitive than his ego, but tonight it was curiously refreshing. Apart from reminding him of a whole world where what he did meant knob-all to people, it was an unexpected comfort that they seemed pleased to see him simply because they remembered him from school (and presumably did so with some modicum of fondness). More disarming still was remembering how much he'd once liked some of *them*.

Somewhere amid the throng he fielded a catch-you-when-this-whole-thing-calms-down nod from Allan Crossland, the only person present who he'd kept in any kind of contact with. Admittedly this hadn't gone much beyond a few pints at intervals of up to three years, but the effort and intention had always been reciprocally appreciated. It wasn't like they lived around the corner from each other, both of them knew that.

There was another such long-distance wave from Charlie O'Neill, someone else Matt was hoping for a long late-night blether with, and not just because he was now playing for Arthurlie. In a school full of hardmen and would-be hardmen, big Charlie had been like a guardian angel to vulnerable short-arses like himself, being the sort of guy only the most psychotic (i.e. Davie Murdoch) would pick a fight with. He carried respect because of his size and strength, as well as for being about the best footballer the school had ever produced, all of which perhaps explained why, unlike many of his peers, he never acted like he had something to prove. An indefatigably good-natured character, he never threw his weight about, and consequently one of his few intolerances was those who did. There'd been once or twice Matt had seen studio execs bawling out an underling and found himself wishing big Charlie could step out of the shadows and 'have a wee quiet word'. Whatever he got sent off for last week, it was a safe shout the Pollok player deserved it.

Perhaps ironically, perhaps not, the most awkward thing was talking to those who *were* clued-up about his stuff, as their deference to the iconic Matt Black threatened to become an impediment to having a conversation with plain old Matthew from St Mick's. He felt especially embarrassed and unworthy when Ally McQuade produced a copy of the *Thatcher's Funeral Party Fund* CD for him to sign, having brought it along on the off-chance that Matt would show. Ally had been a lot funnier at school than Matt ever was onstage. He wanted to tell him that, but couldn't imagine doing so without sounding like a patronising prick.

Instead he tried steering the conversation away from the subject of himself ('So what about you, Ally? You married?'), but Ally steered it back so consistently that Matt began to suspect the guy was hiding something. He took this irrational notion as a further symptom of his own sustained self-loathing: he was actually having difficulty getting his head round the idea of people liking him.

In fact, Matt was finding himself the unaccustomed recipient of so much goodwill that it had been perversely reassuring when Brendan Mooney demonstratively blanked him during his chat with Ally. 'Buckin'' Brendan had been standing nearby with an austerely gaunt and colourless female Matt recognised instantly as Mary-Theresa Devlin. She hadn't changed a hair since she was fifteen, but then in those days she hadn't so much been fifteen as fifteen-going-on-forty-five. The matching wedding bands on their fingers were a message from fate reminding Matt that *it* was a more drily vicious comedian than he'd ever be, even if its gags tended towards the obvious now and then. Buckin' Brendan, God's holy altar-boy, had married MTD-LWT, the one person in the year who was arguably more ascetically religious than he was.

In third year, Brendan had complained to the headmaster about their English teacher, Mrs Laurence, showing the class a video of Polanski's *Macbeth*, as it contained 'scenes of nakedness', or 'durty bits' as the more tarnished members of the class referred to them. Ally McQuade had questioned the reliability of Brendan's account, on the grounds that he had theatrically covered his eyes at the offending moments, to shield them from an occasion of sin. 'Either that or you were peekin' and you'll go to the bad fire.'

Unfortunately, the headmaster, Mr Flaherty, was far less critical, being the same arsehole fundamentalist who'd taken a black-marker to all the biology textbooks and obliterated any reference to contraception. Polanski was replaced by the evocatively minimalist (i.e. zero-budget) BBC version, thus denying future classes the invaluable aesthetic enlightenment that was Francesca Annis's tits. Somehow, for all her towering theatrical presence, Judi Dench's 'unsex me here' speech lacked a certain *je ne sais quoi* by comparison.

Buckin' Brendan had been morally self-righteous before

144

he could pronounce it. Matt always assumed his familially indoctrinated loathing of all things sexual would lead Brendan down the well-worn and traditional path into the priesthood, where ultimately his long-repressed and now thoroughly distorted sexuality would assert itself in the equally well-worn and traditional priesthood practice of buggering small boys. Instead he'd managed to find a lifestyle potentially even more grimly asexual than holy orders: he'd married LWT (Legs Welded Together), of whom Matt had once heard a *teacher* say 'If she sooked a lemon, the lemon would go "fffft-oooh".'

Ally mischievously tapped Brendan on the shoulder, saying, 'All right, Bren, my man? How you doin'? You remember Matt Black, here, don't you?'

Brendan's face contorted in much the same way as the aforementioned lemon. He didn't look Matt in the face, which gave away that he'd already noticed him. 'I wouldn't have the man's records in my house,' he declaimed highly. 'We've got children, you know. Come on, dear.' And away they went, a spoor of piety buffeting in their wake.

Ally smirked, then they both burst out laughing.

'Sorry, Matt, that was a bit naughty of me. I ran into Brendan in a supermarket two or three years back, must have been no' long after you'd that sitcom pilot.'

'Not impressed?'

'Fair to say, naw. But I don't imagine he'd been a big fan before that, either. He got quite het up on the subject of yourself, actually.'

'So what did he say aboot me? That I'm . . .' They started laughing before Matt could finish, both aware of what was coming. '. . . a buckin' disgrace?'

'Buckin' obscene,' Ally corrected, doubling over.

'Ach, critics. They know buck-all.'

The pilot was never likely to have been a hit in the Mooney household, Matt guessed, not that that would put them in any kind of minority. The ill-starred *Harmony Row* was about two abominably bigoted families from either side of the Lanarkshire sectarian divide – the O'Learys from Coatbridge and the McWilliams from Larkhall – who by bureaucratic error were rehoused in either half of a semi-detached. One Scottish critic called it 'the most hate-filled thirty minutes of television I have ever had the misfortune to watch'. Another, of course, simply shat in Matt's luggage.

He'd admit his characterisation was both stereotyped and sadistically cruel, but would assert in his defence that such sadism was only possible because the truth hurts.

He depicted the devoutly Catholic O'Learys (Catholics are, exclusively, 'devout', Protestants exclusively 'staunch'; lexicography has yet to explain it) as the most joyless family on the face of the planet. They were all anaemically pale, thin and hollow-faced, wearing a uniform expression of resigned suffering, with the exception of their teenage daughter, who simply looked suicidally depressed. The interior of their house was desolately sparse, with the only items of ornamentation on display a series of grue-somely graphic crucifixes. The drab white walls were bare apart from three pictures. One was a painting of 'The Sacred Heart', a standard image showing Jesus with his face turned upwards, his hands holding open his robe to reveal his chest, on which was visible a heart surrounded (and punctured in places) by thorns. Any time Matt saw one he always wanted to caption it: 'Check this for a tattoo, big man.' The second picture was of the Pope, and the third was of Tommy Burns.

They went to mass as a family group twice a day, spent

146

all their holidays at shrines in Ireland, and conducted family prayer vigils every Saturday afternoon, beseeching the Blessed Trinity and the Virgin Mary to grant Celtic a holy and deserved victory. Their only permitted pleasure was the satisfied contemplation of the reward that awaited them in Heaven, where there would be no Masonic referees because there would in fact be no Protestants, and where Celtic would win the League for all eternity.

None of them had ever been to Parkhead.

The teenage daughter *did*, in fact, commit suicide at the end of the pilot episode, after her parents finally noticed that she was a little down in the mouth and suggested cheering her up with a family day out: a visit to the shrine at Carfin grotto. It was Matt's intention to bring her back and have her top herself in oppressed despair shortly before the closing credits every week.

The McWilliams, in bludgeoningly unsubtle contrast, were a study of bloated self-indulgence inside their matching, amply filled Rangers shellsuits. They sat around watching endless Rangers games on Sky TV, drinking cans of McEwan's lager, belching uncontrollably, farting enthusiastically and every so often declaring, 'We arra peepel!', to assert the ethnic superiority of the Scottish Protestant.

The interior of their stone-clad semi was like a museum of contemporary cultural vulgarity. It was filled to bursting with the most hideous kitsch the props department had been able to lay hands on, starting with the painting of the green-faced oriental lady and working down the taste ladder from there. Pride of place, however, went to the enormous portrait of King Billy on his white charger, which took up most of one wall above the fireplace. What space wasn't thoroughly cluttered with accumulated tat accommodated official and unofficial Rangers FC merchandising,

147

the relentless purchase of which had the family mountain-ously in debt. In the pilot, the mid-season release of a third away-strip led to a crisis meeting in which it was democratically agreed that they would live on dog food for a month to pay for the new gear.

None of them had ever been to Ibrox.

The only dissenting voice was the family's teenage son, a closet homosexual with frustrated artistic aspirations, who would, to retain a sense of balance, *also* commit suicide at the end of every show.

Harmony Row didn't quite reach *Brass Eye* complaint levels, but if the number of calls to Channel 4 from Scotland had been matched across the UK, it would have probably taken footage of a necrophiliac having his way with the late Princess of Wales to beat the figure. However, it did set a new benchmark in death threats. Also, four members of the cast were assaulted in public the week after the pilot aired, apparently another broadcasting record. Unimpressed even by these televisual high-water marks, Channel 4 didn't commission a full series.

In time another nearby gathering went supernova and Ally was swallowed by the resulting black hole. He backed away with a smile and a roll of the eyes that acknowledged how this was still the whirlwind meet-and-greet stage. Matt felt happily confident that there'd be time for a bit more than that later: all night, if required.

He barely had time to raise his glass to his lips before there was a tap on his shoulder and he found himself facing Lisa McKenzie.

'So, how *you* doin', Matthew Black?' She took his arm as she spoke and led him back a step, as though there was some seclusion to be found that extra two feet nearer the wall. There was nonetheless an intimacy about the gesture, or maybe Matt merely hoped there was. They'd never been anything like familiar way back when, so Lisa was being at least a *little* forward. He looked at her face, matured into features elegantly sharper than he remembered, her eyes glinting with a conspiratorial knowingness. There was momentarily a hollow feeling in his stomach, an increase in heart rate at the pitiable but mandatory anticipation of I've-been-waiting-years-for-you scenarios.

'Oh, I'm doing . . . better than I expected at this thing, anyway,' he replied, dying to steal a glance below face-level. In his peripheral vision he could make out a blur – yellow dress, slim body – but couldn't escape her gaze long enough to bring it into heart-aching focus.

'Here on your tod?' she asked.

'Yeah.' Please say it, please say it, please say it.

'Aye, me too.'

Yyyyyyes.

She took a sip from her champagne glass and smiled. 'Yeah, afraid I didn't feel I was quite ready to parade myself and my dyke bidie-in before the sophisticates of Auchenlea society.'

Nnnnnno.

Matt, despite the wallop, knew he was being paid some kind of compliment. If he missed a beat, he made sure it didn't show. He smiled back with reciprocal conspiracy. 'So why are you coming out to me?' he asked.

'I'm out to a lot of people, but not in this company. I've seen enough of your stuff to take a flyer on you being cool about it.'

'That may be so, but I might still ask if I can watch.'

She laughed. 'Sure you might, but only in a terribly clever, post-modern, self-deprecatory kind of way.'

'Something like that, aye.'

'You surprised?'

'Disappointed, for purely selfish reasons. And please take that as a compliment.'

'No bother.'

'I must admit,' he confided, 'drivin' up here, it went through my – admittedly prurient – mind to do the arithmetic and figure out that, statistically speaking, there ought to be at least two or three of our peer-group who are in the queer-group. I was thinking more of the guys, right enough.'

'Ha!' Lisa said with a sneer. 'In a town like Auchenlea? Forget it. Not out, anyway. There'll be a few trapped-in-a-loveless-marriage tragedies, the poor wife wonderin' why he never comes near her, but I don't think there's any danger of a Pride march up Harelaw Street.'

Matt laughed. 'Good line. I'll probably steal it. So anyway, what you doin' with yourself? You went off to do law. Strathclyde, wasn't it?'

'Yeah. I'm working in Edinburgh for the PF's office now . . .'

Matt listened attentively as she chatted, ironically able to steal the occasional glimpse at that sleek, yellow-clad form now that it had been so unequivocally ruled out of bounds. Inside, he was laughing, sufficiently self-aware these days to appreciate when the joke was on him. He'd been daft enough to indulge in 'what if' retro-teen fantasies, and reality was deservedly ripping the piss out of him for it. Fate was on killer form tonight, just *banging* out the gags. Lisa turning out to be gay was a brammer of a punchline, but you had to give credit for the build-up, too: she was the third and final of his one-time crushes to be declared unattainable tonight.

Time to grow up.

He'd seen Eileen Stewart pass by on a balding hubby's arm about ten minutes before, chubbily up-the-stick and babbling vacuously about her other two spawn. The image of her outside that exam hall was erased forever then and there, though the phrase 'Simple Minds' would probably continue to chime. But fate had kicked off the routine well before that, before the party even started, in fact.

He'd been early, one of the first to arrive at the pick-up point. His plan had been to stop and hang out in Inverness for a while, then set off fairly punctually for the last leg of the drive. Unfortunately, the 'Capital of the Highlands' didn't prove sufficiently enticing to spend more than about twenty minutes in, enough for a pee and a hastily drunk cup of coffee. The place was heaving with blimp-like American tourists, en route to the Loch Ness Monster exhibition at Drumnadrochit, where they'd be ripped off for the privilege of looking at some blurred photos of ducks, old tyres and dead trees, snared by the greatest scam in the history of Scottish tourism, maybe even world tourism. Matt decided just to proceed directly to Kilwhateveritwas. Floating or not, there was still a hotel room waiting for him, an environment in which he was massively experienced at killing time.

He was flown across to the Floating Island Paradise Resort by helicopter in the company of six other early arrivals. He recognised a few of them, but there was little in the way of greeting, just a few shy smiles and hullos. Everybody was a little nervous and awkward, all correctly guessing that it would be poor etiquette to get gregarious before context sanctioned it. After they touched down they were greeted by two smiling young female staff in matching blue Delta Leisure t-shirts and beach shorts. The group was then led from the landing pad, through the Lido swimming-pool complex and up to the Laguna Hotel's lobby. Matt knew he should have been more horrified by the place. Either it was the jet lag or he'd been spending too much time in California.

He'd loitered a few yards back as the the rest of the group approached reception and were assigned rooms. A man and a woman were waiting by the desk, shaking hands, smiling and chatting with the new arrivals. He couldn't see the woman's face because the bloke was standing just in front of her. He was wearing a designer suit that looked more like it was wearing him and was thinking of trading up. That was one thing you *couldn't* get sensitised to in LA: people who thought spending a fortune on their clothes absolved them from the consideration of whether they looked any good. Matt assumed that this must be the manager of the joint, then did the equation and worked out that it was, in fact, Gavin Hutchison.

Gavin's face became increasingly familiar the longer Matt looked at it, though he couldn't remember much more about him than that. No incident or anecdote sprang to mind; Matt didn't even remember him being beaten up by Dilithium Davie. He'd obviously risen to a good bit more prominence these days, though, and it was Matt's guess that he wanted everyone to know it, too. He could make out the ungainly G-shaped face of a gold Gucci watch on Gavin's wrist, then as the man stepped back a pace, Matt noticed that it wasn't the only trapping of success he had on display: the woman with him was, unmistakably, Catherine O'Rourke.

In time they made their way along the informal queue and reached Matt. Catherine seemed pleasantly surprised to see him, but then she'd seemed pleasantly surprised to see everybody. Either she was overcome by the occasion or she worked in PR. However, if she seemed surprised,

Gavin looked astonished. He flapped a little, then recovered enough to manage a thin smile, trade some small-talk and say, unconvincingly, how glad he was that Matt had come.

'I suppose you're one guest who won't be short of a party piece,' he added with a polite laugh, which Matt translated to mean 'I think you're a smart-arse and you'll be escorted from the building if you even *attempt* to go near a microphone'. Gavin then latched on to the couple in front once again, leaving Matt facing Catherine.

'So, how long have you and Gavin been together?' he asked, surprising himself with how friendly he sounded. He felt unexpectedly anxious to please her. Partly this was because he was worried his new-found disdain for Gavin might have been as obvious as Gavin's more deep-seated antipathy towards himself; but mainly, Matt suspected, it was because he was talking to Catherine O'Rourke and the teenager he used to be was desperate for his older self to make a good impression. He'd really have to watch that, he warned himself. There was a long night ahead.

'Oh, Gavin and I aren't "together",' Catherine said, gesturing the quote marks with her fingers. 'Although we *are* friends. The company I work for are doing the resort's PR and we organised the party, so I'm here half as a guest and half on duty. But don't worry, I'm still allowed to drink!'

'So you can get *half* cut,' Matt said, wincing at the line. It was hard to be nice *and* funny. Catherine laughed anyway, but then that was her job.

'I'll tell you who Gavin *is* together with,' she said. 'Do you remember Simone? Simone Draper?'

Did he remember Simone Draper? Did Pelagia remember Captain Corelli?

'Vaguely, I think.'

'Well, Gavin and her have been married for years. They were friends since childhood. Two daughters: twins. Simone's here just now. Upstairs getting dressed for battle! So what about you? I see you haven't brought anyone along, but is there perhaps someone . . .'

Talking now to Lisa in the ballroom, somewhere beyond her left ear Matt could see Gavin doing the rounds. He'd noticed him a few times, in fact, with Catherine always at his side. Matt was starting to wonder about the 'professional capacity' aspect, particularly as he was aware of not having spotted Simone yet. Sure, there was an argument for the PR representative (even only half of one) escorting the host, but he'd have expected the host's wife to be somewhere in the immediate vicinity too. Unless, of course, she was being co-host elsewhere in the ballroom, in the company of another PR bod, but such a possibility wasn't putting the brakes on Matt's relentlessly carnal imagination. At the very least, he guessed his initial impression regarding Catherine's ornamental value – particularly in this context – had been right on the money, wife or no wife. This, of course, had consequences for how Simone must have turned out – which thought made it an unfortunate moment for Eileen Stewart to bumble back into his line of sight.

He could see Eileen notice Lisa out of the corner of her eye, and a tap on the shoulder later there was another high-voiced kiss-hello greeting. The incidence of such squeakiness was starting to grate: so many of them were acting like it was the biggest surprise in the world to run into people they used to know. Hadn't they appreciated the significance of the word 'reunion' on the invites? Lisa in retreat gave him roughly the same look Ally had, and turned away.

Matt was alone for the first time since walking in, and

only appreciated how long that had been when he finally managed a sip from his champagne and found it to be halfway flat. He was looking for a place to put it down when a hand appeared and took it from him.

'Can I relieve you of that, Mr Black?' said a female voice.

Matt looked from the hand, along the bare arm and upwards at her face, powerless to resist taking in a few microseconds of chest and neck en route. It took effort not to gape, swallow or just burst into tears. Eileen Stewart turning into Mrs Mothercare, he realised now, was a mercy; this was crushing. Jennifer Jason Leigh had grown up into Kristin Scott Thomas.

'You didn't look like you were enjoying it,' she added, handing the glass to a nearby waiter. 'The drink, I mean. As opposed to the party.' Her voice dripped a smiling scorn as she surveyed the room, looking away from him. Matt took the opportunity to study her features, a brightness about her eyes belying some of the years, but experience had etched a sly keenness too. Her face wore precisely the look of ironic detachment from proceedings that he'd vowed to keep off his own. He wanted to throw himself at her feet.

'The artist formerly known as Simone Draper,' he said, channelling his stage-act cool into hiding the nervous teen-ager from view. 'I'd say how good you look, but I think Sir Walter Scott would be struggling to do you justice tonight.'

'Must be the wonderbra,' she replied, her eyes flitting busily away from him and back again. 'It said on the packaging it would have men invoking dead poets.'

'Sorry, I'm not normally so flowery. I think it's the occasion. There's so much overwrought emotion goin' round and they're not even pissed yet. But that notwithstanding, it's great to see you.'

'To see *me*? I'm surprised you even remember me. We hardly said a word to each other in school.'

'You still made an indelible impression. Anyway, at that age it was more my style to worship from afar.'

Now she trained her gaze on him, undistracted. The aloofnes had softened, but he couldn't read her look. His slight panic at maybe having said the wrong thing wasn't conducive to his judgement.

'No point pulling the I-used-to-fancy-you-at-school line with me, Matthew. I'm a married woman, remember.' Her tone creaked with ambiguities. She sounded far from flirty, but even further from sincere.

'I know,' he assured her. 'I wouldn't have said anything otherwise. But I'm not making it up; I'm surprised you don't have burn marks on your left cheek from me starin' at you in Chemistry. You're probably the reason I failed the Higher.'

She laughed. Relief swept through him, greater than had his audience been in the thousands.

'Aye, that'll be the reason,' she said. 'Nothing to do with that answer you wrote about . . . what was it? Name three properties compound A and compound B have in common? Neither of them can drive a tractor, neither of them shot JFK, and neither ever turned out for Accrington Stanley.'

Matt had harboured no hopes of Simone telling him 'I used to fancy you too' (well, maybe a very small one), but this was worth much more.

'I still think that was a grave injustice,' he said, returning her smile. 'I'll admit it wasn't the three properties they were looking for, but my answer *was* factually correct. I'm very impressed at you remembering.'

'Well, it stood out. There weren't many laughs to be had in Mrs Deacon's class.'

'God, Mrs Deacon. That was her name. I can picture her now that you've mentioned that. You know, I took a walk round the old school this morning; I know, what the fuck was I doing, you're thinking. Some kind of preparatory exercise for this, I don't know. It brought so much back, though. You don't realise how near the surface the memories are until you actually have a wee delve.' Matt realised he was rambling. Simone still looked attentive, however, and it sent a wave rippling through him every time he looked in her eyes and found them sparkling back. He couldn't credit how good it was making him feel to be standing there talking to her, making her smile, making her laugh. If it was down to emotional immaturity, then emotional immaturity had received a bad press.

'I thought about what we were all like back then,' he told her. 'I thought about the fact that, as you said, we didn't really talk to each other, boys to girls – all wee shy Catholics – and I thought that was a shame. When I said it was great to see you, I meant . . . I was hoping you'd be here tonight, you know, now that we're grown up enough to actually have an intelligent conversation. That make any sense?'

'Yes. Although if we have an intelligent conversation, we'll be the first tonight.' The mocking look returned to Simone's face, a malevolent smile creeping across her mouth. 'No one else seems to have got past how amazed they are to see each other after all these years.'

'Well, I suppose nobody knew for sure who'd turn up tonight,' Matt mitigated, wondering at the same time where he'd mislaid his misanthropy. 'Things'll settle down once everyone's over the element of surprise. Then they'll remember they didnae actually like each other and we can all go home.'

157

Simone laughed.

'So, did you meet Gavin?' she asked. Matt couldn't help but analyse the association. He noticed her eyes flitting away again towards the throng. He couldn't see Gavin himself, but Simone had a wider view of the room.

'Aye, he was welcoming us all aboard when we arrived.' Matt was conscious of specifically not mentioning Catherine.

'He and Catherine O'Rourke,' Simone stated, not quite neutrally.

'Yeah, she's the PR person,' Matt added, trying to neutralise for her.

'Gavin surprised you made it?'

'Eh, yeah. He seemed pretty taken aback. I suppose he thought if I was in America, it was a long way to come for one party.' Matt was impressed with his own diplomacy.

'No, I think it was probably more to do with the fact that he didn't invite you.'

'What?'

'I'm serious. He didn't invite you.'

His feelings of confusion and disorientation were tempered to the point of irrelevance by the look of delicious disdain in Simone's eyes.

'This isn't a party,' she said, the twinkling scorn remaining, though her eyes were now trained somewhere in the crowd. 'This is a contest. This is the night we count up the scores and see who did best in the game of life.'

He understood. He said nothing, but Simone looked at him again and it was obvious she knew that. They both laughed.

There was a squeal of feedback and a bassy clatter through the PA system. Every head turned to see the head waiter adjusting a mike stand at the far end of the ballroom, in front of where the as-yet-untouched buffet was impressively laid out. The head waiter asked for the room's attention and began introducing their host, who stood a few feet away, looking extraordinarily pleased with himself.

'And now's the part when Gavin crowns himself champion,' Simone concluded. The applause rang around their ears as Gavin took hold of the mike. In Simone's eyes Matt could see the vivacious scorn fading, replaced by a weariness, a sadness and not a little hatred. He watched her take a determined step forward, as though she was about to march away from him, then she stopped and sighed. She turned to face Matt, everyone else staring towards the front.

'I don't think I want to witness this,' she said. 'I'm going outside for a walk. Care to join me?'

Matt nodded, struggling to restrain the size of his grin.

A walk. On a summer's night. With Simone Draper. It might be fifteen years late, but what the hell, it was here now.

■ 19:51 ■ beneath fipr ■ column 4.9 and turning ■

Jackson cut off the outboard and they coasted in silently over the last thirty or forty yards. It still wasn't quite as dark as he'd have liked. None of them had ever operated this far north before, and the problem wasn't just how late it got dark but how long it took for the night to descend. Down near the equator it was like 'lights out, ten seconds' – zap. Here, the twilight seemed to hang around to the point of loitering. Still, nobody up top would be watching the water, and even if they were, what were they going to

159

see? Three guys in a dinghy – so what. Connor was right about that much. This would be the least-defended place they'd ever gone into. Way out here, the revellers wouldn't even be worried about gatecrashers.

The dinghy ran out of puff as it drifted beneath the titanic structure. The legs of the installation were like medieval towers, austere and formidable keeps, at each base a sub-aquatic oubliette. Jackson lifted the paddle from the fibreglass floor and with a few firm strokes, eased them towards the jetty at the centre. The scale of the thing was unsettling, making him feel like a gnat preparing to attack an elephant, but he had to stop thinking in military terms. It wasn't a fortress, it was a holiday resort, and he wasn't attacking the elephant, he was attacking other gnats who happened to be on its back. Unarmed and unsuspecting gnats, he didn't have to remind himself, the thought spinning, spinning, spinning, ceaseless like the ringing in his ear.

The dinghy bumped against the buffered jetty. Gaghen clambered out first, crouching down and doing a quick 360, scanning the spider deck above before he tied the boat to an aluminium mooring. The landing platform ran in a wide square around the central of the installation's five giant legs. The jetty was made up of five wooden sections per side, each linked to a coupling system that allowed it to move with the waves independently of its neighbour. A flexible mesh surrounded these sutures to prevent careless feet slipping through the gaps, where they might be ground between the segments. On two sides, further floor sections led right up to the central leg, cushioned by rolling buffers where they met bare wall. Ten or twelve feet above these buffers were two large rectangular panels: entrances to the elevators, but currently inoperable because the water was

160

correspondingly deeper at the resort's intended destination. The entire floating square was secured to the platform's central leg by a hydraulic suspension system, steel arms absorbing all movement up or down. According to Connor, the hydraulics could also lift the thing right out of the drink as a precaution against storms, and for the purposes of moving the rig. It wouldn't be going anywhere tonight, but there was definitely a storm on the way.

Connor pulled on his ski-mask and gestured them to follow suit. There would be cameras all over this place, and although they'd be removing the tapes, you might never be sure you'd got them all. One stray and you'd be banished to non-extraditionland for the rest of your naturals.

'Safety all automatics,' Connor said. 'If we encounter any resistance at this stage, neutralisation must be clean and quiet. Pistolas only, gentlemen, and I want them wearing condoms. Do it now.'

Jackson slung the Ingram's around his back, tightening the strap so that it was snug to his body. He unholstered his Nagan and screwed on the suppressor. They called them condoms because they were a pain in the arse to put on and it felt more natural without one, but sometimes it was better to be safe than sorry. With its short hand-stock, the Nag looked all the more disproportionate encumbered by the extra length of pipe. It reminded him of a plastic ray-gun he'd had as a kid, which in turn, depressingly, reminded him of a recurring dream. He was in a close-quarters firefight, stuck on his own, two marks bearing down on him, both changing clips and getting ready to finish him off. In his hand he had the plastic ray-gun. It was black, sleek, heavy, an evil-looking weapon. He pointed it at the marks and pulled the trigger furiously, but all it did was go click, click, click, click, click.

'Right, let's make ourselves useful,' Connor said quietly, leading them off.

There were two steep temporary stairways leading from the jetty to the spider deck, where the elevators were accessible. The lifts ran all the way up the central leg, but since they emerged at the general resort reception area, Alpha Team wouldn't be using them. The spider deck was a network of narrow gantries about forty feet up from the water, encircling and interconnecting all five giant legs. In common with everything else to do with this monstrosity, it was a sight more elaborate than on smaller rigs, where the spider level might consist more simply of four walkways forming a square.

They ran up the stairs, the metal underfoot ringing dully against the insulated contact of heavy soles. Having reached the spider deck, Connor nodded them in the direction of the north-western leg, above which they could access their point of entry: Hotel B, unfinished, unmanned and out of bounds for the evening's guests. Gaghen put a hand on Connor's shoulder, restraining him from proceeding.

'Closed circuit,' he said, pointing upwards. Neat, grey cameras were attached higher up the legs, trained directly on the spider deck. 'Probably to make sure none of the punters jumps off rather than completes their sentence. Might not be turned on yet, but—'

'No, you're right,' Connor ruled. 'Acks, if you wouldn't mind?'

'Pleasure,' Jackson replied curtly. Connor, no doubt still rattled by his and Gaghen's abortive abort, was heaping on the camaraderie. He'd called him 'Acks', short for 'Action', a barrack-room nickname of old. Jackson couldn't decide if it sounded cloying or just desperate. His real mates knew him as Smogmonster, after his Middlesbrough roots.

He took aim with the silenced Nag and shot out the nearest camera, then circled the gantry around the central leg, repeating the drill on all potentially prying eyes. In each case the only sound was the breaking glass of the camera lens, preceded by the smothered report of his handgun. The trigger, irritatingly, just went click, click, click.

Jackson's withering sense of scale was not dissipated by the jog to the north-western leg. The gangway felt like it was extending the further down it he went, reminiscent of another, less frequent but nonetheless dick-shrivelling dream. The three of them were like fairground ducks running along there in a line, isolated and exposed. If this place had been militarised he'd have been shitting himself with every step.

They made it to the north-western leg, where they found the door to its interior stairway locked. Connor stepped aside wordlessly as Gaghen moved in, removing a compact power-drill from his pack and applying it to the lock. Jackson imagined the squealing and reverberation being carried all around the structure, but looking back across the spider deck, he estimated that you wouldn't even hear it at the next leg along, never mind up-top. He studied the underside of the platform, its look of grim, ugly industrial functionality making him almost sceptical that the resort complex Connor described would turn out to be up there.

He felt a thump and looked down to see that Gaghen had removed the lock and dropped it deliberately on to his foot.

'Wakey-wakey, Acks,' he said, pulling open the door.

They followed Connor inside. The man was definitely

in a take-charge kind of mood, but then he was the one with the most riding on this. They emerged into blackness, Gaghen reaching for a torch before Connor located a switch for the lights just inside the door.

The leg's interior added to Jackson's incredulity about what awaited at the top. The refurbishment programme either hadn't reached this place yet or it simply wasn't on the list because they weren't expecting the paying customers to have cause to check it out. A metal staircase spiralled up the circular wall, straightening out into a landing every time it came back around in line with the door. One storey below them, the wall jutted inwards like a ring, four feet wide and two deep, with a circular steel surface spanning the centre. Jackson wasn't sure whether its purpose was as a floor or a lid. The stairs continued below spider-deck level, disappearing through an access gap in the ring. There was a chemical smell permeating the place, strong enough to catch the back of the throat.

'The oil guys use these legs for storage,' Connor said, indicating the ring and the floor/lid below. 'They pump all sorts of crap into them. The tanks go right down below sea-level. Delta have cleaned out the south-western leg for storing the resort's fresh-water supply. I don't know what they keep in this one, but I'm not planning to light up, I'll tell you that.'

They followed the spiral around; the first landing skirted blank wall, but the second featured a door, beside which the words 'Hotel B sub-level 4' were handwritten in yellow paint. Beneath them a faded and rusty signplate alluded to the place's history with the words 'Cellar Deck'. Connor led them past the doorway and continued climbing until they reached Hotel B sub-level 1.

While not quite emulating the iceberg principle, the resort

had utilised a great deal of space below the platform's topside surface. According to the plans, there were three floors of accommodation below deck, in rooms abutting the outside walls, so that all of them boasted a sea view. The remaining floorspace of those three sub-levels housed leisure facilities not reliant on natural light, such as cinemas, night clubs, bars, shops and restaurants. It was like one of those hotels that has a swimming pool and gardens on the roof, except that on the roof of this place, as well as pools and gardens, there were actually more hotels, going up six or seven storeys, with balconies on the rooms facing the Lido. Officially, the sub-level rooms belonged to whichever hotel sat atop them. This, Jackson presumed, was so that the brochure could show you a picture of the sun-kissed and pool-fringed joint upstairs, but when you arrived, unless you were paying top whack, you'd end up in the dungeon.

He'd seen an item about the resort on TV, though he couldn't remember whether it had been *Tomorrow's World*, *Holiday* or *Eurotrash*. What he *could* remember was swearing he wouldn't be seen dead in the place. With that cautionary thought, he slapped a new clip into his pistol.

Gaghen drilled the door and they slipped through, finding themselves in the darkness of a service corridor. Flicking on his torch and taking the lead, Gaghen scanned the walls for a light switch, but instead found another door. They emerged into a bright and freshly painted hallway.

'Lights are on,' Gaghen observed pointedly, probing Connor as to whether this was expected.

"Sokay, it doesn't mean anyone's around. The sub-level lights are always supposed to be on. Even if the main power goes down, there's a temporary back-up supply.'

Connor got out one of his maps, unfolding it a couple of panels wide and placing it against the wall. He traced a finger along it and rotated it back and forth through ninety degrees until he had satisfactorily oriented himself.

'Right. There's a stairway ringing Hotel B's two elevator shafts, but it goes up through the lobby on the ground floor and the lifts run directly behind the reception desks. You have to pass right in front of the desks to get from one flight to the next. We'll be emerging into plain sight for approximately eight yards – that's if anyone happens to be looking into Hotel B from the Lido area, which is open to the guests tonight.'

'What about the emergency stairways?' Jackson asked.

'Alarmed. All of them. Officially for fire notification, but mainly to prevent pissed punters taking a short-cut down an exterior staircase and falling right off the fucking rig. We'll cut all the alarms later when we take Hotel A – that's where the controls are. Come on. Left at the end here, then the main stairwell should be directly ahead. Halt one flight before the ground floor.'

Connor led off again, Gaghen behind, Jackson at the rear. They took the left Connor had directed and found themselves in another telescopic hallway, this time flanked by card-operated doors on one side. Running along the wall opposite was a prefabricated tiled mural, depicting bronzed holidaymakers splashing in the sea; a curious choice given that the resort's punters weren't going to be getting anywhere near a beach themselves.

Connor had reached the lifts when Jackson heard a door open and close behind him. He turned around and saw a kid of about nineteen standing six yards back along the corridor, dressed in waiter's garb apart from the walkman clipped to his belt and the in-ear headphones that had prevented him hearing three heavily armed soldiers stomping past his room.

The kid looked up and saw Jackson ahead of him, fatigues, boots, ski-mask, bandolier and, most entrancingly, silenced semi-auto pointed at his head. The orders had been clear. It was imperative that they remain undetected at this stage: stay out of sight, and if you *are* spotted, the witness must be neutralised, eliminated, or – if all that Orwellian stuff wasn't your thing – shot dead in cold blood. Jackson looked at the kid's face. He saw surprise, fear and confusion. He saw also that the kid was frozen to the spot. The moment stretched on and on, not elasticated by emotion but because time was actually passing and Jackson hadn't acted.

'Jesus, Acks,' came a voice from behind. The kid sprang from his paralysis as Connor moved into his field of vision, breaking the spell. The poor bastard had barely turned on his heel when four bullets ripped into his back and dropped him to the carpet.

Jackson still hadn't moved.

'Come on, let's get him out of sight,' Connor said, crouching down beside the body and lifting the plastic keycard from the kid's still-twitching hand. 'The fuck happened to you?' he demanded, swiping the card through its slot and reopening the door the kid had appeared from.

Jackson breathed in and out, buying a second's pause he wasn't sure he could afford.

'Gun jammed,' he said. 'Sorry.'

He couldn't see Connor's eyes as they carried the body into the bedroom, couldn't see whether he was believed. Jackson's mind rewound to the north-western leg, outside the door to that service corridor. Had they seen him change clip? If they had, they'd know he was lying. Who ever heard of a gun jamming when there'd been nothing in the chamber ahead of the first new round?

There were crumpled clothes discarded carelessly about

the floor; ghetto-blaster on one bedside table, an ashtray straddling two piles of cassettes; Glasgow Rangers team posters Blu-tacked to one wall; framed photo of a smiling girl on the dresser. On top of the duvet there was a *Viz* annual strewn with tobacco strands and the debris of a ripped-up fag packet.

'Resident staff must have been given rooms down here,' Connor muttered. 'We weren't to know. Gaghen, you'd better knock a few doors, see if there's anyone else, and if so, deal. All right?'

'Gotcha.'

'Should have been upstairs in A with the rest, son,' Connor said under his breath, closing the kid's eyes and walking out.

Should have, yeah, Jackson thought. Poor sod had just nipped down on his break for an illicit spliff. Now here he was, dead on the floor, shot in the back.

He watched Connor outside in the hallway, stooping down to pocket the spent shells, like a fucking hit-man. An unaccustomed disgust flooded through Jackson. The kid's eyes stared back every time he closed his own, but it wasn't the look in them that was doing it. He'd seen that look before, dozens of times – the terror, the helplessness, the paralysis – and it had never stayed his hand. He'd shot people in the back himself, as well as in the face, chest, limbs and every other part of the anatomy. He'd thrown grenades through windows into huts where he'd already blocked the only door. He'd cut the throats of sleeping men and held a silencing hand over their mouths as they died. And he could do any of it again, he knew, without feeling what he was feeling now. The difference lay in one small word.

War.

He'd killed men of just about every colour, ideology,

religion, loyalty, height, weight, shoe size or whatever else might distinguish them as individuals. But the one thing every last one of them had in common was that they were all soldiers. Rebels, guerillas, professionals, mercenaries, even conscripts: like it or not, they were all in the game, and they all knew that, too. It wasn't an issue of whether you bore weapons, either; Jackson had killed plenty of empty-handed men. Once you were in the game, being armed was your look-out, at all times. You couldn't ask for quarter just because you'd left your gun in your other jacket.

But the kid wasn't armed, he wasn't in the game, and this certainly wasn't a fucking war.

Connor *had* told him up-front that the op was going to be on British soil and illegal. Leaving aside pedantic quibbles about the soil part, he couldn't complain he'd been misled. He'd chosen to take part of his own volition, tempted by the money, pure and simple. It was a handsome purse that Connor had dangled in front of him, a shitload more than the adventurer clowns would be getting, and doubtless more than Connor would be offering in future. The man needed his outfit's first op to be a success, and therefore needed to secure a few first-rate personnel in a hurry, so the money was kind of a golden hello. It was intended also to soothe those niggles about making the transition from mercenary to criminal. He would have said 'temporary transition', but he was philosophical enough to understand that whatever your future intentions, you can't temporarily lose your virginity.

Connor, in Jackson's experience, was a solid enough man, someone whose judgment he generally trusted. He hadn't suspected Connor was holding back any details about the job when he made the offer; even now he remained pretty sure of that. It was he who'd been naïve, who hadn't fully thought it through. The way the plan had sounded, yes, sure, it was criminal, but he'd reckoned they could pull it off with an acceptable minimum of fatalities.

But when he saw the assembly at the farm, he instantly began to re-evaluate his projected casualty figure. Apart from this raggle-taggle band of amateurs being so impatient to get killing that they had started on *each other*, the fact that Finlay Dawson was ultimately in charge had unnerved Jackson even more. Not only had he always considered Dawson a thoroughly nasty piece of work, but he tended to have the destabilising effect upon Connor of turning him into a junior sibling who was always trying too hard to impress his bigger brother. That was when Jackson first started thinking about bailing out, finding an ally in Gaghen, who had a reliably sharp eye for the logistics of these things, and who had been privately vocal to Jackson about his misgivings.

When they confronted Connor in the dinghy, the boss had sounded reasonable enough, and made sufficient sense for Jackson to start revising the casualty projection back down. But it was only in that corridor, looking into that kid's eyes, that he understood precisely what figure constituted an 'acceptable minimum', and two seconds later Connor had exceeded it.

Connor snapped the plastic keycard and dropped it on the floor, then closed the door on the shameful little scene. Gaghen reported back that there was no further sign of life in the surrounding rooms. On they went.

They made it to the stairs and climbed to just below where the steps reached the lobby's carpeted floor. Slowly, Gaghen crawled upwards and stuck his head above ground-level. He reported that the lights were on but there was no sign of any movement outside. Connor signalled to Jackson and he scuttled low across the front of the reception desks, eyes always on the glass doors. Jackson took up a crouching position close to the foot of the next flight, and looked up the staircase. There was no-one there, not that he had decided what he would do if there was. He felt like he was on autopilot, detached from his actions but doing them because so far he hadn't sussed out any viable alternatives. He gave the all-clear. Connor crossed the floor then headed quickly up the flight and out of view. Gaghen followed upon a further signal and then Jackson was the rearguard once more.

There were lights on in the first-floor corridors, but it was dark from the second upwards, so they were able to concentrate on haste rather than caution as they made for the top. The main stairs stopped at the fifth floor, where Connor consulted his plans once again and directed them to the end of another corridor, where a door marked DAN-GER – AUTHORISED PERSONNEL ONLY succumbed to Gaghen's drill. Beyond it was one last flight of stairs and, at the top, one more door. They climbed to the summit and violated another lock before emerging finally on to the roof.

Their goal was right before them, fenced off in a pen that also encircled the door they'd just come through. Beyond that, there was only common sense to keep you back from the edges and the drop, which on the north side went all the way to the water. The pen accommodated two huge satellite dishes, but it was the hardware for sending signals *out* that they were interested in. A towering radio aerial reached highest, tapering from a base resembling a miniature pylon into a gently swaying single steel shaft. However, in this day and age an equal priority went to its shorter neighbour, a two-way transponder for amplifying and relaying mobile phone service signals.

On Connor's order, Jackson and Gaghen exposed and disconnected the power supplies to both; also, in the case of the radio aerial, ripping out all feedlines from the base. Connor, meanwhile, delicately connected the severed ends of the transponder's power cable to a remote-controllable circuit-breaker, allowing him to switch it back on later, when required. Still squatting next to his handiwork, Connor pulled a mobile from his belt and tested for a signal, then clipped the phone back in place and stood up.

'Thank you, gentlemen. Stage one is complete. You can now run back down the stairs naked and singing if you feel like it. Nobody on this rig can tell anyone who's further than earshot. Except, of course,' he added, reaching for his radio, 'ourselves.'

Then he said the words Jackson had been dreading since that sub-level corridor.

'Beta Leader, this is Alpha One. Alpha team has achieved primary objective. Commence incursion.'

■ still sort of meanwhile ■ fipr ■ if onlys ■

'You're a brazen, bold, bad article.'

That was what Simone's mum always said when she'd done something naughty, usually accompanied by the time-honoured ritual of the circular spanking (mother takes child's wrist in left hand, aims swipe at bottom with right, child evades in an anti-clockwise motion, mother pirouettes on left heel; repeat until dizzy).

Bad she'd always understood. Little scope for moral relativism in the era of the pushchair. Bold she wrongly assumed to be a tautology, until she learned the distinction between doing something wrong and knowingly doing something wrong. Brazen she didn't really get. It just became part of the phrase, brazenboldbadarticle. Similarly her father used to jokingly call her wee brother 'Rank Bajin', after a Glaswegian cartoon villain. She grasped the 'bad yin' part, but 'rank' in its adjective form had fallen from common usage at the time, so it became a meaningless prefix: all bad yins were rankbajins.

Tonight, however, she knew *exactly* what brazen meant. And Jesus Christ, did it feel good. Not that she was exactly into scarlet-woman territory here; she was just ignoring her husband's big moment to take the air with another man, who was, well, obviously, not her husband. But there was an enervating sense of liberation about it, a delicious taste of a better life she was ready now to live.

She put her right arm through Matthew's left as they exited the function suite, relishing the inquisitive look on the face of Jamie, the already discomfited receptionist. If being bold was knowingly doing something naughty, then being brazen was enjoying it.

Simone had never felt quite so confident as when she walked into that party, alone, Gavin having *had* to be down there earlier, darling. It wasn't just about how she looked (although she did not feel inclined to be modest about that tonight), but who she *was* and what she intended to do. She quickly spotted Gavin in his constant gravitational orbit around Catherine, working the floor as the guests circulated. Once, she feared, she might have cut the pathetic figure of the mousy missus, cowering in a corner, ignored, people politely pretending not to notice her to spare all parties the embarrassment of acknowledging what was so obviously going on. Not tonight. Simone worked the floor herself, appropriating co-host status and earning several satisfying glares of bemused exasperation from her husband.

Despite the emotional eruptions taking place all around her, she felt largely detached from the occasion, immune from the nostalgia that seemed to be engulfing everyone else. She suspected this was because, to an extent, she was acting a part. Nonetheless, she was enjoying giving the performance, and contrary to what Gavin might assume, she was playing solely to herself. The others were not the audience: they were the extras. However, she decided to promote one of them to a cameo when she happened upon Matthew Black standing on his own.

She'd admit to pleasant surprise that he'd turned up, but back when she added his name to the invitation list, she hadn't done so in the hope of actually speaking to him, as she thought he'd probably have no recollection of her. She just thought it would piss Gavin off to see him there, inevitably the centre of far more attention than himself.

Simone had noticed Matthew arrive, edging almost reluctantly into the room with an unexpected air of sheepishness that bordered upon the apologetic. However, her frequent glances in his direction confirmed that there was indeed a steady stream of guests approaching him in turn; but far from holding court, his manner appeared to be deferential.

When her own circulations eventually took her close by, fortuitously he had just been robbed of his previous companion. It was a night when anyone was allowed to go up and talk to anyone else, pretext not required, but she still felt rather nervous about approaching him. That whole 'ken't his faither' thing, the traditional Scottish dismissal of the local boy made good, wasn't working for her. Matthew

Black might once have been in her class at school, but he'd also once had an affair with Juliette Armstrong. Phrases like 'best actress nominee' and 'seven million dollars per picture' flitted unhelpfully into her head.

They flitted straight back out again when he demonstrated how vividly he remembered her. She put up her guard when he started the fancied-you-something-rotten patter, thinking how affable he'd already been with everyone else and suspecting he was switched to auto-charm; working on TV in LA, he'd have to be a black-belt schmoozer. But there was a perceptible nervousness about him that was miles from his practised stage persona, and that suggested a lot more genuineness than her own cool-as-ice act. Besides, she remembered vividly that fifth-year Chemistry class, saw the layout in her head, those big science-lab tables, high wooden stools instead of the usual plastic bucket-seats, gas taps punctuating the worktops on three sides. She sat nearest the aisle on the front right-hand table, Annette Strachan on her right, Lisa McKenzie next to Annette. Matthew Black and two other boys sat at the front-left table, staggered a couple of feet back. Her left cheek would indeed have been in burning range. This might only have been because it was in the way of Annette's, but either way, he'd noticed her enough to remember.

Also confirming she had his full attention was the fact that she'd twice noticed him trying to see down her dress. She didn't let on; truth was, sexual-political implications aside, she felt flattered. Some might say it was letting down the sisterhood, but having so long been neutered by Gavin's inattentions, it was reassuring to know someone still considered her dress worth looking down in the first place.

Despite her affected aloofness, she knew exactly what Matthew meant about being able to talk to one another

175

now, unfettered by the teen-years self-consciousness that jammed all transmissions to the opposite sex. As soon as he said it, she felt that if they talked all night, it still wouldn't be long enough. Then a reality check intervened, enquiring what she thought her contribution to this momentous meeting of the minds might amount to: Hi, I'm a housewife with two kids and a sham of a marriage. That's my life up until now.

But no, she decided, watching Gavin prepare to take centre-stage. That was her life up until yesterday. From today onwards it was going to be different.

'Before you all trample me in your understandable desperation to get to this *splendid* buffet, laid on by our *wonderful* chef, I'd just like to say a few words . . .'

This was it, she'd thought, a knot forming in her stomach as she did so: Gavin's big moment, her revenge, her new beginning. This was it.

She took a determined step forward, then stopped in her tracks.

Did she freeze? Did she bottle it? She didn't think so. So many things were going through her head in that moment, it would have been impossible to pin it all on stage-fright. All around her, everyone seemed so happy to be there, happy to see each other. People who'd barely got along fifteen years ago were blethering away like the closest friends. Maybe it was that they'd gone through that whole rites-of-passage thing together, some kind of war-vet bond of having come through the same ordeal (which secondary school undoubtedly was). Maybe, like she and Matthew, they felt they had a lot to say to each other, backed up from a time when they found it a great deal harder to communicate. Maybe they were just wellied. Whatever, when it came to the moment, she didn't feel right about

176

souring the whole affair just to put Gavin's nose out of joint. There'd be plenty of time to do that. And besides, this wasn't about him, it was about her.

They strolled slowly around the Lido under the darkening sky, the warmth of late summer and the music from inside the Laguna making it possible to believe they were in some far-off destination, if admittedly an extremely tacky one. Simone had lifted a chilled bottle of champagne from the table by the door as they left. She gripped it by the neck, swinging it gently as she walked, but so far there'd been too much talk for either of them to have a swig from it.

'I know everyone's probably saying this, but I'm really surprised that you're here. I know I was the one who invited you, but I wasn't exactly optimistic about you actually turning up.'

Matthew laughed, she wasn't sure at what. Maybe that everyone else *had* said the same thing, maybe at something else, something personal.

'I'd have to admit I'm surprised myself,' he said. 'When the invite arrived, well,' he laughed again, looking away from her, his expression difficult to read. 'I remember thinkin' I'd rather kill myself, but . . . I guess I was wrong.'

'So what made you change your mind?'

'Eh, I had a pretty weird couple of weeks, safe to say. I dunno. Bad attack of soul-searchin', somethin' like that.'

'Sounds serious. Five thousand miles is a long search. Hope you found something.'

He laughed again. 'More than I expected, tonight. And I don't mean you, before you slap me for tryin' to chat you up. I mean, meetin' everybody again – it's been easier than I was afraid of, and it's sure put a few things in perspective.'

'What, like seeing how far you've come compared to everyone else?'

Simone surprised herself with her sudden acidity. She was about to apologise but Matthew wasn't showing any signs of taking it personally. Either he was too egotistically thick-skinned or he was perceptive enough to know who she was really angry at. His conduct so far had suggested the latter.

'No, that was the part I was afraid of, in fact: people thinkin' I was turnin' up here as the famous Matt Black, celebrity and TV star. I'm not a big fan of his these days.' Matthew's smile turned bitter. 'I preferred his earlier stuff, you know?'

Simone did know. She could see a tiredness in his face that was deeper wrought than jet lag, and deduced also that anyone finding spiritual solace in an event such as tonight's had to be in a pretty bad way before they got here. That he had travelled so far in search of it was not a good sign either. Such reflections put the brakes on her intended scorn over how hard it was being famous.

'Career crisis?' she asked.

'Aye, somethin' like that. At least, I thought so, anyway. Pathetic, isn't it?' He stopped walking. They were on a wooden bridge, arcing over an illuminated blue water-channel. Matt rested his back against the handrail and faced her. 'That's what I meant about gettin' a sense of perspective tonight,' he said. 'All the stuff that had been botherin' me, all the stuff that seemed life-and-death important out in Hollywood . . . a wee blether to a few normal folk fae Auchenlea an' you realise: nobody gives a fuck!'

'I don't follow.'

'Sorry, hard to explain. But the thing about perspective is that what looks from the inside like a career crisis, looks from the outside like a guy with his head up his arse. I needed to see that. I'll put it in a nutshell: I hate

178

what I'm doin'. I want to go back to bein' a comedian again.'

'So what's the crisis? Afraid you'll miss the money? Have they got you on a long-term contract?'

Matthew shook his head, seeming to mock himself. 'No, I'm just scared,' he said. 'Worried nobody's gaunny take me seriously now that I've been Mad fuckin' Matty for two years.'

'I didn't think comedians were supposed to be taken seriously,' Simone offered, unable to resist.

Matthew bowed. 'Thank you,' he said theatrically. 'That's exactly what I mean about perspective. I've been beatin' myself up about what the critics will say, what the media reaction will be if I get back behind the mike. "Can Matt Black go back from being an anodyne sitcom star to a hard-hitting stand-up?" Then I come here tonight and folk are sayin' to me: "Heh, Matt, that American show you're on is fuckin' awful, nae offence. By the way, when you goin' back on tour?"'

'So are you resolved to do it?'

'Not quite, no. There's still that theory-and-practice leap of faith in front of me, you know? It's one thing shootin' the shit with Ally McQuade, but standin' up in front of a crowd's a different story. And, of course, the perspective thing swings both ways. Talkin' to people who actually fuckin' work for a living, I started thinkin' I should thank my lucky stars, stick with the sitcom and count the money. But I know that's just a cop-out. I can't go on with the sitcom, I'll end up . . .' He sighed. 'It's not an option. I need to get back onstage, but the truth is I *am* scared.

'Anyway, listen to me, Mr Self-Absorption. I'm out here under the stars with you and a bottle of champagne and

179

all I can talk about is me. Egotistical wanker. I'm bored of me. Can we talk about you?'

Simone would have been happier sticking to the previous subject. Here was Matthew apologising for laying his problems on her, but from where she was standing, this was a half-decent conversation. Gavin would never open up to her like that, because what could *she* possibly know, what could she possibly say that would make any difference? The closest she got was being the audience as Gavin soliloquised. Maybe Matthew was right, though: maybe he *was* an egotistical wanker, and would lay all this stuff on anybody because he believed everybody must be interested. However, in her experience of egotistical wankers (or, to be accurate, her vast experience of one egotistical wanker), they *never* got bored of 'me'. Nonetheless, it was worth putting it to the test.

'What do *I* think of you, d'you mean?' she asked, straight faced.

'Boom boom. Walked into that one.'

That scored a pass, for now. He stood away from the railing and they commenced walking again.

'Nah, come on, fifteen years,' he said. 'Anybody who reads the papers knows mine – what's the story of *your* life?'

Simone shrugged. 'Not my favourite subject, right now.'

'No, sorry, I'm not thinkin',' Matthew said. 'I guess the garden cannae be rosy, otherwise you wouldnae be out here doggin' it from your husband's big self-vindication fest.'

'You got that right.'

'He's screwin' Catherine O'Rourke, isn't he? Or at least he wants everyone to think he is. Oh Christ, I'm sorry. I can't believe I just came out with that.'

Simone brushed off his apologies with a shake of her

head, trying to act like it meant nothing, but she could feel herself welling up. This, she realised, was the first time Gavin's infidelity had been acknowledged out in the open, and in that moment it went from a private hurt to a public humiliation.

She stopped and took a drink from the bottle, buying herself a moment, hoping her eyes weren't reddening.

'I am sorry,' he reiterated.

She nodded. 'Yeah, so am I,' she said. 'He is screwing her. I was over the betrayal, but I'm just hitting the embarrassment phase now, you know? Mind you, look who I'm talking to. I can't begin to compare notes on embarrassment and humiliation with a man who appears on *There Goes the Neighborhood* every week.'

Matthew laughed quietly. 'That was low,' he said, offering a smile.

Simone sniffed and wiped a tear from her right eye. 'Well, I'm wounded and cornered. Self-defence. Don't mess with me when I'm hurting.'

'I won't.'

He reached into his pocket and offered her a handful of tissues. She refused, for some reason grudging him the gentleman role.

'Come on, you're gaunny snotter all over the champers,' he added.

Simone giggled, which did indeed provoke further nasal precipitation. She accepted the tissues and blew her nose.

'You want these back?' she joked.

'Christ, don't. Fifteen years ago, I'd have fuckin' framed them.'

'Eeeewww. Gross.'

'You started it.'

'Yeah, fair enough. But look, it's all right, you can knock

off the teenage-crush motif now. We're outside the reunion. You're officially out of context.'

Matthew looked genuinely bashful. 'Sorry. It's just that I'm still gettin' this weird buzz out of bein' here now, talkin' to you.' He put up his hands. 'I'm *not* tryin' to chat you up, honest. Just . . . please allow for the fact that I'm suddenly dealin' with a bit of an emotional backlog here.'

'Oh, come on. Am I not supposed to be the one who's freaked out about being in *your* company? Mr Superstar?'

'No,' he said, grinning. "Cause you know I'm just another Auchenlea scrote. It's nothin' to do with who I am or who you are. It's who we used to be. They're like gatecrashers tonight, disruptin' the party. See, the guy I used to be fancied the girl you used to be, so he's givin' me gyp. You're all right. The teenage you didnae fancy the teenage me, so she's leavin' you alone.'

'Who says she didn't?' Simone asked, a tone of indignation preventing her from sounding coy.

'Oh, don't gie's it,' he protested.

'I'm not kidding. If you'd asked me out back then, I'd have been walking on air.'

'Oh don't, don't, don't,' he said, laughing through a pained expression. 'You could crush me to death here wi' this stuff. No, please, have mercy . . .'

'I'm sorry, but it's true. It wasn't a solitary distinction, if that makes you feel any better. Andrew Reilly would have done too. I even had a wee thing for Ally McQuade. But I didn't imagine I'd a chance with any of you. Still, let's not start on "if only"s, for God's sake. I've got too much to regret in that department.'

'No, agreed, absolutely. That way madness lies. Let's look on the bright side. We're here now and it's not too late for us to be pals.'

Simone liked the sound of that. She turned to face him. 'I'll drink to that,' she said.

'Me too.'

'In fact,' she added, upon an impulse, 'let's go somewhere and share this stuff, just the two of us.'

'That would be nice. Where, though? I'd suggest my room, but, you know, wrong connotations. It wouldn't look good if we were spotted.'

'Oh, fuck how it looks,' she said, thinking of taking him up to her own accommodation. Let Gavin walk in on them, sitting on the terrace together, that would certainly rain on his parade. Then she remembered that bedside light, left on from Gavin and Catherine's last little tryst, and the idea went sour. 'No, you're right,' she decided, suddenly inspired. 'Let's not go back to the Laguna. I know. Follow me.'

Simone led him across a couple more footbridges, around the high-walled wave pool and up to the entrance of the Majestic Hotel. She had a quick look around to make sure they remained unobserved, then led him through the glass doors and into the lobby. Once inside, she handed him the bottle and ordered him to stay put as she approached the wide reception counter, flanked by staircases on either side.

'First class,' she said, pointing at the flight going upwards. 'And steerage,' she added, indicating its descendent counterpart.

Simone leaned over and unlatched the waist-high access gate, then walked behind the desks to where the reception PC sat, picking a plastic keycard from a box next to it. She toggled through some menus and selected a room on the first floor, then swiped the card through the computer's encoding device, a smile widening on her face.

They walked up the stairs to the first floor and used her now-programmed keycard to enter one of the bedrooms, three doors along from the lifts. Matthew flipped a light switch to no effect. She explained that you had to slot your keycard into the NRG-Sava device to operate the room's electricity, but opted not to do so in case any of the staff noticed the light from outside and came to investigate.

Simone went straight for the bathroom and unwrapped the Cellophane from two plastic tumblers, holding them up and clicking them together as she emerged.

'Classy stuff, eh?'

'Simply the best,' replied Matthew.

Opening the sliding glass doors to the balcony, she discovered with a mixture of disappointment and amusement that there were no chairs out there. She had a look behind her at the room's two-seater sofa. It looked just the ticket but it was going to be a job moving it.

'Floor all right?'

'Aye, grand.'

Matthew poured them a tumbler-full of champagne each and they sat down on the concrete floor, backs against the balcony, facing into the room. The submerged illuminations of the Lido caused rippling patterns of light to play on the building's walls. The effect reminded Simone of dining-hall school discos, an impression enhanced by the Culture Club music booming from across at the Laguna.

'Gavin's special reunion-party Eighties compilation,' she remarked. 'He made it himself on recordable CD. It's quite a line-up, let me tell you. Thompson Twins, Kajagoogoo, Howard Jones, Spandau Ballet, Duran Duran – all the greats.'

Matthew laughed. 'I think I experienced a different

Eighties, musically. Probably just as embarrassing, but . . . different.'

'Let's not open up that particular treasure-chest of memories, shall we? I was a pseudo-Goth. I had all the records but my hair was too fine for back-combing. Had to make do with a Sisters of Mercy t-shirt and bad eye make-up. I could pull that part off, but not necessarily by intention.'

'I've a very vivid image of you going around in a Clash t-shirt,' Matthew told her, causing a tingle down her spine. She remembered the t-shirt herself, even remembered buying it in the old Virgin in Union Street with a birthday record-token, along with the 12-inch of 'Vengeance' by New Model Army. But the fact that *he* remembered her wearing it made her feel, well, she wasn't sure. Touched, flattered, regretful all at once. If onlys.

'Oh Jesus, what's this?' he asked as another not-so-golden oldie began thumping from across the Lido. 'I don't believe it. "Break My Stride". Christ. That skinny wee guy with the bad 'tache. Matthew Wilder, that was his name. This isnae nostalgia, this is recidivism.'

He began to sing along, moving his hands to the moronic beat. Simone was doubled with laughter, trying not to choke on her champagne. Then he got to his feet and began dancing, beckoning her to join him, the pair of them useless with giggling.

'Oh, we're away noo,' he said. 'Look, mammy, I'm dancin'!'

'Oh God no, stop,' she implored, unable to continue. She squatted on the floor once more. 'It's too awful for words.'

'What? The music, or my dancin'?'

Matthew sat down again and took a sip from his drink, then looked across at her with the kind of easy smile she

185

hadn't shared with a man for years. It wasn't too late to be pals, he'd said. She and Gavin had never been that. She leaned over and kissed him. It was soft, tentative, fragile. Precious.

Oh shit.

When she opened her eyes she was relieved to see that he didn't look bewildered or appalled. Surprised, certainly. Even a little afraid.

This was the moment to put the brakes on and take stock, she knew. To say 'Oh, sorry about that', and make jokes about pretending it never happened. This was the moment you took your pleasure back to the shop and spent the refund on guilt.

A night charged with nostalgia, that least trustworthy of emotions; a marriage falling apart; the regrets and if onlys of a needlessly unrequited teenage crush; and not forgetting champagne on an empty stomach. Simone knew all the reasons kissing him was a bad idea, not least because of where it was likely to lead. But just once, couldn't she do the wrong thing now and worry about the consequences later?

'Are you sure you—' Matthew began to say, but she stopped his mouth with another kiss.

Simone got to her feet and led him back into the bedroom, closing the doors and the curtains behind them. Then she turned around and kissed him again, putting her arms around his neck, pulling her body up against his, and noticing with some satisfaction that the comedian, not having previously had a microphone in his pocket, was extremely pleased to see her.

She pushed Matthew not-so-gently back on to the bed and lay on top him, shivering at the touch of his hands on the back of her neck. Pyrotechnics, thunderbolts, shooting stars, all that carry-on. A solitary note of doubt sounded somewhere in her head, enquiring as to the difference between passion and desperation; after all, marriage to Gavin would turn Anne Widdecombe into a fuckmonster. It was quickly silenced by the feel of his hand against her breast. Passion or desperation, did it have to matter? Couldn't she just enjoy it, for once in her bloody life?

She leaned on one elbow and began unbuttoning his shirt. At that point Matthew broke away from her kiss and restrained her hand from descending any further.

'Hang on, hang on,' he said, shaking his head. 'We can't do this.'

Oh Christ, some luck, she thought. Finally unshackled from her over-developed sense of responsibility, she'd thrown herself at a known philanderer, only for the philanderer to choose that night to develop some moral responsibility of his own.

'Why not?'

'I don't have any protection.'

Simone caught the apologetic laughter in his face and joined in, mainly out of relief. They weren't beaten yet.

'All is not lost,' she whispered. 'This is a holiday resort, remember. There's machines in all the public toilets. The nearest ones to here are on the ground floor.'

She reached to the bedside table for the keycard and handed it to him with a kiss. If he was quick enough, he might get back before her conscience kicked in.

Matt quietly closed the bedroom door and stood motionless in the corridor for a few moments. He didn't know
whether to breathe a sigh of relief or punch himself hard
in the face. That morning on the Baja, when he resolved
to embark upon this turning-over-a-new-leaf caper, he'd
envisaged the morality tests starting off a wee bit easier
than the object of his teenage dreams popping up, looking twice as beautiful, and flinging herself at his dick.
That he'd probably passed didn't feel like much of a consolation.

He reached into his jacket for his wallet, removing the
three-pack of condoms he habitually kept there, 'for you
know not the day nor the hour when the master needs
to come'. He dropped them into a nearby bin. Whatever
happened later, it wouldn't be good for her to find them
on him.

So, he'd lied. What you gonna do. He needed to get out
of the room, buy some time. He needed to let her cool off.
He needed to get his fucking head examined – he'd just
walked out on *Simone Draper*.

Calm down, he told himself. This was about as spitefully
unfair as life got, one of those Russian-linesman moments.
Deal with it.

He had done the right thing, but not completely, and
that was the hardest part. He didn't say no, didn't stop
it dead; merely interrupted it in a manner that sounded
plausibly temporary. He could tell himself it was letting
her down gently, giving her time to contemplate what

188

she was getting into, but that wasn't the whole truth, was it? When he returned in five minutes, a huge part of him wanted to find her calm, collected, rational and completely unclothed. The question now was whether to fill that time by actually going downstairs to the condom machine. His options remained tantalisingly open. As John Cleese once said, it wasn't the despair. He could handle the despair. It was the hope.

It wasn't right, though, he knew that. She was vulnerable. The woman's arsehole husband was knobbing someone else, and tonight the bastard was practically advertising the fact to his assembled guests. Matt would have been happy to oblige her with a revenge fuck if he believed that was all she needed, but no matter how hard his dick got, he knew he couldn't convince himself that that was the case.

And maybe that wasn't all he was content to offer her, either.

She was vulnerable. Not long ago that wouldn't have meant a fucking thing, but it sure did tonight. And the scariest question was how much of that was down to him having changed, and how much was down to 'she' being Simone?

He began walking. He couldn't go straight back in there and lay it down, not least because another of those kisses might vaporise his resolution in one exquisitely damning moment. He couldn't give it too long, either; whatever was going through Simone's mind right now, it would be a difficult time for her to be alone. He'd head for the ground-floor gents as instructed. A splash of water about the face might help, but not as much, he suspected, as a conscience-galvanising wank.

He padded quietly back along the corridor and down

the main staircase, cushioning his footfalls. He didn't want Simone to hear him and suss that he'd been hanging around outside, procrastinating.

When he reached the halfway landing, he heard the static burst of a walkie-talkie and reflexively lifted his eyes from the carpet. Down in the lobby there was a bloke in combat fatigues and a black balaclava, standing in front of the main doors with his back to the stairs. He was holding a radio to his face with his left hand, dangling a pistol by the trigger-guard with his right. Resting at his waist, suspended from a shoulder-strap, was Israel's most successful and destructive export since Christianity: an Uzi 9mm sub-machine-gun.

'Hotel B secured at ground-floor lobby. That's a green from me,' he was saying.

Large man bearing arms in lobby. ICI down four-and-a-quarter.

Matt had freeze-framed on the landing in mid-step and mid-breath, explanations whizzing through his head like path-names on a computer search-routine. File not found, it concluded. As the man's head turned slightly, Matt could see that the balaclava was of the eye-and-mouth-holes design, as opposed to the simpler and more commonplace 'child-humiliation' model. As a fashion item, the former definitely made more of a statement. The statement was RUN LIKE FUCK.

Matt retained sufficient composure to be aware that he hadn't been noticed – yet – and a spontaneous clatter of feet would be more than adequate to revoke that fragile status. The guy hadn't heard him come down, so a similar stealth should ensure he didn't hear him creeping back up, either. The glass doors and various polished surfaces throughout the lobby threatened to relay any sudden flash of movement, so his retreat would have to be slow as well as silent. It was like being in a class full of Mary-Theresa Devlins, all just dying to grass him to the teacher.

He took one delicate step back and was about to edge sideways out of sight when his stomach, slighted by his decision to eschew the buffet in favour of more sentimental appetites, traitorously avenged itself. It sold him out with a sonorously gurgling rumble; betrayed him with borborygmi. The man turned around immediately and they stared at each other for a mutually indecisive second. Matt was seldom stuck for an opening line, but the prospect of lead-heckling instantly caused him to dry. He decided to exit stage-left as Action Man raised his pistol and pointed it up the stairs.

'Stop right there,' he shouted, sending a couple of bullets along with the words in case they proved insufficiently persuasive. Matt didn't hear any reports as he ran, just dull slaps as the slugs tore into the plaster behind where he'd been standing. He figured he could now plausibly abandon the theory that Gavin had booked a military-themed male-stripper cabaret. Ski-masks. Radios. Uzis. Silencers. Something extraordinarily bad was happening.

Matt could hear the thump of the guy's boots in pursuit, which was when that philosophical conundrum confronted him, as it inevitably did all who ran away: where was he running to? At that stage he knew only where he *couldn't* run to: the first floor, where Simone was sitting in a bedroom, oblivious to what was going on. He ran around the lifts and continued up towards the second storey, hoping to Christ that Simone didn't stick her head out the door to investigate the noise just as Action Man went past.

On the second-floor landing, as with the first, there were

corridors leading off in two directions. Locked doorways lined up grimly on either side, unable to offer any assistance. Matt kept climbing, both thighs beginning to grumble their discontent. From below he could hear the rattle of metal as the spare clips, and whatever else the man was carrying, shook on his pursuer's belt. He was talking into his radio again: 'Stray subject in Hotel B. I'm dealing.'

The grumbles of discontent had escalated to a threat of mutiny by the time Matt approached the fourth storey. His lungs remained loyal to the cause, but he knew that if he kept climbing he'd get slower with every stair. At some point he was going to have to run along one of those corridors and pray he made it around the first corner before Action Man reached the landing and lined up a clean shot. His efforts so far had bought a few further seconds on the more burdened gunman, but as he tired he'd lose them again soon enough. Now would be the best chance he'd get. It occurred to him that there might be a dead end around that vital first corner, but as there would *definitely* be a dead end when he ran out of floors, he had to go for it anyway.

Matt's thighs applauded the decision with a pumping burst of speed along the flat, making him understand why the late Jock Wallace used to run Rangers players up and down sand dunes all day. He suddenly halted two-thirds of the way along, having encountered a set of double swing-doors and noticed electric light shining upon a stairway beyond. It was a tight, zig-zagging affair with a railed banister, offering faster ascent or descent than the wide spiral encircling the lifts. This was what he'd been relying upon, having as a child spent many a wedding reception playing hotel-tig, a more strategically complex variation on the simple cat-and-mouse game, due to the randomising element of having two staircases. Where the plan fell down was that this guy's parents weren't going to show up and take him home after a while.

Matt went through the swing-doors, gripped the banister and resumed climbing. Simone had mentioned something about there still being work in progress on the upper levels, so with nothing but locked doors further down, it sounded like his only chance of somewhere to hide. He burst back through the corresponding swing-doors on the fifth floor and looked in either direction: the tiny red lights of more card-locks twinkled at him along the passageway.

He turned back and climbed the final storey, reaching the top landing as the double doors flew open two floors beneath and the gunman charged through, aiming up the stairwell with his silenced pistol. A bullet struck the banister two feet away, another embedding itself in the ceiling above. Matt jumped backwards and fell halfway through the swing-doors – legs on the landing, head and torso in the corridor – as the crunch of boots on concrete reverberated around the narrow shaft. There were no card-lock lights on this level, but that was because there were no lights at all, and as far as he could see, no doors either. Nonetheless, as he turned around on to his front he could make out the identifiable shape of a fire extinguisher, sitting in a niche just inside the corridor. He ripped it from its Velcro strap and lugged it through the double doors with both hands.

Action Man had almost reached the fifth floor, hugging the inside of the banister in search of a clear shot upwards. He could see the gun, gripped in two hands, moving along the railing like it was on a track. The man himself was out of sight, but that meant so was Matt. He waited for the tell-tale change of pace as the gunman reached the next flat section, then hurled the extinguisher down and jumped back again.

There was a deep tolling sound and a sharp cry as the vessel struck, then further peals as it rolled and tumbled down the next flight. The footsteps ceased, breathy moaning and swearing taking their place. Matt looked down through the railings, edging cautiously nearer the banister until something other than grey stairs was in view below. The gunman was crouched on the landing, clutching at the lower half of his left leg. He noticed the movement above him immediately and aimed the pistol, rolling on to his back and loosing off three more rounds. They all zipped into the ceiling, but Matt felt a rush of air terrifyingly close to his cheek as the first one passed.

He clattered back through the swing-doors and looked either side of himself. This time, to his right, he noticed that there was dim light shining in two shafts on the corridor floor, between where he stood and the main stairs. Open doors. Had to be. A sign opposite the stairwell read 'Mayfair and Splendide Suites', above an arrow pointing right. Matt began running again, figuring that with Action Man limping a little, he'd get to the main stairs before he was in range again. If he kept leading him round in circles, perhaps the guy would die of boredom.

Matt reached the entrance to the first suite as he heard the inevitable crash of his pursuer emerging behind. He dived through the open doorway, skidding across the tiled floor as the ricochet of another bullet zinged along the corridor. His heart was hammering and his brain couldn't spare even one synapse to wonder what the hell this was about. He was operating on reflex and sheer survival instinct, and the grey-matter Pentium was channelling all processing power into simply keeping him alive.

Matt climbed to his knees and looked around the interior

of the suite, the shuffling gait of now-limping footsteps like a countdown. He had until zero to improvise.

The suite was, as Simone suggested, still undergoing work. Unfortunately, the joinery tasks in progress had not required the use of a chainsaw or a nailgun. The door had not been hung yet, presumably held off until they had finished carting certain bulky items in and out. It stood resting at an angle against one wall, next to a two-seater sofa wrapped thickly in polythene. The room's king-size bed, also mollycoddled in plastic, had been shunted undeferentially into a corner to create working space. Lengths of timber lay schematically around where a walk-in wardrobe was under construction, next to one of two robust and heavy-looking workbenches, which sat three or four yards apart. The one nearer the wardrobe bore a hammer, a plain and an electric drill, the flex of which was plugged into a socket by the doorway, via an extension. Exposed back-boxes elsewhere in the skirting demonstrated that the electricians hadn't finished in here either.

The second workbench sat at ninety degrees to the doorway, forming a channel between itself and one wall, leading towards a set of patio doors, beyond which was an exterior terraced area. Two paving slabs and a fine covering of masonry dust rested on top of the workbench; but still no chainsaw, nailgun or grenade launcher. There was, however, some kind of circular sander lying on the tiled floor by the bench. Maybe he could buff him to death.

The shuffling countdown continued. Matt had another desperate look around, like there might be another exit he'd missed the first time. There were two sets of patio doors leading to the suite's terrace, a section of blank wall between them. What if he could climb down to the balcony below? he wondered, but the answer to the corresponding 'what if he couldn't?' made him drop the idea.

Matt looked at the workbench and the electrical flex again, and had what in the circumstances passed for an idea. He ran to one set of patio doors and pushed them slightly open, just enough to squeeze through, then retreated to behind the workbench, where he crouched down and gripped the power cable.

He could only see Action Man's legs as he entered. He was dragging the left one behind him, a dark dampness staining the bottom of his trouser leg. Matt feared there'd be a yellow dampness staining his own, a bit higher up, as the gunman paused just inside the doorway, looking around. If Matt was spotted, it was over. The moment stretched to unfeasible duration. Leaves fell from trees. Winter set in. Lambs gambolled in the springtime. Rivers dried. Generations were born and died. Civilisations rose and fell. Man abandoned religion, explored space, cured disease, ended conflict, evolved to a higher plane of existence, and at the end of it Matt was still stuck cowering behind a bench waiting to see whether this fucker would clock the open patio door or notice him and blow him away.

The fucker clocked the open patio door and began moving purposefully towards it. Matt yanked at the flex, pulling it taut at shin-height as planned. Not planned, as soon as Action Man's right leg hit it, the plug came flying out of the socket. Before Matt's bowels could respond accordingly, the cable snagged under the gunman's descending boot and tightened again, tangling further around his ankles as his left leg caught up. He tumbled forward, spinning as he did so, and landed on his back on the floor. Before he'd hit the ground, Matt was already charging the workbench to tip the thing sideways on top of him.

Matt spilled to the floor alongside it, sprawling flat-out next to the electric sander. The bench was now on its side between them, the weight of its worktop pinning Action Man to the deck at his right shoulder, so that only his arm was visible from where Matt lay. Matt hauled himself up to his knees in time to see that the arm, though trapped, was laboriously turning to point the pistol in his direction. Still kneeling, he grabbed the sander in both hands, but it was about five times as heavy as he was expecting, and the weight of it toppled him forwards again. He gave a diaphragmic grunt of effort as he fell, and managed somehow to land the device on the outstretched limb.

The gunman roared with pain, but still he gripped the gun and still his wrist slowly turned, the trigger-finger squeezing off shots closer and closer to Matt's head. Matt was flat-out and face-down on the tiles, the end of the silencer just out of his reach. About ten more degrees and it would be pointing between his eyes. He looked to his outstretched hand, still resting on the sander, and noticed the lettering on the device's distinctive semi-circular protruberance. This informed him, better late than never, that the sander was in fact a masonry saw.

Click. Whirr. Spray.

Disarmed.

Matt wiped the blood from his eyes, the gunman's cries slightly muffled by the screening effect of the worktop. He turned the saw off again and crouched beside it. The severed forearm lay absurdly on the floor nearby, its hand still gripping the pistol. It was a bit late for being squeamish, but he couldn't yet bring himself to prise the weapon from its fingers.

There was a grinding rumble of wood and metal on tile, accompanied by a bellowing scream. In a rage of anger, pain and sheer desperation, the gunman had hauled his shoulder and the stump of his arm from beneath the worktop and got to his knees. His left hand reached to the floor for the Uzi, the strap of which was tangled around one of the bench's legs. Matt hefted the saw once more and threw both it and himself across the barrier at the gunman, flicking the switch as he fell.

Action Man's howls were matched by Matt's own primal, animal yell as he pinned his pursuer under the saw, which tore ravenously into his chest and upper abdomen. The man's screams were suddenly silenced when blood began flowing up out of his open mouth, at which point Matt estimated it was safe to turn the saw back off. He stood up woozily, shaking and shivering, looking down in awestruck incomprehension at what he had wreaked. He was soaked from the crotch upwards in blood and fuck-knew what else. Even his hair was wet with it.

Matt stepped unsteadily away and rested his bottom on the edge of the toppled worktop. He was breathing heavily through his nose, the sound seeming to fill the room. The shivering continued, even though he was sweating from exertion, and his hands trembled like he had the DTs. He gripped the bench to right himself, feeling like if he sat on the floor he might fall off the world. Blood continued to seep from the corpse, puddling towards his feet.

'Oops,' he said throatily.

His attempts to reinvent himself as a more morally responsible individual didn't appear to be going quite to plan. He'd managed to resist taking sexual advantage of a vulnerable female, but had ended up slaughtering someone instead. That was the big weakness when fate played the comedian: once it was on a roll, it tended to get carried away with itself and its sense of irony became less and less subtle.

He needed air. He desperately needed air. He stumbled over to the patio doors and through the gap he'd left.

The dim glow lighting the suite and the corridor was from the Lido's illuminations beneath, darkness now having fallen across the highland skies. Over in the Laguna, there was one lonely light shining up in the residential floors, its empty rooms also equipped with Gavin's NRG-Sava system. 'Welcome to the Pleasuredome' pounded out from ground-level.

Matt walked to the edge of the terrace and looked over the balcony, then ducked immediately back out of sight. He crouched on the uneven floor, still missing some slabs, and peered down through the railings. There were two more guys in combat gear outside the Laguna's main entrance, evidently standing guard, or standing by.

A radio crackled on the deceased Action Man's belt.

'Booth, this is Jardine. Come in, over.'

'Christ,' Matt muttered, walking back inside. Revulsion turned once again into fear as he remembered the gunman telling his radio-buddy he was 'dealing' with 'a stray'.

'Booth, this is Jardine. Are you there? Over.'

Matt took a deep breath then crouched down by the body, unhooking the blood-spattered radio and lifting it to his blood-spattered face. He pressed the Talk button.

'Yeah, Booth here,' he growled, trying to remember Action Man's accent. He hadn't heard enough to get more precise than 'English', but what the hell, everyone sounded much the same on these things.

'Did you lock down the problem?'

'Yeah, I got him.'

'Is he dead?'

Matt looked at the Sam Raimi special effect beside him on the floor. 'Safe to say, yeah.'

'So the area's secured?'

'Yeah. Hotel B secured.'

'Good. Remain in your position until further orders. Out.'

Matt exhaled very slowly. He wasn't going to waste brain-time asking himself what this might be about, but he knew one thing for sure: it was only beginning.

Bad-ass perpetrators and they're here to stay.

He pulled the Uzi free of the workbench and slung it over his shoulder, then removed the spare clips from the dead man's belt and stuffed them into his trouser pockets. Slung around the man's back there was also a compact pump-action shotgun, which he tucked under his arm. He attached the radio to his waistband, then moved around the workbench again and ungripped the pistol from the fingers of the severed arm.

Such a sweet thing . . .

You said it, Alice.

No more Mister Nice Guy.

Matt pulled the keycard from his back pocket, then thought better of it as he noticed the state of his hand and remembered what the rest of himself looked like. 'Out damned spot' wasn't going to make it. He gently knocked on the door, covering the spyhole with his hand.

He heard footsteps, then Simone's voice: 'Matthew?'

'Simone, it's me. Don't open the door.'

'What?'

'I mean, when you do open the door, don't scream.'

'Why would I—'

The door opened and Simone breathed in sharply. Matt

couldn't be sure whether she was restricting herself to a gasp or gearing up for a lung-burster, so he placed a bloody hand over her mouth and backed her into the bedroom. Horror and confusion lit up her wide eyes. He was relieved, for practical reasons, to see that she was still fully dressed. All other ramifications were now a long way from relevant.

'Something very, very bad is happening,' he said, looking into her eyes but still covering her mouth, 'and I need you to keep the heid. Okay?'

She nodded. He took away his hand.

Simone looked him up and down in aghast disbelief. She struggled for words, making a few false starts before managing a bare whisper of 'What's going on?'

Matt shook his head. Blood whipped from his hair and streaked the wall.

'I don't know,' he said. 'But I'll tell you this much: it's the last time *I* practise safe sex.'

■ 21:12 ■ orchid suite ■ the uninvited ■

Gavin's party wasn't proving quite as enjoyable as he'd hoped. He was wise enough to know that when you look forward to something so much, a sense of disappointment is almost inescapable when at last the reality arrives. But nonetheless, it was difficult not to feel hard-done-by about the way certain things were turning out.

Simone, of course, had screwed things up for him, but that was to be expected. That was her *raison d'être* these days. Her jealousy of his success had eaten her from within

201

and left a rotting hollow where the woman he loved used to be. She couldn't appreciate that his successes were *their* successes, that everything they had together was the product of *their* marriage, not of his achievements. He'd always understood that her role at home was as important to their success – *theirs*, not his – as his activities further afield, but then he had always thought marriage should be a partnership. Unfortunately that can't happen if one party sees it as a contest.

For a while he thought he'd simply been naïve, too idealistic, but upon reflection he became determined that, damn it, an equal relationship – partnership – *should* be possible. However, for it to work, he realised, the partners had to be equal in the first place, and that was the problem. It was a painful thing to admit, but the honest truth was that Simone perhaps wasn't quite cut of the right cloth to be the wife of someone like himself. She had too many insecurities, and had consequently grown resentful of his pre-eminence, envious that he had turned out to be – for want of a more modest term – a more gifted individual than she. He wasn't saying she should have been content to bask in his reflected glory, but perhaps a stronger woman would have seen how that glory brightened up the place for both of them, rather than wish she was the one doing the shining.

It was little wonder he'd been driven into the arms of others for comfort.

She knew how much this reunion meant to him. That was the danger when someone so close goes from ally to enemy: they know best how to hurt you. Therefore she had been determined to ruin it for him. He could see that now; in fact, couldn't believe he hadn't better anticipated it. Up until tonight he thought the extent of her sabotage had been her insistence on tagging along, even though he knew she'd no desire to see these people again. She never talked about them and she certainly didn't share his interest in seeing how their lives had worked out, something he found distastefully cold.

But she had done a load more than just tag along – she had gone behind his back and invited Matt bloody Black, for a start. There he'd been, Mr TV star, large as life in the lobby, all bloody full of himself, blissfully unaware that he wasn't wanted. The man wasn't even funny. Gavin had seen one of his videos, and as far as he could make out it was just filth and gratuitous abuse. It was the emperor's new clothes: people laughed because they didn't want to be seen to be not 'getting it', Simone among them. Same as the bloody awful music she listened to. Emperor's new clothes and a dose of snobbery thrown in. The irony, of course, was that she forgot how it was Gavin's understanding of the tastes and likes of normal, ordinary people that had made him what he was today. So if M People were good enough for Tony Blair, they were good enough for him.

Also, rather than let him and Catherine get on with their more official role as hosts, Simone had been swanning around the ballroom like she owned the place, all dolled up to the nines too. She looked surprisingly good, he had to give her that, but it did occur to him rather bitterly that if she'd made the effort to look that way for him now and again, their marriage might not be in the state it was these days.

And to worsen matters still, Simone's high profile had been making Catherine uncomfortable about accompanying him around the ballroom. Catherine even suggested that she should be the one who took a back-seat, letting Gavin and Simone play hosts; or that the three of them should work the floor individually. Gavin had insisted Catherine stick with him – he wasn't letting that bitch spoil everything – but she hadn't been very happy about it. It wasn't obvious to the party-goers, of course, Catherine being far too professional for that, but in a way she was *too* professional, as there wasn't much chemistry on show to get people speculating.

Not everything was down to Simone, though. There'd been a very disheartening lack of rapport between himself and his guests, most of whom had shown a uniform ambivalence about the hotel industry. Only a paltry handful had turned up for his tour, the rest opting to stay in their rooms, at which point he'd made a mental note to check whether some idiot had stocked Buckfast in their mini-bars.

They'd not been overjoyed to see him once the party commenced, either. Sure, they'd been polite enough and expressed gratitude for him organising the soirée, but once the initial pleasantries had been dispensed with, they'd often seemed desperate to latch on to someone else's company. Eventually, he'd decided if you can't beat 'em, join 'em, and cottoned on to a couple of larger groups himself. Unfortunately, all they wanted to talk about was their days at St Michael's, rather than what everyone was doing now. It was sad, really, to be so obsessed with the past.

The tales featured the same old tired cast of over-celebrated characters and exaggerated incidents. Glory days on the football pitch, playground misdemeanours, resultant beltings from teachers, pubescent sexual innnuendo and juvenile pugilism. He did his best to join in but found he had nothing to contribute; or at least nothing involving himself, just witness testimony of stories already being told in the first person by those around him. The only point at which he had become the focus of attention was when it emerged that he was unique in never having been assaulted by David Murdoch.

'He must have had a fuckin' force-field roon' him,' remarked one.

'Either that or he was invisible,' offered another, that smart-arse McQuade. 'Are you sure you were in oor class, Gavin? Maybe you've invited the wrang year to your reunion.'

Yeah, yeah, laugh it up, he'd thought, watching them clutch the last remnants of that once-upon-a-time when they were somebodies in a limited little world. But who's fucking invisible now?

Things finally started to look up during his speech, when he noticed Catherine slipping quietly out of the main doors, judiciously choosing her moment when all eyes were on him. That was the Catherine he knew and loved: going up to her suite to prepare for a private little reunion just between the two of them, while everyone else would be busy tucking into the buffet. The lustful glances she'd been receiving all night had made him all the more frustrated that she wasn't making the true nature of their relationship a little more obvious to those who were admiring her. However, once he'd seen her leave the room, the thought of those glances made him all the more horny, as though he was the receptacle of everyone else's cumulative desire.

He'd cut short the speech, declared the buffet open and headed for the lift. There were tingles running through him by the time it reached the top floor. That gorgeous tight dress she was wearing . . . dreadful waste to take it off. Just ride it up. around her middle, maybe against the back of the chaise longue . . .

There was no reply when he knocked at the door, but then she'd more likely be waiting for him to enter, as the master of the house shouldn't need to be asked. He swiped his card through the slot, another ripple of anticipation pulsing through him as the lock clunked beckoningly open.

He made his way inside to find the suite in darkness. Enticing, he thought, but tonight he wanted to see her. He placed the keycard into the NRG-Sava and flicked on the lights.

The place was empty. Catherine's overnight bag lay next to the dresser but the bed was undisturbed. He called her name twice to no reply. Unless, he suddenly thought, she had gone to *his* suite. It was out of bounds with Simone in residence, but maybe she was being a naughty girl, perhaps even by way of demonstrating who really ought to be in his bedroom.

Gavin was about to go along the hall to find out when it struck him that he hadn't seen Simone for a while, either, the bitch making a point of not being present during his big speech. The nightmare scenario entered his head of her going upstairs and finding Catherine in their suite, until he remembered that Catherine had no way of getting in. So where the hell was she? He picked up the phone. Idiot Boy Jamie the Geordie receptionist answered it.

'Hello, Jamie, it's Mr Hutchison here. Do you happen to know where Miss O'Rourke is?'

'Ehm, I think she went to check on a guest who didn't come downstairs to the party. She asked me for his room number. It's still on the screen. Room 322.'

'And which guest would that be?'

'Ehm, let's see. Just callin' up the details. Right. The name is Murdoch, David, Mr.'

'—'

'Are you all right, sir? Sir?'

Gavin went straight to the fridge and poured himself a

very large whisky. He'd vowed to stay straight all night so that he was at his brightest, opting to drink in the occasion instead. But that was before the occasion began to taste like yesterday's sick. He knocked it right back and had another. And another. After so many kicks in the groin, no-one would deny he needed analgesia. Not only was that ego-on-toast Matt Black here, at the behest of his backstabbing bint of a wife, but so, it turned out, was that uber-psycho turned 'victim of society' Davie Murdoch, who despite terrorising every last one of them, was being talked of almost with reverence by the assembly of losers downstairs. And as if his balls hadn't quite been sledge-hammered enough, Catherine had fucked off in the middle of his big speech to go to the bastard's room!

Was there anything else that could possibly go wrong tonight? Not that he could think of. Apart from one of the guests turning out to be a serial killer and topping the whole sodding lot of them, but then he wasn't so sure he'd consider that a bad thing right now.

Well, he thought, the warmth of the whisky beginning to course through him, he wasn't going to just sit here and take it. He'd a good mind to throw these uninvited tosspots off the edge of the bloody rig. Gatecrash a place like this and you had to think about the downsides, didn't you? Bastards. He'd show the lot of them.

■ 21:12 ■ laguna room 322 ■ the uninvited ii ■

Davie flipped through the channels again, barely watching what was flashed before him as he clicked ahead to the next one. In time he switched the thing off and returned the remote to the bedside table. He sighed, placing his hands either side of his face, elbows resting on his thighs, feeling a mixture of failure, depression and embarrassment. He had travelled a hell of a long way for a quiet night in. He wanted Collette. He wanted to see her smiling at him across their living room while Geni and wee D walloped him about the head and body with inflatable plastic zoo animals.

The blank screen and the blank walls mocked him in his useless solitude. His jacket sat accusingly on a chair by the door, like a sulky child who'd been promised an outing then been let down by Daddy at the last gasp. He'd even got as far as gripping the handle before hearing other doors open and close in the corridor beyond. Footsteps and voices.

'Is that you, Tommy?'

'Allan! Christ, how you doin', Aldo? You're lookin' great. Allan, this is my wife, Lorna.'

'Pleased to meet you, Lorna. This is Nadja.'

'Hello.'

'Hello.'

'Hi there.'

'We're not married. Actually, I got her from an escort service, and she doesnae speak much English.'

Thump.

'Oow.'

'Ha ha ha ha.'

'Leave the jokes to your friend Matthew, darling, huh?'

'Aye, sure, honey.'

'God, it's amazin' to see you, Aldo, it really is. I suppose we'd better get used to this or we'll be sayin' it all night. Every five minutes. "Wow! I cannae believe it's you!" "Jesus, look who it is."'

208

'Yeah, till we remember we all hated each other.'

'Aye, right enough. Paul Duff works in the bookie's on Auchenlea main street. Wonder if he's offerin' odds on how long before the first barney.'

'So I heard you're in criminal law these days, Tommy, is that right . . .'

Davie had let go of the handle and stepped back from the door. Tommy Milligan and Allan Crossland. He'd smashed Tommy's head off one of the massive bins behind the dining hall; punched and kicked Allan down the big steps to the football pitch. He didn't even remember why, if there had ever been a why.

He couldn't do this.

When he arrived, he'd loitered at the back of the group while the others queued to check into their rooms. He'd been last off the bus, last off the helicopter, back of the line, out of sight. A bloke he'd assumed to be Gavin Hutchison was talking to people as they waited around the reception area, accompanied by a woman he recognised but couldn't put a name to. Caroline sounded plausible but he wasn't sure it was quite right.

'Catherine' he heard someone call her. That was it. She was saying hello to everybody, individually, while Hutchison was cherry-picking longer conversations. Davie's stomach hollowed with the understanding that she'd inevitably get to him, and when she did, this charmed spell of anonymity would forcibly be broken. It seemed crazy, but he felt scared.

Actually, maybe it wasn't that crazy. In the days when he knew these people, he'd always been scared. The difference now was that he'd learned responses more sophisticated than sticking a boot in their faces. He exercised one of them then, slipping away quietly to the toilets and waiting there until the voices died and everyone had dispersed.

More sophisticated, yes, but not much more constructive. It would be easier later, at the party, he'd told himself. And it probably would have been, if only he'd had the front to go downstairs and enter the bloody thing.

Still the jacket sat there, but he knew he wasn't putting it back on.

Coming here at all had been a mistake, he thought, then retracted that. It had been right to try. Better to make the trip and find the gates closed than spend the rest of your life wondering. He could go home to Collette and the kids now and never look back again. Wasn't that what he'd wanted anyway?

Then there was a knock at the door, causing him to sit up straight. He didn't reply, relieved the TV wasn't on any more. They'd go away in a minute. No-one knew he was here, so whoever it was had the wrong room.

The knock was repeated.

'David?' called a female voice, tentative, nervous, like she might run away if he did open the door. 'David Murdoch?'

Which changed everything. She knew he was in there, knew *who* was in there. Taking a deep breath, he got up and opened the door. She didn't run away. They stood and stared for a long second, mutually aware of there being no going back now that they had seen each other.

'Can I come in?' she asked eventually.

Davie searched for the right way of saying yes but failed to find one involving words. A bewildered nod and a standing aside served in lieu. She walked in but didn't seem any less awkward than had she stayed out in the corridor.

'Catherine, isn't it?' he managed.

'Catherine O'Rourke,' she confirmed. Something fell into place.

'You're the . . . I mean, you're "RSVP Catherine O'Rourke, Clamour PR".'

'That's right. Business unavoidably mixed with pleasure. Except that you didn't.'

'Didn't what?'

'RSVP.'

'I know. Sorry, I—'

Catherine was effusive in heading off his apology, appalled that he thought she was chiding him. 'No, no, I'm just saying. I had no idea you'd be here until I saw you in the lobby earlier. Then you disappeared. I thought I'd catch up with you later, but you didn't materialise at the party, so . . .' She bit her lip, devoid of the professionally affable poise she'd shown downstairs. There was something going on here that Davie didn't get.

'So what, are you contractually obliged to say hello to everybody on the guest list, no matter where they are?' he asked. The atmosphere badly needed humour, but his own awkwardness sabotaged his delivery. Accompanied by such a faltering apology for a smile, it could as easily have been a put-down.

She reciprocated with an equally unconvincing attempt.

'No,' she said. 'But I *was* aware that you hadn't appeared at the ballroom tonight, and I was wondering . . .' She sat down on the edge of his bed and sighed, blowing air through her lips like a pressure valve. She looked up at him for a moment, then looked away again as she spoke.

'I was wondering why you had come all this way and then not shown up at the party, so I thought I should see whether there was something wrong. Then I remembered your vanishing act at reception and it struck me that if there *was* something wrong and you didn't want to see anybody, the solution wasn't for me to go bothering you.'

Davie felt there was an obligation to acknowledge the obvious and invite an explanation.

'But you did anyway.'

She nodded. 'You couldn't face them, could you?' she asked.

He shook his head.

'But somehow you feel you must.'

Davie nodded, this time with a half-decent smile in reward for her perceptiveness.

'Well, same goes for me,' she explained, making what was obviously a testing effort to look him in the face. Whatever was going on, he still wasn't getting it.

'*You* couldn't face them?' he asked.

'I couldn't face you.'

Davie was lost. He moved his jacket to one side and sat down opposite the bed.

He remembered Catherine O'Rourke. It was hard not to: she'd been one of the most attractive girls in the school, and he couldn't imagine her getting kicked out of anyone's bed for farting these days either. He recalled the name now as much as the face, a necessary adjunct to changing-room sexual discussion. A byword for beauty, lust and impossible desires, as much as his had doubtless been for violence, anger and fear. What he didn't remember was ever having any kind of interaction with her whatsoever.

(Unless)

'None of the others know you're here,' she told him. 'Or that you're missing, rather. You weren't on that big guest list in the lobby.'

'Oh yeah, because I didn't RSVP,' he replied, smiling,

further confused but half-hopeful that she was changing the subject.

'No, because you were never on it,' she explained, apologetically.

'Eh?'

'It's Gavin's party, you see. He submitted a list of names to me, and yours wasn't one of them. Please don't be offended.'

After watching her sit there, so portentously burdened, Davie couldn't help but laugh that this was what had been worrying her.

'Never bother,' he said. 'I wouldnae want me at my school reunion. Why d'you think I'm skulkin' aboot up here?' He looked in her face for the appropriate smile of relief but, perplexingly, it wasn't forthcoming.

'So who invited me?' he asked. 'You?'

'Well, not quite. My PA came in kind of sheepishly one morning and told me Gavin's wife, Simone, had phoned to request that invitations go out to a couple of people he hadn't put on his list. One of them was you. She also asked that Gavin be kept in the dark about it. The two of them aren't the most happily married couple in the world.'

'Why me?'

'She was mischief-making, I think. She invited you and Matthew Black because Gavin specifically didn't want either of you here.'

'Gavin didn't invite Matt Black? Me I can understand, but I mean—'

'I brought it up myself when I saw the list. He was afraid there'd be tabloid reporters crawling all over the place if it got out that Matt Black was coming, and he said he could do without the resort getting drug-party headlines before it had even opened.'

213

'But you went ahead with Simone's requests, anyway. Both of them.'

Catherine nodded.

'Even though she'd have no way of knowing if you hadn't.'

She nodded again, this time biting her lip once more. Davie still wasn't getting it, but suspected whatever 'it' was, he was heading in its direction.

'Like I said, Matt I can understand,' he continued. 'He's a big star and everybody would want to see him on the off-chance he turned up. But why me, Catherine?'

(Unless)

'This isn't easy for me,' she said. She ran a hand through her hair, as though composure without would substitute for composure within. 'Even when I approved the invitations, I suppose I thought it would make no difference, as you weren't likely to travel all the way from America just for this. I didn't hear back from you, so I'd got used to the idea that you wouldn't be coming and I wouldn't need to have this conversation after all. Then boom, there you were in the lobby.

'When you didn't appear at the party I was sort of relieved, but then I realised that if I didn't talk to you now, I'd be carrying this around for the rest of my life.'

She shook her head.

'What is it, Catherine?' Davie asked softly.

She took a breath.

Then what sounded like a volley of gunfire beat her to breaking the silence. They looked at each other suddenly, then burst out laughing at the fright they'd got, the noise having broken the growing tension in the room.

'God,' she said, holding a hand to her chest. 'Fireworks. I thought for a moment—'

The noise repeated itself, then again, then more frequently. Screams could be heard mutedly through the
windows. Davie got to his feet and reached for the sliding
door to the balcony. The crackling bursts and the sounds
of hysteria became clearer as soon as he pushed the panel
back a few inches.

'Jesus fuckin' Christ, what's gaun' on?'

He moved rapidly to the edge of the balcony, Catherine
emerging just behind him. As soon as he caught a glimpse
of the scene below, he pushed her back and ducked out of
sight himself.

They scuttled inside, bowed low, and tumbled to the
floor together once they were through the doorway. Tears
were forming in Catherine's terrified eyes as the sounds of
screams and gunshots continued to rise from the terrace.
Her mouth attempted to shape words but got nowhere.

'Wh – what are we going to do?' she managed in a broken
whisper.

Davie climbed to his feet and looked around the room,
though for what he wasn't sure. He'd left his big book of
escaping from terrorist situations at home. Hide, was the
first answer that came to mind, but it seemed like a poorly
defined concept. He needed specifics.

'We've got to get out of *here*, that's for starters. We're
like rats in a trap. Come on.'

Davie reached down and helped Catherine to her feet,
then put a silencing hand over her mouth as he heard the
approach of footsteps in the hallway outside. He motioned
her into the wardrobe and closed the door after her, then
looked about for a chib, but it was too late: the footsteps
had halted. The card-lock whirred and clunked.

'. . . 'an it's still nothin' each, right? They've hit the bar aboot six times, the posts are practically fawin' doon wi' the leatherin' they've had, an' that's no' the only thing fawin' doon: they're divin' like fuck every time they get intae the penalty box. Except, the ref, he's clocked how desperate they're gettin' an' he's giein' them fuck-all, right? So they're goin' fuckin' mental an' their fans are wan decision away fae a pitch invasion. Noo, we've no had a shot at goal the whole gemme, an' they're the Ayrshire league champions, so the way we were playin' that season, we'd have been happy comin' away wi' anythin' less than aboot five-nothin'. But five minutes left, Ger Milligan punches it oot tae me an' I first-time it up tae Billy Ross harin' up the right wing. Tam Keenan's makin' a run through the middle, an' their defence is chargin' back like fuck. The ref's a fuckin' *mile* back an' there's nae linesmen in a wee first-round gemme like this. So Billy fires the cross in an' Tam gets in ahead o' the defender, except he's no timed it right for the header, so he just sticks the haun oot an' punches it intae the net. Ref saw fuck-all 'cause Tam'd his back tae him, so he gies the goal. They aw go mental, an' the berrs roon the touchline are startin' tae sharpen sticks, you know? So Franky, the manager, he goes tae the dressin' room an' just piles everybody's gear intae the minibus an' drives it right up behin' oor goal wi the back doors open, wavin' tae us tae aw pile in soon as the whistle goes. Trouble is, that stupit cunt Billy's only gone an' won us a corner, so we're aw up the other end when the ref blaws the final whistle. Noo,

216

by this point the berrs have noticed Franky's escape plan an' JESUS FUCKIN' CHRIST—'

Bursts of gunfire erupted deafeningly around the room. The sound was so loud it seemed to be everywhere at once. Then the screams started, and they *were* everywhere at once. The gunmen swept into the function suite from the main doors at the front, moving swiftly to encircle the gathering almost as soon as their initial discharges had rung out. People ran into each other, falling, tangling, totally and understandably losing it. There'd been no time for moments of disbelief, just an instantaneous transition from social discussion to mortal terror, erasing in less than a second all the evening's events, words, context. It was probably the clothes, Ally reckoned, rather than the guns; more the semiotics than the semi-autos. Ski-masks and camouflage gear: paramilitaries. Terrorists. Real terrorists. Indigenous, unexotic, common or garden. Not fuzzy-picture-quality news-report towel-heads, but the green, green (or orange, orange) terrorists of home. And so what if their heyday was over, this was proof in action of 'race-memory'.

Plaster dust fell in clouds from the ceiling where the heralding bursts had struck. Ally swallowed. In real life, the bullet-deadliness quotient was always set to maximum. Around him was mayhem. People ran like sheep, erratically, unthinkingly, finding every direction blocked by gunmen. Still the shouting and screaming continued, amid occasional further bursts of machine-gun fire over their heads. At the front entrance, uniformed staff from the lobby, together with Jim Murray (who'd been at the bogs), were being prodded into the mêlée by still more bad guys.

The hysteria would exhaust itself, he knew. Panic would give way to fear and resignation. He could hear it already as

217

the screams and shouts diminished. A few more moments and all would be still. A few more moments and he would be a hostage. If he wanted to swap the Bonnie Bedelia role for the Bruce Willis one, he had to find a way of doing so now or never. The question was, did he? Never mind heroism – from a purely self-preservational point of view, making an undetected run for it didn't seem quite the obvious option it did on celluloid. He wasn't paralysed by any inability to think of what to do, but rather by an extremely vivid ability to think about the consequences. Take your chances among the no-threat extras as they wait – obediently and cooperatively – for rescue, or single yourself out for the seek-and-destroy treatment.

Even the moral obligation aspect was greyed-out. If the opportunity arose, did he risk all in a heroic attempt to rescue the others, or did he have a greater duty to Annette and their unborn child to take whatever course would better assure his personal survival?

He looked at the gunman closest to him. His head was turned away, towards the baffled and terrified 'prisoners' – Jim Murray et al – being escorted into the ballroom's equally baffled and terrified throng. No-one, good guys or bad guys, was looking at him. There wouldn't be another chance.

Ally was no action hero, not even a hard-man. By his own admission, he couldn't fight sleep. Stinging remarks and spectacular vomits had been his only sources of notoriety in youth, a smart mouth and a weak stomach ensuring the traffic of bile was constant in one form or other. Neither was going to be of much use here tonight. The only skills he had to offer were electrical, so short of botching a rewire on their houses, there was little threat he could present to these sturdily beweaponed adversaries. Nonetheless, instinct and experience told him the odds were always better in the field than in the abattoir.

He dropped to his knees and rolled out of sight under the floor-length drape of the buffet tables, which ran almost the width of the room at one end, a couple of yards in front of the bar. The moment of action, of conscious, decisive defiance, sent his insides lurching in nauseous fear of detection and reprisal. Between that and three glasses of champers on an empty stomach, following a day spent on a coach, he felt imminently liable to surpass his legendary Linda Blair up-chuck in second-year RE, after Paddy Greig ate his own scab.

Ally quietened his breathing, stilling himself on hands and knees as dozens of feet shuffled uneasily, inches away from the drape. When he'd first rolled underneath, he half expected to find a dozen others already cowering there, telling him to fuck off and find his own hiding place. So far, fortunately, this was not the case.

The screams and shouts were giving way to a low babbling, which would inevitably be silenced when whoever was in charge announced himself. On the other side of the buffet, Ally could see a pair of heavy boots marching along the channel between the tables and the back wall, heading towards where he crouched. He shivered, holding his breath. The best he could hope for now was humiliation as he, the wretched and selfish coward, was dragged from his hiding place and thrown back among his despising peers, but even that seemed over-optimistic as he heard the sound of a machine-gun bolt being drawn back, and watched the boots stomp closer and closer.

They stopped right beside him. Ally put his hands behind his head in a gesture of surrender, looking at the drape and waiting for it to be whipped back. Instead the boots turned on one heel and there was a crash as the gunman kicked at what Ally's geography estimated must be the door leading behind the bar. There were two more loud crashes, but the door, not having seen any action flicks, refused to splinter open. A burst of small-arms fire ensued, followed by another couple of kicks and a lengthy volley of swearing. Still it remained locked and closed.

'Fuck,' the gunman said breathlessly. The boots backed towards Ally's table again, their owner bumping against it and sliding the thing a few inches along the polished floor. Ally had to execute a nimble sideways bunny-hop to avoid contact and exposure. His heart rate was accelerating so much that he was weighing up whether surrender would offer better survival odds than the impending coronary.

The boots moved away again, at pace this time, then disappeared with a grunt as the gunman dived over the bartop and into the room beyond. Here were squeals of 'Don't shoot, don't shoot, please don't shoot', accompanied by growls of 'Unlock that fuckin' door', as the refugee barman was finally apprehended. The bad guy's accent was Northern Irish, sending another cold note of authenticity chiming through Ally's head. He tried to deduce a plausible motive, a political cause-and-effect context that would make sense of the developing scenario, but precedent brought his speculation to a bleak, stomach-turning halt: IRA, UVF, whoever, they'd none of them ever gone in for hostages. They just murdered people. No tooling around with negotiators when everyone already knew their demands; the stake was always who they might kill *next* time.

He watched the boots frog-march a pair of Adidas trainers past the buffet tables. Five or six feet away, the door to the bar remained open. The gunman had his back to it, but he'd probably turn around again once he had ushered his captive into the middle with the rest. Ally had very little time left to evaluate his options: the bar didn't lead any- where, otherwise the barman wouldn't have been nabbed, but nonetheless, hiding under the table wasn't much of a long-term strategy either. Besides, he thought, what better hiding place than somewhere they've already searched?

He scrambled across the gap, stealing a glance to his right where the gunman's back remained reassuringly in view. Behind Ally, the standing captives had their backs to him, facing the main entrance at the front, shielding him from the other bad guys' lines of sight. He rolled inside the bar, away from the open door, the theft of those few more yards further lifting his cardiac tempo and sending another bilious aftershock shuddering through him. Ally felt sure he was going to puke, could swear it was rising in his throat. He put a hand to his mouth in anticipation, thinking he'd probably end up choking to death on the stuff at precisely the moment Gavin Hutchison revealed it all to be an elaborate wind-up.

The feeling receded (or maybe just the boak did), and he looked at his surroundings. Bar, pumps, drains to the front. Shelves, optics, fridges behind. To his left was the way he'd come in, and to his right a second open door, leading to a compact storeroom, where the barman had no doubt been cowering less than a minute ago. He crawled into the store. Even without the music, the hubbub sounded like it could still be a party, dozens of excited voices talking loudly and quickly, all at once. Trouble was, the gatecrashers wanted to play party games.

'Everybody sit down on the floor. Everybody down on the floor *now*.' The bloke didn't say 'Simon says', but Ally was sure everyone would comply. His accent sounded different from the last one, but it was hard to place with the guy just barking out an order like that.

Ally looked up. There were crates of beer, boxes of wine, plastic-wrapped pallets of mixers, all littered unsystematically about the shelves and the floor, more like a giant carry-out than the stock of an organised bar. But then, that's what this was: a party in an empty new-build before the residents moved in. Doesn't matter if you mess things up a wee bit, long as you clear the place out later. Plus, there are no neighbours to call the polis if things get wild. Normally, that last part was considered an advantage.

The thought offered a possibility beyond hiding and hoping. Polis. Assistance. Help. But wouldn't these guys be contacting the authorities themselves? he wondered, before recalling with a wince his reflections on Ulster terrorist hostage-taking, or the previous lack thereof.

Right. In that case, definitely get the polis. If bargaining was what they had in mind, then let it commence sooner rather than later, and hopefully they could all go home alive. And if it wasn't, then all the more reason to call. They were sitting in the middle of the Cromarty Firth, he reasoned. If notifying the authorities wasn't on the terrorists' game plan, then the buggers might be forced to trade their hostages for a chopper off this bloody thing.

He needed to get to a phone. Ally looked behind the bar again, like a phone was the kind of thing he'd have missed in a situation like this. Of course, there was nothing. In that case, he had to find a way out. He stood up, glancing down at the storeroom's floor. This was a bar. Bars had cellars. He lifted the end of one of the pallets on the floor and slid it to one side, but as a trapdoor failed to reveal itself, it dawned depressingly on him that if there had been such a way out, then the barman would surely have made use of

222

it. The entrance to the beer cellar was probably that door right next to the one he'd scrambled through from under the buffet table, but there was no point in mourning missed opportunities, because it would almost certainly have been locked.

However, with the pallet moved to one side, he noticed for the first time the battleship grey of a ventilation shaft built into the wall, obscured by the shelves of booze as it rose from floor to ceiling. Ally frantically pushed cartons and boxes aside until he revealed a mesh panel between two shelves at about waist-height, at which point he almost took a step back in awe. Right in front of him was the sacred conduit of the lone action-hero, from John McClane to Duke Nukem: the Holy Grille. It even looked wide enough to fit inside.

There were screws at each of the grille's four corners, too tight to yield to even the most painful and stoically determined thumb-and-finger pinching. On a shelf behind the bar, however, there was a steel tray bearing a knife and some freshly sliced lemon wedges. Ally retrieved the knife, moving slowly and softly on the balls of his feet. The chatter continued outside, unaccompanied by any further orders or prompts. The bad guys' main man, whoever he was, had presumably not put in an appearance yet.

The first screw refused to budge as Ally applied pressure with the blade. He had plenty of elbow-grease in reserve, but was terrified of the thing giving off a squeak when finally it gave. The sweat oozing around his palm and fingers wasn't doing much for his grip. He twisted a little harder and the screw loosened, emitting the tiniest metallic yelp. After that it wound out easily, and the other three reacted in kind. Mercifully, the panel began to fall away through sheer gravity once the two top screws were removed, so once all four were gone, there was no noisy heaving or scraping required to pull it free.

Ally stuck his head inside. The shaft disappeared into darkness above and below, but he was sure he could make out a junction with a horizontal passage a few feet up, slightly higher than what he estimated to be ceiling level. It ran at ninety degrees to the back wall of the ballroom, heading away from it. Any route, however awkward, heading away from the bad guys, was an improvement on the status quo. He took off his jacket and hid it under a box of vodka bottles, then stuck the knife through one of his beltloops.

He had to execute a sort of backwards limbo-dance to get in, squeezing his head, shoulders and then full torso inside the shaft as his bottom rested on the shelf beneath. It was one of those rare occasions when he was grateful for being a skinny short-arse who spent all day crawling about under floorboards. He pulled himself further up until his feet were on the edge of the open panel, whereupon he breathed in and rotated himself ninety degrees, so that he'd be facing the gap when he reached it. He pressed his hands to the walls of the shaft, palms-out at waist-level, taking his weight off one foot and then the other to see whether this was going to work. He failed to drop, screaming, into the blackness below, so began to climb by pushing his feet against the sides. His scuffing movements reverberated around him, his breaths echoing through the tight chamber with equal volume. Ally stopped still, his guts heaving once again, convinced the noise must have betrayed him. He waited for the sound of footsteps from the bar, but none came.

Recommencing, he strained silently to haul himself into the adjoining passage, his left knee causing a dull thump as he rattled it sharply against the junction. He breathed in sharply between tight lips in lieu of a groan, tears coming to his eyes, but the pain was tempered by the relief of having made it to the horizontal vent, apparently undetected.

A swimming motion propelled him forwards into the dark. There was no quick way of doing this, so he concentrated on stealth, keeping his movements as soft and fluid as the cramped space allowed. Soon he could see nothing, and the only sound beyond that of his own exertions was of one muffled voice. He couldn't quite make out what was being said, but the directness of the tone suggested that the hostages were being addressed, so he guessed the baddie-in-chief must have turned up. It would be the usual everybody-stay-calm-and-cooperate-and-this-will-soon-be-over shtick. Heard it.

Ally's fingers struck steel ahead of him. He flapped his hand around in panic to confirm whether he had succeeded in holing himself up in a dead end, but found free space before he needed to contemplate whether he was capable of reverse. The passage turned hard left, and further along it there was a dim glow of light, suggesting another grille-panel.

In the darkness it was impossible to estimate how far he had travelled, but the door to the bar was only a few yards from the ballroom's left-hand wall as you faced the back, so he had to be somewhere above the parallel corridor outside. He could no longer hear the muffled voice, which meant it was out of earshot, so at the very least he'd cleared the function suite. Maybe he'd even made it to the restaurant on the other side of the hall, Mariner's, or whatever the fuck it was called. He'd see when he reached the grille.

He edged further along, closer and closer to the glow of light. Initially, all he could make out was ceiling-tiles and the cross-hatching of another grille beneath. One more heave brought his face directly above that, and he was able to look through both grids at what was below.

What was below was the ballroom, where the hostages were sitting in gun-enforced silence upon the insistence of their captors, several of whom were scanning the ceiling in one corner of the room to isolate the source of the loud, metallic thumping sounds they'd been hearing from above. Ally stopped still, halting even his intake of panicked breath. There was a gunman only four feet below him, but the double-grille and the darkness inside the vent meant he still hadn't been seen.

The fright and the ensuing tension proved more than his historically cantankerous alimentary canal could deal with. He barfed on a tidal scale. The two grilles filtered out what diced-carrot content there was, but that still left a bucketload of thick fluid to splash down on to the balaclava-clad head of the gunman standing underneath. There was an indecisive, will-he-give-a-penalty pause while the intruders watched the deluge cover their comrade, as though no-one was quite sure the whole thing – noise and all – wasn't down to a plumbing problem. Then Ally sent down another volume, this time accompanied by an involuntary diaphragmic retch.

The drenched gunman took a step back as the liquid hit the floor, then aimed his machine gun upwards at a steep angle. An ear-bursting fury of tearing and exploding metal erupted around Ally, sending shudders through him which at first he thought must be bullets. The deafening volley continued and continued and continued, gouging and hacking at the aluminium less than a foot from his head, until something gave above him and the shaft split open with a sudden lurch. The vent dipped sharply forwards and sent him sprawling head-first through the ceiling-tiles. He landed face-down in the giant centrepiece commemorative reunion cake, baked in the shape of the St Michael's school building.

This sort of thing never happened to Bruce Willis, not even when Luc Besson was directing.

Ally felt a sledgehammer blow to his back as the bevommed baddie bore the butt of his machine gun down upon him in vengeance. He recoiled and rolled off the cake-splattered table to the floor. His assailant rammed the stock into his mid-section, winding him and doubling him over in breathless agony. Ally covered his head with his arms, then reflexively pulled them away again as a boot was driven down with all weight into his shins. His head again exposed, the gun-stock was sent into his face, smashing bloodily into his cheek.

The building cacophony of pain in Ally's head and body was amplified by the terror of understanding that he was being beaten up by someone professionally proficient in violence, and there was no reason why it should stop. After all, he'd just been sick on the guy. There was another crushing impact on his ribcage, then a blow to his nose and mouth that sent blood welling over his lips and chin, causing him to splutter as it ran also into his throat.

'Leave him alone!' shrieked a voice, high, shrill and loud, insistent rather than appellant. The gunman stopped in surprise and turned to see where it had come from. Ally looked across the floor in his daze. Mrs Laurence had climbed to her feet and trilled out the order in that universal classroom register, comparable with Jedi mind-control. Grown men – terrorists, even – might not obey it now they were adults, but they were powerless to ignore it.

'That's enough, Bill,' commanded a voice. 'Put him with

the others. Give him a handkerchief or something.' The accent was impossible for Ally to place, especially with the ringing in his ears and the pain searing through his body. It was definitely on the plummy side, though, like a Brit golfer who doesn't spend much more than the odd fortnight back in Blighty and is reaping the tax benefits as a result.

Ally's assailant, 'Bill', pulled him roughly to his knees and handed him a clutch of paper napkins from the nearby table, muttering 'here' as he thrust them at Ally's bleeding face.

'Oh, the humanity,' Ally muttered, holding a napkin to his nostrils.

'Don't push it, pal,' Bill warned, urging him into the centre of the room. Charlie O'Neill and Mrs Laurence both moved forward to help him, but they were instantly ordered back to the floor. Ally wasn't sure what kind of assistance they were planning to offer, but he appreciated the gesture. He stumbled across and sat down between them.

'So what'd I miss?' he asked, wincing as various throbs beat out a continuous tattoo all around his body. He placed his hands in his lap, about the only spot where they wouldn't be resting on something tender. His elbow scraped a hard object under his shirt, which had been pulled outside his trousers. It was the knife, still tucked into the beltloops and concealed by the M&S polyester and cotton. He felt another wave of nausea at how close he might have come to disembowelling himself when he fell.

'No' much,' Charlie replied. 'Your man there was just tellin' us tae sit at peace an' toe the line before you dropped in. I must admit, I was wonderin' where you'd got to, but

then I saw spew comin' oot the ceilin' an' I says tae mysel',
"Aye, that'll be Ally."'

'Very fuckin' funny.'

'Silence!' It was the bossman who spoke, standing tall
in front of the main doors. Now it really *was* like being
back in school: assembly in the big hall, everyone sitting,
legs crossed, on the floor, and some blowhard at the front
abusing his authority to compensate his ego for a lifetime of
inadequacies. It was likely there'd be prayers before long,
as well, though not aloud.

'Now,' the bossman continued. 'Could Mr Gavin Hutchison
please make himself known to one of my assistants?'

There was a tense, expectant silence, which lengthened as
Gavin failed to emerge. After a few seconds, people began
looking around for their erstwhile host, but sure enough,
he wasn't to be found.

'Oh, do come on, Mr Hutchison. The sooner you iden-
tify yourself, the sooner we can get this whole business
over with.'

Still there was no response.

'All right,' the bossman sighed. He stepped forward and
grabbed Lisa McKenzie by the hair, dragging her to her
feet and sticking a pistol to her temple. 'Point him out,'
he demanded.

Lisa scanned the room, her eyes flitting hurriedly from
face to face. Ally could see the desperation as she looked
again and again for someone who wouldn't be found.

'He isn't here,' she said, her voice little more than a
mumble.

'What?'

'He isn't *here*,' she stated more firmly. 'I think he left the
ballroom shortly before you arrived.'

'Christ,' he hissed, then backhanded Lisa, knocking her

to the floor. Ally noticed Charlie bristle, his shoulders moving a little, but he was restrained by the sight of all that hardware. Charlie's face burned with rage and shame, the humiliation of helplessness.

One of the gunmen was doing a head count, the total of which he related to Bill, the bloke Ally had been sick on. Then another came in from the lobby, carrying a sheet of paper.

Bill approached Bossman. 'We've a print-out of the guest list,' he said. Bill's accent was unmistakably Scottish, further confusing Ally's political speculations. He couldn't guess at a region, but he was definitely north of Carlisle. 'We're four short. Two males, two females.'

At that point there was a loud thump from behind Bossman, followed by a low groan. One of the gunmen yanked the drapes away from the 'Welcome' table nearest the main doors, heaving with mostly empty champagne bottles. A familiarly blotto Kenny Collins was dragged out from within, eyes entirely failing to focus through sleep and drink.

Poor Kenny had failed to subvert anyone's memories or expectations, ending up by his early thirties a pathetic if not pitiable fixture around the pubs and street corners of Auchenlea. It didn't really sound adequate to say he was an alcoholic, as that didn't cover the wide spectrum of drugs Kenny was widely known to be using, dealing or cadging at any given time. When he turned up at the coach, Ally was aghast that he'd been invited, and took it to be evidence of either admirable altruism, poor memory or staggering naïvety on the part of their host.

Ally's evasive action in grabbing a seat beside Mrs Laurence had proven partially unnecessary and partially ineffective. Kenny had sat himself down immediately on a free double seat and proceeded to use it as a homebase for forays up and down the vehicle, bothering everybody in turn with dismally incoherent attempts at conversation.

'Aw right? Aw right? Aye, I mind o' you, ya cunt. Fuckin' brilliant. Fuckin' brand new. Mind me? Aye. Aw right? Mind me? Fuckin' brilliant. Any cunt got a spare fag?'

Which was about as interesting as it got. He'd been fairly anonymous throughout the party, remaining obstinately within a short radius of the free bar and choking back a quite valiant number of shots before deciding it was 'a fuckin' celebration' and stumbling off to the front in search of champagne.

'Make that one male and two females,' Bill corrected, as the thoroughly confused Kenny was escorted past him. 'And I'm assuming that's not our man.'

'Fuckin' hauns aff me, ya cunt,' Kenny grunted, belatedly deducing that he was being manhandled. He threw an arm back to ward off his molestor, the effort causing him to trip and fall forward to the floor. Kenny climbed unsteadily to his feet again and turned around, eyeing Bill and Bossman with drunk but concentrated scrutiny.

'Fuck are yous cunts?' he asked. The import of the weapons had clearly failed to register, if he could even see them. Ally feared the worst. ''Sno a fuckin' fancy-dress pairty.'

'Get him out of the way,' Bossman urged testily.

'You fuckin' talkin' tae, ya black bastart?' Kenny challenged. 'You want your go, ya nigger cunt? I'll fuckin' take yous aw, right noo.'

One gun-butt later, he was out cold. Sometimes terrorism did bring its compensations, though it was actually one of the less enthusiastic gubbings Kenny had ever talked his way into.

Gunman Bill unclipped a walkie-talkie from his belt. 'What's the score with the staff headcount?' he asked the man with the list.

'All present apart from two males.'

'Including the guy downstairs?'

'Oh yeah, sorry. That would make it one male unaccounted for.'

Bill raised the radio to his mouth. 'Booth, this is base, come in, over.'

He waited a few seconds then repeated the call. Eventually a screechy hiss came in reply, but Ally couldn't make out the message. Bill continued.

'That stray you retrieved. Please tell me it was staff, and not our Mr Hutchison.'

There was another screech.

'Good man. Out.'

'Right, Bill, so we're missing Mr Hutchison and two women,' Bossman confirmed. 'Well, I suppose it *is* a party. Chances are he's upstairs screwing one or indeed both of them. Okay. I want three men keeping this lot in order and the rest can get on with finding our shy host. I'm going to take the air for a while. I expect Hutchison to be here by the time I get back.'

Ally watched the delegated search party march urgently out of the ballroom, spare clips, knives and radios jangling weightily on belts and bandoliers. *Please tell me*, he thought, remembering what the gunman had said, calculating the horrible logic. Please tell me that stray you retrieved *wasn't* Mr Hutchison? The very man they're looking for?

Good man.

It could only mean that the poor bastard who *had* been

232

'retrieved' was now in a condition that was, well, irretrievable. And as for 'the guy downstairs', it didn't sound too good for him either. Ally didn't know who these men were or what they were up to, but he was damn sure of one thing: this was no posturing, no stand-off. The killing had already begun.

■ 21:18 ■ laguna room 322 ■ true confessions ■

Davie made a light hop on the balls of his feet to position himself just inside the door, a microsecond before it flew open with angry force. The intruder took one determined step inside and was instantly seized, Davie pinning the man's wrist to the small of his back with one hand and placing another just below his nape. He charged forward and slammed the intruder face-first into a wall, unknowingly eradicating Gavin's sole distinction among his St Michael's peers.

'Who are you?' Davie demanded as his captive's face recoiled from the plasterwork.

'Ccchh-gllg . . . I'm Gavin,' he spluttered, his breath ripe with whisky.

'Fuck, so you are,' Davie observed, letting him go and stepping away. Catherine emerged uncertainly from the wardrobe, looking pale despite the make-up.

'Oh for God's sake, hiding in the cupboard,' Gavin mocked, eyeing her with some distaste. 'It's like a bloody sitcom. How could you do this to me?'

'Do what?' she asked.

'And you,' he grumbled, staring dazedly at Davie. 'What

233

the hell do you think you're doing? It's not enough to gatecrash my party, you have to fuck my girlfriend and beat me up as well? Christ, it's not a sitcom: it's a bloody teen movie.'

Davie grabbed him around both shoulders, causing Gavin to flinch and his eyes to close, evidently terrified Davie was about to send the head in.

'No, Gavin,' he told him, sharply but quietly. 'It's something a wee bit more serious than a teen movie. And we cannae have very long before it becomes a snuff movie, so quit babblin' and sober up. We're in a lot of trouble.'

Gavin swayed a little, a tipsily bemused expression on his face. 'What the hell are you on about?'

Davie decided the newcomer hadn't grasped the gravity of the situation. He frog-marched Gavin out to the balcony and stuck his head over the side for half a second, then pulled him back in and sat him down on the edge of the bed. That Gavin began hyperventilating assured Davie he had not failed to notice the gunmen standing guard outside the Laguna's main entrance.

'Wh-who are they? What do they want?'

'Does it matter?' snapped Catherine, having had a little longer than Gavin to assess the situation.

'C-can't you do something?' He looked at Davie, desperation and booze dilating his pupils.

'Like what?'

'Well, I mean, you're . . . aren't you . . . weren't you . . .'

Davie rolled his eyes. 'Aye, Gavin. I'll just nick doonstairs the noo an' kick fuck oot the lot o' them. Just the sound of my name'll have them shitin' it. Get a fuckin' grip.'

'I just thought you'd have had more, more . . . *experience* with this sort of thing than us.'

'No, Gavin, I've the same amount of experience with

terrorists as you: about two fuckin' minutes. If it was half-a-dozen screws comin' in wi' their truncheons raised, then yes, I could give you an object lesson on how to lie on the floor and take a quality doing. But it isnae, so the way I see it, the only thing we can do is stay out of these people's way.'

Gavin nodded eagerly. 'You're right. You're right. Hole up and wait for help. Maybe they don't know we're up here, right?'

A loud ratcheting resounded from the hallway, like two dozen hammers hitting two dozen lumps of wood at once. The three of them exchanged looks in a moment's silence.

'What the fuck was that?' Davie's voice dropped to a whisper, his breathing speeding up by the second.

'I think it was the doorlock override,' Gavin offered, his voice wavering. 'For emergency evacuations. You can unlock every room in the hotel from . . . from the computer downstairs.'

'Is it automatic?'

'What do you mean?'

'Is it triggered automatically – by the fire alarm or anything?'

'No.'

'Then they're comin' to get us. They know we're up here: or at least they know *some*body's up here.'

'Oh God,' Gavin whimpered, lying down on the bed and burying his head in his hands. 'We're going to die.'

'Come on, Gavin, fuck's sake, chin up. You know this place better than I do. We need you thinkin' straight.'

'We're going to die,' he moaned again. Davie tried to pull a hand away from Gavin's head, but he lashed out and squirmed a few feet further along the bed. 'Oh God. Oh Christ, why is this happening?'

235

Davie shook his head disparagingly and looked at Catherine instead. Her eyes were moist with tears, but she was keeping it together.

'Okay, think fast,' he told her. 'We've still got some time. If they knew exactly where we were, they'd be here already, right? What are our options?'

'Well, kill the lights for a start. Bloody homing beacon.'

Davie pulled the card from the NRG-Sava. Gavin let out another quivering howl as darkness engulfed them.

'They're gaunny be lookin' for hidin' places,' Davie said. 'They're gaunny check every room. Is there a way oot o' here apart fae the stairs an' the lifts?'

'There's emergency stairs running down the outside of the hotel at the back and either side.'

'No, we'd be too obvious. Anythin' else? A waste-disposal shaft or somethin'?'

'The laundry chute,' Catherine remembered, her voice rising and taking Davie's hopes up along with it. 'It's at the far end of the corridor, round the corner. It goes all the way down to sub-level three.'

'So that's – Christ – six floors?'

'Seven. Straight down. But it's all we've got, unless you fancy crossing the corridor and jumping out the window: only a hundred feet down to the Cromarty Firth.'

'Well, let's check the chute out first, eh?'

Davie felt himself smile. Christ knew he didn't feel like it, but the faintest glimmer of possibility had always found reflection in his eyes. He was an indefatigable believer in DIY salvation, and having saved himself from himself, saving himself from anyone else could surely never present the same challenge.

'Right, Gavin,' he declared, dragging his ex-schoolmate

236

upright from the bed. 'Dry your eyes or I'll boot your baws.' Gavin gave out a sniff, but he seemed alert. 'Catherine, take him to this chute affair an' start climbin', quiet as you can. I'll be there in a sec.'

'A sec? What are you going to do?'

'Buy us some time. Get goin'.'

Davie checked his watch. It had been two minutes. He had to go. There was other stuff here he could use, but time was more important, and the terrorists might not go for it, anyway. He slotted the keycard back into the NRG-Sava and headed for the patio doors.

Climbing quietly and carefully on to the balcony railing, Davie noticed that one of the gunmen was gone from below, perhaps reassigned to search-party duties. It was unquestionably Gavin they were after. Davie hadn't said anything about it, because the poor bugger was already falling apart in front of him without adding a personal element to the encroaching danger. But whoever these people were, they'd want to talk to the man in charge, and Davie guessed the longer that didn't happen, the better the chances of the cavalry arriving in time.

It was only a four-, maybe five-foot jump to the next balcony, but the forty feet of fuck-all underneath added an unwelcome note of excitement. Davie counted to three and dived across the gap, landing with a palm-grazing tumble on the concrete of the next terrace. He picked himself up and pushed the handle of the patio doors, which remained fastly closed.

'Fuck.' He'd assumed this keycard-override business downstairs would open everything, but he'd forgotten that the sliding panels were on a plain old manual lock. There were a couple of one-time petermates of his who'd be pissing themselves if they could see this, career house-breakers who lapped up tales of burglary incompetence. He decided he wouldn't begrudge them their laughter if he actually lived to tell them the tale.

Two more jumps, two more balconies, one lightly sprained wrist and a bloodily stinging collection of grazes later, he made it to an unlocked portal and charged inside.

As he neared the end of the corridor he failed to spot any kind of hatch for a laundry chute, and he remembered with growing alarm that Catherine had said it was 'round the corner'. His route had taken him three rooms along, so it was possible he was in the wrong hallway altogether. Worse than that, there was a stairwell just a few yards away, and he could hear the sound of footsteps from it, though he couldn't be sure how far above or below they originated.

He looked around again. The door nearest him was marked Private, and lacked the brass fittings that dis-tinguished the residential rooms. It opened to reveal a cupboard packed on one side with cleaning utensils – mops, brushes, buckets – mostly still wrapped in Cellophane, and on the other side sat a blue canvas laundry cart. Right in the centre was the hatch he was looking for, sunk into the wall, four feet back from the door. The shaft itself sat behind a good six inches of concrete, which was why he hadn't heard anything from within. Neither, he hoped, would the pursuers.

Davie climbed inside and pulled the hatch closed behind him, supporting himself by pressing his feet and one hand against the sides. The darkness was total, for which he was grateful. The drop was twice what had been beneath him on the balconies, and this time there were two people for him to hit on the way down. He began his descent very slowly, edging his feet lower by tentative increments and nervously pulling his hands away from the sides, only to replace them quickly each time he felt the sensation of gravity upon his body weight. A yard or so down, his feet encountered one of the braces that held the chute's sections together, and after finding another one the same distance down again, he had the confidence to move more easily, allowing himself to slide until reaching the next indentation. This allowed swifter and more assured progress (admittedly unmeasurable in the dark), the slides soon becoming more like bounces in a pseudo-abseiling descent. He'd therefore built up both a rhythm and a momentum by the time his feet landed on fingers and his exposed groin crunched into the corresponding head.

The obstruction instantly disappeared from beneath him, then he also began to fall, his legs temporarily unable to apply pressure after the blow to his testicles. His arms were forced uselessly above his head by the drop, and he slid for several terrifying yards until power returned to his thighs, upon which he was able to brake with the outsides of his feet. He thumped hard into the next brace and came to a halt there, breathing fast and heavily with fright.

Looking below for further sign of whoever he had struck, he saw only a bright white square at what had to be the bottom of the chute. He granted himself a few more seconds to let his balls recover, then bounced quickly down the final few yards, dropping out on to a soft bed of linen and towels. At the other end of the laundry hopper lay Gavin, semi-conscious and groaning incoherently.

Catherine's face appeared, peering over the side. 'Is he all right?' she asked, keeping her voice low. 'What happened?'

'I think he's just sore and a bit pissed. I landed on his

head comin' doon the shaft. I reckon my balls got the worst of it, but he lost his grip and fell the last couple o' floors.' Gavin gave out a muffled moan, his face half buried in towelling cotton. 'Lucky for him this thing wasnae empty, or he'd have broken his legs. Come to think of it, why isnae it empty? I thought this place wasnae open.'

'I'm sure Gavin's made, ehm, a few overnight stays,' Catherine explained, her cheeks glowing a little, perhaps from her exertions.

'Well, at least he didnae fall into someone *else*'s dirty laundry, eh? Anyway, do you want to gie me a hand gettin' him out?'

Catherine shook her head. 'We might as well leave him be if he's comfortable. We're not going anywhere.'

'What d'you mean?'

'The doors are locked from the outside. I'm sorry. The only way out of here is the way we came in.'

Davie gripped the top of the hopper and pulled himself over the side, dropping to his feet on the floor beside Catherine. The aqua-blue of her dress was streaked with dust, and was ripped around her left shoulder, where a little blood also stained the fine material.

'Thank God for lycra, eh?' she said, acknowledging his concern. 'If I'd gone for a taffeta ballgown I'd be stuck in that chute till doomsday.'

She looked back at Davie's attire, grime and blood-stains smearing his white shirt where he'd been wiping his grazed hands. Both his trouser legs were torn below the knees, and he could consider his new shoes thoroughly 'christened'.

'Don't know how James Bond manages it,' he said.

'At least you kept your tie on,' Catherine observed.

'Forgot I was wearin' it.' He patted at it with one hand

then pulled the thing free. 'Miracle I didnae strangle masel'.' Davie dropped the tie to the floor, which was when he noticed that Catherine was in her bare feet.

'Dropped the shoes and tights down the chute first,' she explained. 'Mother Bridget in RE always said high heels would be the ruination of us St Mick's girls, but I don't think this was the outcome she had in mind. Of course, the bloody things landed in all this laundry, and there was me at the top listening for them hitting the ground, to hear how far down it was. Endless bloody silence. I started wondering whether the chute went right down and opened out into the sea.'

'It must have taken some bottle, goin' first too. You did well.'

'Oh yeah, David, I did great. Led us all into a locked room.' She walked away from the hopper to the heavy double doors, demonstrating with a push that they were locked.

Davie looked around the room. Apart from shelves stacked with clean linen, and a small fleet of laundry carts, there wasn't a lot to the place. 'Where's all the machines?' he asked.

Catherine looked apologetic again. 'This isn't actually a laundry as such,' she said, sitting down deflatedly on the bare floor. Davie squatted beside her, his back to the wall, still scanning the room for possibilities. 'It's a "laundry depot" or "laundry station" or something, I can't remember the term. The resort's got one big central laundry servicing all the hotels; it's on this level somewhere. This place is where the Laguna's dirty stuff is supposed to get sent from and returned to. So the good news is that there are corridors on this deck linking all parts of the resort via the central laundry. The bad news is that the corridor leading

241

from this one starts on the other side of these doors. I've dropped us in it. Literally.'

Davie looked at Catherine as she sat and stared miserably into space. Interrupted upstairs before she could unburden herself, the woman was sure hell-bent on taking the blame for *something* tonight.

'I don't remember anyone else havin' any brilliant suggestions,' he told her. 'We needed a hidin' place and that's what you gave us. Plus, they're less likely to look for us somewhere that's locked from the *oot*side. You kept the heid up there. I'd say I owe you one.'

'No, David.' Her eyes lost their blank glaze and focused sharply upon him. 'I'm about the last person on this earth that you owe anything.'

Catherine turned her head towards the back of the room, glancing at the hopper wherein Gavin lay. There was no sign of him stirring, which Davie considered a mercy for all parties. When the poor bastard did wake up, it would be with a family-size variety pack of headaches. Then he'd remember that they were the least of his worries, and wouldn't that be a fun moment.

She looked back at Davie. 'That night,' she said with a resigned sigh. 'The night of the Easter disco, when you, I mean, when Derek Patterson—'

'Saturday, March 24th 1984. I don't normally have a great memory for dates, but for some reason that one sticks in my mind. That's the night you're talkin' about, isn't it?'

She nodded. Davie smiled, trying to let her know it wasn't sacred ground. He knew what she was going to tell him.

'You were the girl,' he said, saving her the strain. It was a rough enough night already.

242

'You knew?' Her voice was a horrified whisper, her eyes reddening again. 'You always knew?'

Davie took one of her hands in his own, gently shaking his head. 'Not until tonight. I never saw your face. I don't think I even looked. It wasn't a priority at the time.'

'I was so scared,' she whispered. 'I was so, so scared. I was coming back from the toilets and he just appeared from behind and pulled me into the art room. I think I'd knocked him back for a dance; he was in the year above, I didn't even know who he was. He'd some kind of art knife in his hand, and he said he'd cut me if I made any noise. "I'll mark you, hen," he kept saying.' Catherine twisted her expression in an angry parody. '"I'll fuckin' mark your face." Then he began touching me. To this day I don't know how far it would have gone if you hadn't appeared.

'When the two of you started fighting I just ran. I went back to the toilets and locked myself in and sat there crying, for ages. I tried to cry quietly so's no-one would knock on the cubicle asking what was wrong. By the time I came out, everyone was in the car park. There were police cars, an ambulance, God, all the lights. But when I heard what happened, I said nothing. I didn't tell anyone. I was too ashamed.

'There was a policeman and a policewoman came round the classes on the Monday. They split up the girls from the boys and she asked us to come forward at lunchtime if any of us "knew anything" about what happened on the Saturday night. They were looking for someone to back up your story, and presumably Derek Patterson wasn't going to own up to his part. But I couldn't come forward. I didn't want anybody to know what had happened to me, what he'd done. I'm sorry, I'm so sorry.'

Catherine wiped away her tears, sniffing a little. 'As

243

time went on, every time I heard or read about what was happening to you, I always felt so guilty. You'd barely turned sixteen by that night, and maybe you wouldn't have ended up on that . . . downward spiral if, if . . .'

She ran out of words, sighing, closing her eyes. When she opened them again she was looking away. Davie felt banjoed by the sheer weight of what she'd been carrying around with her all this time. He watched her blink away more tears, then reached into his pocket for a paper hanky.

Seek no absolution: his penance and his protector; his pain and his strength; and, most of all, his guide. But still, it didn't say anything about dishing it out. The very least she deserved was the truth, the substance of which forced out a small laugh.

'What?' she asked.

'I think you must have gone aboot school wi' your eyes shut, Catherine,' he told her. 'Do you no' remember who I was? The way you're talkin', it sounds like some storybook act of chivalrous gallantry, for which the hero was unjustly imprisoned. It wasnae. I was a fuckin' nutcase, an absolute class-A bam. I was on aboot ten last warnin's fae the polis an' the panel an' everybody else by the time that happened. An' if I hadnae been sent away for that, then it would have been for somethin' else no' long after.

'Get this straight: I wasnae comin' to your rescue that night. I was in the art room because I was bored o' the disco an' I was lookin' for glue to sniff. When Deek dragged you in, I didnae see your face, because all I needed to see was an excuse. Bang: you were my maw, he was my da, if you want some cheap retro-psychology. I just waded in. You'd nothin' to do wi' it.'

Catherine looked even less sure of herself, but that was

understandable: he'd thieved her sackcloth, so now she was naked. She tried to steal some back.

'But you must have hated me – hated whoever the girl was.'

'Oh Christ, aye. Fuckin' bitch. This was what I got for tryin' to help somebody. If I'd just left that lassie tae her fate, nane o' this other shite would've happened. All that stuff. Loads o' that stuff. Damn right I hated whoever she was – it was a big comfort to have somebody else to blame for everythin'. Better that than if I'd got sent away just for hammerin' some poor bastard who never deserved it.'

Davie shifted position on the floor, turning to face her more directly.

'See, the biggest fuck-ups you meet inside are the guys who cannae stop hangin' on to one wee thing that wasnae their fault, one wee thing that they think, if it hadnae been for that, everythin' would be different. "If that tube had just minded his ain fuckin' business, I'd never have ended up glassin' him, an' I wouldnae be in here." Because no matter how long or short you're inside for, you never really get out – up here, I mean – until you cut all that shite loose.

'I did terrible things, Catherine, believe me. Inside an' out. I tortured people. I mutilated people. I inflicted damage an' pain like it was a fuckin' religion. I could've improvised a lethal weapon oot a bag o' marshmallows if it was the only thing to hand. That's who I was; and I know that that's who I still am and always will be. But the difference now is that I can choose not to do those things, a choice I couldnae make until I'd accepted that the person makin' it was me. I could blame the prison system for a lot of it – an' I still do blame the fuckin' prison system for a lot of it – but it had to be *me* that changed. Otherwise I'd still be there, in

245

the endless circle of gettin' fucked by it, retaliatin', then gettin' fucked again.'

Catherine squeezed his hand. 'I feel kind of daft now,' she said. 'But it's been with me for so long. Now and then I'd forget about it, but something would always bring it back, so when this reunion thing came along . . .'

He returned the squeeze. 'Cut it loose,' he told her. 'Cut all the shite loose.'

She nodded, even managing half a smile.

'Okay. Consider it cut.'

'Good. Now all you need to worry aboot is gettin' oot o' this place alive.'

■ 21:44 ■ laguna hotel ■ hunt the cunt ■

This stuff went all the way back to his schooldays, he knew. He'd never been able to shake it off, it had always transmogrified itself to become part of whatever he was doing; in fact, when he looked back now, he saw that it had probably *dictated* what he was doing. Since he was eleven years old, William Connor had been striving to impress Finlay Dawson. The stupidest thing was that he didn't even fucking like him.

He and Dawson had met at Craiglethen College, south of Edinburgh, where mere alphabetical juxtaposition threw them together in their first class, seating Connor, last of the Cs, at a double desk next to Dawson, first of the Ds. It was as arbitrary as that. Very few of the boys knew each other, so for the eternity of that first morning, the person you'd been plonked beside was the only one you could talk to.

Dawson was probably as lost and apprehensive as everyone else, but Connor found himself looking up to him almost immediately. He always had just that little bit more: a few centimetres taller, a few months older; he was a boarder while Connor was a day-boy; his father was a colonel while Connor's was a farmer; he'd been to Murrayfield while Connor had only been to the Melrose Sevens.

Thus began the unfulfilled life-long quest for his approval.

Connor made schoolmates that he got on better with, that he had a better laugh with, but if anyone asked who his best friend was, he'd have told them Dawson, even though he knew Dawson was unlikely to give a reciprocal answer. It wasn't that Dawson had better friends; more that Dawson wouldn't have a 'best friend' anyway. He was always very self-sufficient and even slightly aloof, which in retrospect Connor could see made his endorsement all the more desirable. It was also, however, eternally unobtainable.

In later years he heard someone say of Dawson's haughtiness, 'If he hasn't eaten it, he's fucked it', but that expression usually carried the inference that the subject was lying. In Connor's experience, Dawson had always been hard to impress because he usually *did* have something that beat your hand. For instance, when Connor finally persuaded his parents to buy him a Chopper like Dawson's, with its nifty three-speed stickshift in the middle, he returned after the summer to find that Dawson had moved on to a racer, with drop-handlebars and a *ten*-speed lever-gear system.

And, of course, when it came to their shared fascination with and ambition of soldiery, Dawson, with his family's military background, was always at an advantage. Connor owned a Dinky model of a Chieftain tank; Dawson had been *inside* a Chieftain tank. Connor had been to the Imperial War Museum; Dawson's house *was* the Imperial War Museum.

Even on the rare occasions when he was bested, Dawson had a way of making you feel that the things you were good at mattered less than the things *he* was good at. Connor may have won the mile race, but it was the sprint that was the big one. Connor might be better at the javelin, but the discus, well, that was the event that took *real* skill.

Military life had been much the same. As things worked out, they didn't see that much of each other down the years, but when their paths did cross, Dawson was always that rank higher; his unit had always seen that bit more action. Then when later they both turned mercenary, Dawson always seemed to be making that bit more money, operating that bit higher up the chain.

Christ, he thought, here he'd been, all his days, trying to measure up to this indifferent cypher, in whose presence he felt instantly inadequate. It was pathetic. He reflected that if he became a billionaire and he found Dawson rotting in a gutter, he'd probably start wondering why he'd never had the vision or the balls to throw away all the pressures and trappings for the free life of a tramp.

When Connor decided to put together his own outfit, harvesting some of the respect his career and abilities had sown among his peers, there was an excruciating inevitability that Dawson should turn out to be his first employer: that one bloody place above him again. It also seemed inevitable that things wouldn't go to plan, the way you were bound to have your worst game on the rugby field the one day your girlfriend came along to watch. For that reason he should have passed on the job, spared himself the grief and waited until he had the right personnel before tendering for any business.

Nonetheless, there were bigger reasons why he couldn't refuse, not least the huge payout that was up for grabs at a time when start-up capital would come in very handy indeed. There was also the low-risk factor – unsuspecting, unarmed civilians; isolated location; limited response options – ideal for a debut outing. (This was countered ever so slightly by the operation being criminal rather than military, but that was an issue of morality, not logistics.)

However, the most irresistible reason was, quite simply, that Dawson needed him. No matter what shine he wanted to put on it, or how patronising he would doubtless act, for once Dawson couldn't do without Connor, and the self-satisfied bastard knew that. Since the old sheik snuffed it and the new regime turfed him out, Dawson had found himself at a bit of a loose end, having been effectively off-the-market for such a long time. So when some dodgy associate of Dawson's threw him the floating-resort scenario (in exchange, no doubt, for a reflective slice of the proceeds), he knew his next alternative pay-packet could well be a long way off: short notice or not, he had to grasp the opportunity. And to do that, he needed the help of his old school chum, William Connor.

This morning's fiasco had been everything he feared, presided over infuriatingly by Dawson's practised look of laboured, pitying tolerance. However, since then, Connor had delivered a smooth and ordered operation, the pieces slotting into place seamlessly and on schedule. The set-up was necessarily more streamlined on account of the various personnel they had lost, but, if anything, he felt it was running more efficiently as a result. In the field it was

249

often the case that the less room there was for mistakes, the less you tended to make them.

Dawson could have little reason for complaint.

Primary incursion: undetected and bang on schedule. Communications rendered inoperable, telephone links under control.

Secondary incursion: undetected and bang on schedule. Defensive rocket teams in position. Watch details deployed. Elevators and alarm systems deactivated. Even the inevitable rogue factor – a stray member of staff spotting Booth in Hotel B – had been dealt with cleanly and without raising alarm.

Assault on ballroom: hostages brought swiftly under control, no casualties, bang on schedule. The only blemish (literally) had been that bloke in the air vent puking on him, but compared to what Connor had already been soaked in that day, it wasn't worth getting too upset about. He'd been obliged to give the guy a bit of a going over, *pour encourager les autres*, but decided to cut it short when that woman intervened, mainly because he didn't want Dawson thinking he'd lost his cool.

The fact that there were still a few civvies unaccounted for at that stage was nothing to be alarmed about: they couldn't have expected absolutely everyone to be conveniently assembled in the ballroom when they made their move. That one of the strays happened to be Hutchison was unfortunate, but hardly a crippling setback. They'd get him soon enough. Everything was under control.

Dawson's announcement that he was going for a walk was a typical piece of pantomime. Connor had delivered on everything else, so the prick had to make a big deal about the one little detail that wasn't quite there – *yet*. But it would be. Damn right it would be.

250

Connor decided to lead the search himself, determined that they should get a result before Dawson came back from 'taking the air'. The pompous bastard might be wearing a ski-mask, but Connor knew he would still be able to read that can't-you-get-anything-right expression in his eyes if Hutchison was still missing when he returned.

He put Jackson in charge of the hostages: given Acks' earlier reservations, it was the best way of ensuring the situation in the ballroom stayed calm and stable. If the other two monkeys started fucking around with the prisoners, Jackson would rip them a new one.

Connor deployed sentries on each stairway, then divided the rest of the men into two units: one would start from the bottom, the other from the top. He reminded them that stealth was still a consideration, because if their target was several floors up, he might not have heard the gunfire and could be blissfully unaware of what was going on below. Very blissfully, if Dawson had guessed right about what Hutchison might be up to. There was even a chance, in that case, that when they overrode the doorlock system, it would bring Hutchison downstairs of his own accord, to investigate what was going on. However, realistically he might also be cowering in a cupboard, so the orders were to comb every inch.

Connor's team worked from the top, Gaghen's from the bottom. The computer had said Hutchison was quartered in the Orchid suite, so Connor started there. No booting-down-doors stuff: they quietly turned the handle and moved rapidly inside. The bed hadn't been slept in – or indeed anything else. Connor looked underneath it while Dobson went through the walk-in wardrobe and Pettifer checked the terrace. Dobson climbed on a chair to remove one of the ceiling tiles, then Pettifer gave him a leg-up to

251

investigate whether anyone was hiding in the cavity above. Still no joy. Satisfied that it was empty, Connor pulled them out and they began repeating the drill methodically, suite by suite.

They laboriously swept four of the bloody things without finding so much as a fugitive midge, all the time Connor glancing anxiously at his watch. Then he got a call from Jardine, who was posted outside the Laguna's front entrance, to say that he'd noticed lights on in one of the rooms. Connor ordered his own men to continue their systematic search, then headed downstairs to meet Gaghen, Quinn and McIntosh on the third floor.

Jardine described the location relative to the central stairway ('fourth balcony to the left'), so that they were sure they had the right room. The four of them moved along the corridor in near-silence, barely the clink of a belt-clip to be heard as they delicately cushioned their footfalls. Quinn and McIntosh took position either side of the prescribed door, from beyond which they could hear nothing. Gaghen looked to Connor for a signal. He gave the nod. Gaghen gripped the handle and quickly turned it, throwing the door to the wall and charging inside. His speed meant he'd gone four or five feet before they noticed that the room was in complete darkness.

Connor closed his eyes, took a long, deep breath and counted to ten before reaching for his radio.

'Jardine, is that light still on?'

'Yes sir. Fourth on the left from the centre. Hasn't changed.'

'And would that be your left looking in, or our left looking out?'

'Ooh. Sorry. I assumed that—'

'Shut up.'

Swiftly, silently, *again*, they made their way back along the corridor and took up position outside the corresponding door. Room 322. Again, Quinn and McIntosh took position either side. Again, Gaghen looked for the nod. Again, Connor gave it. Again, Gaghen gripped the handle. The next bit was different this time.

Gaghen began shuddering and trembling, like there was an earthquake and he was the only one feeling it. Connor was about to tell him it was no time for taking the piss, when he noticed the buzzing sound and the smell of burning. Gaghen's face was contorted into a soundless scream, his eyeballs vibrating in his head.

'Jesus!'

Connor shouldered him, but Gaghen's hand remained immovably clasped to the metal handle. Quinn then tried to grab him, but leaped back as the current ripped through him too. In the end, it took two of them rushing Gaghen at once to dislodge him, all three tumbling untidily to the floor in the tight corridor. Connor rolled away from the tangle and looked down. Gaghen was still jerking a little, but there was little doubt that he was dead. Connor climbed to his feet and took firm hold of his Ingram's.

'FUCKING BASTARD!' he bellowed, peppering the handle with rounds until the clip was empty. Then he kicked the door with all his anger and strength, but to his further frustration, it refused to budge.

'He's fucking barricaded himself in,' he spat.

Connor kicked open the next door along and stomped inside, heading straight for the balcony. Once out there, he slapped a new clip into the breech and slid the bolt, before diving across the gap to the adjacent terrace. He landed with an expert roll that took him back up to his knees, from where he opened fire on the sliding doors, aiming upwards into the ceiling inside. The glass shattered and rained down in thousands of tiny fragments, tinkling on the concrete along with his ejected shells.

He marched through the empty frame. Room 322 looked like it had been tipped on its side, with most of its contents ending up piled against the front door: mattresses, the dressing table, even the television, its flex ripped away. He could see the missing cable also, plugged into the mains at a socket two feet outside the bathroom. The wire disappeared behind the furniture blockade, where presumably it was connected to the door handle.

It certainly beat the shit out of a Do Not Disturb sign.

Connor picked the television off the pile and threw it against the wall with an accompanying scream. He had to spend his rage, had to restore focus. He'd lost one of his best men, a friend too, but the time for emotion was not now. Nonetheless, harsher tactics were definitely called for. This bastard Hutchison was smart. He knew what was going down, and he'd made it plain by killing one of Connor's men. Well, *he* could play dirty too. Enough of this stealth-and-restraint shit.

He tore the offending flex from the wall and began furiously dismantling the barricade, casting its components behind him with further growls of strain and anger until the doorway was cleared.

'Resume your search,' he ordered Quinn and McIntosh. 'We need Hutchison alive, but remember, the cunt doesn't need kneecaps to be able to talk.'

'Yes sir.'

Connor bounded down the stairs several at a time, heading back to the ballroom. A resort like this would have an extensive PA system, he reasoned. Well, it was time for an announcement. 'Hi de fucking hi, campers. Here's the rules of tonight's party game. The redcoats are going to execute one hostage every five minutes until Mr Gavin Hutchison does the right thing and crawls out of the woodwork.'

In fact, the chief redcoat was going to execute the first one right away, partly to let Hutchison know this wasn't a bluff, and partly to teach him the dangers of messing about with electricity.

He rounded the foot of the last flight and crossed the floor of the lobby. This was what he should have done the minute they realised Hutchison was missing. For a job like this, he had to think less like a soldier and more like a criminal. Never mind all this running around, the best thing was to keep it simple. You put a gun to a hostage's head and you get what you want. What could possibly go wrong with that?

Connor unholstered his pistol, threw open the double doors dramatically and strode into the ballroom.

Unfortunately, there were no longer any hostages in it.

■ **21:52** ■ **laguna ballroom** ■ **fuck this for** ■

Jackson looked upon his new 'unit' with a perverse satisfaction as they readied themselves to move the hostages out: a less likely bunch he'd never seen, but he felt more like a soldier among them than he had among the last shower. McQuade, O'Neill, McKenzie, Potter. Frocks, dress-shirts, hairspray and Uzis. They looked awkward, clumsy and scared out of their minds, but as a CO of his once said, 'Show me a troop who's not scared and I'll show you a liability who doesn't appreciate what he's up against.'

Jackson knew they were outnumbered, outgunned and untrained, but he also knew that he'd rather fall with these people than stand with Connor's scum. This was about more than life or death. This was about who he was and who he'd been.

He was a mercenary, a hired gun. Other people's dirty work a speciality. Fighting fights that weren't his, often in countries he'd barely heard of a fortnight before he was waist-deep in their bloody conflicts.

He'd always told himself he had ethics, always told himself he was on the side of the good guys. He didn't simply fight for whoever paid the highest: he fought to establish democratic regimes, or to restore them, or to defend them. And he justified the acts he committed with the belief that he was saving the world from men far worse than himself. But in truth the sum of it all had just been a big pile of bodies. Toppling one tinpot dictator to replace him with another; putting down insurgence only for it to rise somewhere else, like air bubbles on wallpaper. He hadn't saved the world from anybody, least of all himself.

It was long since time to grow up. That was why he'd accepted Connor's offer in the first place: as a way out. Grab a decent chunk of change so he could find something better to do with his life, and not get sucked back into the next shithole that decided to have itself a civil war. The illegality wouldn't bother him, he'd reckoned. After the things he'd 'legally' done in conflict, it was hard to imagine shedding a tear over a few spoiled businessmen getting ripped off for money that they'd claim back from their insurers anyway. But he knew now: tears would be shed over the kid Connor blew away downstairs, tears would be shed over the poor bastard Booth had taken out, and tears would be shed over however many others these trigger-happy psychos deemed expendable.

He'd looked at the two pricks guarding the ballroom with him, two ex-paramilitaries for whom punishment beatings and rubbing out rival drug dealers hadn't proven a satisfactory replacement for the excitement of the glory days. There they were, happy as Larry, once again doing what they did best: pointing guns at unarmed victims and getting off on the power.

Carrion fowl. Men of violence who'd be fucked in a world without war.

At the start of every armed struggle there was a time when, with a heavy heart, men of conscience reasoned that they had fruitlessly exhausted their peaceful and democratic options, and had therefore no option but to take up arms in pursuit of what they saw as justice. Once the battle had been going on for twenty-odd years, however, it was difficult to imagine everyone who picked up a gun going through the same tortuous ideological maze as their forebears. Most simply grew up indoctrinated, and their only question was 'Who do you want me to kill?'

Jackson had encountered their kind around every festering conflict on the planet, Belfast to Bosnia: vicious little bastards who'd be no-marks in a normal world, stuck doing a shit job for shit money like the poor sap they grew up next door to. But as 'paramilitaries' or 'freedom fighters' they got kudos, they got respect, and best of all, they got to run around with a rifle, shooting people, blowing things up and generally kidding on they were James Bond. Whatever those men of conscience had been seeking all those years back was now irrelevant, if it was even remembered. For the carrion fowl, this wasn't a struggle, it was a way of life.

The so-called 'adventurers' were made of much the same stuff, they just grew up in a different neighbourhood. Psychopaths with little or no military training, who went travelling in search of war because there wasn't one at home. They were poorly paid – usually the same as whatever the local grunts were getting – because their employers knew they weren't in it for the money: they only wanted the opportunity to kill people.

But Jackson detested the carrion fowl far more, because for men who liked to call themselves soldiers, they tended to be extremely shy of a fair fight. From Omagh to Warrington to Lockerbie to the Valley of the Kings, it seemed the principal criterion denoting a 'legitimate target' was the target's inability to retaliate. The cunts wanted to play the game, but they didn't fancy playing it toe-to-toe.

And now here he was, standing shoulder-to-shoulder with them, facing a room full of terrified hostages. He'd come all this way, all these years, to end up pointing a gun at some defenceless fucker's head and saying 'Gimme all your money'.

No ideological hair-splitting could colour this conflict: tonight he was on the side of the bad guys. And if he was one of the bad guys tonight, then maybe that was who he'd always been. Not a soldier, not a professional, just a thug who killed for coin.

Well, as Aristotle put it, 'To do is to be'; and more to the point, as Zappa put it, 'You are what you is'. It was time to define himself. As soon as the search teams were safely departed, he reattached the suppressor to his Nagan and called his fellow guards towards him.

'What's that phrase you boys use? Oh yeah. Nothing personal,' he said, then shot both of them through the middle of the forehead.

Sorry, guys, but once you're in the game, you're in the game.

There were gasps of shock from the floor, and one woman began screaming.

'Christ's sake, shut her up or she's gonna get us all killed,' he said stiffly, pulling off his ski-mask. The man beside her, presumably her husband, stared back helplessly as she filled her lungs for another volley. 'I'm on your side,' Jackson explained, by which time the woman next to her had covered her mouth with a hand and was telling her to calm down. Jackson gave her a thumbs-up.

He then pointed at the bloke who'd fallen through the ceiling. 'What's your name, mate?'

'Ally. McQuade.'

'Well, you looked like you had some initiative earlier on, and I'm gonna need a bit of help. Grab that guy's Uzi. There'll be a handgun on him, too. Get that and whatever ammo he's carrying.'

McQuade looked a little startled, but he nodded and moved off towards the indicated corpse.

'Anyone here got any combat training?' Jackson asked. It was worth a shot. 'TA, anything.' No response. 'Paint-balling? Clay pigeons?' Still nothing. Jesus. He looked to McQuade. 'Who can I rely on?'

McQuade swallowed. 'Charlie,' he said, pointing towards the bloke who'd helped him after Connor beat him up. He'd have been Jackson's first choice, anyway: he looked ballsy, alert and fit as a butcher's dog.

'You up for this?' Jackson asked him.

He got to his feet. 'Aye. And I'll see *you* later,' he told McQuade.

'Good man,' Jackson said. 'What's your surname?'

'O'Neill.'

He indicated the other body. 'Get yourself tooled up, O'Neill. We're gettin' out of here.'

Jackson surveyed the floor again. The clock was ticking, no time to work out who among them could best handle this. He looked to the woman who'd shut up the screamer – she'd been ahead of the game then, so she was as good a shout as anyone. She nodded back nervously once he'd caught her eye, then stood up and walked forward.

'What's your name?'

'Lisa McKenzie.'

'I'm Jackson. McQuade, give her your handgun and any spare clips.'

McKenzie walked across to where McQuade still squat-ted, pulling items from the dead guard's belt. He handed her the Beretta, gripping it by the barrel, which Jackson took to be an encouraging sign: at least he knew which end the bullets came out. McQuade then passed her the three clips he'd been able to find. Having no pockets in her dress, she slipped them into her evening bag and slung it over her shoulder.

'There's one more gun, so might as well have one more volunteer,' Jackson announced. He walked closer to the huddle of resort staff. 'Who here knows the layout of this place?'

An unsure hand went up, some teenager who looked barely old enough to be legally in work. Jackson thought of the kid downstairs, with his roaches and his pin-ups. At least this one would get the chance to shoot back.

'I don't know it well, like,' he ventured. 'I've just takken a few walks aboot the place.' Jackson recognised the Makkem accent with a smile.

'What's your name, son?'

'Potter. Jamie Potter.'

260

'O'Neill, give Potter that pistol. Maybe there's someone from Sunderland who can get his shots on target.'

Jackson checked his watch, estimating he could allow himself all of ninety seconds for basic weapons training. Tactical tutorials he'd have to carry out on the move.

'Are you . . . an undercover agent or something?' McQuade asked.

'No, I'm just a bad guy havin' a crisis of conscience. Keep your fingers crossed it doesn't wear off.'

'So what's this all about?'

'Later. Right now we've got to get everybody out of this place before the search parties get back. McKenzie, O'Neill, get everybody lined up two-by-two, we're goin' out the side door there. Do you both know how to use those things?'

'This is the safety here, right?' McKenzie said, correctly indicating the switch.

'Yeah,' Jackson confirmed, taking the gun from her. 'Potter, you watch this too. When your clip's empty, you press this release, slam the new one in, then pull back here. McQuade and O'Neill, I want you holding those things with both hands at all times. I know you've seen guys firin' them one-handed in the movies, but believe me, that's the magic of Hollywood. If you tried it, the recoil would have you shootin' into the ceilin' after about three rounds.'

'What do you do if it jams?' asked McQuade.

'Pray that your partner's doesn't. Potter, we can't go near the front, so where can we get to from here?'

'There's lifeboats at the back of the hotel on this level.'

'No good. There's look-out teams at the north-east and south-west corners.'

'Aye, but if we're already away—'

'They're armed with rocket launchers. They might even have worked out how to use them. We need somewhere

261

we can make a stand. Elevated position, good lines of sight, with access channels we can control.'

Potter looked blank.

'All right, I'll settle for whatever's the furthest point on the rig from here.'

'The Carlton, then. It's the hotel at the north-western corner. There's no electricity there, though.'

'It'll do. If they can't see us, that makes us harder to shoot. Can you get us there?'

'Aye.'

'I mean, without using the surface level? Without going outside?'

'Aye.'

'Good man. All right, listen up. McQuade: you, me and Potter will take the front. O'Neill and McKenzie, you guard the group from the rear. Everybody else, keep your mouths closed, your feet moving and your eyes open. Let's go.'

■ 21:55 ■ fipr ■ a game of soldiers ■

Ally was glad he'd nothing left to puke. The Uzi was heavy in his hands as he ran, a solid weight of cold steel and responsibility. Seeing Jackson alongside him should have been a reassurance, but in fact it only made him feel worse, as the soldier's expertise thickly underlined how little Ally knew what he was doing. As soon as they'd got out of the ballroom's side door, for instance, Jackson had waved him and Potter ahead while he crouched in front of the exiting group, covering them against anyone appearing in the corridor that led back to the lobby. He'd made it to the front again by the time Ally and Potter reached the stairs, where he nipped nimbly through the door first, pointing his machine gun up then down the stairwell in a blink of the eye. After that he'd practically glided to the level below, and signalled that they were clear to follow. They descended again to sub-level two, where Potter said there was a staff access-corridor linking the Laguna's lower reaches to the central entertainment complex.

Every corner threatened Ally with the dry heaves, as it seemed the more of them they turned without meeting confrontation, the greater the likelihood that it would be found around the next one. The drill was becoming no less terrifying for its increasing familiarity: he and Jackson approached ahead of the group, Ally crouching on the floor tight to the wall; then after a silent, gestured count of three, Ally would stick his head and his gun around the bend to provide potential covering fire, while the big man dived across the gap and righted himself into a kneeling position on the other side. After that they'd signal Potter to bring the party forward; or rather, Jackson would, while Ally gave himself CPR.

'You're doing all right, McQuade,' Jackson assured him, presumably when he was looking particularly liable to barf up his actual stomach now that its contents were all gone.

'What's the plan?' Ally ventured to whisper, breathing out again after another bend mercifully failed to yield a firefight.

'Plan?' Jackson replied, his voice a low burr. 'We get to the Carlton, we barricade ourselves in, we shoot anyone we don't recognise and we hope they run out of bullets first.'

Ally swallowed. He was hoping for something a little more Jerry Bruckheimer and a little less *Zulu*. He knew

263

Michael Caine's mob won that one in the end, but doubted tonight's assailants would be as likely to retreat in tribute to their opponents' bravery.

'That's *it*?'

'So far, yeah. Unless you had some scheme in mind for once you'd finished ferretin' through the ventilation ducts?'

'Well, can't we try and contact the police or somebody?'

'Telephone transponder and radio transmitter have been disabled.'

'How do you know?'

'I helped disable them.'

'Oh. What about your radio?'

'The range is too short. It operates on a limited frequency too, so the cops can't hear us. Outside contact was something we took great pains to prevent. It's unfortunately one of the few things we actually pulled off tonight.'

They got to their feet as Potter caught up again. According to him, the staff access-corridor was dead ahead.

'So what is this about?' Ally asked.

'What do you think?'

Ally remembered the mix of accents: Irish, Scots, English; there might even have been a Yank. Politics could make for strange and varied bedfellows, terrorist politics more so, but for *that* perverse an orgy, there could be only one lubricant.

'Money.'

'Correct.'

'How?'

'The usual. Give us some or we'll blow your head off.'

'Gavin?'

'All of you. But it's his show, so all the transfers were to go

264

through him and thence to the time-honoured unnumbered offshore account.'

Ally didn't quite follow the technicalities, but the principle was familiar enough.

'That's all this is about? Fuckin' robbery?'

'Extortion, technically, but yes.'

'Christ, if I'd known Gavin was worth that much I'd have mugged him myself,' he muttered. Jackson gave him a look he couldn't quite read, but he looked away before Ally could enquire further.

The access corridor was unlit, smelled strongly of gloss paint and was only wide enough to travel one-abreast. Jackson went first, pointing a small torch, Potter next, blocking Ally from what little light the beam spared. Behind Ally the rest of the group were filing in and along as fast as they could, hand-to-shoulder, enveloped completely in darkness. It felt like walking down the barrel of a gun. Fifty-odd people crammed into a tight passage with no idea whether there were killers waiting for them at the end. Tactically speaking, Jackson said, it was Russian roulette: nothing to worry about if the chamber's empty, but no getting out of the way if it's not.

Potter recommended that they keep going past the first door they reached, which accessed the multiplex ('a bloody rabbit warren'), and take the next one, into the bowling lanes. Ally didn't fancy extending this march through the blackness, but as the latter route sounded like it would involve fewer corners, he counted his blessings when Jackson opted for it.

Once through the door, Jackson handed Potter the torch and told him to find some lights: 'The bare minimum – we don't want it to look like bloody Blackpool.'

Ally watched the beam bob away along one wall, leaving

265

them in darkness as the rest of the group began to spill one-by-one from the door. Potter flicked a switch somewhere and a row of lamps came on at the front of the hall, above some of the pool and air-hockey tables, on-hand to gobble your change while you waited for a lane. Jackson signalled that it was enough and Potter returned. The three of them stood to one side as they waited for the whole party to reassemble intact before progressing further.

Jackson looked darkly at Potter. 'There's something you should know, lad,' he said in a low, hoarse tone. 'Those two blokes missing from the staff head count – they're dead.'

Potter nodded solemnly. It didn't look like it had come as a huge surprise, but Ally suspected few things would tonight.

'Who were they?' Jackson asked. 'Did you know them?'

Potter nodded again. Even in the half-light Ally could see tears glistening. 'Stevie Grant. He was same as me – just here for the summer, skeleton staff, like. Christ. Stevie.' He swallowed. 'And Mr Vale, the security bloke.'

'Security guard?'

'No, he's – was – some sort o' consultant. I didn't know him, meself. I knew Steve, though. Steve was a mate.'

Jackson put a hand on Potter's shoulder. 'I'm sorry to lay this stuff on you, lad, but it's best that you know now, so that if you get any of these shitehawks in your sights, you won't have any little moral dilemmas about pullin' the trigger.'

Potter nodded, wiping his eyes. 'Who are they?' he asked with a sniff.

Jackson sighed. 'Oh, a real advert for the human race. Mercenaries, thugs, what you call "adventurers". The couple I bagged back there were ex-terrorists. IRA or UVF, I don't even know. They're all the fuckin' same under the balaclavas: vicious little cunts who like shootin' people. Their excuse used to be politics. Tonight it's money.'

'And who are you?'

'Don't ask, lad. Don't ask.'

Jackson shook his head and looked behind, to where Eddie Milton and Allan Crossland were emerging from the access corridor, bearing the unconscious figure of Kenny Collins. Eddie had his torso, Allan his legs, and Ally realised they must have carried him like that all the way from the ballroom.

Eddie shook his head as he caught Ally's eye. 'Never even liked the cunt an' here I am savin' his life,' he said. 'Bet he's no' even fuckin' grateful.'

'Aye,' Ally replied, 'but think of all the people who love him.'

Eddie stared back sternly. 'I'm tryin'. I'll gie you a shout if I come up wi' wan.'

Lisa McKenzie and Charlie O'Neill appeared finally at the rear, at which point Ally feared the insanity of the evening had begun to infect his perception: each of them was starting to appear less incongruous holding a gun. Charlie had his sleeves rolled up, Uzi cradled in his muscular arms, steely expression, close-cropped bullet-head: Ed Harris, *The Rock*. Lisa, party dress, pretty face, evening bag, hand-cannon: Ann Parrilaud, *Nikita*. Ally didn't feel he merited an equivalent comparison. He was wearing a white shirt but he suspected it might as well be a red jumper. He even had the poignant, all-to-live-for, baby-on-the-way back-story, and was grateful that he hadn't shared that with anyone yet, as it invariably sentenced you to a bullet in the next reel.

All present and correct, Jackson gave the signal to get moving again. They headed to the doors through a seated

267

snackbar area that overlooked the polished, unused lanes. The smell of wood varnish would have had Ally hallucinating if things weren't mental enough already. All around, the floorspace was cluttered with polythene-wrapped bundles of skittles, and larger, moulded-cardboard pallets of brand-new bowling balls, like enormous egg-boxes.

Potter guided them along a tiled corridor lined with empty shopfronts, familiar names on many of the signs above the doors. Obviously Gavin was the expert when it came to resorts and all that, but Ally couldn't help wondering if he'd ever heard the phrase 'getting away from it all'. This place would be like going on your holidays to the St Enoch's Centre. He imagined how hilarious Annette would have found the place, then put the brakes on the thought. When he pictured her face, it drove home everything he had to lose, and everything she had to lose too. Images of his pregnant fiancée standing by his graveside were not constructive. He had to keep her out of his head, and concentrate solely on the matters at hand.

'By the way,' he therefore asked Jackson, 'why *have* they got rocket launchers?'

'Emergency measure. Part of the contingency if the authorities find out what's going on. They're for taking pot-shots at anything that comes near this place, air or sea, to deter attempts at intervention. After that, it would be a matter of negotiating hostages' lives for a helicopter out of here.'

'But that's Plan B.'

'Yeah. Plan A was – is – to get in an' out of here without anyone knowin' about it. That's apart from you lot, who can't contact the mainland and aren't due to be picked up until tomorrow morning, by which time the bad guys – who you can't describe because they were wearing ski-masks – will be long gone.'

'Sounds like the better bet. I'm no' sure you could negotiate a helicopter against a bunch o' scrotes fae Auchenlea. Be lucky to get a rowin' boat.'

Again, Jackson gave him that quizzical look. 'What?'

'Just a joke.'

After that they had to negotiate another blind chicane along a second access corridor. The good news this time was that it was only about half as long. The bad news was that there were no lights to switch on at the end of it, Potter having been right about the Carlton's lack of electricity. There was, however, a staircase only a few yards away from the exit, flanked by windows that looked out the back of the structure, over the water. The pale glow of the moon somewhere above seemed ample illumination after such total blackness. Ally reckoned that if he could see his own pupils, he'd look like Betty Boop.

According to Potter, half of the top floor was taken up by an open area earmarked for a restaurant, as opposed to the standard warren of rooms and corridors. Jackson decided they would make their stand up there. Ally didn't imagine this was well received by the Kenny-bearers, but no-one was in much mood for dissent. Up they climbed.

'What's Auchenlea, by the way?' Jackson asked, his voice rising above a whisper for the first time since the bowling rink. 'Is that the name of your company?'

'Eh? Naw, it's where we're all from,' Ally told him. 'Just ootside Paisley.'

'*All* of you are from there?'

'Originally, aye. This was a school reunion, remember. Until you lot fronted up.'

'This was a *what*?' Jackson hissed, stopping dead.

'A school reunion. St Michael's Auchenlea. It's where we all know Gavin Hutchison from, although nobody seems to

269

remember much aboot him. Christ, they'll no' forget him efter this, right enough.'

Jackson began moving again, now aware that the whole group froze every time he hesitated. 'Wait a minute, let me get this straight,' he said. 'This is a school reunion?'

'Aye, how many times—'

'Not a hospitality junket for investors in the floating-resort project?'

'Whit?'

'And you're not all wealthy venture-capitalists, here to be entertained while you greenlight the electronic transfer of investment funds to Gavin Hutchison's company?'

'Eh, not that I'm aware of.'

'Oh.' Jackson was smiling. 'Well, I know of a number of individuals who're going to be very disappointed to hear that.'

Ally totted up the logic.

'You mean, you thought, the bad guys thought . . .'

Jackson began nodding. 'It appears somebody some-where has got their wires very badly crossed,' he said. 'And I don't think they'll be very pleased when they find out.'

'So you cannae see them just packin' up an' apologisin' for the inconvenience?'

'Not likely, no. And unfortunately I can't see them believin' it, either. It would be like a mugger believin' a victim who said he left his wallet in his other coat.'

The restaurant area went from the front of the building all the way to the rear, with full-length, floor-to-ceiling windows affording the hypothetical diners a view of either the sea or the rest of the resort. The intended layout of the tables and decorative furnishings was marked on the floor with blue electrical tape, the furniture itself still in

270

flatpacks piled at one end of the room. Jackson delegated several groups to lift the packs and barricade all stairways one level down, giving them an elevated angle of fire on the area that intruders would need to breach.

While the rest got on with that, Jackson assembled his neophyte gunmen to teach them a little more about how their weapons worked. It was Ally's estimate that few crash-courses had ever been so head-on.

'Do they know about us yet?' Ally asked him.

'No, but I'd guess that we're down to minutes. I've been monitorin' Connor's radio channel. He's the guy you spewed on. It's his ball and he wants it back. They've just spotted a light on in one of the third-floor bedrooms and they're checkin' it out. If Hutchison's in there, the search parties'll be back downstairs as soon as they've nabbed him. Even if it's just one of the women, they'll have to bring her down to join the other hostages. Then the fun starts. Who are they, by the way? Do you know?'

Ally shrugged. It had been a wee bit hectic for calling roll, and after everything that had happened, he could hardly remember who was here in the first place.

'Simone, Gavin's wife was one of them,' Lisa McKenzie said. 'But I'm not sure your boss's head count was right. He said one man and two women, but we're also missing a guy called Matt Black. I saw him and Simone leave the ballroom together and I haven't seen either of them since.'

'When was that?' Ally asked, trying to think when he'd last seen Matt himself.

'During Gavin's speech. I know this is hardly the time for prurient speculation, but, well, maybe I wasn't the only one who noticed – maybe Gavin went off to look for them, if you see what I mean.'

Potter was shaking his head. 'Nah. Mr Hutchison went off

271

lookin' for Miss O'Rourke. He called me, askin' if I'd seen her, not long before everythin' went off, so that probably means she's missin' too. *And* the bloke she went to check on, which would makk your head count even less accurate.'

'What bloke?' Lisa asked.

'Oh God,' Potter said, grimacing. 'I'm pretty sure he was on the third floor. That's bound to be the light they've seen.'

'What bloke, Jamie?'

'Bollocks, what was his name? A Mr Mullen? Murtaugh?'

Ally felt his stomach lurch and his eyes widen. To his surprise, he realised the emotion he was feeling was hope, daft as it seemed. It wasn't as though the man could make much difference in a situation like this, for God's sake, but for some reason the notion reassured him. Possibly it was the thought of the scariest person he'd ever met being on *his* side, inside the tent pissing out. But it couldn't be – it was impossible. He hadn't even been there tonight. Had he?

'Murdoch?' Ally asked.

'That was it.'

'*David* Murdoch?'

'Aye, that's right: Murdoch, David, Mister. Room 322.'

'Jesus fuckin' Christ,' gasped Charlie. 'Davie Murdoch. He's here.'

'Who's here? Who is he?' Jackson asked.

'He's a rather celebrated reformed criminal,' Lisa stated, pre-empting Ally's own, more colourful description. 'And former fellow pupil of ours.'

'What kind of criminal?' Jackson demanded. Lisa stared at Ally in admonishment, but her silence deferred him the floor.

'Think of the most mental psychopath you ever met in

272

your life, then multiply that by the hardest bastard you can imagine,' Charlie said, beating him to the punch.

'First he terrorised our school,' Ally explained, 'then he grew up and terrorised the Scottish prison system. In his heyday, Satan would've shat it from Davie.'

'And then, as I said, he reformed,' Lisa interrupted, shooting both of them a chastising glare. 'He became a painter, highly acclaimed. He's a different person. He's got a family now.'

'Well, if he wants to see them again,' Charlie observed, 'he might have to regress a wee bit.'

Jackson looked sceptical. 'It doesn't matter how tough this bloke is, or was. He's not gonna do much against a bunch o' guys with machine guns.'

There was a short burst of static from Jackson's radio, followed by a voice bidding him to respond. This is it, Ally thought: the game begins. All of them exchanged apprehensive looks as their leader held the device to his mouth.

'Jackson here,' he answered calmly.

'This is McIntosh,' squealed a frantic voice. 'It's Gaghen. He's fuckin' dead. Electrocuted. Some bastard wired a door handle to the mains. Connor's gone ape. He's on his way down.'

'Received.' Jackson clipped the radio back on to his belt.

'You were saying?' Ally asked.

There's nothing quite like a man covered in blood to cool your ardour, unless perhaps you're Robert Mapplethorpe. The vision of Matthew returning from his contraceptive quest, his terrified face, hair and shirt dripping with red, had initially made Simone fear she was suffering a hallucination induced by the residual guilt of her long-abandoned Catholicism. The one time she'd dared to do the wrong thing, she was being confronted by this gory chimera, reminding her with gruesomely overwrought symbolism that the wages of sin is death. Maybe she'd mingled too long with Brendan and Mary-Theresa earlier on.

Not that her ardour's temperature hadn't already taken a swallow-dive, anyway. As soon as Matthew exited the room, the matronly chaperones of conscience and responsibility had taken his place and commenced their prudish tutting.

Left alone to contemplate her actions and intentions, Simone reflected that the unrivalled prophylactic properties of the condom might be based less on barrier-method contraception than the intermission their use necessarily imposed, during which one or both parties could capably have a volte-face. It was the Windows dialogue-box of human sexuality: 'Are you sure? Yes No.' Matthew's extended absence therefore took her well past changing her mind, beyond worrying how she'd tell him when he came back, and on to the further, harsher terrain of wondering whether he was coming back at all.

She couldn't blame the champagne, empty stomach or not. She hadn't had *that* much, as evidenced by how

274

instantly the aforementioned chaperones were able to sober her up. No, the fault lay with something far more intoxicating. Despite all her calculated detachment, she'd fallen under the spell of nostalgia tonight as much as anyone else.

What was this power, she asked herself, this aura that was visited upon people simply because you once sat in a classroom with them? It could strip you bare, magnify your vulnerabilities, shout your secrets to the rooftops. It rendered beauties of the plain, heroes of the mediocre, legends of the spent; and, mercilessly, it made its martyrs of the unfulfilled.

Simone wasn't yearning for Matthew Black: she was yearning for her own youth, and his presence merely promised to reconnect her to it. What she saw in him, what he saw in her, what so many of the people at the party saw in 'best friends' they'd barely ever known was a glimpse through younger eyes at a world still full of opportunity. Not the people they were now, nor even the people they were then, but all the people it once seemed each of them could become.

What she saw in Matthew was a distant reflection of the many possible selves she'd thought she might be by now. They reintroduced themselves like it was her own, personal reunion party, and seeing them again after so long was an emotionally charged affair. They all still looked like her, and the happiest among them still had Rachel and Patricia around, but not one was a mousy housewife married to a man who didn't love her. Not one was dependent upon anyone else.

Given that, Simone reasoned there couldn't be anyone on the rig tonight who was more susceptible to the lure of the past.

But she was wrong.

'Do you believe in second chances?' Matthew asked her.

They were sitting on the floor, their backs against the bed, not knowing what else to do or where else to go. It was after the horror and confusion parts were exhausted; after the gibbering and the stupid questions, uselessly enquiring what it was all about.

'Who are they?' Simone had asked, stupidly, uselessly.

'How the fuck should I know?' Matthew had replied, chaos behind his eyes. 'Taste vigilantes maybe. Judith Chalmers and Katie Wood with serious PMT: they're here to blow the place up so they never have to report from it.'

He stood before her, trembling, shivering, bloody, the Uzi round his neck, the shotgun in one hand, a pistol in the other.

'Have you had some kind of combat training?' she enquired. 'Some weapons-handling experience? Maybe in Hollywood? Was there an episode of the sitcom where you were in a siege or something?'

'No.'

'Then put all that stuff down before you blow both our heads off.'

Simone led him, like a zombie, to the bathroom, sitting him on the edge of the tub as she unbuttoned and removed his blood-soaked shirt. She was able to remain calmer than him at this point (all things, of course, being relative) because the reality had been driven home to Matthew a lot more, well, viscerally. He wouldn't say how he'd managed to overpower his attacker, but the evidence suggested something with a sharper edge than one of his trademark put-downs. She dabbed a sponge gently about his face, during which he began to emerge from his daze and took over the ablutions for himself. After that he bent over the tub and held the shower nozzle behind his neck, rinsing the blood from his hair.

'Christ, like fuckin' *Psycho*,' she heard him mutter, watching the dark liquid circle the plughole.

Simone handed him a towel. When he lifted his face from it she could see tears in his eyes.

'I just killed somebody,' he said with a shocked, humourless laugh. 'Not bad for a professed pacifist, eh? Jesus Christ.'

She took hold of his hands. Further volleys of gunfire were audible from the Laguna. 'Listen to it, Matthew,' she said softly. 'What else could you have done? Impose sanctions?'

He withdrew from her grasp and walked away, sitting down on the edge of the bed, his back to her. A voice issued from the walkie-talkie, which was sitting on the floor among the discarded guns and ammunition. Matthew slumped down to the carpet and picked it up.

'Yeah, Booth here,' he said.

'That stray you retrieved,' crackled the radio. 'Please tell me it was staff and not our Mr Hutchison.'

'Staff,' he mumbled, staring at the wall.

'Good man. Out.'

Simone sat next to him on the floor, again reaching out a hand and taking one of his. This time he returned the grip and gave her a half-smile of gratitude.

'They think you're . . .'

Matthew nodded. 'Booth was his name,' he said quietly. 'Not much of an assassin, though.'

'The man on the radio mentioned Gavin.'

'Aye. Figures – it's his gig. Whatever they're about, they'll

277

want to deal with the boss. He must have given them the slip, though. They were worried I . . . *he*, Booth, the guy I, you know . . . had killed him, so the good news is they must want Gavin alive.'

'They'll be looking for him, though, won't they? Everywhere.'

'They think Booth's still guardin' this part of the complex, so until they suss otherwise, we're probably safe here. Safe as anywhere else, anyway.'

Matthew dropped the radio back down among the weapons, then sighed and closed his eyes, as though trying to block everything out. He looked very, very tired. He swallowed then spoke again.

'About a week ago, I was on the verge of killin' myself,' he said.

Simone's back straightened: this she had not been expecting.

'Went through the whole wringer,' he continued, resting his forehead against one palm, elbow on his thigh. 'Down in Mexico. Fuckin' typical: I decide against it, an' noo they're queuein' up to do the job for me.'

Simone was familiar with the cliché of the depressive comedian, but she would never have thought of it applying to him. There were plenty of comics who made endless play of their own such vulnerabilities, but Matt Black onstage was the savage antithesis of self-pity. She realised in retrospect that a little basic psychology ought to have tipped her the wink, and was therefore acutely aware that he was unlikely to have volunteered this admission under less extraordinary circumstances.

'Suicide?' she asked (stupidly, uselessly). 'Why?'

'Probably because it's the ultimate act of self-indulgence and I'd already tried all the other ones.'

278

He turned his head to face her, and that was when he asked it: 'Do you believe in second chances?'

'I . . .' Simone breathed in then out, searching for an honest answer, searching for the truth. 'I'd *like* to,' she said.

Matthew nodded. 'I'd like to as well. I suppose that's why I came here today. Tryin' to remind myself of who I used to be and what the road looked like from the startin' point.'

Tell me about it, she thought.

'I know you must be thinkin' what does he need wi' second chances, he's the guy who got his dreams, but . . .' Matthew closed his eyes again for a second, laughing sadly at himself.

'I was Mr Nice Guy way back when,' he said. 'Always such a good boy at school. I was never *bad*, you know? Never answered back, always worked hard, didnae break the rules. Didnae smoke behind the dinner hall like the bad boys; didnae drink Woodpecker down the swing-park. I was pretty quiet, too, really. Too shy, too geeky to get any interest from girls.'

'Can I dissent here?'

'Thanks, but you know what I mean. Then bang, just a few years down the line I was suddenly the wean who got the key to the sweetie-shop. Fame, notoriety, money, acclaim, women, booze, drugs, whatever you like. But do you know what happens to the wean who gets the key to the sweetie-shop? He becomes a fat, bloated, selfish bastard, with his teeth rottin' oot his head, and he's always ill because he never gets any decent nourishment. An' the worst part is that he's no happier than when he was outside, starin' in the window at all the things he couldnae have, because at least back then he knew what he wanted – or at least what he thought he wanted.

'I had all this success, all this money, all this *talent*,

and basically all I did with it was pamper myself. No, *compensate* myself, compensate some fifteen-year-old for all the things he never got because he had to be a good boy. I used, devoured and discarded, whether it be drink, drugs, friends or women. Especially women. They were all just sweeties in the window. Couldn't have them back then, so I wanted as many as possible once I had the keys.'

'In that case, maybe you deserve to come back as me. A sap married to a philanderer. Faithful to a cheat, with an over-developed sense of responsibility.'

'Don't knock the last part, Simone. I could seriously use some responsibility. I've been livin' in the land of do-as-you-please for so long, I'm surprised nobody else has noticed the fuckin' donkey ears growin' oot the top o' my head. Oot my box every night, pissin' a fortune up the wall with the good-time crowd, so-called friends who're off like an electric hare if your star falls and your money runs oot. But they're the only friends I can find these days because I've alienated all the real ones. And as for my career . . .' He laughed bitterly and looked away.

'I started out tryin' to be Lenny Bruce – and I was even getting there for a while – then ended up turnin' into Dennis Leary. I'm supposed to be a comedian and it's two years since I was on a stage in front of an audience. I've been sellin' cheap notoriety instead, like I'm a Disney-animated version of myself. It looks like me, but you don't have to worry about it sayin' anythin' controversial – or funny.'

He turned to look at her again, holding her hand tightly as though afraid she'd abandon him.

'I blew it, Simone. Totally fuckin' blew it. I woke up – must have been five, six days ago – on a beach in the Baja California. I couldnae remember who I'd been with the night before, and I mean I couldnae remember their *names* or their faces, even though they'd been the best friends in the world a few hours before. I realised I had nothin'. I mean, yeah, there was still a bank account with a few Gs – well, a lot o' Gs, actually – to spend on more sweeties, but nothin' else. No friends, no wife, no "significant other", no kids – nobody who would miss me if I decided not to be there any more. And that included me. I realised *I* wouldnae miss me, the person I'd become. I hated his guts for what he'd done with my life, and I wanted to kill him for it.'

'But you didn't.'

'No,' he said with a sad smile. 'I couldnae – I'm a pacifist.'

'How close did you come?' Simone asked.

The smile became that bit more self-deprecatory. 'Probably no' that close. I will admit that the feelin' of wantin' to die might have been somewhat exacerbated by the extent of my hangover. But I knew I didnae want the life I *had* any more, that was for certain. I wasnae ready for a monastery either, right enough. I do like bein' a comedian. I *miss* bein' a comedian. I do like gettin' drunk, too, but I decided maybe once in a while would be spiritually and physically healthier than every night. I also decided I should probably lay off the unregulated pharmaceuticals as well: coke, I have come to realise, was just my version of Woodpecker down the swing-park.

'I went back to LA, gave up the place I was rentin', plus what was in it. Told the landlord he could keep the stuff or sell it. I decided I was startin' again from scratch. I flew in yesterday with just the clothes on my back and some spare Ys in my bag. Spent the night in a hotel at Heathrow, then this mornin' I took the shuttle up to Glasgow and hired a car. I figured if there *was* such a thing as second chances, then this thing tonight was as good a place as any to look for them. Hasnae quite gone to plan so far, but some parts have been no' bad.'

He gave her hand a squeeze. The platonic, near-fraternal gesture felt like an affection between some old married couple who'd been through it all together; their earlier kisses now a mere memory of distant, frivolous youth.

'I was going to start again tonight too,' Simone said, Matthew's silence having denoted that his own confession was over. 'I was going to tell Gavin I'm leaving him. I wanted a second chance: a chance to find something better than the life I've got with him. I felt I deserved it. I felt my daughters deserved it too. Oh God. Rachel and Patricia. Oh Jesus Christ.'

At last the brutal reality that Matthew had found in another man's blood struck Simone, right to the heart, the womb, the once-suckling breast. Maybe it was the sheer impossibility of what was unfolding, maybe it was a psychological self-defence mechanism, but either way, the danger to her own life had so far seemed at a remove, almost theoretical. Now she saw Rachel and Patricia bereft: their tears, their pain, their clouded future. That was the moment when the threat became immediate, tangible. That was the moment when the guns in front of her were transformed from mere objects to instruments of murder. But the weirdest part was, it was also the moment when she ceased to feel fear. The need to protect her daughters became paramount, and the desire for *all* of them to have that second chance became something she was prepared to fight for.

To the death.

Simone took hold of the shotgun and got to her feet. The weapon was very similar to the one Timothy Vale had taught her to use at some hellish outdoor event where there was a clay-pigeon range. She'd been abandoned by Gavin, as usual, and had put her respectable score that day down less to beginner's luck than to imagining his face on the flying targets.

'What you doin'?' Matthew asked.

'I'm not prepared to let my twins grow up without a mother. I've been outside that sweet-shop myself, Matthew, being a good wee girl, behaving myself, lying down and taking all the shit. But now I want the key, and I'd rather die trying to get it than cowering in this bedroom. You say the bad guys don't know we're here, right? They think this Booth person's guarding the place?'

'Yeah.'

'Well, if they don't know we're here, they're not gonna miss us if we leave. Let's see if we can't get off of this thing, get to shore, raise the alarm.'

'How?'

'These guys must have come here on boats, and if so they'll be moored on the central jetty. We can get down there through the sub-levels.'

'You're right,' Matthew said. He pulled his jacket on over his naked shoulders and reached down for the machine gun. 'Better than waitin' in here like Vladimir and Estragon. Your gory bed or to victory. Live forever or die in the attempt.'

Simone knelt on one knee and began slotting shells into the breech, picking them from a scattered pile on the carpet in front of her. The barrel rested on her thigh, cool through the fine material of her dress. The physical sensation of it was dulled by more than lycra and nylons, however: there was a numbness blunting all feelings, all emotions. She was way past fear and into a place of cold resolution beyond, where she was already dead but her life was there to be won back if she battled hard enough.

The shotgun had been almost full, only accepting three more cartridges. Simone gathered the spares into a disposable drawstring bag for 'feminine hygiene items' that she'd found in the bathroom. She slung the bag around her wrist and stood up again, pumping the shotgun to chamber the first shell.

Matthew slipped a finger around the Uzi's trigger-guard, spare mags bulging his jacket pockets. With his chest bare underneath, he looked like some under-developed Chippendale.

'You all right with this, morally, Mr Pacifist?' she asked him.

'Oh, I think all normal morality has been suspended for at least the next hour and a half.'

'Good. Shall we?'

'You askin'?'

'I'm askin'.'

'Then I'm dancin'.'

Whistling in the dark, laughter in the trenches.

Simone opened the door and out they went.

■ 22:18 ■ laguna ballroom ■ plan b plan c plan d ■

It was a few moments before Connor could speak. He stood facing the gaping expanse of the room, outraged and incredulous at the bare-faced, impudent emptiness of it. He gasped. He spluttered. He snorted. He blinked. He shut his eyes for a few seconds to see whether the disappearance of upwards of fifty people was perhaps merely a trick of the light. He opened them again. It wasn't. The desertedness proved chronic.

'—'

'I mea—'

'Bu—'

'Kkk—'

He dropped to his knees, feeling the closest he had been to tears since he was twelve. It just wasn't fair. It just wasn't fucking *fair*. All his work, all his strategy, his precision, his resolution. It had been going fine, it had been going absolutely bloody fine. Incursion undetected, communication links controlled, hostages taken. *All bloody fine*. Then he turns his back to sort out one other thing, and, and—

'Oh, fuck,' he moaned, deflatedly, remembering that Dawson would be back any moment, and would be expecting to find him in possession of *all* the hostages, including Gavin Hutchison. That he was now in control of none whatsoever was something Dawson was unlikely to let by without comment.

Maybe he could just shoot him, Connor thought. Yes. That would be the simplest thing. Blow him away before he could open that smug fucking mouth of his. Or even wait until he'd come out with whatever withering indictment he chose to pass upon poor, pathetic William's latest failure, then unload a full clip into his face to finally shut him up and, for once, have the last word.

Raising his head, he noticed from his lowered perspective that the bodies of two of his men were lying motionless under the buffet table. They still had their ski-masks on, but he didn't need to see their faces to know who they were – or rather who they weren't.

285

Jackson.

All that shit on the boat, and then his hesitancy downstairs in Hotel B when they were spotted by that kid. It all added up. The treacherous swine had turned fifth column on him. Connor looked at the holes expertly drilled in the centre of the two corpses' foreheads. It was well seeing the bastard's gun hadn't 'jammed' *that* time. The fucking overgrown boy-scout had decided to be a hero, had he? Well, in that case, there was a full clip with his name on it too.

'Unit Leader, come in Unit Leader,' came a voice from Connor's radio. He grabbed it hurriedly from his belt, desperate for information.

'This is Connor,' he responded. 'Who's this?'

'Harris, sir. Look-out team one. I've got a vessel leaving the rig, heading south-east away from us.'

'One of ours?'

'Well, the boat isn't, but I think the driver is. It's the small motor launch that was moored below, and I'm pretty sure the occupant is Mr Dawson. He's in fatigues but no mask. I've had a decent look at his face through the binoculars and I'm fairly certain it's him. Is everything still on-track, sir?'

Connor stared into space, digesting the news. How very Dawson, he thought, miserably. How bloody quintessentially Dawson. The one time he decides to shoot the bugger rather than listen to his sneering disgust, the self-satisfied tosspot communicates it all the more humiliatingly by walking out without a word. He'd even taken the spare boat rather than one of their own dinghies, a gesture that he wanted nothing more to do with them.

Connor looked at his watch, which told him he'd wasted the best part of an hour chasing around upstairs. Dawson had returned to find the embarrassment of the empty ballroom and – again, typical of the pompous prick – decided that retrieving the situation was less worthwhile than taking the opportunity to convey his total disdain for Connor and his set-up.

Well, fuck him and fuck Jackson too. Connor still had the bank codes, he still had control of communications, and he still had several hours of darkness. The situation was eminently retrievable, he'd show Dawson. It's not only about plans and contingencies: it's about adapting and improvising, and it's the end result that matters. They'd still get their money and they'd still get away clean to spend it. Then he'd see how superior that stuck-up bastard was feeling after being told he could whistle for his share.

'Sir? Is everything still on-track?' the voice on the radio repeated.

'Yes, Harris. Everything is still on-track. But if you see any more vessels leaving this place, blow them the fuck out of the water.'

'Yes, sir.'

The situation *was* retrievable, but the game had changed, and tactics were now crucial. Despite talking the rest of them up, Connor knew that, apart from himself, there had been only three soldiers here tonight worthy of the name. Now one had fled, one was dead and the other had become the enemy.

Jackson was only one man, but the threat he posed could not be underestimated, and it went beyond the disruption he could cause here and now. He could name everybody, and he would, unquestionably: between that and his selfless heroics, it would probably earn him a cosy little immunity when the investigations and recriminations began. And even if they took Jackson out, there was no way of knowing how much he might have already told the hostages. In that case, Connor was looking at either life in prison or no life in non-extradition shitholes for the rest of his days. He wasn't even sure the latter was achievable: if they destroyed all communications and pulled out right away, he'd still have to make it to Glasgow and on to an international flight before the alarm was raised. Left unguarded, Jackson and the hostages were bound to find some way of doing that long before morning.

'All units, all units, this is Connor,' he stated grimly, that last thought still in mind. 'Booth, I want you to proceed immediately to the comms pen. Acknowledge. Booth? Booth? Acknowledge.'

'Acknowledged.'

'Pettifer and Dobson, both of you join Booth. Acknowledge.'

'Acknowledged.'

'Acknowledged. Have you found Hutchison then, sir?'

'Shut up. Repeat: join Booth at the comms pen. Kill anybody who attempts to approach it. And I mean *any*body.'

'Yes, sir.'

Restoring comms would be Jackson's first possible strategy. Connor knew he'd be listening, so he was letting him know who still held all the cards. His second would be getting ashore.

'Look-out teams, remain in place. Destroy any vessels leaving or approaching the rig. Do not wait for authorisation from me. Shoot first and ask questions later.'

Connor then told everyone else to drop what they were doing and head for the ballroom, where he could debrief them without Jackson listening in.

There was no option now but to finish what they had started. If they played this right, Connor was confident they could still neutralise Jackson, recover the hostages and get what they had come for. But whether or not they managed that, the primary objective now was to ensure that when he and his men evacuated, no-one else was left alive.

■ **22:27 ■ cromarty firth ■ merrily merrily merrily ■**

Molly's prescription of a large dram and an early night sounded just grand. McGregor sipped the measure sitting up in his bed, his wife reading the paper alongside. She was absolutely right. After the day he'd had, the only sensible strategy was to get the head down and put everything behind him. Unwind and forget about all of it. Relax with a generous glass of Speyside malt (he couldn't drink Islay whiskies any more – too many painful memories) and chase from his mind all the torments and frustrations he'd been forced to endure on this, his first official day of retirement.

Such as being knocked unconscious by an independently airborne limb. Such as trudging ankle-deep into a pool of blood, cowshite and God knew what else trying to discover what had happened to the rest of the arm's erstwhile owner. Such as attempting to flag down a lift looking like Dennis Nilsen. Such as nearly running himself over with an abandoned Renault. Such as getting chased by a helicopter and demolishing a police roadblock with the aid of a bouncing sheep. Such as getting shot at and arrested by an Armed Response Unit. Such as being interrogated by hapless dunderheids and then patronised by some suit-full-of-fuck-all who was treating him like he'd advanced-stage senile dementia just because he'd been off the job a fucking fortnight.

'It's not unusual for men like yourself, Mr McGregor, who've been in the force for so many years, to undergo certain difficulties during that initial transitional period, as they begin adjusting to everyday civilian life. You may feel a little left out of things for a while, and you may tend to overreact to what incidents you do find yourself at the centre of, for which there will always turn out to be a perfectly reasonable explanation. It's not unknown for former officers' imaginations to run away with themselves a wee bit, perhaps to compensate for the sudden lack of excitement and responsibility.

'You were unfortunate enough to be witness to what appears to have been a tragic accident this morning, an accident we will be doing our utmost to get to the bottom of. But what you have to accept, having retired, Mr McGregor, is that investigating it is *our* job from now on. And though I'm very sure the force will miss you, it *will* manage without you. So please, trust us to get on with it ourselves. We know what we're doing. We're the police.'

'Wee wank,' McGregor muttered, placing his empty glass down on the bedside table

'What was that, dear?'

Know what they're doing my arse, he thought. An unfortunate accident? Where was the rest of the body, then? What about the bullet holes all over the place at the farm? What about the spent shell he had found? What about the blood inside the shed? Did the mystery dead punter go in there for a wee bleed before taking a walk outside and spontaneously combusting?

'Fuckin' idiots.'

'Did you say something, Hector?'

290

'Sheep-shaggin', carrot-crunchin', tumshie-munchin', teuchter half-wits,' he declared, getting out of bed.

'Are you going for another whisky, dear? Hector?'

'I'll no' be a minute,' he told Molly, pulling his socks back on.

'Where are you going?'

'Just ootside for a wee look at somethin'.'

'Oh, Hector, come back to bed. It's after ten. Just leave it.'

'Five minutes, Molly.'

He shuffled into his shoes at the front porch and lifted his raincoat from the hook, pulling it on over his pyjamas. Exploding teuchters. Pools of blood. Bullet holes. Thirty-odd years on the force, and if there was one thing he'd learned, it was that there's no such thing as a 'perfectly reasonable explanation'. Throughout his career, even in the explanations that made incontestable logical sense, reason had always been the last thing to factor into the equation.

The available evidence couldn't tell him what had actually taken place at that farm earlier today, but what it did say to him, in big, bright, blood-red neon capitals, was 'BAMPOTS AT WORK'.

He trudged out of his house and into the garden.

'I don't think we need lose too much sleep over mad bombers. I mean, what could terrorists find to interest themselves around here?'

From his front driveway he could see the moonlit silhouette of one corner of that holiday-resort place, the rest of it obscured by the spur of Kilbokie Brae. McGregor's new cottage was less than a quarter of a mile from the water's edge, and even in the half-light he could make out the shape of the rowing boat that came with the place, resting down on the shingle.

It wouldn't hurt to take a wee look. Just get that bit closer, round the spur, see what he could see. The fresh air would do him good, help clear his head. And besides, he knew himself too well: he wouldn't get any sleep until he'd at least had a wee nosy.

The night felt warm, like Edinburgh during the Festival, except he'd always put that down to the accumulated bodyheat combining with kebab grills, pizza ovens and self-immolating performance artists. Maybe this keech about 'micro-climate' was true. The weather had been un-Scottishly hot up here for a few days now, and even the breeze was warm. It was a night for moonlit walks, midnight swims and knee-tremblers in the woods.

He'd half a mind to go and get Molly and suggest she come for a wee boat trip under the stars: prove he wasn't going to turn into some curmudgeonly old pensioner just because he'd retired. Ach, maybe tomorrow night. Or maybe later on, once he'd satisfied his own curiosity.

McGregor pushed the boat into the water and clambered in, inadvertently dooking one shoe while he did so. As his momentum carried him the first few yards out, he was relieved to find that there were oars inside, having failed to check this first. For a horrified moment, he had images of Jimmy Johnstone heading helplessly into the Irish Sea, one of the more imaginative ways a Scottish internationalist had attempted to flee the inevitable horror of a World Cup campaign.

He settled into a rhythm, ploughing the surface with his back to his destination and meeting little resistance in the way of wind or current. Now and again he'd glance over his shoulder at the approaching monstrosity. The place was silent, with no lights visible other than the glow that peeked between the structures on the platform's 'ground' level.

Apart from that it was simply a big, dark mass blocking out the stars.

As he drew ever nearer and there remained nothing more specific to see, McGregor had to confess to himself that he had no idea what he might actually be looking for. Blisters were beginning to form on his hands from the rub of the oars, and he was aware that every further stroke he took now, he'd have to duplicate to get back. He was beginning to feel a bit daft, in fact, floating out there in his bloody pyjamas and raincoat. If he did discover anything untoward, he was hardly going to cut a very credible figure confronting it. Worse, if something went wrong and he had to be rescued, the last thing he wanted was those numpties from Rosstown nick finding him in this state and reinforcing their impression that he was some attention-seeking headbanger.

With that thought, he stopped the boat and turned to face the other direction. He flexed his shoulders a little and rubbed the smarting palms of his hands, then gripped the oars again to begin his return journey. Now that he was looking *towards* the floating hotel, he therefore had a perfect view of the rocket-propelled grenade that had been launched from it and was fizzing through the night sky towards him.

'Sufferin' Christ!'

The missile plunged into the water only a few yards to the left of the boat, sending out an arc of spray and a circular wave that pulsed powerfully underneath. McGregor heard the fizzing sound again, and saw that a second projectile had been fired from the platform. He let go of the oars and dived over the side of the boat, kicking downwards to take himself deeper into the water, where he struggled free of his shoes and the now somewhat moot raincoat.

The shock of the cold jolted through McGregor's body, electrifying him into frenetic, energised thrashing and clawing, which took him further away from the grenades' intended target. To his enormous relief, he could tell that his body temperature was non-fatally readjusting to that of the water, but he estimated that you'd need an electron microscope to see his scrotum at that point. A few seconds later there was light and sound from above him as the boat suffered a direct hit, exploding into matchwood third time lucky. It was a small but important consolation that the explosion at least reminded him which direction the surface lay. He stayed under for as long as his complaining lungs would allow, all the time swimming further away from the wreckage.

McGregor's head emerged from the waves with a gasp and he began to tread water. He'd learned that, God knows how many years ago: treading water. They taught you it at life-saving classes, during which he'd always been extremely sceptical about the instructors' insistence that you jump into the swimming pool clothed in your pyjamas. Well, he knew now: never let it be said they were anything less than prescient at the Leith Vicky baths.

Debris was bobbing on the surface a few yards away. Watching it, McGregor was fairly confident that he could now supply an accurate but strictly non-reasonable explanation for what had happened to puddle-man back at the farm.

'An unfortunate accident.'

'It's not unknown for former officers' imaginations to run away with themselves a wee bit.'

Fuckin' arseholes.

He glanced around himself, turning in the water. He was a lot nearer the rig than the shore, and in recent years the most strenuous swim he'd attempted was a couple of lengths before lunch in Majorca. On the other hand, there were men with explosives complicating his alternative. He was truly caught between the devil and the deep blue sea.

McGregor looked closer at the giant construction, focusing between the pillars that jutted up from the water. Around the central support there appeared to be three rubber dinghies, equipped with outboards. If he could fire up one of those, he would be a lot harder to hit, moving fast and zig-zagging erratically all the way to shore. It had taken them three goes to blow up a near-stationary rowing boat, so it was definitely worth a shot. He trod water for a few more moments until he was happy he had his breath back, then he began a cautious breaststroke towards the rig.

He kept his gaze trained on the central pillar as he approached, gradually making out the encircling jetty that the dinghies were moored to. There didn't appear to be anyone guarding it, which made him all the more nervous of where else his approach might be observed. The rockets had been launched from platform-level, and he was confident that he was now beneath their line of sight, but there were decks and gantries above him, any of which might be patrolled. He turned on to his back for a few strokes. He couldn't see anyone, but that was hardly reassuring. Snipers generally didn't tend to be extroverts.

His arms were starting to seriously ache from the combined efforts of rowing and swimming. The sleeves of his pyjama shirt weren't proving very aqua-dynamic, but pulling the thing off while in the drink would be like trying to do origami with clingfilm. In space. He trod water for another few breath-restoring seconds, then, heartened that he hadn't been machine-gunned yet and that neither had he seen any heavy ordnance for a good ten minutes, he summoned up renewed effort and crawled the last twenty yards.

McGregor reached the nearest of the dinghies and threw an arm over the side, preparing to climb in. The rubber tube compressed flacidly under his weight with an incontinent rasp of air, causing him to slither helplessly back under the water. He came up and tried again, gripping the dinghy a bit nearer the front, but with similar results.

The thing was barely afloat. The weight of the outboard motor was slowly pulling the boat under from the back, a process McGregor had accelerated by assisting the deflation of the air chambers on one side. He swam to the jetty and hauled himself up, water gushing from his pyjamas and pouring with a steady cadence on to the wooden boards.

Standing upright, he could see that all of the dinghies had been sabotaged, each of their air chambers slashed in several places. Someone had made damn sure nobody was leaving this rig, including, now, McGregor. He was cold, drookit, and worst of all for a Leither, marooned.

'Christ,' he muttered. 'If I'd ken't it was this much fuckin' fun, I'd have retired years ago.'

McGregor had another look at each of the boats, as though he might have failed to notice the first time that one of them was actually fine. They remained consistently jiggered. Short of sticking one of the outboards up his arse, lying on his back and opening his legs, it looked like he was here for the duration. He sighed heavily and began walking around the jetty to see where it led.

On the other side of the central column there were two shoogly looking stairways leading to the deck above. Lying in front of these was a dead man in cammy gear and a black balaclava, sporting holes for the eyes, the mouth and the bullet-wound in his forehead. In a way, McGregor found it comforting to meet someone who'd had a worse night than himself. Nonetheless, he was mightily confused to discover a corpse kitted out in the classic terrorist away-strip. McGregor wasn't complaining, but he'd been kind of expecting any dead people he encountered to be wearing civvies.

To further confirm which team the dead man was on, he still had a machine gun strapped to his shoulder, though his hands evidently weren't on it at the time of death. McGregor's confusion grew. Either he'd been drilled from distance – which seemed unlikely, given the pin-point position of the plug-mark – or he'd been taken by surprise, which seemed equally unlikely, as the only approach was via the two stairways he was lying in front of. It was of course possible that he was just a shite sentry, but that still begged the time-honoured question: whodunnit?

McGregor knelt down beside the body and pulled off his soaking pyjama top, dumping it with a splat on the boards. Removing the man's machine gun, he noted with a shudder that the corpse's temperature suggested he hadn't been dead an hour. The man's camouflage-vest was therefore still warm as McGregor pulled it over his own head, a sensation similar to, but several million times less comfortable than, sitting on an already tepid lavvy seat.

The man's boots were too small for him, as were, even more frustratingly, his trousers. McGregor tugged manfully at the waistband to get it beyond his thighs, but after tumbling to the deck twice and almost spilling into the water, he was reluctantly forced to squelch back into his pyjama-breeks. Between those, his bare feet, the cammy-semmit and the machine gun, he reckoned he must look like

297

the leader of the Demented Geriatric Liberation Front. With that inspiring thought, he bounded up the gangway.

■ 22:54 ■ fipr ■ radioheadgames ■

'Jackson? Jackson? Jackson, come in, over. Jackson, come in, over. Oh look, stop playing hard to get, you bleeding-heart Geordie tosspot. I know that you and your new best friends are listening to every word I transmit, and every word that's transmitted to me. So in that case you'll have heard your former comrade-in-arms Mr Quinn a few minutes back, informing me that he'd captured the elusive Mr Gavin Hutchison. No doubt you also heard me order Quinn to bring his prisoner directly to the ballroom. Well, Jackson, bugger me backwards with a banana if they aren't both standing in front of me right now. So here's how it's going to be. You tell the hostages to come out from wherever they're hiding, or else their gracious host will be forced to take his leave of them. It's kind of an it's-my-party-and-I'll-die-if-I-want-to scenario. You pass the message on: they've got five minutes to show up in front of this hotel and do business with me, or Mr Hutchison here does business with the Desert Eagle lead-export company. Five minutes, I said, starting now.'

'Jackson? Jackson? I mean it. I'm going to drill him right now. I thought you were the big hero, Jackson. Do you want this man's death on your conscience? Do the hostages want his death on theirs? Did you even tell them the situation? Maybe you should let me talk to them. Maybe they should be told how your recklessness is likely to get them all killed, whereas if they just give me what I want, nobody has to get hurt.

'That five minutes is up, Jackson. Time's run out for Mr Hutchison, here, I'm afraid. I just hope if I'm ever in his position, I've got better friends than he has tonight. Unless, of course, his friends would like to intervene and request a stay of execution. I'm sure I could grant another five minutes' clemency if somebody spoke to me really nicely. Maybe I'll give Mr Hutchison thirty seconds more, just in case that plea comes. Then again, maybe I won't.'

■ 22:59 and thirty seconds ■

'Jackson? Are you listening? You callous bastard. You've just signed Mr Hutchison's execution order. I want you to know that his blood is on your hands as much as it's on mine. It didn't have to be this way, you know. A simple negotiation, that's all it would have taken. This is just so unnecessary. Maybe if you had seen sense, if the hostages had seen sense, it would never have come to this, but here we are—'

'Oh look for fuck's sake, Connor, knock it on the head, this is pitiful. We know you don't have Gavin Hutchison, so stop making a cunt of yourself. You can tell Quinn his acting's fuckin' shite. And *don't* call me a Geordie again, you ignorant Scottish get.'

'Ah, so you've found your voice at last, Acks. But I can assure you that I *do* have Mr Hutchison. I'm looking at him right this second, down the barrel of my gun.'

'Aye, sure, Bill. Tell you what, then: we'll trade him for Lord Lucan here. He's bound to be worth a few bob more. We'll throw in Shergar as well. Can't say fairer than that.'

'All right, Jackson, you smart-arsed prick. We don't have Gavin Hutchison, but what we do have is a truckload of guns and about twelve hours before this rig is due any contact from the outside world. I've got units scouring every inch, and there aren't that many places you can hide fifty people around here. We'll find you soon enough.'

'I don't doubt it. But I reckon you'd be better usin' your time to get out of here. You might have twelve hours, but this isn't hide and seek, mate. We're not hidin', we're dug in. Cut your losses, Bill. This was all a daft mistake. I saw that, and it sounds like Dawson saw it too. Be smart, Bill. Call it off.'

'Hmm. Actually, know what, Acks? You're probably right. I *should* call it off. I might have put a lot of planning and effort into this, and there's millions of pounds at stake, but I suppose you do have to look at the bigger picture sometimes, don't you? And right now that bigger picture is showing how futile it would be for me and my men to even *attempt* to take on an elite fighting force such as you must have assembled and trained in the past hour. Perhaps I should let my men know what they're up against, rather

300

than ask them to go unwarned into a fight they couldn't possibly win.

'All units, be advised. All units, be advised. This assault will bring you up against adversaries who are *trained* catering contractors. I have reason to believe there may even be a crack corp of travel agents and several venture capitalists in their ranks. Any man who feels this mission would be suicide has my permission to stand down. Anyone? Anyone? Oh, I suppose not, then. Sorry, Jackson. I guess these guys of mine just don't know when they're beat.'

'Well, they'll know soon enough.'

'Connor, come in, over. Connor, come in, over.'

'Connor here. What is it?'

'It's Booth, sir.'

'Yes, Booth, what is it?'

'No, this is Dobson. I mean the issue is Booth.'

'What issue?'

'Well, primarily, I suppose, the issue of who disembowelled him with a circular saw, then made off with his guns and his radio. He's dead, sir. Very, very dead.'

'But I've been speaking to Booth on and off for the past . . . *Jackson.*'

'Don't blame me, mate. I don't know anythin' about that one. Can't claim credit for Conroy down at the jetty either – I notice he's not been answerin' his calls, so I'm assumin' the worst. It's not lookin' good, is it? Face it, Bill. This whole thing's comin' down around your ears. You've lost Dawson, you've lost Gaghen. Who does that leave? You and a bunch of fuckin' amateurs. Did you all hear that out there? Fuckin' amateurs, the lot of you. Like Booth was an amateur. Like Conroy was an amateur. Well, unless you bail out, it's me and my amateurs against you and yours, and we haven't lost any so far. I'll take those odds, Bill, what do you say?'

301

'I say ten out of ten for bravado, Jackson, but we'll see how tough your new pals are once the shooting starts. It's amazing how they can lose their stomach for the fight after one of them's lost his stomach altogether.'

'Aye, well, like I said, we haven't lost any so far. Go an' ask Booth how *he* feels about your chances.'

'Fuck you, Jackson.'

'Right back atcha, Bill.'

'You doin' all right there, McQuade?'

'Oh aye. Is there a military term for shitin' yoursel'? Whit was aw that aboot?'

'Just talkin' smack, mate. Just talkin' smack. He's tryin' to scare me, I'm tryin' to scare his lot.'

'Why didn't you tell him who we really are, seein' as it sounds like the baw's on the slates already for these guys. Might sow that bit of dissension in the ranks.'

'No chance. These idiots'll do whatever Connor says, no matter what, believe me, because they're fuckin' lost without him. But more to the point, as long as he believes you lot are rollin' in cash, he's got an interest in keepin' you alive, so it wouldn't be the wisest idea to disabuse him of that particular notion.'

'Understood.'

'But havin' said that, it'll only be a tactical consideration for a little while longer. He has no idea how much I've told you lot about him, so he'll assume the worst. He'll assume that at the very least you know his name, so whether he gets money out of you or not, he needs you silenced afterwards. My guess would be he's already set himself a time limit for recapturin' you all alive. Once that's past, it's a straight fight to the death. Us or them. All or nothin'.'

'How many of them are there?'

302

'Let's see. Dawson's gone, Gaghen's dead, Booth's dead, the two from the ballroom, probably Conroy too, by the sound of it. That leaves eleven.'

'Eleven! All with Uzis an' stuff?'

'Uzis, shotguns, and don't forget the rocket launchers. Connor won't use those until his time limit's up, but when he does . . .'

'Yeah, I've played a lot of *Quake*. The guy with the rocket launcher usually wins. So you're sayin' we've not only got to hold out – we've got to win this fight, an' win it before a deadline expires, against a clock that only the other guy can see?'

'That's what I'm sayin', lad.'

'Can't you go back to talkin' smack?'

Ally watched Jackson walk away, striding off with that imposing gait to check on maybe Lisa or Charlie at one of the other barricades. He felt all the more scared and helpless as soon as the big man left. It was selfish, but he wanted it to be his post Jackson was closest to when . . . whatever happened, happened. Selfish, but natural: they were all kids tonight, and Jackson was the only adult.

The ever-bleakening picture he painted shouldn't have come as a surprise: the darkest-before-dawn rule of action flicks dictated that the situation always got one level more scary than the trailers and even the plot so far had previously hinted. Ally just hoped that had been it.

He looked at his watch, though it couldn't tell him anything pertinent to the timescale he really needed to know about. Less than two hours had passed since he was standing drinking champagne with old friends, happily immersing himself in the past for a night because there was the rest of his life to deal with the future. Now it felt like he'd never had that past, just seen it on video like

303

any other empty and irrelevant tale. Now there was no past, there was no future, and time existed only in another man's mind.

It was shite.

■ 23:04 ■ laguna laundry depot ■
■ machine-gun etiquette ■

Matt Black used to do a routine about male aggression on all scales, from the battlefield right down to the playground. Davie had felt the hairs tingle on the back of his neck the first time he heard it, live in New York, fearing what cameo he might be about to play in the monologue; fearing even more the possibility that Matt had clocked him in the audience and was improvising as a result. But he wasn't spotted, and Davie later heard the routine on one of Matt's albums, *Didn't Cry for Di*, confirming that it was a standard part of his set at the time.

He'd quote Oscar Wilde's assertion that 'patriotism is the virtue of the vicious', then follow it up with his own admission that 'pacifism is the cause of the cowardly, the yen of the yellow, the shibboleth of the shite-bag'. His objection to war and violence was not, he said, based on Christian principles of love and forgiveness, but on the self-preservation principle of not wanting to get hurt. 'I'm being straight with you here. My pacifism comes with no added self-righteousness. I'm not in it to save the world. I'm in it to save the me. My objection is not conscientious, it's rational: I don't want to *be* where the bullets are.'

'Live forever or die in the attempt', ran the quote from Joseph Heller on the back of the CD.

The comedian related an imaginary dialogue with a militarist: '"If everyone in this country was as cowardly as you, we'd be goose-stepping up Argyle Street under a swastika."'

'"Yeah, but if everyone in the *world* was as cowardly as me, there'd be no wars, and violence wouldn't exist."'

Matt would then confess to countless acts of apparent forgiveness throughout his childhood and later life, occasions when he sought and obtained a diplomatic solution, as being nothing to do with strength of character and everything to do with weakness of body. 'Maybe that was Gandhi's big secret: he just didnae want to get into it with anybody. Look at the fuckin' size of the guy, for Christ's sake. He couldnae have fought an infection.'

Like most of his material, there was a disarming honesty about it that sounded self-deprecatory until you realised how widely it applied. With Matt Black, cotton wool usually concealed fish-hooks. He said he turned the other cheek because he was too scared to hit back, 'forcing me to confront my anger and my grievances, forcing me to make peace with myself and then search for alternative paths, so that I might eventually discover a non-violent way of . . . [big, long, reflective pause] . . . fucking the guy's life up forever. And I'm not alone – I think that's why there are so many lawyers in this world . . .'

Matt was admitting that he had to pursue non-violent alternatives because violence had never been an option open to him; but the barb in the candyfloss was that whether it was down to cowardliness or weakness rather than wisdom or vision, it didn't make it any less right.

Davie had an uncommon, even opposite, perspective on

305

the pacifism routine, but one which far from negated it. To Davie, violence had *always* been an option, and the ability to fight meant that he hadn't needed to consider alternative responses, even when he knew they were available. However, his facility for violence wasn't always what dictated his recourse to it: sometimes – often – it had felt like there *were* no alternatives. Childhood and beyond, whenever he felt threatened, violence had seemed like the only possible response. Changing that hadn't merely been about learning the alternatives, but about learning not to feel threatened in the first place, learning when no response was required.

However, what Matt Black knew as well as he was that not everyone in this world *was* as cowardly as Matt: there *were* wars, and violence did exist. Davie had learned not to see a challenge in every face, a gauntlet in every remark, but there were still times when he had good reason to feel threatened. Tonight, it was fair to say, fell into that category. The big question – the question in which there might even dwell some of that absolution he did not seek – was whether sometimes there *were* no alternatives to violence. He'd admit he hadn't paused to think of any as he wired that door handle to the mains, but what if, indeed, there were none?

Honest to the last, it was a question Matt Black didn't pretend to be able to answer, acknowledging that circumstance had thus far never asked it of him. 'I really don't know what I'd do,' he said. 'But I'll tell you this, there cannae be many things more tragic than bein' a martyr to pacifism. You die *and* you lose. In fact, I'd say if you're a pacifist, you've got a fuckin' ideological obligation *not* to die from violence. And like all ideological obligations, unfortunately no guidance is offered as to practical application. Actually, if you're a pacifist and you

306

do find yourself in that situation . . . let me know how you get on.'

Cotton wool and fish-hooks again. The cotton wool was admitting he didn't know the answer. The fish-hook – and indeed the gag – was in the possibility that there might nonetheless *be* one. Perhaps, Davie thought, that was the true measure of a pacifist: someone who would always find a non-violent solution, no matter what the circumstance. In that light, the deeds of his past sank all the further into shadow, and his action in that bedroom tonight flinched also from the glare.

(*Offer no excuses, seek no absolution.*)

As Davie watched the black-and-white surveillance images on Tim Vale's laptop, it came as quite a surprise, then, to observe that the pacifist comedian had at last been forced to address that big, no-longer-hypothetical question. His answer involved grabbing a 9mm machine gun and spraying bullets around like it was a garden-hose.

Presumably, Matt's latent pacifism was manifest in his apparent inability to hit a coo's arse with a banjo.

They had heard footsteps approaching the laundry room. Davie instructed Catherine to hide as the sounds grew louder, taking up position himself to the right of the door. He'd looked around for a chib, but the only thing to hand was a thick pile of fluffy towels, and despite PE teachers' dressing-room warnings that 'you could take somebody's eye out with one of those', he didn't think they constituted lethal weapons, even when rolled up and wet.

The door opened and Davie leapt upon the emerging figure with all his weight. The man's form seemed to disappear from beneath him, and Davie felt his own momentum carry him helplessly, spastically forward into a stack of shelves. He threw up his arms to cushion against the impact, crumpling to the floor as his feet skidded, slipped and tangled with each other. Davie scrambled to turn and face, all the time expecting a blow to arrive, or as likely a bullet. None came. He looked up at his assailant. It had been several long years since he was at the peak of both his skills and his activity in the field of personal harm, and Davie had not expected his abilities to be instantly restored, but nonetheless he was a little alarmed to see that he'd just been effortlessly brushed off by someone of retirement age.

He hadn't even managed to ruffle the guy's hair, and to further rub it in, the bloke was actually holding a briefcase. Whatever he'd just done, he'd done one-handed, and looked sufficiently cool about it to suggest even *that* hadn't required special effort or concentration.

The man walked over, still holding the damn briefcase, and offered him a hand up.

'Sorry about that, old chap,' he said. 'Bit of confusion was inevitable, I suppose, what with all that's going on. I'm Tim Vale, by the way. Security and surveillance consultant.'

What with all that's going on. He sounded like they had plumbers in or something.

Davie felt the power in the man's grip as it pulled him to his feet. Vale was, yes of course, smaller than him, but he was also clearly in far better shape. Not that Davie's being out of practice made any difference: he was instantly sure this guy could have utterly owned him at any time in his life. He didn't know what career path had taken Vale to being a 'security and surveillance consultant', but he was confident it hadn't involved slave-wage night shifts on a building site.

'Davie Murdoch,' he offered deferentially.

'Mr Vale,' said Catherine, emerging from behind a table, evidently familiar with the newcomer.

'Ms O'Rourke. Good to see you. Quite a party so far, I understand.'

Gavin's hands and then flushed face appeared above the rim of the laundry hopper. 'Christ, Vale, what on earth's going on?' he asked, climbing clumsily over the side. Davie was reminded of a toddler escaping from a barred cot.

'Ah, Mr Hutchison. I was going to ask you much the same question.'

Vale spoke like this was a business meeting. Davie wondered momentarily whether the man was missing something – such as the presence upstairs of armed maniacs in ski-masks – but strongly suspected otherwise.

'And where the hell have you been?' Gavin demanded. Presumably, as security consultant, terrorist disposal was Vale's remit and Gavin's tone suggested two hours was an unacceptable delay in discharging his duties. Davie wouldn't have spoken to the man like that from behind a cannon, but he guessed Gavin's vocation had moved him in circles where sharpness of tongue was not checked by the real and immediate threat of burst nose.

'I'm sorry, I rather missed out on things,' Vale remarked. 'I was working on ironing out some of the bugs in this new surveillance software. I needed somewhere quiet, away from the noise of the party, so I retreated to one of the admin suites on sub-level two. Time just dissolves when you're working with computers, I find. You get caught up in the most pernickety little operations and before you know it, it's the middle of the night.'

'Are you *aware* of what's going on here right now?' Gavin asked.

'Latterly, yes. I only decided to boot up the system about

309

half an hour ago, to see what difference my dabblings had made. I almost shut it straight down again – there was no response at all from the spider-deck cameras, which at the time I assumed to be a software fault. You're lucky I toggled through a few of the others or I'd still be in there, trying to reconfigure the compatibility settings.'

'Didn't you hear all the gunfire?'

'Not a thing. I had my discman on, you see. I need to be mainlining Prokofiev while I work with computers, otherwise I'm terribly inclined to put my fist through them.'

'Computers?' Davie asked.

'Yes,' Vale said, holding up the 'briefcase', which turned out upon closer examination to be a laptop PC. 'It's our pioneering, frightfully clever and right now deeply flawed Nodal Network Video Surveillance System. It's really just closed-circuit TV with knobs on, except most of the knobs don't work at the moment. That's why I'm stuck here, instead of shooting in the Highlands. Of course I might get some shooting done yet, by the look of things.'

'How does it work?' Davie enquired.

'Well, I'll have to fire this up to check the coast's still clear, so I might as well show you.'

Vale flipped open the laptop and set it down on a nearby work surface, elbowing a pile of bedsheets to one side to make room. He then squatted down next to one wall, scanning along the skirting board for something. What he was looking for turned out to be a small junction box, similar to a telephone socket. Vale plugged a cable into it and attached the other end to the back of the laptop, then began working the keyboard.

'Instead of all the security cameras connecting directly to one big surveillance room full of TV screens,' he explained, 'the nodal system allows you to monitor activity from any point on the rig.'

'Resort,' Gavin corrected. 'We don't call it a rig,' he explained to Davie.

'The signals go to a central server and get converted into digital feeds,' Vale continued, opening up a window on the colour LCD screen. 'You can plug into the network at any "node" on the ri– resort. The place is simply far too big to rely on one central observation room.'

'So could any of the punters plug into this?'

'Not without this cursed software.'

'What about the terrorists?' Gavin asked. 'They'll be able to access the computers in the surveillance room upstairs.'

Vale shook his head. 'The system's up just now, but you can't see anything without a username and password.' He keyed the aforementioned into a dialogue box. 'Now, this is how I knew to come and let you lot out of here.'

The window he had opened now displayed a black-and-white image of four figures hunched around a laptop. At the top of the window was a blue bar with white text reversed out of it, stating 'hotela/laundepot/sublev3/ 23:02:36'. Davie looked up and noticed a lens staring back from high on the wall behind them.

'It defaults to the nearest camera,' Vale explained. 'But you can switch to any image in the place – apart from the Carlton, where the electricity's off, and apart from the gantry decks, where I'm just getting static. Probably vandalised by our visitors. You should, in theory, be able to remotely pan and refocus the cameras using the laptop's track-ball and the shift keys. The fact that you can't was merely one of the faults myself and the late Mr Prokofiev spent the evening attempting unsuccessfully to remedy.

311

Anyway, as I was saying earlier, I rebooted the whole system and was toggling through the cameras when I noticed Mr Hutchison here, lying face-up in a laundry hopper. I noticed Ms O'Rourke too, but the presence of yourself, Mr Murdoch, alerted me that something was mysteriously amiss.'

'What? The fact that we were stuck in the laundry room wasn't suspicious enough for you?' Gavin protested. 'Isn't that rather credulous on the part of a security specialist?'

'Well, you see, Mr Hutchison, my cameras *have* on occasion spotted you and Ms O'Rourke tarrying together in quite the oddest locations.'

Catherine blushed deep red and closed her eyes. Gavin's peepers, for their part, threatened to burst from his skull.

'For future reference, the lure of adventure aside, I'd advise restricting such activities to the bedrooms, unless of course the pair of you tend towards exhibitionism. No cameras in there, you see. As opposed to the lifts, for instance. Or the Laguna's indoor pool.'

'I think I want to die,' Catherine groaned, mortified.

'Well, you certainly picked the right night for it. A quick scan of a few other cameras showed me a number of heavily armed individuals whom I suspect would be only too happy to oblige you. What they are doing here, I cannot even begin to speculate, but I'd find it hard to imagine their intentions are benign.'

'Do you know where they are?' Gavin asked.

'Only where they're not. I used this to make sure my route down here was clear. So far, so good.'

'What about the others,' Catherine said. 'Can you show us the ballroom on that thing?'

'It was the first camera I called up as soon as I suspected something was wrong. There was no-one there.' Vale stared sternly at Gavin. 'My credulity didn't stretch to accepting total desertion as being entirely plausible, even given the quality of your house champagne.'

'Can't you rewind the footage?' Gavin asked. 'Find out what happened?'

Vale sighed, barely tolerant. 'Again, that's one of the features I . . .' He made a dismissive gesture with his free hand.

'So where the hell are they?'

'I *am* looking,' Vale replied, hitting the tab key. Each time he did so, the window blacked out for a second, then picked up the digitised feed from a new camera. The images were summoned and dismissed, heralds with no news. Empty corridors, stairwells, walkways. Then they saw a perspective upon part of the Lido, the absurd complex of interconnecting swimming pools and water-channels that was gouged into the platform's surface deck like a crude respiratory system. There were three masked men walking along the terrace, carrying the standard complement of automatic weaponry.

'Oh dear,' Vale said quietly. He sounded as though he'd just read a slightly disappointing cricket score. All things being relative, Davie took it to be a very grave sign.

The intruders walked out of the camera's line of sight.

'Where have they gone?' Gavin asked. 'Get them back!'

'Looks like they're heading for the Carlton,' Vale murmured. He tapped the tab key again. The gunmen reappeared at the corner of the new image, moving closer to a group of four more bad guys in front of the darkened hotel building. 'I'd guess that must be where your guests have gotten to. I wonder how they managed to elude these individuals in the first place?'

'They didn't,' Catherine stated. 'The terrorists went straight in the front of the Laguna, all guns blazing, by the sound of it. We heard screams coming from the ballroom. They couldn't *all* have escaped. There were about fifty of them, for God's sake.'

Vale opened a second window, retaining the previous video-feed in the one beneath. Using the track-ball, he placed the cursor on the new window's blue bar and keyed 'hotela/func1/levg', then hit Return. After a moment's pause, the interior of the Laguna ballroom appeared in the frame.

'As you can see, there's no-one around,' he said.

'What's that?' Davie asked, pointing to part of the screen. 'Can you zoom in closer?'

'No. The software isn't speaking properly to the cameras, I'm afraid. I can blow up the image we do have, though.' Vale's fingers tickled the track-ball and a dotted square appeared around the area Davie indicated. He clicked on an icon at the side and the window filled with a fuzzy blow-up of the highlighted section. The image definition was badly reduced, but they were nonetheless able to make out that there was a masked man lying motionless under the buffet table.

'No-one, but not no*body*,' Davie observed. 'That, to me, looks very much like a dead bad guy. Question is, who got him?'

'Curiouser and curiouser,' muttered Vale. 'Maybe he tried the cold meats. You didn't get them from that James Barr fellow I read about, did you, Gavin?'

Their decreasingly gracious host simply glared.

'Only joking, old chap. No, this one died from something far more acute. And I think he may not have been alone. Does that look like a leg just behind his head, there?' he asked Davie. It did.

314

'Make that two dead bad guys,' Davie confirmed.

'Which might explain the subsequent haemorrhage of hostages from the vicinity. Let's see what else we can find.' Vale delicately fingered the tab key again. More corridors, more walkways. Lifts. Restaurants. Bars. Bowling lanes. Cinema auditoria. Rows of empty shopfronts. He was about to tap the key once more to dismiss the current image, when some movement stirred in the current picture, staying his hand.

'More baddies,' Davie mused, looking at the silhouettes of two armed figures, their backs to the camera. The pair then scurried across the hall and crouched for cover in a shop doorway opposite, their unmasked faces now clearly visible. And very, very familiar.

Davie's surprise at seeing Matt Black squatting there, determinedly gripping an Uzi, was matched only by Gavin's at recognising the shotgun-toting woman beside Matt as his own wife. Both of these, however, were thoroughly eclipsed by Gavin's appalled astonishment as he watched the pair exchange a brief but unmistakably affectionate kiss.

'I'm sure that was just for luck. A heat-of-the-moment thing,' Vale offered, with gleeful insincerity.

'What the hell are they doing?' demanded Gavin, as they made a dash to the next corner and disappeared from the frame. Vale opened another window and tiled all three frames on the screen, keying a location shortcode into the blue bar above the newest one. Another row of shopfronts appeared, but no people.

'Damn,' he muttered. 'Wrong one.' His fingers rattled the keyboard, cycling through different images in two of the windows. Matt and Simone became visible again a few seconds later, by which time they were positioned in opposite doorways, firing their weapons towards one

315

end of the hallway. Spent cases were cascading around Matt's ankles like popcorn, while Simone pumped and fired, pumped and fired on the other side. Ahead of them, glass was shattering in surreal silence, spraying all over the tiles in front of the ravaged window-frames.

'Oh my God,' gasped Catherine. 'Oh my God.'

Davie was silent, Gavin speechless.

Vale continued to toggle the spare window, trying to find a view of who or what they were shooting at. After two more stretches of empty mall, he revealed another scene of flying glass and splintering debris, another Uzi-blazing gunman at its centre, madness in his angry eyes.

'Oh, God help them,' Catherine breathed. 'He looks like a maniac.'

'Quite,' Vale agreed, a degree of surprise detectable even in *his* phlegmatic tone. 'I've come across a few armed lunatics in my time, but I must confess, I've never seen one in tartan pyjamas.'

■ 23:13 ■ fipr ■ gunfight at the k-mart corral ■

Dear *Matthew Black*,

'Let's meet up in the year 2000!'

Your former classmate Gavin Hutchison cordially invites you to an unmissable reunion event. Join your fellow ex-pupils from St Michael's Auchenlea in the incomparably luxurious surroundings of Delta Leisure™'s Floating Island Paradise Resort on Saturday, August 12th, for an evening of food, drink, dancing, reacquaintance, reminiscence and nostalgia.

316

Oh yeah, plus murder, mayhem, hijackers, machine guns, power-tools, dismemberment, disembowelment, destruction, horror, terror, insanity and lots and lots and lots of bullets. Thanks a fuckin' bunch. Wouldn't have missed it for the world. Let's do it again soon. It's been very.

Matt shook more tiny nuggets of glass from his hair, grateful that the panes had been shatterproof, otherwise he'd have been either impaled or flayed alive by now. The tinkle of the falling fragments subsided eventually, a few moments after the last volley of machine-gun fire from down the hall. The sound of his own breathing seemed deafening. He could see neither Simone nor the enemy, just wrecked shopfronts and piles of glinting glass. Their own private Krystalnacht.

He was supposed to have provided covering fire while Simone made a run for the other side of the mall, part of a zig-zagging retreat strategy they had devised to get themselves out of this potentially non-metaphoric dead end. The most impressive aspect of his weapons-handling so far had been that he hadn't shot himself, so it was no surprise when the Uzi jammed after two rounds, with Simone only a few paces out of the doorway, caught in no man's land. The trigger clamped stiff against the stock and refused to release, nothing doing at the business end.

There'd been a slow-motion pause for one eternal, infernal moment as all three parties sussed what had just happened. Simone must have responded a fraction of a second before the bad guy, or maybe she was merely lucky that the bad guy initially aimed towards the doorway from where Matt's truncated burst had issued. Whatever, she blew out the window opposite with her shotgun and dived through the gap, out of sight.

The bad guy's continuing volley seemed to go on and on,

completely demolishing the two semi-hexagonal frontages that jutted out in front of where Matt was crouched. The enemy was positioned somewhere inside a shop at the end of the corridor, where it formed a T-junction with the adjoining stretch of vacant lots. Matt was, it appeared, just outside his angle of fire, but he could do nothing more than cower there with his arms around his head and wait in hope for the shooting to stop.

He glanced across towards where Simone had disappeared, looking for movement, any sign of where she was. There was nothing, only more shattered glass, and shadows beyond where the lights of the mall reached into the darkened shop. He had to get over there. She could be injured, unconscious, out of ammo, anything. There was ten or twelve feet of open floor to cross, but he felt he had no option. The danger seemed temporarily outweighed by the need to get to her, the need to know she was all right. It was an unaccustomed emotion, this selflessness. Blame it on extreme circumstances, he told himself, nothing else.

He dropped the useless Uzi to the ground and pulled the pistol from his belt. Holding it in both hands, he leaned out of the doorway and began firing in distraction, preparatory to making his move. The pistol jammed, same as the Uzi, after two rounds.

Matt threw himself back against the double doors as a retaliatory burst issued from down the hall. He examined the handgun, trying to think of what they did on telly when their weapons jammed, then remembered with a shudder that the answer was usually: get shot.

'Fuck,' he grunted, looking down at the ugly hunk of metal. It offered no clues, as all the lettering on it was Cyrillic. He then felt his stomach lurch for the hundredth time that evening, and quickly realised that this was

318

because he was actually falling backwards. The double doors had opened suddenly and he tumbled through them, before being grabbed under the oxters and dragged further inside the shop. He attempted to struggle, but the man, whoever he was, had already loosed his grip and scuttled swiftly forwards to retrieve the discarded machine gun. Going by the lack of a ski-mask and the fact that Matt was still alive, he was able to deduce that the newcomer was on his side.

'Are you—' Matt's voice had caught whatever disease he'd given both guns, jamming after two words. He cleared his throat. 'Are you Jackson?'

'No, Tim Vale's the name, surveillance and security consultant. Delighted to meet you, Mr Black.' He offered Matt a hand to shake. 'I'm a friend of Simone's. Where is the good lady, by the way?'

Matt pointed across the hall, through the empty window-frames. 'She's over there. I'm not sure how she's doin'. How did you know we were here?'

'Trade secrets, old chap. All in good time.'

'But how did you get in here?'

Vale pointed behind himself and Matt saw that the shop was S-shaped. Around the corner more light was streaming in from where a second entrance gave on to a parallel corridor.

'We can stealth your friend along the hall here with a bit of a pincer-movement,' Vale said. 'But we'd better hurry, because with all the racket you've been making, the chaps upstairs are bound to take an interest at some point.'

'What do you mean, at some point? Who do you think's shootin' at us?'

'I honestly couldn't say, but I'm rather sure he's not one of them.'

'How?'

'As I said, all in good time. Which is somewhat of the essence at the moment, so, ehm, may I?' he asked, indicating the handgun.

'By all means,' Matt obliged. 'Be safer for both of us.'

Vale turned the weapon over in his hands. 'Nagan automatic. Nice. I take it it's not yours.'

'I procured it earlier.'

'Quite a heavyweight. Massey-Ferguson of the gun world. I'm sure its owner would have been disappointed to lose it.'

'Aye, he was gutted.'

'KGB assassination favourite, once upon a time. Those were the days. Now they're all over the bloody place, since the Wall fell.'

'It's jammed. So's the Uzi.'

Vale flexed his thumb and an empty magazine dropped from the pistol-grip. 'No, just out,' he said. He picked up the Uzi and did the same thing. A cartridge clattered to the floor.

'I thought they went "click" when they were empty,' Matt said sheepishly. 'The triggers both stuck. I thought – never mind.'

'Any more ammo?' Vale asked. His tone was optimistic rather than desperate, as though Matt saying "no" *wouldn't* be a total fucking disaster. The man's calmness was almost disconcerting.

Matt reached into his jacket and handed Vale a mag for the Uzi, then fished a clip for the Nagan from one of his trouser pockets. Vale slapped the magazine smartly into the stock of the machine gun and offered it back to him.

'You'd best stick with this one,' Vale said, grinning. 'Play the percentage game.'

Matt delicately placed the handgun clip upright on the floor beside him, freeing both hands to hold the Uzi once more.

'Aye, fire off another couple of hundred rounds and I might even *fuck*—'

Vale's eyes had suddenly gone from the glint of a smile to the glint of cold steel as he reacted to movement elsewhere in the shop. Matt saw him grip the Nagan by the barrel with his right hand and slam the squat stock down on top of the waiting clip, then flip the gun a hundred and eighty degrees with a flick of the wrist, simultaneously grabbing the slide with his left, slotting the first round into the breech. He pulled the trigger the first of six times almost before the slide had returned to cock the hammer.

In the time it took Vale to spot the intruder, load his pistol, prep it and prolifically ventilate the guy, Matt had just about managed to turn his head and watch the dead man fall. To his credit, he had also managed to pull the trigger on the Uzi, mainly by reflex, but less impressively, it was pointing at Vale at the time. Fortunately, once again, nothing issued from it.

'Good thing for me you forgot to slide the bolt,' Vale remarked, indicating a lever on the weapon's right-hand side. 'You're lucky I don't confiscate it until you've learned to use it properly. Fortunately for you, this fellow over here won't be needing his any longer, so there's one going spare.'

Matt stared open-mouthed. Up-close, Vale looked like some RSC thesp who'd played his last Dane and would now unavoidably be moving on to the Lears and Shylocks. But in action, Jesus. Schwarzenegger wouldn't spill this guy's pint.

'Who *are* you?'

'There isn't time,' Vale replied, stripping the dead intruder of his armaments. 'I need you to do the talking. You look like you've had a more interesting evening than me so far, so why don't you tell me about it. And quickly.'

'All right,' Matt said, mentally rewinding, still aghast at what was on the tape. 'I'll give you the edited highlights. I killed a guy named Booth and took his guns and radio. I've been listenin' into the show ever since, and replyin' to his messages. They know he's dead now, but the fact that they bought my voice up until then suggests they're not the best-acquainted bunch. I don't think they're terrorists. Nothing political's been mentioned, and one of them said somethin' about there being millions of pounds at stake, so my guess is they're here to shake Gavin down: a ransom-for-hostages deal.

'But it's not exactly runnin' like a dream so far. One of them, somebody called Jackson, switched sides and freed all the hostages while the others were away searchin' for Gavin. Not the kind of development your average bad guy generally has a contingency against. They're dug in somewhere, ready to make a stand.'

'The Carlton,' Vale stated, getting up from the dead gunman. 'There's a siege getting underway there at the moment. Potentially rather messy.'

'Right. Also, someone called Dawson has buggered off on a motor-boat. I got the impression he was a main player. From what was said, he took off because he clocked which way the wind was blowin'. The leader, name of Connor, didnae sound too pleased aboot it. On top of that, they've suffered a few casualties: as well as laughin' boy in the corner there and the guy I lit up, they've lost two to this

322

Jackson punter, one to electrocution, and there's another one MIA.'

'Electrocution?'

'Somebody wired a door handle to the mains. Gavin, presumably. That's who they were lookin' for at the time. Impressive bit of improv, if you ask me. He's still on the lam, far as I know.'

'Yes, he's downstairs in the laundry, where I've just come from. The mains trick doesn't sound much like him, though. Perhaps the other chap.'

'What other chap?'

'Murdoch, I think he said his name was.'

'*Davie* Murdoch?'

'Yes, that was it. He struck me as rather more practical-minded than Mr Hutchison.'

'That would be one way of puttin' it, aye. Anyway, Simone and I reckoned our best bet was to try to get ashore an' raise the alarm. We were makin' our way down to look for a boat when we ran into your man, here. That's the story so far: now we go over live.'

'Very well,' Vale said. 'Here's the plan. I want you to fire down the corridor at two- or three-second intervals, in short, controlled bursts, aiming high, to keep our man distracted while I go around the other side. When I give you the shout, you cease firing. Think you can handle that?'

'Short, controlled bursts. Two or three seconds. Aim high.'

'Good. You ready?'

Matt took a breath and nodded, lying. He felt about as ready as King Ethelred. 'I don't tend to get a lot of this in, you know, in the average week,' he explained.

Vale grinned and slapped him on the shoulder.

'By the way,' he said, pulling the double doors open for

Matt, 'how did you two manage to evade the hijackers in the first place?'

'We weren't in the ballroom when it all went down. We were over in the Majestic.'

He nodded, a little too sagely for Matt's liking.

'I know it's none of my business,' Vale said quietly, 'but I'm rather fond of Simone. So if you don't treat her as she eminently deserves, you'll have me to answer to.'

Matt swallowed. 'Got it,' he said.

He crawled through the gap and knelt just outside the doorway once again. Noticing movement across the hall, he looked up. Simone was staring back at him from inside the shop opposite, pulling spare shells from her sanitary disposal bag and feeding them into the shotgun. She had cuts on her forehead and down the left side of her face, and her dress was ripped at the left shoulder.

'You all right?' he mouthed.

Simone rolled her eyes and shrugged, as though to say 'You mean apart from this?' Matt signalled to her to get down and stay put, then commenced firing, ducking in and out from his covered position to do so.

He glanced back across at Simone during each of the prescribed two- or three-second intervals.

'What's going on?' she mouthed.

Matt leaned out and fired again.

'Vale,' he mouthed back.

'Wha?'

Another burst.

'Vale,' he mouthed again.

She shook her head, a look of frustration on her face.

After the next volley, Vale's voice sounded loudly from down the corridor. 'That'll be all, Mr Black, thank you.'

Simone furrowed her brow upon hearing it. 'Tim Vale?'

she said in apparent disbelief. Matt nodded with a wry smile. He hadn't been the only one in for a surprise, and he suspected Simone wouldn't be the last.

'Sir,' Vale called out. 'Man in the pyjamas, are you listening?'

Matt and Simone exchanged gestures of bewilderment.

'We know you're not one of the hijackers,' he continued. 'We'd like you to know that neither are we, so it would be a dreadful shame if we shot each other, don't you think? Now, we have you in our sights from two directions, and in light of that advantage, I'd advise you to throw your weapon through the front of the shop and come out with your hands raised. You'll get the gun back as soon as we've all become sufficiently acquainted as to be sure you're not going to kill any of us, at least not intentionally.'

Matt couldn't see where Vale was, neither could he see the man he was alleging to have in his sights. He assumed that at least Vale knew what he was doing, then assumed that he'd find himself assuming that a few times more before this horrible night was over.

There was a few seconds of silence, then: 'Get tae fuck. D'you think I'm an eejit? If you can fuckin' see me, fuckin' shoot me.'

Matt heard Vale fire two rounds from his handgun. It was met by a yelp of 'Jesus fuck!', then followed immediately after that by the sight of an Uzi flying through the air and skidding along the hall amidst the squillion pieces of glass.

'Close enough?' Vale asked rhetorically. 'Now, come on out, and quickly, before the balaclava brigade get down here *en masse.*'

'I cannae.'

'Why not? Are you stuck?'

'Naw, but I've got nae shoes on, an' I'm up tae my fuckin' arse in glass.'

Vale appeared at the end of the hall and picked up the machine gun, then summoned Matt and Simone forward. They climbed through the shop's ruined frontage together, guns raised, and found themselves standing over some old punter on his knees, wearing a camouflage-vest and, true enough, tartan pyjama trousers, which were wet through. Matt hoped this wasn't because the bloke had peed himself, as they were clearly going to have to carry him over the debris until it was safe for him to put his bare feet down.

'I'm Tim Vale, security consultant,' Vale said, offering the man a helping hand. 'This is Mr Matthew Black and Mrs Simone Hutchison.'

'Hector McGregor. Lothian and Borders Police. Retired.'

'How long?' Vale enquired.

'One day. Don't ask.'

Vale returned the discarded Uzi and gestured to Simone to take the vanguard. He and Matt then picked McGregor up in a sitting position, one hand each under his thighs.

'Left, Simone, then first right,' Vale directed. Simone held open what was left of the shop's front door until they were through it, then resumed her position in the lead, shotgun held at shoulder level each time she approached a corner.

'How did you get here?' Vale asked McGregor.

'Rowin' boat. They blew it up wi' a rocket launcher. I had to swim the rest.'

'A rocket launcher? Oh dear. Can't say I like the sound of that. Do the authorities know about the situation, then? Someone must have seen the explosion.'

'Not that I know of, I'm afraid. I live just over the water, but mine's one of only three hooses in a five-mile radius. The only thing likely tae be payin' any attention roon here

326

is coos, sheep an' fish. I was investigatin' off my own back, based on a couple o' suspicious incidents earlier in the day.'

'In your pyjamas?' Matt was compelled to ask.

The man just glared.

'So what's the score?' he asked Vale.

'Ehm, in short, hijackers. Not particularly competent, but extremely enthusiastic and very heavily armed. After money, we believe. *Quelle surprise*. Fifty or so civilians dispersed variously about the resort, at their mercy if not exactly under their control.'

'Give us some money or we kill you?' McGregor summarised.

'Something like that.'

'We were plannin' to sneak ashore in one of their boats when we ran into you,' Matt added. 'Good job we didnae make it, I suppose, if that's what they did to yours.'

'There's nae boats doon there,' McGregor informed him. 'Well, there were dinghies, but somebody's knackered them.'

'Somebody's sabotaged *their* dinghies?' Simone asked.

'Well, whatever dinghies were doon there, aye. And the wan that was guardin' the jetty's deid, as well. That's where I got this machine gun. He'd been shot right through the foreheid.'

'Jackson's work?' Vale asked Matt.

'Nah. Jackson's been with the hostages the whole time. Wait a minute, though. This Dawson bloke left in a motor-boat – I heard the look-outs tellin' Connor. But why would he sabotage the remainin' dinghies? And why would he kill one of his own men?'

'Never mind aw that shite,' McGregor interrupted, putting his feet down again at last. 'Whit aboot the bomb?'

327

Matt and Vale stopped dead and stared at each other. 'What bomb?' they both asked.

■ 23:26 ■ laguna laundry depot ■ oh, *that* bomb ■

Vale and McGregor made it back to the laundry room less than five minutes behind the rest of them, both breathless and the former about as ruffled as Matt ever expected to see him, which was nonetheless not very. During the intervening time, the tight little room had played host to another reunion event that, in Matt's opinion, more genuinely reflected the true spirit of such affairs than its grander predecessor. He and Davie Murdoch accounted for a frugally ameliorating dose of awkward but genuine amity amidst an oceanic deluge of bitterness and recrimination, all of which was ebbing and flowing around Gavin.

'Long time no see, Davie, fancy meetin' you here.'

'Well, you know me, Matt, wouldnae miss a good barney.' He looked down at the Uzi. 'How's the pacifism hangin' these days?'

'Ach, it's more of a hobby than a lifestyle, you know?'

'And where the bloody hell have you been?' Gavin was meanwhile demanding of Simone.

'Where does it look like I've been?' she fired back, indicating the shotgun, the cuts and the rip in her dress. The presence of armed hijackers and mortal danger had been about the only thing capable of stopping Matt trying to kiss the area of shoulder that the rip had tantalisingly exposed. He was already starting to resent his earlier good conscience.

'The party got a wee bit out of control,' Simone continued. 'A few gatecrashers. Black attire, not quite dinner dress. Don't know whether you caught any of that.'

'I mean, where were you that you weren't in the ballroom when the terrorists appeared?'

'Would you rather I *had* been? Don't answer that. And where, I might ask, were you? Again, don't answer that. Hi, Catherine.'

'Hi, Simone,' Catherine mumbled, looking like she'd rather be facing the hijackers. Her eye kept straying to the shotgun.

'And as for you, Mr Comedian,' Gavin challenged, 'what the hell do you think you're doing with my wife?'

'Ehm, tryin' not to get shot, mainly.'

'I saw you kissing her.' He pointed to the laptop computer nearby, which was displaying surveillance images on its LCD screen. Very cute. Presumably secret agent Vale's. It probably turned into a motorbike if you pressed the right button.

'Well, that's a sight more than *you*'ve done for a long time,' Simone butted in. 'Which is not a complaint I'd imagine *she* could level at you.'

'What on earth are you talking about?'

'Oh for Christ's sake, Gavin,' Catherine chided. 'Act your age. She knows. Probably always has. Sorry, Simone, I really am. It was just one of those—'

'Oh, give us a break. You want him? Fine. You should just have asked. He was going spare anyway. Or at least he is now. Gavin, darling, I know this is not the best time, what with everything falling down around us, but . . . actually, on second thoughts, I'd say this actually *is* the best time. I'm leaving you. If we get out of this ridiculous, hellish bloody place alive, I'm leaving you, and I'm taking the girls.

Do you remember them at all? Short, dark hair, passing resemblance to me, striking resemblance to each other!'

'You're . . . you . . . I . . .'

'And, Catherine, if you've any regard for me or my children at all, I'll be expecting your full cooperation when I name you in the divorce.'

'You got it,' she said, her eyes still hypnotised by the pump-action mistress-dispatcher.

'God, Catherine, have you no loyalty?' Gavin growled. 'But then, of course, I now know you've been sneaking around behind my back, carrying on with Mr Psychopath there.'

Matt was momentarily impressed with Gavin. Not only was he ignoring his wife's firepower, but he was now noising up Davie Murdoch. This was either bravery worthy of a VC or recklessness worthy of Ford Prefect. Matt was 'Mr Comedian'. Davie was 'Mr Psychopath'. Another thirty seconds of this and Gavin could easily be 'Mr Bleedingslowlytodeath'.

It was a fortunate time for the two stragglers to make their appearance. During a hasty round of introductions, Vale tapped intently at his computer, then maximised one of the windows so that it took up the whole screen.

'So what is it?' Matt asked, though he knew the range of plausible answers was depressingly limited. The image on the screen was of a corridor in the shopping mall, one evidently not visited by himself and Simone as it didn't look like a bomb had hit it. Yet.

'It,' Vale said gravely, 'is approximately eighty to a hundred pounds of C4 plastic explosive, plus timer, detonators, the works. Our gratitude to Inspector McGregor here for discovering it. It's sitting in a shop doorway on sub-level two, and it's going to be making things very interesting for anyone in its vicinity in about seventy-two minutes from now.'

The collective intake of breath must have reduced the room's atmospheric pressure enough to threaten implosion. Vale didn't need to repeat himself. 'Explosive' was the only word in the English language not witheringly diminished when you preceded it with 'plastic'.

'Can you defuse it?' Gavin asked him.

'No. Can you?'

'Jesus Christ. Jesus Christ. Well, I mean, what constitutes the vicinity? Can we get to a safe distance?'

Vale sighed. 'It's been positioned pretty much bang in the centre of the installation. The explosion will smash through the sub-levels and cripple the platform from the middle. The whole place will begin to fold in on itself. But that's only the start. The blast will hit the resort's electricity generator. That'll go up with another big bang, taking out whatever happens to be left of the eastern sub-levels and ripping through the hotel structures above. The destruction of the generator will ignite its oil supply, and that will burn all the way back to the reservoirs in two of the platform legs. Then, if they haven't gone up already, the resulting conflagration will explode the two hundred bottles of cooking gas stored on the west side of sub-level three.'

'And is there a *down* side to this?' Matt asked.

'Actually, yes, as a matter of fact, and it's that this bomb was not designed for remote-detonation: it's on a timer and the timer has been started. No surrender, no negotiation, no ransom is going to stop it. Unlikely as it sounds, it would be my contention that our unwelcome guests tonight don't actually know it exists. Why else would they be wasting their time chasing around this place, trying to pin down

331

hostages, when they could simply tell them to cooperate or the place goes sky-high?'

'But I don't understand,' said Gavin, before being cut off by Simone's prediction that that would be his epitaph.

Matt understood, but that was because he'd been listening to the radio all night.

'Dawson,' he said.

Vale nodded.

'Who?' asked Davie.

'They've been fucked over by their own man,' Matt stated. 'Somebody called Dawson was one of their heidbummers. He took off earlier in a motor-boat – not according to plan, going by the reactions. We thought he'd just bailed out because the hijack had turned into *Carry On Shooting*. But Mr McGregor here says the bad guys' getaway dinghies have all been sunk, and the guard they posted down on the jetty has been shot dead. It sounds like this Dawson character's marooned everybody here with his surprise party-popper, and as a bomb's not the kind o' thing you'd just happen to have on you, we can assume levellin' this place was his objective all along.'

'Absolutely,' Vale agreed. 'He's also done his homework extremely well, too – unless you believe it to be a coincidence that the bomb has been placed in the precise spot where it would trigger maximum damage to the rig. This is not a hijacking, this is a demolition.'

'But why?' Gavin whined, even more appalled now that he knew his *true* beloved was the real target. 'Who would want to demolish this place?'

'Anyone in their right mind,' Matt muttered.

'Is there anythin' you're not tellin' us, Gavin?' Davie enquired. 'You've not been the subject of some grand-scale protection racket, have you?'

332

'No,' Gavin insisted.

'Well, I hope you're insured. Even if it's your weans that are gaunny be cashin' the cheque.'

'He is insured,' Simone stated, her tone suddenly very deliberate. 'Or rather, this place is.'

Gavin nodded. 'Against everything. The premiums are colossal. Fire, storm, earthquake, tidal waves, anything.'

'Including war,' Simone added, retaining the flat, analytic register. 'The resort is covered against destruction through military conflict or terrorist action.'

'Why?' asked Matt. 'Was it gaunny be a Club 18–30 joint?'

'Oh ha-ha,' Gavin snapped. 'It's because we're locating off west Africa. A potentially volatile part of the world.'

'No,' Simone countered. 'It's because Delta insisted on it. That's why Tim was brought in: the insurers wouldn't underwrite unless you installed a state-of-the-art security set-up. And when did Delta insist upon it, Gavin?'

'Two or three months back. But what's that got to do with it? There's a bomb ticking on this place, for God's sake.'

'Yes,' she said. 'And I've just worked out who planted it. Or who ordered it, anyway. Remind me, Mr Vale, when exactly were you brought in?'

'I've been on the project since May.'

'And what happened at the end of April, Gavin?'

'I don't know.'

'Well I do. Delta announced their annual figures, that's what. And with them up to their arse in debt from building this monstrosity, their stock nose-dived and the market smelled blood in the water. May was when the rumours of a hostile take-over started. The only way to fight that off was to come back after the next quarter waving massive bookings for this place, so that the stock would recover.

But Delta weren't confident of that happening, so they took out a little insurance. You never knew it, but I'd say you probably had until about the end of July to come up with good news. Instead all you had for them were more delays and bigger bills.'

'B-but . . . that's insane. Jack Mills is a friend. He was the only one who truly understood my vision.'

'Jack Mills is a scumfuck, Gavin, and I've just understood *his* vision: this is an insurance fraud, plain and simple. Except they couldn't just torch the place. With the resort gobbling up money and showing no sign of making it back, the insurers wouldn't believe something so convenient didn't happen deliberately. But no-one's going to suggest it was an inside job if the place blows up while the man behind the whole project is onboard, hosting his school reunion party, surrounded by his wife and dozens of friends. We're supposed to die for added plausibility.'

'But what about the hijackers?'

'Unwitting accomplices in the scam,' Matt ventured, hoping that if he could speed up the whodunnit discussion, they might more quickly proceed to the howarewegettingoutofit one. 'It went by me at the time because I'd other things on my mind, but one of them described the party guests as being "venture capitalists". My guess is this guy Dawson is workin' for Delta. He hires a bunch of semi-competent, expendable eejits and convinces them this is a party for serious movers and shakers here tonight. They go in, thinkin' they're there to demand money, and they play their role to the full: takin' hostages, wavin' guns, the full song-and-dance number. Then Dawson exits stage-right an' the place goes up, takin' everyone with it except maybe a couple of survivors, who live to tell a hazy tale of hijackers an' extortion. The disaster investigators find a few machine

334

guns an' dead guys in ski-masks among the rubble, and conclude that it was a shake-down that went wrong. Delta gets their cheque. Ploy explained. Can we get back to that bomb now?'

■ 23:30 ■ laguna laundry depot ■ cometh the hour ■

'How long before detonation?' Gavin asked dejectedly. The feeling of abject loss was beginning to dull that of terror. Previously, Gavin had been in fear for his life. Now he knew that if he survived, his life wouldn't be worth living anyway. Vale had laid it down unequivocally, never a man to unnecessarily alarm or exaggerate: this bomb was going off, end of story. The Floating Island Paradise Resort was about to be destroyed.

Even if Gavin didn't, his dream would die tonight, snuffed out by the man who had helped him nurture it: a brutal, bloody, late-term abortion. And even if he survived, he'd be left with nothing. Now that Mills' crooked intentions had been uncovered, there would be no insurance settlement, no compensatory cheque winging Gavin's way to allow him to start over again. Pursuing Mills or Delta would be so futile as to be absurd. This Dawson swine had already disappeared, and even if he was captured, proving a conspiracy would be impossible, especially via the American legal system.

Vale looked at his watch. 'Sixty-eight minutes and fourteen seconds,' he announced.

'Well, surely this changes everything,' Catherine reflected. 'The hijackers have been stitched up – we're all in the same predicament now. Surely we can come to a deal with them?'

Airhead. This was why the shiny, smiley, presentational side of business was Catherine's natural habitat, rather than the hard-nosed, back-biting reality. What, did she think they could all close their eyes and give the baddies ten to get away later, in exchange for them helping everyone safely back to dry land? Probably. She was already under the impression that her new hero, the allegedly reformed Neanderthal, was capable of saving them all with a single headbutt.

'Unless they relish the prospect of a long spell in jail, it is in the hijackers' best interests that we all die here tonight,' Vale explained, far more tactfully than Gavin could have managed. 'If we tell them about the bomb, they will cease trying to recapture their errant hostages, and dedicate their energies to two things: getting themselves off this place, and ensuring that everyone else is still onboard when it blows up. Our energies should be dedicated to one thing: contacting the authorities on the mainland, which will of course be tricky, as the hijackers have taken out all our means of communication.'

'Taken out, but not destroyed,' Matt Black corrected.

The so-called comedian was no doubt disappointed that there wasn't a mirror nearby, to admire his own coolness as he posed around with that machine gun, talking like he was the only one who knew what was going on.

'How do you know?' Vale asked.

'Connor sent extra guards to somethin' he referred to as "the comms pen" as soon as he discovered Jackson had swapped jerseys. I'm assumin' that's communications.'

'Yes,' confirmed Vale. 'All the transmitting hardware is in a pen on top of the Majestic.'

'He must have been afraid Jackson would try to restore the link, so that means the link *is* restorable.'

'How many guards?' asked the Neanderthal.

'Two.'

'Well, we've got seven people, three Uzis an' a shotgun,' Murdoch reasoned, such base arithmetic of brutality the only equation his faculties could process.

'It's not as simple as that,' cautioned Vale. 'The pen's on the roof, with only one stairway and one door leading to it. If you approached quietly enough, the element of surprise might buy you half a second as you come through the door, but you'd have to take out both guards in that time. And even *that* is only if both guards are on the roof. If one's at the foot of the stairs and one's at the top – which is how *I* would deploy – you might get the first, but the second one would have time, warning, cover and a clear shot. It could be suicide.'

'Are there any alternatives?' Simone asked.

Vale said nothing.

The Neanderthal shrugged. 'Well, the way I see it, if I'm gaunny die anyway, there's nothin' to lose. Somebody gimme a gun.'

'No,' Catherine protested, physically intervening to prevent Murdoch reaching for Simone's weapon. 'There must be something else we can do.'

In that moment, Gavin realised that this was no longer the laundry depot, no longer the Laguna, no longer even the Floating Island Paradise Resort: this was Room 101. This was his personal hell.

Like it wasn't enough that the vision he had strived so long and so hard to realise was about to be obliterated, and like it wasn't enough that he'd probably be sitting front-row when it happened, he had also, in the meantime, to suffer an intolerable humiliation, which, to turn the knife one more sadistically ironic degree, was entirely of his own making. He had gathered the ex-pupils of St Michael's together in order to exorcise the ghosts of his schooldays, but had instead seen all of those ghosts once more rendered flesh.

Once more, he was the anonymous supporting player while others – the *same* bloody others – took centre-stage. There was Davie Murdoch, then the notorious hard-man, now also the selfless and courageous hero, the guy everyone wants on their side. Catherine, then the unattainable beauty, was once again miles distant. She'd been offhand all through the party, and now she was acting like Gavin didn't exist. All her admiration was reserved for Murdoch, the pair of them opening their hearts to one another as Gavin lay silently in a skip full of dirty bedsheets, feeling like he was a kid eavesdropping on his big sister and her boyfriend while they talked grown-up talk.

His wife had shown up with Matt Black, both of them blood-spattered and carrying weapons. They'd been in the thick of it, sharing God-knows-what experiences together, from foreplay to gunplay, while Gavin's role had been restricted to trying not to wet himself.

Across at the Carlton, this white knight Jackson would inevitably have chosen deputies to bear the spare arms they accrued, and Gavin didn't have to be there to picture the scene. First choice would be Charlie O'Neill, muscular and composed, ever the natural fucking leader. And no doubt Ally McQuade would be the one keeping everyone's spirits up with jokes and smart-arse remarks.

If somehow they all got through this thing, those were the ones whose roles would be remembered. School all over again: the same faces, the same characters, the same names. Davie Murdoch, Catherine O'Rourke, Matt Black, Charlie O'Neill, Ally McQuade. If Gavin was remembered at all, it would be as the idiot who put them all in that spot in the first place; or, if Catherine squealed, the wimp who turned into a quivering jelly in that bedroom before Davie Murdoch took charge and rescued them all.

His dream was going to die, his wife was going to leave him, his lover had betrayed him and he was once more an anonymous nonentity. There was therefore only one way he could redeem himself, one way he could turn things around. It would take balls of granite and a resoluteness far beyond anything he had known before, but in such moments is destiny forged.

It was time to grow up. Time to prove to himself what kind of man Gavin Hutchison could be.

'There *is* an alternative,' he announced. Immediately, he had the floor, all eyes intently upon him, all mouths silent.

'However gullible they've been, these men still couldn't have come here tonight expecting to walk away with cash. If they thought we were all financiers, they must have been planning to perform their extortion electronically. The reason the communication links are restorable must be so that money transfers can be arranged.'

Gavin paused, looking at their faces to see whether the import was sinking in. It was.

'I can get them to restore the phone lines if I give myself up and start talking dosh. While I chat to the money-men, you can call the police.'

'Then what happens to you?' Murdoch asked.

'I'll string things out with the bank – God knows I've had to often enough before. At this time of night, it'll take a while to raise the right people anyway. By that time the cavalry should be on the horizon. Then I'll tell the hijackers about the bomb, so that they know there's no time for a stand-off.'

'They might use you as leverage to ask for their own helicopter,' Vale warned. 'And, if so, they'd take you with them as insurance. That's if they don't just shoot you on the spot.'

'Well, that's the chance I'm going to have to take. To quote Mr Murdoch here, if I'm going to die anyway, there's nothing to lose.'

Gavin walked through the door, the slap from Murdoch still tingling between his shoulderblades.

'You're a fuckin' hero, man,' he had said.

Vale had offered him a gun, suggesting he could conceal it somewhere about himself, but Gavin refused, reasoning that if they patted him down, it wouldn't bode well for negotiations if he looked like some Trojan Horse.

There'd been words of good luck and gratitude from everyone, even Simone, though she hadn't stretched to a kiss. He'd wondered whether she . . . but no. Don't be stupid.

Gavin walked along the corridor and out through another door to the stairs. Doorways, portals, rebirths. He had been plunged helplessly into that laundry depot from a dark passage above; scared, fragile, vulnerable, a hostage to the actions of others. A child. But when he emerged from it, he was a man.

There *was* an alternative. An alternative to dying and an alternative to losing everything. An alternative to tonight's humiliation and an alternative to ever again facing those people who'd never respected or appreciated him: including the mistress who'd jilted him and the wife who'd spent

340

years disappointing him, then had the fucking *temerity* to walk out on him.

What chance would these clowns have, anyway? Vale had his head screwed on right, but he was only one man. Look at the rest: Murdoch, Black and some looney in wet pyjama trousers. If they managed to raise help, how were they planning to overcome the bad guys while they evacuated fifty-odd people? They'd the same odds as Murdoch's suggested suicide mission on the Majestic roof.

No. So far tonight there had been only one man who really knew what he was doing, and his name was Dawson.

Now there were two.

■ 23:42 ■ fipr ■ cometh the man ■

If there hadn't been grown men around, Connor would have sat on the floor and buried his head in his hands. He wished he was home in his bed. This whole night had turned into the biggest waste of time in his entire life and he could now simply no longer be arsed. Death was starting to look like an attractive alternative to anyone he knew ever finding out about his role – starring role, male lead, even – in this mortifyingly embarrassing snafu, but as death wouldn't actually prevent that, and he didn't fancy the idea of posthumous mockery much either, there was no option but to get on and get out. Maybe he could cheer himself up later by hunting down Dawson and feeding him his own entrails.

Jardine was standing beside him, waiting for a response. Waiting for an order. Waiting for some kind of fucking direction because, like the rest of these amateurish, infantile, useless cunts Connor had saddled himself with, he couldn't have managed an independent thought any more than he could have sucked his own dick.

As he predicted, Jackson and his new friends hadn't been difficult to find. You wouldn't lead that many people to hide and hope somewhere in the labyrinths of the sublevels, which left either Hotel B or Hotel C. Dobson and Pettifer had failed to turn up any huddled masses en route to the comms pen on the roof of the Majestic, finding only another dead amateur, so that had left what the unlit neon sign advertised as the Carlton.

He'd sent a couple more expendable arseholes below stairs anyway, to have a hunt for this Hutchison character and whoever had seen off Booth. One of them, Ritchie, radioed back with a report of gunfire on sub-level two, then went off in search of the source. He hadn't reported in since, so it was depressingly reasonable to assume he'd located it the hard way. Neilsen was still wandering around down there too, but Connor resisted asking him to investigate Ritchie's disappearance and decided to leave him to his own devices: if the bastard could get killed on his own, without directions, it would be the first piece of initiative shown by any of them all night.

Quinn and McIntosh had led the sortie into the dark halls of the Carlton, being about the most dependable personnel he had left. Neither was a professional, but at least they were low-handicappers. Quinn had trained with one of those paranoid American militia groups, and McIntosh had been in the shit alongside Connor in Sonzola, acquitting himself respectably in as much as he came out alive.

When they'd found what they were looking for, they'd remained in position and sent Jardine back downstairs with

342

the story, so as to keep Jackson out of the loop. The news was, of course, bad. Jackson's little army were playing a very well-organised game of king-of-the-castle on the top floor. They had erected barricades on all the main approaches, and they had a nice downward angle of fire on anybody who came a-knocking. Quinn and McIntosh had shown the good sense not to try.

This was the final, inevitable confirmation of what had become more and more apparent as the evening wore on: the most he could expect to walk away with tonight was his life and his liberty. Nobody was going to make a poxy penny.

He indulged himself a sigh as Jardine waited beside him on the terrace.

'What do you want to do, sir?' Jardine asked. Again.

Connor had a look around the place, up at the three looming hotel buildings, down at the swimming pools, jacuzzis and fountains. He pictured the tourists gathering here for fortnights at a time, and was minutely consoled by the thought that thousands of others would have a far worse time on this shithole than even he'd suffered tonight.

'Get Harris and Forrester up here with their rocket launcher,' he ordered tiredly. 'Bring all the spare ordnance they've got. There's nothing to celebrate, but we *will* need the fireworks.'

'Yes, sir.'

Jardine turned around to go, then stopped immediately where he stood, raising his machine gun.

'*Sir*,' he hissed, drawing Connor's attention to what he was looking at. A figure was walking towards them among the swimming pools, his hands raised in surrender. Connor drew his pistol nonetheless, and ordered the man to stop

343

where he was. He did, instantly, keeping his hands in the air.

'Are you Mr Connor?' he called out. 'Because if so, I can assure you that shooting me would be the most expensive – and possibly final – mistake of your life. My name is Gavin Hutchison. I have an offer that may interest you.'

After everything he had been through today, Connor reckoned the veracity of the phrase 'better late than never' was about to undergo an extremely exacting test.

'Mr Hutchison. Pleased to meet you at last. Do come closer,' he instructed, keeping his pistol trained on the man's head. 'But I should stress that I'm more in the business of taking than of being offered, and my patience is not at its most robust after the way this evening has unfolded thus far. So whatever you've got to say, I'd better be smiling underneath this ski-mask by the time you've finished talking.'

'I'm not sure I can guarantee that, given what I have to tell you about a certain Mr Dawson, but as I said before, I think you will be interested.'

Connor felt his eyes bulge at the mention of the name. 'What about him?' he said flatly, straining to keep the emotion from his voice.

'Well, as time is very much at a premium, I'll break it down as simply as I can, and please bear in mind that the less you interrupt, the quicker I can explain matters. Firstly, there are no venture capitalists, bankers or money-men on this facility tonight. This man Dawson sold you a line to get you here as involuntary but necessary extras in a very high-stakes insurance fraud. Before he left this evening, he shot whoever was guarding the jetty, then sank all of your dinghies, but that was only *after* he planted a bomb downstairs that will soon blow this place to buggery.'

Connor was about to tell him he was talking bollocks, but the rising bile in his stomach indicated otherwise. Hutchison was ready for the doubt anyway.

'I don't expect you to take my word for this, so I'd advise you to send someone down to confirm it while I talk to you up here. It's on sub-level two, in a doorway somewhere in the shopping mall.'

Connor stared into Hutchison's eyes. He could read nothing, and feared this was because the other man was telling the truth. He signalled to Jardine. 'Grab Whitely. The two of you get down there and check it out. Use the radio, but just say "yes" or "not so far" when you report. Don't refer to what we're talking about. Go.' He looked back at Hutchison, pointing the gun between his eyes. 'If this is an ambush, you lose your head.'

'It's not, Mr Connor. It's a bomb. And it goes off in less than an hour. Dawson is working for an American businessman, a Mr Jack Mills, my supposed partner in this floating-resort project. Mr Mills needs to liquidise his assets to stave off corporate predators, and the quickest way to do that is to demolish this place and claim the insurance. Evidently, it was decided that an extortion attempt gone wrong would be a convincing enough scenario for the underwriters to cough up. Unfortunately, for it to look realistic, a large number of innocent civilians plus a corresponding group of wicked, nasty hijackers would need to die in the explosion. And among the former would be Mr Mills' business partner, not only providing added plausibility, but also ensuring one fewer claimant to split the insurance cheque with.'

Connor put his finger around the trigger-guard rather than the trigger itself. He'd been gripping the stock of his gun so hard, there was a very real danger he'd accidentally shoot the fellow in his growing rage.

Dawson.

Despite his anger, Connor now understood what was the true difference between them, understood even why Dawson would always be one rung up the ladder, one step ahead. And it wasn't that he didn't care about anybody, it wasn't that he was more ruthless, it wasn't that he was better connected, though all these things were true. It was very simply that Dawson got it done. Whatever *it* was, and whatever *it* took, he got *it* done.

Connor had put up with years of withering insults, but tonight he'd been paid the ultimate one, and the worst of it was that it wasn't even personal: Dawson hadn't lured him into this death-trap because of any animosity, he'd done it simply because he needed a sucker and Connor fitted the bill. He'd needed someone who would buy into the whole thing, who would play the part with every enthusiasm, so who better than the daft loser who's always trying his hardest to impress you?

Connor and his new outfit hadn't been hired because they were the only help available – they'd been hired because Dawson needed someone he could rely upon to fuck things up. That was why, despite his open disgust, he'd still stuck around after witnessing the incompetent chaos at the farm. Inside, he must have been secretly delighted.

'So what are you after, Mr Hutchison?' Connor asked. 'Do you want me to get you and your friends off this thing out of sheer gratitude for showing us we've been had?'

Hutchison laughed drily.

'I don't imagine you're a man for whom gratitude is sufficient motivation. That's why I'm prepared to offer you appropriate remuneration. Unfortunately, I can't do that without my share of this insurance payout, so I'm afraid – much as I'm sure it would pain you – you'd have to leave my friends behind, along with the disloyal Mr Jackson and the bodies of your fallen comrades. What do you say, Mr Connor? Are you smiling behind that ski-mask yet?'

Connor's radio broke the short silence.

'Sir? Sir, this is Jardine. That's a yes, sir. That's a very big fuckin' yes.'

Connor pointed to the walkie-talkie.

'What *he* said.'

■ 23:49 ■ laguna laundry depot ■
■ song for the dumped ■

Watching Gavin talk down the barrel of Connor's gun, Simone couldn't have been more intent upon the laptop's screen if it had been showing Jeremy Clarkson being publicly executed – or, better still, dying in a car crash. A few minutes later, she was picturing Gavin in the passenger seat.

She had felt her suspicions rise as he was leaving the laundry depot, too eagerly garnering accolades for his sacrifice *en route*, but she suppressed those feelings as unworthy: this had already been a night when a lot of people found out who they – and each other – truly were, what unknown strengths lay hidden inside them, so perhaps Gavin was no exception. Along with the others, she had hardly dared breathe as she watched him appear in the silent video-feed frame, courageously going face-to-balaclava with an armed hijacker. In that moment, she found herself caring for him again, the way she had once upon a time.

It was just one more thing to hate him for when, in

347

the next window, there appeared two bad guys intently examining the bomb. One of them held a walkie-talkie to his mouth.

'Sir?' said a corresponding voice on Matthew's stolen radio. 'Sir, this is Jardine. That's a yes, sir. That's a very big fuckin' yes.'

Simone felt a shudder for every time Gavin had touched her, sick that he'd ever been inside her, disgusted that he was the father of her children. The most horrible part was that she didn't feel all that surprised. Gavin had always been the most selfish person she ever knew. People might not believe that, because they'd seen him throw cash around, but money he could spare, and he was usually looking for some form of return. His selfishness was other than material. It was a deeper, absolute indulgence, a life of votations and libations upon the altar of that vast part of himself that never grew up.

They say we all have a child within, but that didn't necessarily mean some soul of innocence and lost dreams. Having borne two, Simone knew there was nothing more selfish in the world than a child, until that child is forced to learn that it must share the place with everyone else. Gavin had been forced to learn that, but it didn't mean he'd been forced to agree with it, and he'd spent his adult life compensating that child for all the compromises it had endured as a result.

Simone closed her eyes. She didn't want to face the others. Most women only had to put up with their husband embarrassing them by having a few too many at a dinner party. Still, at least there'd be no morning after.

'He's sold us out,' Davie Murdoch said, neutrally, almost as though he was open to contradiction.

'No,' Catherine obliged. 'Maybe he just panicked. They've

got a gun to his head, for God's sake. Maybe he panicked and told them about the bomb.'

Simone opened her eyes again and looked around at the others. They were all seated on or leaning against shelves and table-tops, apart from McGregor, who was standing up straight as he tried and retried the laundry depot's phone, in wait for that vital outside line. 'He *has* sold us out,' she declared. 'Not only did he probably reckon his chances of getting off were better with the bad guys, but it's in Gavin's best financial interests. If he gets off here and this place goes bang, he'd be due a big share of the insurance, plus no doubt payouts from Jack Mills for keeping his mouth shut and in compensation for trying to kill him. We're screwed.'

'We're not screwed,' Vale countered. 'And here's why: the hijackers' boats have been sunk, so they'll need to organise another way of getting themselves ashore. That means they'll have to restore the phone lines at some point.'

'I'll keep trying,' said McGregor.

'I can't remember,' Davie said to Matthew. 'Did I ever leather Gavin at school?'

'No.'

'Fuck.'

■ **23:52** ■ **laguna laundry depot** ■ **murder polis** ■

'I've got a tone!'

'Keep it brief. They'll cut the link again as soon as they're finished with it.'

'Sure.'

Nine. Nine. Nine.

Ring.

Ring.

'Hello. Which service do you require?'

'Police.'

'Transferring you now, sir.'

Ring.

Ring.

'. . . caller's number is 717474.'

'Hello, this is the police. What's the emergency?'

'Oh thank Christ. We've got a terrorist situation in Kilbokie Bay, on . . . whit's the name o' this place?'

'Floating Island Paradise Resort.'

'The Floatin' Island thingmy. Hijackers and upwards of fifty hostages. There's a bomb, due to go off in less than an hour. We need transport immediately. That's the Floa—'

'Excuse me, sir, can I have your name please?'

'My name is Insp . . . Hector McGregor. We need—'

'Ah, Mr McGregor, yes. This is DS McLeod at Rosstown. I spoke to you earlier today, remember? Your wife has been on the phone in the last hour, to report that you had gone missing from your bed.'

'Look, never mind my wife, there's a bo—'

'She was worried that you might be having some sort of breakdown, or perhaps concussion sustained from that blow to the head earlier today. I can share her concern, Mr McGregor, but nonetheless, you're the last person I should be having to remind about the seriousness of wasting police time. I think—'

'Look, I'm tellin' you, there's—'

'. . . said earlier, retirement from the force can be a difficult thing to get used to, but—'

'Will you fuckin' shut up and listen, ya brainless fuckin'

350

sheep-shaggin' hill-billy, in-bred teuchter numpty, there's fifty people trapped on—'

'Brrrrrrrrrrrrrr . . .'

'He hung up!'

'The *police* hung up?'

'Eh, well, there was a wee bit of an incident earlier today, Mr Vale. They're not the most credulous bunch up here.'

'Oh good grief. Give me the phone.'

'No. They're fuckin' useless anyway. I've got a better idea.'

Ring.

Ring.

Ring.

Ring.

'Christ, come on tae fuck.'

Ring.

Ring.

Ri— 'Hello?'

'Dougie? It's Hector, here. No, Molly's fine. Look, I need your help, an' I mean seriously. No, she's no' kicked me oot again. Listen, Dougie, whit shape's the *Ha'penny Thing* in?'

■ 00:02 ■ orchid suite ■ all along the watchtower ■

When he tried with his mobile, Vale got much the same response from the local polis as McGregor. Quoting his former MI6 rank and serial number to the plod at the other end probably had the opposite effect to that intended, massively detracting from his credibility rather than granting weight

351

to it, but at least it allowed Matt some clue as to the man's intriguingly murky background.

The lines were cut again moments later, but not before the mad McGregor claimed to have organised some means of evacuation, on his brother-in-law's fishing trawler. The very pertinent question was whether it would make the trip from Portmeddie, along the coast, in the forty-five minutes they had left at that point. By McGregor's own admission, it was going to be tight.

'I'm sure Dougie'll row his hardest,' he'd said. It took Matt a deeply disturbing second to realise the man was joking.

It had been Vale's recommendation that they get out of the laundry depot and head upstairs, contending that if Gavin had told Connor about the bomb, there was no reason why he wouldn't also have betrayed where they were hiding out. Having ascertained that everyone was up to the ascent, he suggested they make for the top floor, where they could look out for the approaches of the *Ha'penny Thing* and whatever transport Connor had hailed, as well as keeping an eye on what was happening at the Carlton. Vale and Matt handed their pistols to Catherine and Davie respectively, and off they all set in two-by-two cover formation: Vale and McGregor in front, Davie and Catherine next, Simone and Matt the rearguard.

Their climb took them past one end of the Laguna's lobby, from where Matt could see the reception desks and the entrance to the ballroom. The last time he'd stood by the former, the biggest problem he had to contend with was the mildly ironic news that the object of his rekindled teenage yearnings was married with kids. The last time he'd passed through the latter, he was holding her hand, imagining scenarios in which her husband was out of the picture.

This, despite fulfilling the principal criterion, had not been one of them.

Vale set his laptop down on the floor next to the Orchid suite's double doors, having plugged his cable into a 'node' socket outside in the hallway. Davie and Catherine were on the balcony, looking alternately towards the Carlton and beyond the platform at the black waters below. The curtains were closed behind them, to hide the light that was streaming into the room through the double doors. These were open to allow vocal communication between the Orchid suite and the water-side bedroom opposite, where McGregor had shot the glass from the sealed and double-glazed windows. Having delegated computer duties to Simone, Vale joined the ex-cop in leaning out and scanning the view to the south, but so far there was nothing but darkness to look at.

Simone raided the suite's fridge and handed out soft drinks, then returned to monitoring the laptop. Matt stood guard in the doorway, keeping his eyes and his gun trained on the stairhead down the hall.

He looked at his watch with gut-deep dread. He'd just endured the longest couple of hours of his life, only to segue straight into what would undoubtedly be the shortest forty-five minutes. Showtime was twelve thirty-eight. McGregor had raised help at 11:54 and it was already twelve zero-three. There *were* still sixty seconds to a minute these days, weren't there?

'Any sign?' he called to McGregor.

'Ach, naw,' he replied calmly. 'We'll no' see him until he's quite close, anyway. He'll be oot o' sight until he's round the headland.'

Terrific, Matt thought. Maybe they could restart his heart once they got him onboard.

353

'A good thing, too,' Vale remarked. 'Our best chance is if the hijackers have left on their boat before ours becomes visible. They can't afford for us to escape, remember, so if they see the *Ha'penny Thing*, they'll blow it out of the water with their rockets.'

'And what do we do then?'

'Overboard and every man for himself.'

Christ. The phrase had chilling, specific connotations. Thanks a bunch, Ms Bainbridge. Cheers, Mr Cameron. True, it wasn't the North Atlantic in midwinter, but then freezing wasn't likely to be the problem. Forecast temperatures were going to be in the region of three thousand degrees, due to an area of extremely high pressure centred around an exploding oil rig.

It had been decided not to tell the group in the Carlton about the bomb until such time as it would be of any help for them to know. The eventuality Vale just described definitely qualified, and there'd be a very short queue to be the one who broke the news.

Simone glanced up at Matt from where she knelt on the floor by the computer.

'That wasn't bollocks, by the way?' she asked. 'That stuff you said about me being the one you had a thing for at school?'

'Absolutely not,' he assured her, surprisingly able to raise a small laugh. 'Why?'

'Well, I was just thinking: hell of a first date.'

'Aye, you cannae say I don't know how to show a girl a good time.'

'No. But maybe just dinner next time, eh?'

'Sure,' he said. 'Or a take-away an' a couple o' videos.'

Matt looked at her face, seeing again the girl he had once been so unheraldedly captivated by, and the equally

354

beguiling woman she had grown into. He had only caught a glimpse of her tonight, he knew. He realised that he wanted to meet her daughters, to see what they looked like, see her beside them, see her complete. Nothing juvenile, nothing sentimental, nothing daft, nothing heavy: he just wanted to know her, properly, like adults, like grown-ups, like pals. But then what were the chances of that, guns and explosives aside? Tonight had been insane even before the hijackers showed up. Strange and unique circumstances, never to be repeated. If they made it through this thing alive, she wasn't going to let a shambles like him near her new life. And if he really cared for Simone, he wouldn't try and inflict himself on her, anyway.

'Are you up for a next time?' she asked. She was smiling, but her lip trembled a little. 'I mean, you wouldn't want to get yourself involved with one of these single mothers, would you?'

Matt recalled his last thought. If he cared for her, he should stay away. That's what his conscience told him, still diligently operating despite how fucking hypothetical this whole thing was. Then he recalled the last time he'd listened to his conscience – dried, purple-black mementoes of which were still flaking off his trousers.

'Haud me back,' he said.

The curtains billowed suddenly at the front of the room as Catherine stuck her head through them.

'Get Vale,' she said urgently. 'Something's happening downstairs.'

Simone looked back at the laptop and began toggling through the windows.

'Tim!' Matt called. 'Action out front.'

Vale bounded nimbly into the suite and crouched beside Simone to get a closer view of the screen. He had a brief look, then got up and headed for the balcony. Matt made to follow but was curtly ordered to 'Stay at your post'. Matt had littered tours with the smashed egos of hecklers, from Hollywood to Linwood, Brooklyn to Brechin, but this was one night when he'd happily keep his comebacks to himself, especially where Death's Dark Vale was concerned.

'What can you see?' Matt asked Simone.

'They're doing something at the front of the Carlton. There's some of them inside the lobby. I can't see properly. The image is too fuzzy. Oh, shite.'

'What?'

'The ones outside have got one of those . . . I mean, I think . . . have a look yourself. That's . . . isn't it?'

'Jesus. *Vale!*'

'I know, I know, fire in the hold,' Vale said, coming back in from the balcony. 'They've started blazes in the Carlton lobby. They're getting ready to pull out, and this is their version of cover fire – to keep the good guys at bay while they get down to the jetty.'

'No,' Matt said, pointing out the rocket launcher on the laptop. 'I think *that*'s their version of cover fire.'

Vale looked at the screen.

'Bugger,' he said.

■ 00:09 ■ fipr ■ two riders were approaching ■

This was like the sickest kind of psychological torture, Ally thought. Standing there forever, scared out of your mind, waiting and dreading and waiting and dreading, the seconds and minutes ticking on, the tension growing, the pressure building, and still nothing happening. He almost *wanted* the fighting to begin, if only for some kind of release, all the time aware of Jackson's words about what would happen when Connor decided his time limit had expired.

The pressure had been cranked up at least a full atmosphere when Jim Murray, who was on look-out at the front windows, announced that the baddies were amassing on the terrace. It went up another when he reported that a group of them had run inside. Then after that, nothing. Just more waiting, impossible waiting. How long could it take them to climb the fucking stairs? he'd begun to ask himself. He'd even heard footsteps close below at one point, followed by . . . more nothing. In time, Jackson came by again and suggested that Connor's men may have sussed the set-up then pulled back to consider a change of plan.

Aware of how limited those change-of-plan possibilities might be, Jackson pulled everyone who wasn't on look-out or guard duty to the very back of the restaurant, ordering a couple of them to dismantle the rearmost barricade. Jackson transferred Ally to guarding that now most crucial stairway, then handed his own Nagan automatic to Eddie Milton and stationed him at Ally's previous post. Ally decided to keep to himself the tales of Eddie being stung by a dead wasp or knocked unconscious by a pillar while playing tig. Jackson could have done without knowing, and Eddie could certainly have done without reminding. Just as long as he didn't blow his own – or Ally's – head off.

Ally looked to either side of his position, at all his former classmates of a decade and a half ago huddled on the floor, he their assigned protector. What a fucking joke. He'd probably fantasised about such scenarios when he was twelve, but then he'd fantasised about Lindsay Wagner when he was twelve, too. And of being in The Stranglers.

No more heroes.

The waiting was even worse over here. At least at his previous post, he hadn't been forced to listen to Buckin' Brendan and Mary-Theresa muttering endless decades of the fucking rosary.

'Brendan, will you knock it off,' he said eventually, deciding he couldn't take it any more.

'*Some*one's got to pray for our souls, Alastair,' Brendan retorted indignantly.

'Aye, well we're no' deid *yet.*'

Mrs Laurence gave him a thumbs-up. 'Low BDQ so far,' she said, trying to offer encouragement. He held up crossed fingers in reply, but didn't feel much reassurance. He thought of the two guys Jackson despatched in the ballroom. The BDQ was pretty high when the gun was in the hands of someone who knew what they were doing. And as for the *rocket* deadliness quotient . . .

Jim Murray called Jackson to the front. Jackson took one quick look at what was going on below, then grabbed Jim by the shoulder and pulled him away, running for the back of the room.

'Everybody, get down flat and take cover, NOW!' he shouted.

It was not a good time for Kenny Collins to regain the power of his legs, having until then lain flacidly horizontal, intermittently swearing and complaining. In his still-blootered state, said legs took him staggering towards the front windows, ranting at the top of his voice.

'Come ahead, ya fuckin' black cunts. I'll take emdy. Square go, ya fuckin' bastarts.'

Allan Crossland was the first to notice. He got up and began moving towards Kenny, but the fast-retreating Jackson cut across Allan's path before he had travelled two yards, rugby-tackling him to the floor. Jackson's momentum rolled them against the rear windows with a glass-testing thump as the first missile smashed through the front and detonated against the ceiling.

The errant pisshead didn't stand a chance.

'Oh my God,' said Mary-Theresa in horror. 'They've . . .'

'Buckin' hell,' agreed her husband.

The room felt the impact of a second rocket a few seconds later, this time less accurately striking the floor below.

'McQuade,' Jackson shouted. 'Get everybody down the stairs, now.'

'But what about—'

'Go two flights down and assemble in the corridor. I'll round up the others. *Do it.*'

'All right, everybody, you heard him,' Ally said, standing up. 'Behind me, fast as you can. Come on.'

By 'the others' Jackson meant Charlie, Lisa, Eddie and Potter, who were still guarding their barricades elsewhere on the top floor. Eddie was in sight, just outside the restaurant, but he had a dozen yards of open floor between his position and the rear stairs. Jackson hared off in his direction, diving through the doorway as another rocket impacted, this time erring on the high side and striking the outer wall between the top of the windows and the roof.

The stairs were wide enough to accommodate two abreast, but the element of mortal haste was like an Ibrox Disaster repeat in the making. Giant window-panes ran almost the full height of each flight, looking out over the darkness. Ally was picturing the feared pile-up smashing through and spilling out into the black waters below. At this point, all it would have taken was one person to trip. Then Mrs Laurence's voice boomed from somewhere at the back.

'Walk quickly, but don't run,' she commanded. 'Two by

two. Keep an arm's length between you and the person in front at all times. That's it. On you go.'

Ally couldn't resist looking over his shoulder at the astonishing sight of a St Mick's class going down a staircase in a disciplined, orderly fashion. Maybe he'd missed the part where she told them they'd have to read *A Scots Quair* as punishment if they didn't comply.

They heard no further explosions during their descent, and began regrouping in a corridor off the stair-landing. Charlie O'Neill appeared from an adjoining hallway before the last of the procession made it down, having been ordered by Jackson to leap his barricade and rendezvous below. He'd shouted 'Charlie O'Neill, comin' through, don't shoot,' as he approached. Ally, now preoccupied with the larger-scale ballistics, hadn't even raised his gun. Some sentry. He was the guy in the red jumper right enough.

Eddie Milton followed shortly after from the opposite corridor, then Potter, then finally Lisa and Jackson together.

'What now?' Ally asked.

'We head downstairs,' Jackson said. 'They're pullin' out. They've taken the rocket launcher and they're pullin' out. I don't know why.'

'What if it's a trap?'

Jackson shook his head. 'Connor had us by the balls right then. It's not his style to suddenly get cute when brute force is workin' fine. Anyway, we don't have much choice. The building's on fire in about three places upstairs, an' it's spreadin' fast. We have to get out of here.'

'Boy, this just gets more fun all the time.'

'Ah, come on,' said Charlie, rubbing the back of Ally's head. 'You love it, really.'

Aye, he thought. Tell it to Kenny.

'Right,' Jackson commanded. 'Just in case this *is* a trap,

360

I want all guns to the front, and if I give the order, I want everybody else to hit the deck. Got that? Okay, let's move it.'

They went back out to the stairwell and resumed their nervous but orderly descent. Ally was on the outside, nearest the windows. His gaze was focused ahead and below, but he was nonetheless the first to spot movement outside the glass.

'Jackson,' he said, pointing.

There appeared to be two objects moving towards the rig, still a distance away, but visible by their lights. They were both approaching from the east, one travelling much faster than the other, and already nearer. The faster vessel looked smaller than its counterpart, though Ally was only going by their illuminations. They could both be the same size, physically, but only one appeared to have Motörhead's lighting rig attached to its roof.

'Any ideas?' he asked Jackson.

'Dunno. Wasn't in Connor's script. Could be the cavalry.'

'Forgive me if I don't get my hopes up. On a night like this, any light at the end of the tunnel's bound to be a train.'

A few more flights down, Ally's pessimism was crushingly borne out. They smelt it before they saw it, smoke drifting up the staircase to meet them. Charlie leaned over the railing and looked down.

'Fuck, I can see flames,' he said. 'Ground floor, two flights doon.'

Jackson signalled everyone to stop.

'This is why they pulled out,' Jackson spat, furious. 'They'd already got us from above and below. Talk about burnin' it at both ends.'

'So what do we do? Find another stair?'

'If this was their plan, there'll be fires in all of them. They can't have been burnin' long, though. Let's grab every extinguisher we can find and give it our best.'

'We can't,' said Potter. 'There aren't any. Not installed in the Carlton yet.'

Ally buried his face in his hands. He could hear the cries and gasps as the desperate news filtered back among the crowd.

'Oh, for fuck's sake,' cried Jackson. 'Somebody throw us a fuckin' bone here.'

There came a startlingly loud blast of sound from below. Even Jackson flinched, sharing everyone else's fear that it had been a burst of flame. Ally looked over the railing as the noise repeated and continued. Instead of smoke, there was now steam billowing violently around the landing beneath them.

'Hello?' Jackson shouted. 'Somebody down there?'

One more blast, then a figure emerged from the steam, a fire extinguisher in his hands, a pistol tucked into his belt.

'Awright, boys?' he called. 'Heard there was a party. Sorry I'm late. You're Jackson, I take it? I'm Davie. Davie Murdoch.'

'Much obliged. I've heard a lot about you. Love your work.'

'You've seen my *paintings*?'

'No, I meant the number with the door handle an' the electricity supply. *That* was a work of art.'

'Davie,' Ally said. 'Christ, are we glad tae see *you*.'

'Jesus, Ally McQuade. You're lookin' well, sir. Some soirée so far, eh? Big Charlie O'Neill, as well. Howzitgaun, big man? An' Christ, Lisa McKenzie tae. Nice handgun,

362

Lisa. Goes wi' your hair. Anyway, we better save the group hugs the noo. The show's no' over.'

'How did I know you were gaunny say that?'

They followed him through the foam-flecked doorway and on into the lobby, where there were more figures emerging into the half-light from other stairways, also bearing firearms and fire extinguishers. Matt Black was the first one Ally recognised, maybe because he'd seen him emerge from a cloud of steam before, at the start of a live video. The Uzi was a new prop, right enough. Seemed it was the must-have reunion-party souvenir. Ally also clocked Catherine O'Rourke and Simone Draper, the latter not only looking the part with her shotgun, but looking like she'd kicked some as well. There were also two older men he didn't recognise, and conspicuously no Gavin.

Signals were exchanged as soon as they noticed Davie emerge with the erstwhile hostages. They all dropped the extinguishers where they stood and headed out towards the terrace. Matt Black and the two older men were first to reach the new group. Matt's face was streaked with cuts and scratches, but even cumulatively they couldn't possibly account for the volume of blood that was staining the rest of his person. Ally, it surprisingly appeared, had had a comparatively quiet night of it.

'This is Jackson,' Davie told them. 'Jackson, this is Matt Black, Tim Vale, security specialist, and Hector McGregor, ex-polis. Don't ask aboot the jammies.'

'What's the latest?'

'D'you want the good news or the bad news first?' Matt asked. He didn't wait for an answer. 'All right, the good news is there's a boat on its way to take us off this dump. The bad news is it's only got seventeen minutes to get here before the whole place goes supernova. There's a bomb on the rig, I'm afraid. Your man Dawson planted it then fucked off.'

'Figures,' Jackson muttered, gritting his teeth.

'Seems that was always his agenda. The away-team there have just found out about it, an' that's why they've shot the craw.'

A bomb, Ally thought. Of course. Last reel. It always got darkest just before . . . you got blown to chunky kibbles.

'We saw boats from upstairs,' Jackson told them. 'There's two of them on their way here. One a lot quicker than the other, I should add. I take it ours is the slow one?'

'Well, let's hope so,' said Vale, 'because that way your ex-colleagues won't be around to impede our embarkation.'

'Got you.'

'This other boat,' Matt enquired. 'Do you think the bad guys'll be able to see it from down there?'

'I think they'd be able to see it from space,' Ally answered. 'It's got more fuckin' lights than Hampden.'

'Aye,' mumbled McGregor apologetically. 'Dougie's always been a bit wary of sailin' in the dark since thon time he ran aground.'

'Fuck,' was Matt's response. Ally could tell this wasn't an aesthetic consideration.

'What's the problem?'

'They're gaunny blow it out the fuckin' water wi' their rocket launcher, that's the fuckin' problem. They cannae afford for us to get off o' here.'

'We have to stop them,' Vale stated flatly. 'If they sink that other boat, we're dead, simple as that.' He turned to Jackson. 'How many are there?'

'Nine or ten now, I think.'

'Plus Gavin,' Simone said acidly.

'They took Gavin hostage?' asked Lisa.

364

'No, I'm embarrassed to relate, my husband sold us out and joined the bad guys. I'll tell you later – if there is a later.'

'They'll be waiting down on the jetty by now,' Vale said. 'Which way were the boats coming?'

Jackson pointed. Vale threw Simone a radio and told her to go to the barrier and have a look.

Ally listened to Vale and Jackson discuss their tactical options, which amounted to little more than minor variations on a general theme of throwing everything into an all-or-nothing, death-or-glory suicide assault on the jetty. He exchanged frightened looks with Matt, Charlie and Lisa, everyone clearly aware of what was being asked of them. The Uzi started to feel heavier than ever in his hands, scenes from *Full Metal Jacket* and *Saving Private Ryan* playing vividly in his head. But how could he refuse? How could any of them refuse? It was death either way. And greater love hath no man, yadda yadda yadda, even if he hasn't seen half those friends in fifteen years. He swallowed. He wanted to protest, but he could already hear Jackson once more telling him he was open to alternative suggestions.

'I can see them,' said Simone, via Matt's radio. 'The first boat's going to be here in minutes.'

'Right,' Vale said, checking his weapon. 'It's now or never.'

Ally felt hollow. No paralysing terror, no adrenaline-fuelled exhilaration, just a numb void. He ransacked his mind for ideas, but all he found were more old movies, and this was the wrong genre. Bye-bye *Lethal Weapon*, hello *Gallipoli*. Mel didn't make it in that one. Nobody made it in that one.

There had to be another way of doing this. Couldn't they wait and shoot the boat's fuel tank as it left? Aye, right.

From this range? In the dark? Christ, even Renny Harlin would say no to something as shite as that.

The suicide squad got ready to move out, Vale and Jackson at the front. Ally noticed Mrs Laurence standing among the group that he'd started involuntarily to think of as 'civilians'. He found himself replaying their conversation from the bus because he knew he had to think about something to keep Annette's face out of his mind.

Clichés and conventions. Bullet-deadliness quotient. Bad guys coming back for one last fright. And good guys getting shot in the shoulder. That was when he remembered, that was when he got it. *Treasure Island*! The solution wasn't to be found in some American action-adventure – this was a *Scottish* action-adventure. Pirates. Boats. Booty.

And cannonballs.

■ 00:28 ■ fipr ■ strike! ■

Matt could see the bad guys' boat, a souped-up cabin-cruiser affair, from the Majestic's ground-floor sea-view restaurant. It slowed to a crawl as it prepared to pass underneath, between the platform's vast, vanessafeltzian legs. Pootling a couple of hundred yards behind it was the *Ha'penny Thing*, floods blazing with retina-threatening intensity. He looked behind. Still no sign of the others, but his and McGregor's instructions were to shoot as soon as the boat was underneath, regardless. Vale had chosen McGregor for the task due to his shoeless state – not much good for high-speed fetching and carrying. Matt got the gig on the grounds that glass was the one thing he had a track record of hitting.

The cabin cruiser disappeared from view.

'Couple more seconds,' McGregor said, compensating for their angle of view. 'All right. Ready?'

Matt remembered to slide the bolt this time. 'Ready,' he said.

'Fire.'

They stood side-by-side, six yards back, peppering the seaside windows with bullets until there wasn't a pane left. When the noise of firing ceased, Matt heard the heavy thump of running feet behind him. Allan Crossland was first there, just ahead of Jim Murray. Charlie O'Neill was next, carrying two, as were Jackson and Davie when they appeared. The room began to fill up over the next thirty seconds, then on Vale's direction they all took their places along the now glassless outside wall.

Simone sidled in next to Matt.

'You still up for this, Mr Pacifist?' she asked.

'Aye, well, as the man said, if you tolerate this . . . What about you? I mean—'

'I'm thinking of it as a very messy divorce,' she said. 'It's him or us. And the kids won't miss what they never had.'

Vale, leaning carefully out of the window and looking straight down, gave the order.

'ATTACK!'

The prow of the cruiser came into view, gliding slowly out from underneath the Floating Island Paradise Resort and into open water. It was preparing to set a course for the *Ha'penny Thing*, but ran into extreme and unusual weather conditions in the form of a sudden hail of around fifty bowling balls precipitated from sixty feet above.

Maybe one of the balls hit the engine, maybe the spare rockets, whatever. Either way, the boat went bang.

■ 00:33 ■ fipr ■ this never happens ■

The trawler was sailing its way clear of the facility by the time Gavin hauled himself on to the wet boards, aching and bloody. He wanted to shout after them, but he had neither the breath nor the hope left.

The blast had blown him clear of the boat, and he'd flapped limply in the water, watching in a bleary daze as the two halves of the cruiser went under. He had struck out for the jetty as soon as his faculties returned, having seen the second boat go around the wreckage and dock on the other side. If he could only get there in time, he'd thought, even just get their attention . . . He'd made a mistake – a *big* mistake – and he didn't expect forgiveness, not immediately, but they wouldn't leave him if they saw him, would they? That would be tantamount to murder.

It was a moot point, anyway. They were gone long before he reached the jetty. He sat dejectedly on the walkway and started to cry. Then suddenly he heard splashes nearby, and looked up to see another survivor climbing from the water. Gavin ran towards him, crouching down to help pull him on to the boards.

'Where's the bomb?' the man said breathlessly.

'Can you defuse it?'

'Well, I've built a few in me time. Take me to it.'

Gavin ran faster than surely he ever had in his life, ignoring the protests of his pain-racked limbs as they climbed the

368

spiralling stairs encircling the lift-shafts inside the centre support-leg. Reaching sub-level two, he careered through two sets of swing-action fire doors, his lungs threatening to explode from his chest. By the time they reached the spot, he had no breath left to speak; he could only point.

The timer said forty-four seconds.

The other man produced a small knife and began trying to wedge the cover off the detonator housing. It wouldn't budge.

Thirty-six seconds.

He used the knife to tease out each of the two tiny screws holding the cover in place, Gavin's heart jumping every time the blade slipped from the hair's-breadth grooves. The cover clattered to the floor. It revealed a cascade of bare wires, leading from a conduit beneath the timer-device to a number of metal tubes. It looked like a wind-chime decoration.

Twenty-two seconds.

'Fuck, he's daisy-chained the detonators,' the man said.

Eighteen seconds.

'What does that mean? Can you still defuse it?'

'I'll need to cut the lead wire.'

Fourteen seconds.

'Christ? Which one's that?'

Twelve seconds.

Above the wind-chimes, there were two insulated wires, one green and one blue, connecting the timer to the conduit.

'It's one of this pair,' the man said, slipping the knife between them.

Ten seconds.

Nine.

'Green or blue?' Gavin asked.

Eight.

'I don't know.'

Seven.

'Jesus.'

Six.

Five.

'Fuck it, green's me lucky colour.'

Three.

He turned the blade and flicked his wrist.

■ **00:38** ■ **the ha'penny thing** ■ **inevitably** ■ ■

'God 'michty,' McGregor spluttered, ducking and clamping his hands to his ears as the first explosion shook the night.

'Well, that's something you don't see every day,' Vale remarked, barely flinching.

Columns of flame reached toweringly into the sky, accompanied by the scream of tearing metal and the growling rumble of destruction. Every few seconds the inferno would pulse with renewed impetus, in celebration at finding fresh combustibles to consume.

'Now, if we can just organise somethin' similar for Torremolinos,' said Matt.

McGregor laughed, having been thinking along the same lines for Tynecastle.

He began picking his way between the evacuees to reach Dougie at the helm; their gratitude at getting away alive, he noted, had not tempered remarks about just how powerfully the boat reeked of fish. They did have a point, right enough: McGregor's eyes were watering. The ones not commenting on it were only refraining because they had their heads over the sides, boaking for all they were worth.

'Out of the fryin' pan, into the fire, eh, Hector?' Dougie said as McGregor approached.

'Whit?'

'Well, I dinnae think oor Molly'll be in the best mood when you get back.'

Oh bugger, he thought, recalling that his last words to her were: 'I'll no' be a minute.'

'Aye, mibbe I should've taken my chances wi' the—'

McGregor never got to finish his sentence. Beside him, one of the puking punters had sprung back from the edge, shrieking in fright as the last of the balaclava-bampots came clambering suddenly up the side, utterly covered in sick. The bloke must have been hanging on to the old tyres that buffered the sides of the boat, then climbed up when he decided he couldn't take the deluge any more.

McGregor looked frantically about the deck as the man got his first leg over the edge, a pistol gripped in one dripping hand. McGregor was unarmed, having eagerly ditched the machine gun as soon as they pulled away from that jetty. Vale was still tooled up, but he was way back at the stern, and there were dozens of bodies between there and here. On the floor beside his feet, however, there was just the thing.

McGregor reached into the ice-box and grabbed the monkfish by its tail, then spun on one heel and swung it at the intruder's head with both hands. It connected with a splat and a crunch of bone, he wasn't sure of which party. The hijacker crashed to the floor, his gun going off once before it fell from his grip and slid across the deck. The bullet hit the boy McQuade, but he was all right: it only got him in the shoulder.

McGregor pulled the balaclava off the unconscious figure.

'Connor,' Jackson growled, arriving from behind and drawing his pistol.

'No you don't,' McGregor warned him. 'He's my collar. I'll take it from here. There's a plod in Rosstown I'd really like him to meet.'

There were flashing lights all along the front of the liftings yard as the *Ha'penny Thing* chugged slowly into dock: polis, ambulances and the fire brigade, though what the fuck *they* thought they were going to achieve, McGregor wasn't sure. Not without Red Adair, anyway.

Dougie and a couple of the evacuees threw mooring ropes to the party waiting on the pier. DS McLeod was standing among them.

McGregor bent down and reached for the monkfish.

■ later ■

Finlay Dawson was apprehended at Glasgow Airport, attempting to board a flight bound for Newark. He and William Connor were both detained at Her Majesty's pleasure, with the recommendation that once they died, they should be cryogenically frozen until such time as technology could revive them, whereupon they would each begin another life sentence. It was that kind of judge. You can just be unlucky.

Delta Leisure's CEO, Jack Mills, was arrested in the US on charges including fraud, conspiracy and murder, and his company indicted at corporate level. In keeping with the renowned expediency of the US legal system, it is expected that the case will come before a judge some time around March 2009. Prosecutors have apologised for the delay, but have explained that they are unauthorised to pull out all the stops unless Mills does something *really* serious, like get his cock sucked then lie about it.

Ally McQuade, following marriage, honeymoon and convalescence, wrote a screenplay based on his experiences, working successfully in collaboration with his former English teacher, Mrs Angela Laurence. The script was sold to a major studio for a six-figure sum, and is currently in pre-production. Matt Black turned down a lucrative offer to play himself, citing tour commitments. Renny Harlin is directing.